For Julia

ACKNOWLEDGMENTS

Some people don't even know that they have helped, but they have, just by being there.

Thank you; Becky Hayes, Steph Mason, Lorraine Campbell, Anne Bolitho, Sarah Bolitho, Julie Lowe, Janien Brolls, Donna Quinlan & Donna's Dad, Karen De Lastie, Cindy Russell Lee, Angela Love, Alison Kynastons, Karine Genser, Justin Rogers, Mum, Dad, Manon, Anthony, Jesus, Harry & Lilly the dog.

CHAPTER 1

London was drowning in a typically British summer. They'd promised Mediterranean skies and Pina Colada ice creams but that was last Tuesday. People bustled in and out of crowded cafes and bars doing their after work thing. They planned, schemed and networked. This was London and a drop of rain could never stop the all-important buzz of people trying to get ahead. And you could get ahead, boy could you get ahead, if you made the right contacts with the right people at the right time.

In a flat above Kensington Square, the smooth tones of Frank Sinatra drifted out through an open window into the rain. Julia Connors was not one to play by the rules, she had the window wide open and was enjoying watching the raindrops bounce off the windowsill not bothered that the rug was getting soaked.

Anyone looking up from the street, would see the elegant human façade; a statuesque, beautiful woman with a strong air of determination about her. They could never have imagined the pain and sorrow that lay beneath – a deep sadness that was only ever fleetingly revealed if you were permitted to look into the turquoise eyes, at the exact moment that she dropped her guard.

Julia sang along with Frank, her smooth voice suitably melancholic for a rainy day in London, and the things she'd got planned.

She turned and took a good look at herself in the mirror.

Well, there I am; plain dog poo coloured wool dress with zero chance of it clinging anywhere, flat sensible shoes, and a lovely pair of inoffensive earrings that are so tiny they look like well-placed specs of dandruff. Alan will be pleased. Wear something quiet and not too sexy, he'd said. She sighed to herself. Well it was definitely that.

Julia was a London lady on a mission and her life plan was about to come to fruition. Tonight was the night that Alan would propose, she could feel it in her bones and she was making a huge effort to do as she was told.

Humming to herself she wandered back into the kitchen and hesitated over the gin bottle. Dutch courage or cold Turkey? A tough call. Well it wasn't cold turkey in the true sense because she was more of a 'calm the nerves and relieve the boredom with a bottle' than a 'give me a drink or I'll stab you with the kitchen scissors' kind of girl. The Dutch won - they always did. The only clean glass left in the cupboard was a half pint mug. Well, it saved her having to pour another one later. Julia opened the fridge door and glanced gingerly inside, hopeful of catching the yellow glimmer of a fresh lemon. Everything seemed very brown and murky and stank to high heaven so she quickly shut the door again. Yikes. Disgusting, but needs must. She added a bit more gin.

Julia headed back into the bedroom, swaying to the rhythm of the music. The gin was beginning to have its desired effect. She took another look at the dog poo dress in the mirror. No. No, no, no. I can't do it. I can't wear that! Alan might think it's the right thing to do for his banking friends but he's never going to propose to me if I'm wearing that. She took another gulp of gin and pulled off the dress and took a good critical look at herself in the mirror

Those spray tans were a rip off – her skin didn't seem to have changed colour at all. What's the use of having skin that tanned easily when you live under clouds in the UK? No wonder the tanning booths do so much business. And so much for the classic Scandinavian look - that failed spray tan's turned me jaundice yellow. She turned and checked out her bottom in the mirror. Well at least that's OK. Not too bad at all in fact. The painful workouts were worth it. Excellent butt transformation from past its sell by date pear, to pert peach. She turned back around and peered at her face. Wish I'd got the money to get a nose job. Liane, her assistant said it was classic Greek and that it made her photogenic but that probably just meant that she could carry off giant specs and even the worst camera in the world could focus on it. Patience. I just need a bit more patience and as soon as I'm married it'll be first thing on my buckets of money list.

She took another swig of gin, threw open the wardrobe door and pulled out a scarlet silk dress. Bye-bye dog poo. Hello Lady in Red! Jean Claude Vasin, designer to the elite, had really excelled on this one. From the front it was an ordinary little dress but when you turned your back, it was clear that the front was only attached by two

3

sequin straps and you were bare right down to the top of your bottom. Jean-Claude really was a genius. She turned to look at the side view. The edge of the front clung seductively to her boobs and so long as she didn't leap around too much she was just about covered – although anyone sitting beside her would definitely get a ringside view of the rounded curves of her fixed assets.

She wandered back and forth in front of the mirror delighting in the sensuality of the delicate fabric. God I love my job. I get to work with one of the best designers in the world, go to the best parties in the world and even better I get to wear Jacquard, the most expensive clothes in the world, all for free! What's not to like? She looked around the bedroom, at the piles of designer skirts, suits and even lingerie that were deposited like rabbit droppings all over the floor and furniture and she suddenly felt guilty. Note to self. Must try tidying up more. Jacquard would not be impressed and Jean Claude would probably sack me if he saw this. She took another swig of her gin and tonic, feeling the reassuring cooling of her stomach and the calming of her mind. Yes the Dutch courage was advancing nicely now.

She casually stepped over the debris, putting the image into the back drawer of her 'to do' file in her head. She grabbed her bag, switched her lipstick from the dying a death coral to a Monro-esque red and she was ready.

She grabbed her phone and tried to decide what time it was but gave up. Maths dyslexia was such a pain, but luckily she had the Google lady to help and Lady Google never ever shouted at her for being late. 'OK Google, what time is it?' she asked.

'The time is eight o five pm,' replied Lady Google

happily.

Shit, Alan had said be there by eight so by the time she got a cab over to Alan's place she'd be very late.

She rang for a cab, deciding she'd better make it A-Z cars because Express said she owed them lots of money. She felt another churning in her stomach. She took large nervous gulps of her gin and tonic. She was almost there, the peak point of Dutch courage. The point when her mind had moved on from calm to slightly numb and the feelings of inadequacy were anaesthetised. She could never completely vanquish them though, somehow a slight tremor of nervousness always managed to stick around, bubbling under the surface like the lava of a volcano waiting to erupt into a full blown panic attack.

I should be used to it by now. It's really not fair. I've worked so damn hard to get to this point. She twisted a lock of hair nervously and took the final gulp of gin. Oh well. Here goes.

She couldn't remember who was going to be there except that they had all sounded really dull. If Eleanor Cholmondeley was there, Julia knew she would die a slow death being engulfed by the thousands of patio tubs that were the mainstay of Eleanor's conversational skills. And if she had to sit next to her husband William she'd bury herself in one of the tubs voluntarily. But the last straw would be if they brought their dermatologically challenged teenage son Georgie with them. It wasn't really Georgie's fault she supposed. He was only a teenager after all. He should have been at home, safely up to no good, partying with his mates while the old codgers were out. As it was they dragged him with them everywhere they went, introducing the son and heir; the Right Honourable

George, St John, Elspeth, Cholmondeley, to anyone who might have access to an heiress. Poor old Georgie Porgie spent the whole time nervously gobbling his posh words and spraying them on all sides with whatever the dish of the day was. She made a mental note not to stand with her back to him otherwise she'd end up one crispy coated Julia. Yuk.

Her phone rang and she dashed over to check and sure enough it was Alan. She left it to take a message and listened in.

'Hello, Julia darling. Just ringing to see if you've left. Why the hell do you always have to be late? You can't use the maths dyslexia card every time you know.' He sighed. 'And if you're still there listening to this and pretending you've left, there'll be hell to pay.' He changed tack and sounded amused. 'You'd just better hope your cab knows where it's going.' Julia sighed to herself. Sometimes she wondered if Alan had her flat bugged or something, he always seemed to know what she was up to. His voice continued matter of factly. 'The Cholmondeleys are here, oh and Christophe de Flaubert and Cassandra Girault who you haven't met yet. You might know her actually, she has something to do with the Paris Clothes Show. Well, I'll see you later, darling. Bye.'

Julia sighed. Alan was so reasonable. It was no use, try as she might she just couldn't get it together with a guy who was nice to her all the time. It was as if she'd always been emotionally dead. She shivered as she thought back, she couldn't ever remember a time when she'd sought affection; she'd grown up without it from necessity and now it didn't matter anymore because she was old enough and smart enough to do without it. She went to grab the bottle of gin again, knowing that dreadful scene was twitching in the very depths of her memory and threatening to emerge to taunt her again. She put the bottle down. No. Just think of anything and everything to prevent it. No matter how many times it reared its head, haunting her, she could never seem to exorcise it completely. Julia you've got to be strong, she told herself.

Thankfully, her thoughts went back to Alan. He was lovely, but if only he wasn't so exhaustingly nice sometimes...

Julia had come to realise that the only solution to her many crises – her determination not to fall in love, her inability to physically respond to anyone and her catastrophic finances – was to marry money. She would never be poor again and it was to this end that she had started frequenting Sloane Street bankers' dinner parties. It was a very practical solution, and she was determined that she would go right to the top and marry into the toff lot and become Lady Julia Connors, double barrelled Bloomsbury-Connors, top notch posh totty socialite.

The buzzer from the intercom sounded, indicating her cab had arrived and she grabbed her bag and charged down the stairs. She was relieved to find the driver was Bert; he was the only one who did know where he was going.

'Hi, lady. Wow, you look something else!'

'Hi, Bert, thanks. You know where we're going don't you, Bert? Flood Street, Chelsea.'

'Sure, home to the rich, famous and not so nice. I 'ad that Boris Johnson in my cab once you know. You going to a party, miss?'

'No, just high society dinner. You know how it is.'

'Yeah? You the main course?'

They pulled up outside Alan's house and Julia leapt out looking ten times more enthusiastic than she felt. She rang the doorbell and waited, contemplating the toes of her shoes. Why does each pair wrinkle differently around the toes? Your feet are the same inside, aren't they?

Julia began to shiver and got bored with tapping her feet.

When the door finally opened she said grumpily: 'Finally! Alan, I was freezing to death out here.' And she looked up into an unsmiling, extremely handsome, totally unfamiliar face.

'So I see,' came a deep voice as its owner stood gazing at Julia's nipples pointing out under her dress like the Himalayas out of the clouds.

Julia stared thunderously into a pair of guarded brown eyes that stared back at her. Their owner leant his muscular frame back against the open door, as if to let her past, but he was so intimidating it had the opposite effect.

'Well, can I come in?' she asked in annoyance, deliberately folding her arms across her chest. Just who the hell did this guy think he was?

'Of course,' he said standing even further back to let her through. 'You must be Julia Connors.'

'Yes. And you must be Christophe de Flaubert,' she said wafting him her most charming smile as she slinked through the door. She knew everyone else there, so this had to be Christophe de Flaubert and she hadn't expected him to be quite so good looking either – devastating, in fact for a banker. His dark roguish curls, smooth, dark skin and well-sculpted, if slightly rugged features, were the things actors were made of.

She glided through the hall, catching his reflection in the mirror and was highly satisfied to see his eyebrows rocket as he got the full view of her back, right down to the top of her bottom. Take that, she thought smugly.

As she entered the lounge she realised that everybody was assembled and waiting for her. They all turned to look and she smiled, heading straight towards Alan who looked very English and very aristocratic in his dark blue dinner jacket.

'Darling, I've met the new butler,' she said, her eyes mischievously taking in the Frenchman, 'he's simply divine. Where did you find him?' And everybody laughed, Georgie especially – showering his mother with a mouthful of mixed nuts.

'Ah, sorry, Christophe,' said Alan smiling with embarrassment. 'Er, you two have met then?'

'Yes,' came the Frenchman's deep tones as he casually reached over for some peanuts. His eyes did not smile as they met hers. 'I found her on the street and, being a gentleman, felt obliged to help her back into her dress.'

Julia choked on the fistful of cashews that she had half shoved into her mouth and everybody else erupted. My God, that was too near the truth thought Julia, her face chilli-red as she glared at the Frenchman. William Cholmondeley gave a raucous impression of a donkey having a heart attack and the Frenchman just smiled at her. Fifteen all.

Julia continued to glare at him. She was furious and the antagonism she'd felt tripled. She was about to start a full-scale battle when she took a look at Alan's face, fully expectant of the worst and she decided to let it go.

'*Touché*, monsieur,' she said, smiling enticingly up at him and he raised his eyebrows in suspicion.

William had stopped braying and was moving over to say hello to her.

'Don't you listen to him, old girl,' he said, 'he's just a Frog, albeit a rich one and, even worse, a nice one, but he's a Frog just the same. You look positively edible, m'dear.' He pecked Julia on the cheek, and as she expected, she felt his hand slide round the back of her and squeeze her bottom. She shivered, but managed not to outwardly wince. Underneath she cringed and her whole being was disgusted; she'd felt like that for as long as she could remember.

'Do you know, Alan…' continued William, smiling lecherously at her, 'it's about time you married this girl.'

'Do you think so, William?' replied Alan smiling, almost to himself. 'She simply won't have it, William.'

The Frenchman raised his eyebrows in disbelief. He didn't miss a thing, thought Julia, annoyed by Alan's inappropriate choice of words.

'Julia, darling, this is Cassandra Girault, a friend of Christophe's,' said Alan, introducing her to a stunning raven-haired woman who was sitting in a quietly sultry fashion in the corner, displaying a pair of very long, very fine legs.

Julia turned and assessed her quickly. She decided Cassandra was about thirty, had had plastic surgery on her nose and that it was probably because the poor girl had been unfortunate enough to have been born with a silver spoon stuck up it. Julia smiled one of the warm, easy-going smiles that she used so often with difficult Jacquard customers. She was annoyed to see it greeted with one hundred per cent suspicion. So this was an up-front competition. Julia wondered just exactly what the stakes were.

'How do you do,' said Cassandra, her tones as deliberately deep and sensual as her appearance. Poor Georgie couldn't contain himself and was showing his adolescent nerves by gulping down his drink. Julia had already taken in the well cut, very expensive dress that she recognised as being from the Chanel collection quite a few years back and decided to test the water. The woman looked as if she had all the makings of a prime cow.

'What a beautiful dress,' said Julia, smiling. 'Chanel I believe. Rather old, but a vintage year of course.'

William erupted in laughter again and Georgie started to stammer something which everybody ignored so he gulped down his drink again instead. Cassandra smiled wryly but Alan interrupted quickly, trying to tone down Julia's remark.

'Julia is general manager of Jacquard UK,' he said smiling apologetically, 'so clothes are her business.'

'So I see,' replied Cassandra. 'Next time she should maybe wear some.'

Alan looked horrified at the turn events were taking, and Julia just glared at Cassandra, for once lost for a reply. Christophe stood coolly catching dry roasted peanuts in his mouth.

'Erm... er... well now that we're all here, maybe we should go into dinner,' said Alan, loath to make a decision, but desperate to change the subject.

Julia lagged behind so that she could go in with him. 'I'm so sorry I'm late, darling. I couldn't get a cab,' she said, kissing him full on the mouth.

'That's OK, pet,' he said relieved that she had decided to ignore Cassandra's comment. The last thing he needed was a Julia Connors tantrum. He was a bit surprised at her kissing him in public like that though. It usually took him at least three hours to get a peck on the cheek out of her.

He felt encouraged by her behaviour and said, 'Darling I've put you next to Christophe. He's terribly important and I'm trying to pull off quite a heavy deal with him on this South American funding thing. He's enormously influential, especially with the City, so do your best to charm him. He's just bound to fall in love with you; everyone does.' Alan smiled affectionately down at her.

Julia took an enormous gulp of the gin and tonic he'd handed her. She felt like he'd just asked her to charm a six foot Doberman.

'Alan! I didn't come here to play charades with some guy whose ego's as big as his bank balance.'

Her voice trailed off as she realised that Christophe and Cassandra had not followed the others into the dining room at all but had moved across the room and were standing right behind her.

'Cassandra was just admiring your dress, Miss Connors,' said the Frenchman giving her a look that said he'd heard every word. 'Jean-Claude Vasin does have very sensual tastes.'

Julia became immediately suspicious because he hadn't insulted her. But she brushed it aside.

'Yes, you know his collections then?' she asked, smiling with a trace of genuine warmth at the thought of Jean-Claude.

'Yes,' said Cassandra. 'I buy many things at the Paris boutique but of course Christophe and I find some of his things a little too risqué for the conservative banking world. Actually I'm presenting the French coverage of the collections in Paris next week. It will be interesting to see how outrageous he's going to be with next year's collection.'

'Well, if you're here tomorrow, you must come to the show,' said Julia in a fit of enthusiasm and not without some rapid brainwork. Nobody in their right mind refused free publicity. 'We are holding our annual launch of the new summer range,' continued Julia. 'There really are some beautiful things this year.'

'Perhaps I will,' said Cassandra, her black eyes gleaming, not at Julia but at Christophe de Flaubert who was standing so uncomfortably close behind Julia that she felt goose bumps spreading across her bare back

Julia shivered and turned around, her eyes locking with the Frenchman's.

'Somebody is walking over my grave, I think,' she said, shuddering. Then she recovered, smiled and said to Cassandra, 'Give me a ring at Jacquard in the morning if you'd like to come, and I'll get an invitation sent over. It's seven o'clock at the Albert Hall and there's a champagne reception afterwards.'

But Cassandra wasn't listening. Her eyes had followed Christophe's tall figure as he and Alan wandered off into the dining room.

Besotted, thought Julia. Totally besotted. Yet another human being on an emotional suicide mission and what a man to pick – looks by Adonis, body by Michelangelo and ego by Genghis Khan. This dinner party was going to be a nightmare.

The dinner progressed slowly. Cassandra and Lady

Cholmondely, unsurprisingly, became engrossed in the finer points of Provencal patio tubs, and poor Georgie nervously gulped most of the wine totally unchecked by his disinterested parents.

William, Christophe and Alan were heavily into share prices, foreign exchange and Euro bondage so Julia sat quietly for a while wondering how Euro bondage differed from ordinary bondage and if it was as much fun. One of her ex's had liked bondage – so had she really, it took her mind off the whole sexual fear thing while she tied him up. Then, once he was tied up she could taunt him so badly then when they finally got around to doing it, it was all over really quickly. Otherwise just like every other time she had sex, she would have frozen outside and gone mad inside her head.

She glanced down the table. Georgie was not looking good, he'd certainly been calming his nerves with a bottle, his complexion was beginning to look like curdled Hollandaise. Julia reached for the bottle of claret herself and realised it was empty. She stood up to go and get some more just as poor Georgie dived for the bathroom. Nobody else seemed to have noticed so she followed him. Honestly he was far too young to be subjected to this amount of alcohol and social pressure.

Georgie hadn't even had time to close the door properly and was retching in the bathroom. She grabbed one of the towels, wet it with cold water and put it over his forehead.

'Hey, come on, you'll be OK soon. Best to throw it all up, that's what I think.'

'No… No… awful I've been awful. Leave me alone.'

'You haven't been awful Georgie, it's not your fault,

you're a teenager, teenagers do that kind of thing.'

She opened a draw and pulled a new toothbrush out of a packet.

'Believe me, I know Georgie.' And she did know. She started to tremble and feel nauseous herself. Why did she only ever remember the bad things, never the good things in her past? Probably because she couldn't think of any.

She put the toothbrush down on the floor next to him.

'Rinse your mouth and brush your teeth and no one will ever know, I promise.' As she turned to go she bumped straight into the Frenchman who had been standing there watching.

'No one will know will they?' she insisted to the Frenchman as she passed him and went to get another bottle of claret.

Back at the table, Julia's nerves got the better of her and she found herself doing a double act with the bottle of claret. She decided the Frenchman was far too good looking to be ignoring her and she turned to accost him verbally.

'You're a big banker then?' she asked grinning a wide, slightly drunken smile. He turned to her and produced a devastating smile like a magician pulling a beautiful soft endearing rabbit out of a very stiff top hat. Wow! Wow, wow, wow, thought Julia. I'd never have expected that! He's gorgeous. Cassandra looked on suspiciously.

'You're right, Miss Connors,' he said. 'We have spent far too much time talking business and have been ignoring you.' Alan picked up on the cue and suggested they all went into the living room.

By midnight everyone was still there and they were still talking about the South American deal. She'd been bored to death by her own company and everyone else's and had resorted to planning how she would decorate the room if she married Alan, in between polishing off more of the port than she should have done.

'Alan, darling,' she said, sidling over to him and dropping herself heavily onto his knee, 'it really is time all these people were going,' and gave him a meaningful smile. Too much brandy and the shock of Julia being so physical made Alan's eyes stand out on stalks. Julia flopped forward to get a closer look at him, her drunkenness making her even more short-sighted than usual. She suppressed a giggle. His usually serious expression had given way to boyish enthusiasm. He's really quite endearing, she thought through the haze. A bit like a grown-up Hobbit. She did not see the Frenchman's cynical smile.

'Julia. When are you going to marry me?' asked Alan, feeling the most courageous he'd ever felt in her presence.

'Whenever you like, darling,' answered Julia, playing to her audience and kissing him full on the mouth.

'Hoh! Well done Alan!' William's voice boomed out almost shattering the crystal chandelier. 'Well done indeed. Thought you'd never get around to it, Bloomsbury. You're a lot sharper on the exchange – never known you to sit on a good deal before. You lucky, lucky boy.'

'Oh, congratulations, Julia, my dear,' said Lady Cholmondeley, hugging her with tears in her eyes.

'I say that's sss ... super,' said Georgie, who had recovered quickly. He leapt up and started shaking Alan's hand, as if it was a money box with a million dollars stuck in it. 'I sss … so wish I was getting married,' he sighed, his eyes looking yearningly in Cassandra's direction. Cassandra gazed at the heavens, looking for rescue. Everyone was congratulating Alan and he was shaking their hands, looking gleeful. Julia smiled at everyone, accepting their congratulations, and then suddenly excused herself to go to the bathroom, realising the enormity of what she had just done.

As she sat on the toilet contemplating the beautiful brass taps and toilet roll dispenser, the extortionately expensive wallpaper and furniture, she began to shake uncontrollably. She couldn't understand why – it was what she'd worked for. All those years she'd worked it out. The theory was correct, just as she'd always planned. Marry someone rich because she was frigid and would never fall in love anyway, and it would solve all her problems.

Her palms were clammy and she felt nausea rise in her throat. Tears welled up in her eyes and began to trickle down her cheek but she wiped them away with her hand and sniffed determinedly. She forced the thoughts to the back of her mind. Nobody would ever hurt her ever again. She would marry Alan just like she'd planned.

So why did she feel so wretched?

She sat with her chin in her hands looking at the thick carpet and tried to take her mind off things by guessing how many flowers there were in the whole of the room. There were far too many flowers really. It might be expensive but it was dead old fashioned. She bet the Queen had stuff like that in her loo. It didn't matter that she was still on the seat with her dress hitched up and her knickers round her feet. The wooden loo seat felt familiar and safe – besides which it was the most comfortable place to sit in the whole house. She'd decided there were at least ten different flowers in the carpet and that poppies, peonies and the tiny scarlet pimpernel were her favourite, but she would probably only keep the pee-on--knees ones because they were the only ones that were obviously meant to be in the bathroom. Suddenly the door opened and she was horrified to see the Frenchman there.

The fact that she was drunk made her less embarrassed than she normally would have been and slightly irritated she said, 'don't you ever knock?'

She jumped down and hitched up her knickers sulkily and didn't look at him.

'No I don't,' he said. 'Most people I know lock the door.'

'Well most people I know knock politely.'

'Of course, the British,' he said nodding.

'What the hell is uniquely British about not wanting to pee in front of a total stranger?' asked Julia annoyed. 'Aren't you even going to excuse yourself?'

'No.' He said, grinning.

'No?'

'No.' he shook his head

'Why not?'

'Because I'm French.'

'Oh. OK.' Julia nodded understandingly.

'They were worried about you,' he said. 'You've been gone for a long time.'

He took in the liquid turquoise of her eyes that were made even brighter by the smudged dark mascara. She'd obviously been crying and he felt a strange feeling of deep sadness. He held her gaze, hesitating about saying something but then whatever he'd seen had gone and she switched to glaring at him, so he decided against it. Then the eyes turned full on combat green. No, definitely not a good idea to say something.

'We thought you'd done a bunk and left Alan stranded with knee cramp on the middle of the proposal cushion,' he said.

'Don't be ridiculous,' said Julia. 'I was enjoying the peonies.' She dabbed her eyes with a tissue and walked past him back into the hall.

William and Eleanor, bedecked in large overcoats were waiting to say goodbye, and Georgie had mummified himself in an old Barbour jacket. Alan went off to get the rest of the coats and Julia took the opportunity quickly to call herself a cab. She couldn't possibly stay the night. The last thing she wanted to do was dive into bed. He was bound to be feeling rampant and she was so tired she couldn't even bring herself to pretend; she was scared, she so wanted things to work out for them.

Alan came out of the cloakroom just as she got through to the cab company. She could see he was annoyed.

'But, Julia,' he said, exasperated, 'it's our engagement night.'

'I know but I do have to be at the office very early. I've got the whole show to fix, Alan.' She felt terrible … her excuse sounded so lame.

Christophe coughed politely indicating that they were all ready to leave.

The image of herself and Alan standing arm in arm on the doorstep waving everyone goodbye would stay in

Julia's mind forever. William's wine-laden joviality as he staggered off with Eleanor, Georgie's adolescent excitability as he got to kiss Cassandra good night French fashion, and that smart-arsed Frenchman's cynical smile as he took her hand, crushing all her fingers. But most of all, the way she stood rigid in Alan's arms while he kissed her. She felt as they must have felt going down with the *Titanic* — very shocked and very cold.

She sat in the cab and rubbed her lips frantically. It was no use — they'd never worked. She'd never ever felt her knees buckle and her body collapse like a melting chocolate fondant when somebody kissed her — wasn't that what was supposed to happen according to books? Why didn't her lips work? Why didn't she ever get turned on? Maybe they didn't have neurons or something. She should go to the doctor. But how could she? Doctor, I have this terrible problem. I'm one hundred per cent frigid, and I have to marry for money so I'm engaged to a banker and could I have a lip transplant please? But it was even worse than that — she was worse than frigid: she just couldn't bear any human to touch her.

And why, oh why, had she invited that Frenchwoman to the show? It was going to be hell as it was. She was going to have a major hangover. Her right hand woman, Liane was going to have to leave early to get to Paris for the next day's meeting and then she'd got to pack and get to Paris herself. The last thing she needed was to have to entertain one of Alan's banker's bits as well.

When Julia crawled through the door of the flat she couldn't even be bothered to move the clothes off the bed so that she could get in properly. She just got in under the pile and dropped off almost immediately.

As her mind drifted into her dreams, the cynical Frenchman was suddenly there, complete with priest's dog collar, judge's wig and a long black robe, at the front of a musty church – she was on trial.

'Julia Connors. Swear on this bible that everything you say is the truth the whole truth and nothing but the truth, so help you God.'

'Mmm,' said Julia talking in her sleep. 'Yes.'

'Do you take this man to be your lawful husband to love and to cherish, to have and to hold, from this day forward?'

The jury was full of boutique customers all staring at her suspiciously. Then suddenly there was a loud clatter of a keyboard and the sound of the church organ burst into the air. William's flushed drunken face appeared above the keyboard; his laugh erupted, echoing around the church and he smiled lecherously at her.

Cassandra and Eleanor stood, black-robed, beside the Frenchman. Their grey white faces and enlarged eyes stared up at him with the adoration of the insane.

Georgie stood in the blood red robes of a choirboy playing with himself in the cloisters. There was no sign of Alan.

The Frenchman's brown eyes held hers. *'Do you, Julia Connors, promise to love and cherish this man?'* he repeated loudly.

'I do, I … I do' muttered Julia.

'But are you in love with him …?

Silence.

'… I said, "Are you in love with him?"'

'Yes well sort of, sort of like a brother really.'

'Julia Connors: are you in love with this man?'

'Yes, er … yes.'

'Do you promise to share all his worldly wealth?'

'Oh, Yes! Yes I do,' she said firmly.

'Do you swear by almighty God to help him in sickness and in health, for richer, for poorer?'

'Well I don't know; in sickness as well? Don't you think that's a bit unreasonable – I mean …'

Silence again. Then.

'No! No … No I don't love him. I don't. I've never loved him. I've never loved anyone!'

Suddenly Alan was standing there before her, a look of complete horror upon his hobbit face. His face was white and drawn and he was shouting. 'I don't want her! Get her away from me. It's her fault, take her away. Get her out of my sight.'

Julia began tossing and turning to try and get away from the dream. She was in a cold sweat and her hair was damp on her forehead.

The horror continued as Alan's face changed shape, moulding itself into the face of her father and she began screaming. 'No!'

'Take her away from me,' came her father's agonised cry. 'Get her away from me I don't want her anywhere near me. It's all her fault.'

'There rests the case for the defence, your honour,' said the Frenchman, gazing up at a stained glass window of the Crucifixion.

CHAPTER 2

Julia crawled from underneath a crêpe de chine blouse that had wound its way around her head in the night and groped for the tablets that she thought might be resting on the bedside table. Her hands shook and her head killed her. She was exhausted, her body ached from her frantic tossing and turning and she could feel that her leg had somehow been bruised in the night, either that or she'd walked into something. She couldn't find the tablets, but she found her phone instead and picking it up she tentatively half opened one eye to try and read it. She winced as a small beam of light managed to worm its way through the shade of her eyelashes and pierced its way right into her brain. She winced again and gave up. Her maths dyslexia was always worse with a hangover. She asked Lady Google what the time was, her voice dry and croaky.

'The time is six-thirty a.m.,' replied Lady Google happily.

Six-thirty! That was outrageous and totally unjust.

She'd only got to bed at one, for God's sake. Life just wasn't fair. If she went to bed at nine o'clock, a tribe of Scottish football supporters couldn't wake her, even by midday.

She pulled the duvet tighter round her and hid her eyes under the corner. Her head killed her, and when her head killed her this much she dared not reflect on what she'd been doing the previous night. Whatever it was, she'd obviously got the bruises to prove it.

Gradually her dreams began to float back to her. She'd been on trial and that smarmy Frenchman had been there. Even worse he'd been the vicar. Who the hell told him he could be the vicar? It was *her* dream wasn't it? He could clear off and feature in his own dreams in future. He really did make her nervous. He had this air like he was telepathic and knew what everyone was thinking and doing. She pushed the horrific incidents of the end of the dream right to the back of her mind. She'd got to be practical about life. She'd done it, she'd become engaged to Alan. She smiled wryly. Lady Bloomsbury would be furious, the snooty old cow, and that just made it even more worth it. Her plans were going perfectly. So long as she could keep her background a secret from Lady Bloomsbury, all would be just fine. As far as Alan was concerned, both her parents were dead and, as far as Julia was concerned, her father had never really existed. London society and Lady Bloomsbury would not be able to cope if they ever realised that the next son and heir to the Bloomsbury estates had a drunken tramp as a grandfather on the maternal side.

She decided it was best not to think about it too deeply, and jumped out of bed, shocking herself horribly.

Julia stood, hands on her hips, contemplating the mess of the room. Life was such hard work – that's the one thing they never prepared you for. The place was a tip and she hated it but she couldn't bring herself to do a thing about it. Still, it was Eloisa's day to come and clean, and tomorrow she'd be in Paris so it didn't matter.

Poor old Eloisa. She was Portuguese, newly arrived in London and her English was definitely not up to describing what she felt about Julia's ability to carpet the flat with dirty clothes and mugs. As far as Julia was concerned it was the perfect set-up, and so long as she continued to pay her well, Eloisa would keep coming.

Julia held her hand to her head. She'd just got to find some paracetamol. Where the hell had she seen them? She put the kettle on and searched for a clean cup. Not surprisingly there wasn't one in sight and there wasn't any washing-up liquid either. Taking the cleanest of the dirty mugs she cleaned it with hair shampoo. Well, it was all the same stuff.

As she put a spoonful of coffee in the cup and filled it with boiling water, a picture floated into her mind of a packet of paracetamol leaning against a half-dead parlour palm in the lounge, and she went off in search of it.

Empty. She threw it in the bin.

Another image of two loose tablets floating around in the bottom of her handbag appeared. She found them and, as no other images seemed to be about to emerge, she picked the fluff off them and washed them down with her black coffee. It was amazing how appetising black coffee became after a few years of watching milk fester into yoghurt on window-sills and in the darkest depths of an inefficient fridge.

Oh well, she'd just better get started. She had to pack for her Paris trip, check on the set for the show, call in at the boutique for the clothes, check the models and music, supervise the dressing and dress rehearsal and caterers, entertain the guests and still manage to get to the airport for her late evening flight.

Julia dived into action. She'd worked hard pulling herself up from the gutter to get where she was and she wouldn't let herself blow things because of a hangover. She'd spent a lot of time perfecting her manner, her walk and her appearance. She'd learnt the hard way about life. She cringed as she thought back to the sleazy back room in the *Rue Pigalle*. She'd been just fifteen. She could almost smell the damp musty room. The peeling, dung coloured walls and the pungent odour of the landlord as it mingled with the smell of burning crack as he lit a match under it and wafted it beneath her nose. She felt nausea rise in her throat and tried not to think any more, trying frantically to stop the horrific image from coming back into her mind.

This time she could not prevent it appearing. The look in his eye as he had come back that night. His fat swollen body as he had lunged towards her, the smell of stale wine upon his breath as he forced his mouth on hers. The pungent acid of stale sweat, the weight of his bulbous form upon her as he crushed her and forced her legs open. The sobs escaped her and she felt a wave of disgust wash over her. Oh God, why did it always haunt her? She started frantically rubbing and scratching her arms to try and get herself clean. She couldn't get the filth off her no matter how hard she rubbed. And her arms began to bleed. She panicked and the nausea returned, a huge wave rising up from her solar plexus and she ran to the bathroom and threw up.

For half an hour she sat there her head over the sink sobbing and retching, until her body ached. Eventually she was calmer. She pushed her hair back from her face and sniffed. She'd got to stay calm. She'd got to get up and move and get on with her life. She'd got to be logical. Julia sat up determinedly and began to pull herself together again.

She had made a vow to herself that she would never be poor again. She would never have to live in that kind of place. She'd walked down the *Rue Pigalle* that night and had never gone back. She'd been physically repulsed by any male contact ever since, steeling herself for embraces from people she knew could help her move on and move up. She'd used her looks and figure to her advantage. She'd spent every penny she'd earned by washing up and waitressing to take lessons and a modelling course until finally she got her big break. She'd seen Jean-Claude's work in the glossy magazines and she'd rung his offices time and time again at every hour of the day hoping that she would get to speak to him. Eventually late one night she got through to him in person and he'd agreed to see her and he had given her a job. Now she was manager of Jacquard UK, she could do all the things that any privately educated girl could do - riding and playing the piano, she knew about opera, ballet and art. She could move easily in the highest social circles and had a good job in the fashion world. And soon her life plan would be complete; she would marry into the English aristocracy.

She ignored her aching limbs, put cream on her scratched arms, she'd have to wear long sleeves again today, and she drove herself to action. She pulled out her clothes for the Paris trip and threw them into her suitcase; she could get them laundered when she arrived at the Hotel Medici. She dragged her favourite suede suit out of the pile on the bed and hung it up on the back of the bathroom door brushing it frantically with a clothes brush to remove the fluff. By the time she'd finished her bath the steam would have helped the creases drop and it would be as good as new.

She cursed as she couldn't find a clean white shirt with long sleeves and then realised that she had one of the new collection ready for photography in her bag. She laid it out on the bed. The thin collar went perfectly with the straight lines of the loosely cut jacket.

Flicking the radio on, she ran a bath and started humming to the mellow tones of Ella Fitzgerald. She laced the bath with Chanel and lazed in it, enjoying the smell as it wafted around her nostrils. Pure luxury. She soaped herself all over with matching Chanel soap. She shampooed her hair sitting in the bath and then stood under the shower to rinse it. At the last minute she turned the water temperature to cold, forcing herself to stand it for as long as possible and it helped, she was beginning to feel a bit revived.

Twenty minutes later she was ready. Immaculately dressed as every manager of a French fashion company should be, subtly made up as every beautiful woman should be and wearing her darkest *Ray-Bans* to disguise the remnants of a sleepless night, an hour of crying and a terminal hangover.

As she walked through the door, suitcase in hand, she bumped straight into Eloisa. Julia immediately started gesticulating wildly about how late she was and how sorry she was that she couldn't hang around and chat. 'Money in the pot,' she said and dived into the lift.

Eloisa stood hands firmly on her hips shaking her head and tutting knowingly as the lift doors closed and spirited Julia away. Julia bit her lip. Thank goodness she'd remembered to leave some cash; otherwise this time Eloisa really wouldn't come back.

Julia was first to arrive at the Jacquard building and opened up the back way, heading straight into her office. The boutique could wait until Liane arrived.

She dumped her case in the corner of the office, threw her jacket over the chair and sat down to go through the list of guests for the show. The rehearsal was scheduled for two and the show was due to start at five thirty. She'd got Lady Google primed to remind her throughout the day so that she didn't have to keep trying to work out the time. There were ten top and up and coming models lined up for the catwalk and Julia prayed that they all turned up in good form. Some of them were a bit young and hadn't yet developed the professionalism of the older ones but the older ones who'd made it weren't really interested in the catwalk any more, it didn't pay enough.

After about ten minutes the phone went.

'Hello, Jacquard UK. Julia Connors speaking.'

'Hi, Julia, it's Liane. Sorry I'm late. I'm just leaving so I should be there in an hour. By the way, I forgot to send that shirt off to the photographer's for you yesterday – you couldn't sent it, could you?'

'Oh no! Liane, I've got it on. Isn't there another downstairs in the store?'

'Yes but we used it on the last shoot and it's looking a

bit grubby.'

'Oh don't worry, I'll get it express cleaned and get them to deliver it straight there. I'll probably have to go to the Albert Hall and then on to the PR agency by the time you get in, so I'll leave a note if anything needs doing, OK?'

'OK. I've sent off the accounts as we discussed and there's the break down on the show costs on your desk, if you want to check them.'

'Check them? Very funny Liane,' Julia laughed. It was a standing joke between them. The last thing she was ever going to do was check the accounts. It would take her hours and she'd still get it wrong.'

'Thank you so much for doing them, Liane. As always, you are a star and the Champagne is on me.'

'Just name the time and place. By the way how did dinner with Alan go?'

'Well.' Julia paused and took a deep breath, 'I … hum … got engaged.'

There was silence at the other end of the phone.

'Liane? I said I got engaged.'

'I heard. Who to?'

Julia thought she must be hearing things. 'To Alan of course.'

'Oh. Congratulations.' Liane sounded distracted.

Liane had been the one who'd introduced Julia to Alan a couple of years back. She'd known him since they'd been at neighbouring schools.

'Liane, you didn't sound like you meant that at all. Are you OK?'

'I'm fine. I … I've just got a terrible hangover that's all.'

'Oh. Well, that makes two of us.'

'The thing is, Jules, last week you were going on about how half the time Alan was rushing off on business ignoring you and the rest of the time he was being too nice to you. You even said he deserved a nice girl who would marry him, stay at home and look after him, which is the last thing on earth you want to do.'

Liane was silent for a moment then continued, 'Look you know how it is. He's a good friend and I wouldn't like to see him get hurt. Well what are you going to do?'

'Marry him, of course. I mean, I do love him Liane, in my own way.'

Liane sighed. 'I know you do, Julia. I'm just not sure that your romantic ideas are going to be satisfied by Alan that's all.'

If only Liane knew the truth, thought Julia. If only she knew just how unromantic and frigid I really am.

They were interrupted as the other phone started to ring.

'Listen, I'll have to go. The other phone's going. I'll 'see you when I see you' at the show. '

Julia picked up the other phone.

'Miss Connors?' asked a deep voice.

'Yes,' replied Julia, 'Julia Connors speaking.' Then she bit her lip and raised her eyes in prayer. The voice sounded so official, please don't let it be Barclaycard, Access or the bank. I can't handle explaining everything today.

'Ah, hello it's Christophe de Flaubert. How are you?'

'Fine,' lied Julia relieved, 'and yourself?'

He didn't answer but continued efficiently with his own train of thought. 'You mentioned to Cassandra that there was a show on today and she'd very much like to come. Could you send an invitation over to her? It's 5, Eaton Square.'

'Of course,' said Julia 'Just the one invitation?' Won't you be coming then?' she asked, trying to be polite. He laughed dryly.

'No I have business to attend to in the City. In fact I have a meeting with your fiancé this morning.'

'Oh. Yes,' said Julia. How very correct of him using the word fiancé, like that. Although, she was fairly sure she could detect a note of sarcasm in his voice.

'Well, do say hello to him for me,' she said and then cringed again. What was wrong with her? What a stupid thing to say! 'Say hello to my fiancé for me.' He must think her a complete idiot.

CHAPTER 3

Julia launched herself into the preparations for the show. Everything that could possibly go wrong went wrong. Two of the models turned up late and one, Tessa, was totally unfit for the catwalk. It was much worse than drink too. The girl had been taking something a lot stronger and was way ahead of the racy Michael Jackson track that they were using. Julia had a word with one of the other girls who knew Tessa quite well.

'Sarah, is Tessa in as bad a way as I suspect? And she is way too thin now. You know Jean-Claude refuses to take models under a size eight.'

Sarah looked thoroughly miserable as she stood fiddling nervously with the buckle on her suede belt. She did not answer.

'Look, Sarah,' Julia put a friendly arm around her shoulders, 'it doesn't matter what Tessa does in her own time, but I just can't afford to let her go on the catwalk like that; she'd be a disaster.'

'Look, she really needs the money, Julia. She can't afford not to go on. She …. She's in big trouble. Julia please. You've used her before; you know she's good.'

'She used to be good, Sarah, until she got into whatever it is she's on.' Julia looked Sarah in the eye. 'Is it coke?'

Sarah shook her head. 'Worse'.

'Christ,' said Julia sighing. 'She's crazy.'

Sarah grabbed Julia's arm as she turned to go. 'Please Julia? Please don't tell the agency. You know they'll sack her, and she really badly needs the money.'

Julia nodded and thought for a moment. She fished in her handbag and pulled out one of the cards that she kept in an inside pocket. 'I'll get another girl from another agency today.' She said and handed it to Sarah.

'But you tell Tessa from me that if she doesn't ring this number and get help, the agency will sack her anyway and there's nothing I can do about it. The people at the agency aren't stupid, they'll know she has a problem.'

It wasn't much thought Julia but Tessa might just ring the number. Why did they do it? They were so young. The money, fame and excitement went to their heads. And they couldn't cope with the lifestyle – starving themselves to nothing and working solidly for a few years and then being dropped, becoming a 'has been'. Still, that wasn't her problem now, she just had to find another model and teach her the programme.

Later on, halfway through the dress rehearsal, a riot broke out over by the clothes rails. Serena and Danielle, two of the younger models, were arguing heatedly over the star evening dress of the show which was being snatched backwards and forwards between them. Julia stood horrified for a second watching two fake ostrich feathers fly to the floor as Danielle snatched it back again. Julia demanded silence. Her face looking like thunder, she stared at both of them for a second. Liane came in at that moment with the full programme and Julia asked for it in a quiet steely voice, her eyes still on the two models. Serena just stood staring at her, giving Julia the full benefit of watching her chew her gum like a cow on the cud. Danielle's mouth was pouting in a full-blown sulk.

'Right,' said Julia. The two models looked at her warily. 'The programme lists Danielle to wear the dress and if you don't pack it in, neither of you will wear it and Karl Fregère who is going to be sitting front row will think you're just a couple of low-key agency bimbos who aren't stylish or professional enough be in the finale, and neither of you will ever get a chance at doing the *Coco* commercial that we all know you're both angling for.' She smiled sweetly at them and went to check on the seating arrangements for the guests.

They'd been lucky enough to get Richard Blake, the distinguished Welsh actor to do the voice over for the show. His inclusion had all been down to Alan who used to drink in the same local Hampstead pub as Blake. Alan's Christmas card list, Julia had come to realise was like the latest edition of *Who's Who*. Julia wandered over to Richard to wish him luck, and to try and take his mind off drinking the extremely large whisky that was in his hand. He was renowned for his drinking capacity, and a slurred voiceover from Richard Blake would be worse than not having had Richard Blake in the first place.

Ten minutes before the guests were due to arrive, Julia was chatting to two of the leading fashion journalists while re-briefing the camera man when the electrician blew the main spots. He finally fixed them about a minute before they were due to start, by which time the only thing Julia could add to the evening were crossed fingers and a prayer.

As the music started, Julia stood at the back of the hall facing the front of the catwalk. She'd worked hard at this, she'd put her all into it but it didn't seem to make her any less nervous. She glanced down at the front row. Karl Fregère's isolated form as he lounged cross-legged with an unlit cheroot in one hand was as distinctive as ever, the punctuation at only the most important of fashion shows. Julia knew he was only scouting for new talent, a new *Coco*, a new prima ballerina for the Chanel ballet, but his presence anyway was the ultimate endorsement. The Paris couturiers rarely bothered with the London launches of the French collections and his presence meant that Julia's show was worth bothering with.

Julia's arms ached, her back ached and her lungs felt as if she'd been holding her breath since about April.

The finale music finished and Julia let out a long sigh as the audience began their rapturous applause.

She took a canapé from a passing waitress; she'd forgotten to eat all day, and headed over to circulate among the guests. Her real job of the evening was only just beginning.

As she moved towards the guests, the tall figure of Fregère, his greatcoat slung around his shoulders came towards her. He took her hand and asked that she walk with him to the door.

'An excellent show, Julia. Although it could have done without Jean-Claude Vasin's clothes of course.' He smiled wickedly and Julia tutted at him.

'Seriously though, Julia, come and see me next time you are in Paris. I have a proposition for you.' With that he kissed her cheek to cheek and slid into his large limousine.

Julia walked back into the hall stunned. What better endorsement could she ever have than that? Even Jean-Claude would be impressed, although he'd never admit to it.

There was a wonderful buzz in the hall when Julia returned to the guests and she wandered through, chatting to customers and catching pieces of excited conversation. The collection had gone down well and she had already heard customers frantically trying to extract promises of first choice on the evening gowns and suits. Julia had deliberately bought the section of the collection that was smart and chic in subtle shades, knowing her market well. She and Liane might adore Jean-Claude's most outrageous garments but most of her clients were very English and thought them too adventurous.

Cassandra Girault didn't turn up, but Alan did and immediately made Liane introduce him to a Gulf State ruler and his several wives. Julia smiled to herself: there was one thing you could say about Alan, he really did have a nose for money. She was just making her way over to talk to him when Lady Bloomsbury's head of expensively disguised grey hair appeared through the crush of customers. She inclined her head frostily in Julia's direction. Julia smiled and said hello in return and then they collided as they both darted towards Alan.

'Liane, look, I'm sorry. I really don't think this is quite the time ....' Alan's voice trailed off as he saw Julia and Lady Bloomsbury. 'Oh, hello, you two. A wonderful show, darling,' he said, moving to kiss her. Rather embarrassingly they clashed noses as he went to kiss her one side and she went the other.

'Isn't the time for what?' asked Julia remembering the conversation when she'd arrived.

'For discussing weddings and presents,' said Alan.

'I think you should take many wives and many presents, Mr Bloomsbury,' said the Sheik, smiling and indicating his happy household surrounding him.

Lady Bloomsbury's usually frosty face went into a permanent ice age. There was an uncomfortable silence and Alan looked at Julia with raised eyebrows. Liane, Julia noticed, looked very stressed out. Today was not a good day for either of them to have had hangovers and Liane was supposed to be on her way to Paris within the hour.

Julia was just about to make an attempt to cheer her up and get her on her way to the airport when Lady Bloomsbury piped up.

'Liane, my dear, you look beautiful. That dress does look lovely on you. Doesn't it, Alan?'

Liane smiled. 'Thank you Lady Bloomsbury, that's very kind of you to say so.'

'Alan, did you hear me? asked Lady Bloomsbury.

'What? Yes, oh yes, lovely.'

Julia, determined not to be hurt by Lady Bloomsbury blatantly ignoring her yet fawning over Liane yet again, caught sight of Karen Stall, one of the BBC's most influential news presenters, and went over to chat to her.

Lady Bloomsbury really was a complete dragon, thought Julia. She doted on Liane just because she went to school with half the Royal family and had a pair of hips like an incubator stand. Then she chided herself. Liane was sweet, kind and her friend and if it hadn't been for Liane's fantastic mathematical ability neither of them would be where they are today. They really were a perfect team. Julia felt guilty for having such mean thoughts. She made a promise to herself to really do something nice for Liane when they were in Paris.

Alan finally caught up with her after having worked the room methodically, starting with the billions and drawing the line at the millions. Contacts, he always said. Business is ninety per cent about good contacts. He slipped his arm around her waist.

'Sorry about Mummy, Julia. She'll come round. She just, well you know what she's like and you're just not the docile little thing that she'd wanted for a daughter-in-law.'

Before Julia could reply, Lady Bloomsbury appeared again from out of the mêlée.

'Alan darling, don't you think we should set a date?' Julia said smiling in triumph at his mother.

'Mm, I think we should make it later this year; hate all this long engagement stuff. That will give me time to sort this South American thing out and you'll have to work your notice, I suppose.'

Julia was surprised, 'Work my notice?'

'Well you wouldn't carry on at Jacquard, would you? I mean it exhausts you and you have to keep going out to Paris. I thought you'd want to give up work and besides I'd want you to come away with me on business.'

'I can see clearly that you two just haven't thought this thing through at all,' said Lady Bloomsbury smugly. 'Don't you think you'd better both think a little more about it before you set the date?'

'Not at all,' said Julia determinedly. She slipped her hand into Alan's. 'I don't think we should wait one minute; after all you never know what well-bred young debutante may be thrust into Alan's path in an attempt to snap him up.' She smiled sweetly at Lady Bloomsbury.

A little later in the evening Julia was talking to the manager of Crightons, the champagne reception bar and let slip about her engagement. Next thing she knew he was calling for silence from the stage.

'Ladies and gentlemen, champagne is being distributed amongst you, courtesy of Crightons, and I ask you to charge your glasses and toast Lord Alan Bloomsbury and Miss Julia Connors of Jacquard who have just become engaged. Julia and Alan.'

There was a loud cheer. Julia smiled and took a look at Lady Bloomsbury's face which seemed to be turning an increasingly darker shade of purple as people congratulated her too. So this was it, Julia's triumph at last. She would eventually inherit the title of Lady Bloomsbury, along with a few million to set up her home. However beneath her smiles, her face felt drained and she felt hollow inside. In the depths of her gut, something was niggling her and it wasn't due to the canapés, she was sure of that.

She looked up and her eyes caught the familiar guarded stare of Christophe de Flaubert approaching them from across the room. For a moment she felt as if those eyes were boring into her and then realised that she was staring at him. She quickly nodded and gave him a smile of welcome, before squeezing Alan's arm to tell him that Christophe was there.

'Christophe,' said Alan, shaking his hand frantically,

'I'm so glad you could make it. You're just in time for the champagne.'

'So I see,' he said. 'Congratulations, Alan, Miss Connors.' That cynical twitch was still playing around his lips and it annoyed Julia. It was as if he had a world monopoly of knowledge of everything that was going on.

'Cassandra isn't here,' snapped Julia. She was a little irritated. It had been quite a lot of trouble to sort out an invitation at the last minute and then Cassandra hadn't even deigned to come.

'I know,' said Christophe. 'She sent her apologies but she had to take an earlier plane back to Paris, there's been some changes on the schedule for the collection coverage next week. In actual fact I came to see Alan,' continued Christophe. 'We have a little more business to finish off. It's probably easiest if we go to Eaton Square,' said Christophe. 'It's the nearest.'

'Of course,' said Alan, his admiration for Christophe evident in his voice.

Before Julia could interrupt and remind Alan that he had said he would drive her to the airport, they began discussing the South American deal yet again. They must be planning to take over the whole bloody continent, the amount of time they've spent discussing it, thought Julia irritably.

Lady Bloomsbury had disappeared into the crowd, Julia could just see the bobble of her hair piece flitting up and down as she chatted her way to the bar. She's probably hoping the whole thing is a nasty dream thought Julia.

Left stranded between a load of Bolivian pesos and Brazilian cruzados, Julia realised she hadn't eaten properly again and grabbed another canapé and a glass of champagne from the passing waitress. What was wrong with her? Her plans were going so well, earlier on in the evening she'd been over the moon. Now she felt thoroughly miserable. An avalanche of chill went straight through her, and she began to shake visibly. When she looked up, Christophe de Flaubert was staring at her and Alan was sighing in exasperation.

'Julia darling, did you hear?' asked Alan. 'I said I thought October would be the best time to set the date for the wedding.'

'Oh yes, yes of course,' replied Julia enthusiastically. Alan gulped down the rest of his champagne. 'Listen, we are going to have to make a move. I'll call you later.'

'But, Alan, I'll be leaving for Paris later this evening. I thought you were going to drop me at the airport?' said Julia, trying desperately to look endearing.

For a moment Alan looked undecided but then he patted her hand and said very firmly, 'I'm sorry, darling, you'll have to get a cab.'

Julia's eyebrows rocketed. Get *a cab*?

'Anyway I know you hate saying goodbye at airports. I really do have to sort this thing out with Christophe. I'll call you tonight.'

Julia sulked furiously. She couldn't stand not to get her own way. Eventually she gave Alan a peck on the cheek and glared at the Frenchman. Just what was so great about the arrogant old Frog anyway.

CHAPTER 4

It had taken ages to clear up and organise the return of all the clothes after the show. Serena had very nearly got away with the black crêpe de chine and someone had spilt red wine all down one of the ivory satins. Sheena Jones and Guy Taylor from *Society* magazine sat it out until the last of the drink ran out, making her late and when Julia had tried to get hold of Alan he'd already switched his phone off. She'd finally left so late that she'd missed her original flight and was having to catch the last one.

She sat quietly in the corner of the Heathrow airport lounge just relieved to be finally through passport control, luggage check-in and all the other bureaucracy that moving fashion show equipment entailed. She was still hyped up from the show and her mad rush to get to the airport and had arrived only to find that the last flight was delayed due to fog. May, and they were grounded due to fog. England was impossible.

Julia looked around her, miserable from exhaustion.

Airports at night were so different to airports during the day. During the day there was a real buzz of excitement, people going places and doing things. At night they metamorphosed into sad desperate places where people were overtired and impatient. Heavily coated, heavy-hearted executives waited impatiently for their flight calls. A young mother's children wailed with tiredness and boredom, and she stared at the dingy mustard coloured seats, unmoved by their screams.

I hope the weather in Paris is better than this, thought Julia. Even though she now lived in London, she still had a soft spot for Paris, despite what had happened to her. Something always drew her to Paris. She'd run away there three times before the English orphanage had given up on her. Paris was where she'd fought to make herself into something; her mother had been Parisian, and Paris was in her blood.

She remembered that very first day when she had walked into Jean-Claude's office, bold as brass, thinking that the second hand fifties suit that she'd bought at great cost would really do the trick and secure her the job and the fact that she couldn't get past two plus two equals four in mathematical ability wouldn't matter at all. How naïve she'd been. She thought she knew the ropes. She arrived to be greeted by a sour-faced Madame Boucher, Vasin's long-time assistant who sniggered with delight at the shabby suit, the rough, reddened hands and badly cut hair. But Julia had been determined and refused to be daunted, she held her head high and walked with poise, just as she'd been taught. This had only seemed to enrage Madame Boucher even more. Julia could see the hatred on her face now, as if she'd had a premonition of things to come.

She'd insisted that Jean-Claude was out and would not see her. But Julia had an appointment; she had spoken to Monsieur Vasin himself, she'd insisted. Madame Boucher had laughed viciously, her voice cruel with disbelief as she'd said that there really wasn't any point in Julia seeing Monsieur Vasin because she was, well – how could she put it? – highly unsuitable for a stylish company like Jacquard.

Julia had been furious. She'd rung and rung trying to get hold of Jean-Claude Vasin and now that she had an appointment this horrible woman was turning her away. It was so unfair. Her eyes had taken in the room, the dazzling clothes displayed in the pictures on the walls, the plush designer office furniture and the expensive chrome desk and her gaze had moved across to Madame Boucher looking grey and school marm-ish.

'If Jacquard is such a stylish company, how come you work here?' she'd retorted, believing that all was lost. She was saved from Madame Boucher's retaliation by the loud commotion that accompanied Jean-Claude as he emerged from his office in a complete fury. Everything was wrong; he was surrounded by imbeciles everywhere, he'd said. The machinist had made a complete mess of the design and he doubted if it would fit a turkey, let alone look as he'd intended on a human being. They'd sent him a model that looked like a refugee. Didn't they have any models with curves? You know, breasts and hips? He wasn't expecting Bridget Bardot but at least a hint of a feminine figure would do. He couldn't possibly work, it was like trying to fit clothes on a corpse and as he wasn't into designer shrouds, he suggested they find him someone with a bit of flesh on them. And what's more, a corpse would have had more interest in his work too.

Then he had seen Julia standing there, looking warily at an obviously furious Madame Boucher. He eyed her up and down, the long slim legs, full firm bust and delicately curving hips. 'Perfect,' he said 'Come in here, I want to fit a garment on you.'

'But … but' stammered Madame Boucher.

Julia smiled to herself. She'd never looked back since and Madame Boucher had never forgiven her either, the sour-faced old trout. Julia had later found out that Madame Boucher's brother was a shareholder in Jacquard and that was why she was tolerated. Throughout the two hours that Julia had been with Jean-Claude she had set about charming him. She took pains to speak properly but when he accidentally stuck a pin in her she'd let slip a curse that came straight from the street. There was silence for a moment and then Jean-Claude's wrinkled features had creased up and he burst out laughing, saying she was the cheekiest little devil he'd ever seen.

Vasin was wonderful, totally nutty and ridiculously generous too. It pleased him that she had come from nowhere and he took great pains to encourage her. He would often slip her extra cash so that she could buy the beautiful accessories required for a life in the fashion world and so keep up with other managers, most of whom came from a more affluent background. Eventually Julia had won through – to the annoyance of Madame Boucher.

Julia sighed. There was only one thing left to achieve to complete her perfect life-plan, and that was her marriage to Alan.

She sat quietly, and casually looked around her. Across the rows of seats a middle-aged woman sat staring at passers-by and anybody who seemed more interesting than her husband, who was absorbed in his paper.

Later Julia glanced up again and caught the wife looking at her across the lounge. Julia narrowed her eyes slightly and held the woman's gaze. Eventually the woman dropped her eyes in embarrassment. Julia sighed. She should be used to being stared at she supposed, after all that was the objective of high fashion, to cause a stir, but she had never quite come to terms with it. Underneath, she was always nervous and wanted desperately to drop her head and hide from the stares. It was the hardest thing she'd had to learn, walking tall and confident when all she wanted to do was tunnel into a corner and hide. And encounters with this kind of woman were the worst. She'd seen them in Jacquard often enough; negative types who would rather bring the world down to their level than make the best of their own assets. She supposed you couldn't blame her for staring though, there wasn't much else to do and her husband didn't exactly seem to be the most scintillating man on earth.

Julia considered defying all the unwritten rules of airport etiquette by going over and introducing herself politely for a chat.

She watched them for a while, nosiness getting the better of her shyness. The man had to be her husband. They hadn't spoken to each other for over an hour now. Her eye for the fashionable – or unfashionable – assessed them quickly.

He was dressed in an over-worn, over-baggy pinstripe suit with an ostentatious matching red lapel handkerchief and tie (her contribution, no doubt). He kept folding and re-folding his paper over and over again and fanning himself with it.

You could see it irritated her. She'd frown, tight-lipped, every time he re-folded it.

Her supposedly smart navy and white suit was covered with contrasting piping around the pockets and the spatula-shaped, over-wide lapels. It looked brand new. Julia could imagine the scene now; the way she'd bought it specially when he'd finally relented and said, 'Oh if you really must, then come to the conference with me.'

By the look on his face he was regretting his decision.

The woman's suit clashed horribly with the mustard and bottle green upholstery. Julia began to feel dizzy from fatigue and lack of food.

A waft of a dry but pungent cigar smell reached her nostrils and she glanced over to see a portly, Germanic-looking man sucking on his unlit cigar as if it contained the stuff of life itself. He was moving at pace towards the foggy smoking room.

That's what the pinstripe man will look like in ten years' time, thought Julia, glancing back at the couple.

The unrepentantly plastic voice of the tannoy droned on and on, and Julia, feeling tired and irritable, mentally cursed it, knocking her magazine to the floor as she did so.

She bent to pick it up and found herself bumping into a bright smiling face, crowned with reddish, curly hair, and just a trace of freckles over a very long, very straight nose.

'Oh excuse me. If you please.' he said in what amounted to an American accent with a touch of French sentence construction. 'Allow me.' He smiled a charming mischievous smile and flamboyantly passed Julia her *Paris Match*.

'You're French?' he asked, his smile being replaced by a slight glimmering in his eyes.

'Err no, no, I'm English, well half French. Thank you,' she said taking the *Paris Match* from his well-manicured hands.

Julia wasn't conscious of shivering slightly.

'But you speak French, naturally,' he said eyeing the magazine.

'Yes … yes I do,' replied Julia hesitantly. If there was one thing she hated it was strangers who tried to talk to her at airports, or even worse on the plane when she was trapped and couldn't get away.

'You must be on the Paris flight then,' he continued.

'Yes, yes I am.'

God, this guy was persistent. She gave him a forced professional smile that he couldn't help but read as 'get lost' and, to her amazement, he laughed, flopped into the seat beside her and said, 'Good, so am I, so we can be friends then.'

Julia was suddenly conscious that the wife in the navy suit was muttering to her husband and flashing a supercilious smile in their direction. Damn you, she thought and turned her full attention on the Frenchman, replacing her bad mood with one of mischief as she proceeded to flirt outrageously with him.

In the end it turned out to be very entertaining. In fact she had the time of her life. Smiling and laughing she tossed her hair back and kept an eagle eye on the wife who so obviously disapproved of people picking up young men at airports. She could see the woman straining to pick up their conversation as they vied over who'd been to the wildest parties or drunk champagne in the most unusual venues of the world. Freckle Face won hands down with his champagne lobster picnic in the lagoon of Bora Bora.

Julia figured her companion must be in his mid-twenties; just a little younger than herself, but she couldn't be sure, red hair and freckles tended to make a man look much younger than he was. She looked enviously at his thick, reddish curls – many women paid a fortune to achieve that pre-Raphaelite look. He was quite amusing, and a man of discerning taste if the Hugo Boss suit was anything to go by. He said his name was Jaimie and that he was on his way back home to Paris and then travelling on to Provence.

Julia wasn't usually one for making polite conversation, but one more look at the nosy woman's supercilious grin and she found herself agreeing to a bottle of champagne.

It went straight to her head and freckle face soon had her in hysterics with his very rude assessment of everybody in the lounge. He'd decided the woman in the navy suit was an undercover agent for the Russians and her suit was the latest in social warfare, guaranteed to hypnotise any enemy that looked at it; and the portly man with the cigar was an ex Nazi Columbian drug dealer, wanted by the FBI.

Finally their flight was called and Julia found herself being escorted through the boarding gate and into her seat. Unluckily for her, she found herself seated next to the Russian agent and her husband but before she knew it Jaimie traded places with the husband and managed to get Julia the window seat, placing himself next to her. The woman looked furious, but her husband smiled warmly at them. Jaimie suggested that he was probably relieved that he didn't have to sit next to his wife.

Now that the long delay was over, Julia was looking forward to getting off the ground: even now, she still got a thrill when she thought of Paris. She loved to see the tiny lights and the whole city spread below her as the plane neared the airport. Each time her eye would try to find the *Rue Pigalle* and then quickly move on following the roads until she came to the Arc de Triomphe. She would go over the route in her mind, time and time again finally ending up at the Avenue Montaigne, one of the chicest streets in Paris and she would smile. She'd done it. She'd dragged herself from the bottom to the top spot in the world of fashion.

Jaimie caught her smiling to herself. 'Why do you smile like this, *chérie*?'

Julia laughed. 'Oh, no reason really. It's just been a long time and a long road that's all.'

'Ah. And you have worked hard and now here you are and you still have to work hard. Is this true?'

'Yes. But I enjoy it, so now the hard work doesn't matter.'

'But there are other ways of earning a living, a good living, a great living with not so much hard work, Julia.'

Julia looked unconvinced.

'Like marrying for money, this is one, and a beautiful girl like you would have no problems there eh?'

Julia gulped. She wondered if she had "Bloomsbury takeover bid" plastered across her forehead or something.

'And there are even better ways than that. Work is for the sad people who have been born with few attributes, the people born without looks or brains to help them. Think about it Julia and maybe I will tell you the secret of wealth with little effort - if you are nice to me.'

Once they were at Orly, Julia let Jaimie guide her through

baggage and passport control, which were a lot quicker than usual. As they stepped out into the arrivals hall, a flashbulb went off in their faces as the paparazzi moved in. In one swift movement Jamie grabbed the camera from the offending photographer and smashed it on the back of a seat swearing, '*Mais merde! Espèce de gros conard!*'

The photographer stood in front of him, equally angrily

'I'll make you pay for that. This camera cost two thousand dollars.'

'You don't have the right to take my picture!' said Jaimie

'What's your problem Girault? One day you want us to take your picture to make you famous, then the next day you're smashing cameras. Today you come back to Paris with a beautiful new lady and you smash the camera. You're a sick man and you are going to have to pay for this,' he gestured towards the camera.

'No. I'm not paying for that. You should ask before you take pictures and I was only trying to protect my fiancée.' Jaimie putting a protective arm around her.

'Really? Your fiancée? And you think this is not news for us? I tell you what Monsieur Girault…' He pulled out a smaller spare camera from his bag. 'You give me a nice picture and I won't sue you for the camera? OK?'

'Jaimie, I think …' Julia started to interrupt but Jaimie, though furious was already nodding in agreement.

'OK. One picture!'

Jaimie pulled her slightly roughly towards him and smiled lovingly. The smile did not reach his eyes.

'Smile Julia darling, this isn't the way I wanted to announce it but that's the paparazzi for you.' This time his cheeky grin did reach his eyes and Julia began to see the funny side of it. Her laughter was infectious and Jaimie began to laugh too. That set off a whole stream of people laughing and photographing them.

'Oh well,' said Jamie, 'what is it you English say? In for a penny, in for a pound. I adore that expression.'

'Me too,' laughed Julia.

He offered her a lift to her hotel and soon they were heading straight for the lights of Paris in his Porsche.

'I'm sorry about that,' said Jaimie. 'The press drive me mad! They hang around trying to catch you in a compromising situation and then plaster it all over their gossip columns with ridiculous headlines. Anyway that will get that photographer going, I just couldn't think of anything else to say. They are always hounding *la famille* Girault.'

'Girault?' asked Julia amazed. 'Then, are you related to Cassandra Girault?'

'You know her?' asked Jaimie, turning to look at her for a moment. Julia clutched her hand to mouth, wishing to God he'd keep his eyes on the road.

'She is my half-sister,' he said. Where did you meet her?'

'At a dinner party in London earlier this week,' replied Julia.

'She's a darling,' said Jaimie smiling. 'She's my best friend in the world and she is one of the cleverest women I know, except where men are concerned. She's got the most appalling taste in men.'

'You're telling me,' laughed Julia. 'She was at this dinner party with Christophe de Flaubert. Do you know him?'

Jaimie's face went rigid. 'Yes,' he said abruptly.

The atmosphere suddenly felt quite chilled. He obviously didn't like Christophe de Flaubert that much. Well, they had something else in common then, and Julia began to like Jaimie even more. He didn't say anything else so she surmised that he didn't want to talk about Monsieur de Flaubert. At last she'd found someone who didn't think the sun shone out of that infuriating man's backside.

The champagne seemed to have worn off and a slight headache was setting in. Julia became a little edgy. She really shouldn't have drunk so much. She was tired and if she wasn't careful she'd be emotional too; champagne usually made her cry. Sometimes she wondered why she didn't just save herself the trouble and the hangover by just pouring the bottle straight into a box of tissues. She licked her top lip; her mouth felt like a dried up Saharan well and she knew her eyes were turning red from tiredness.

'If I didn't have to be back to the veritable familial residence I'd invite myself in,' said Jaimie, reverting to his charming, smiling self as they approached the Hotel Medici. 'The trouble is I've got to drive back tonight, I have some rather important business to attend to first thing in the morning.'

'What is the family business?' asked Julia quickly. She'd no intention of asking him into the hotel anyway. She was already beginning to regret the little engagement charade. What if Alan heard? Mind you, there was no reason that he should.

'Oh, mainly wine. We have one of the best vineyards in the South of France. Our family have been making wine for over a thousand years. We've had our ups and downs of course but I am working on a new project. It's top secret at the moment... because ... well you have seen how the paparazzi treat us!'

Jaimie pulled up outside her hotel.

'When can I see you again, Julia? It's been so very nice. I feel that you and I could do very well together. You are an incredibly beautiful woman and we have such chemistry.'

Chemistry, thought Julia, what the hell could have made him think that? She didn't have chemistry with anyone. Her lack of chemistry was so profound, if she was a soufflé she'd come out as a pancake.

'How long are you in Paris?' He asked, looking intently into her eyes as he took her hand in his. Julia found herself shivering at his touch. She could not hide it and she pulled her hand away from his, almost too quickly. She gave him a lukewarm smile and rushed into the hotel.

Jaimie followed her, smiling arrogantly to himself as he brought in her bags and handed them over to the porter whilst she checked in. He blew Julia a kiss as she was led off to her room. She could hear him laughing loudly to himself which did nothing for her self-esteem.

They took her bags to her usual room and when she arrived there she found Jean, the concierge, waiting for her with a large bottle of champagne on ice.

'Who left this?' she asked with surprise.

'Monsieur Girault, Mademoiselle.'

Julia grinned; this guy was so over the top it was untrue. She admired his organisation – how the hell had he managed to get a bottle of champagne into her room in the short time she was checking in?

She poured herself a glass and read the note that was attached to the bottle. 'The finest Dom Perignon, to celebrate our engagement, all my love Jaimie.'

She topped up her glass and then said to Jean. 'Would you like a glass, Jean, courtesy of Monsieur Girault.'

Jean smiled warmly at her and shook his head. No thank you Mademoiselle Connors. I do not drink when I am working.'

'Of course. I apologise, Jean,'

'No need to *Mademoiselle*.' He seemed hesitant.

'Is something the matter, Jean?' asked Julia, aware of his unease.

'Err …this man he is how do you say? Young? Impetuous?'

Julia laughed, but underneath was curious. She knew Jean well and he was the most discreet and impeccably mannered concierge she had ever met. Certainly not one for idle gossip, nor for speaking his mind. He obviously had some strong feelings about Jaimie Girault for him to warn her like that. It intrigued her. What was so bad about Jaimie? How wonderful, she'd met a real rebel. She sighed and smiled at Jean.

'It is okay, Jean, don't worry. He only gave me a lift from the airport, and you're right – he is young.'

Jean smiled, nodding to himself and left reassured. He would hate *Mademoiselle* Julia to get mixed up with such as Jaimie Girault.

Julia lazed back against the chaise longue gazing out at the Seine and sipped her champagne, contemplating her trip. Fancy Jaimie being related to Cassandra. She wondered idly why he detested Christophe de Flaubert – probably didn't like him hanging around with his sister.

Although, from what Julia had seen, Cassandra could certainly look after herself – and she absolutely drooled over the arrogant Christophe. And she could keep him, for all Julia cared.

CHAPTER 5

The next morning turned out bright and clear. Julia was up and out early and decided to walk to the Jacquard offices, taking the long route along the Seine and then cutting up towards Avenue Montaigne, home to all the major fashion houses. It always paid to see what the competition was up to.

There is nothing on this earth like the flamboyant shop windows of the haute couture houses. This year they really had taken the spring theme on board – brightly clad models looked down their noses at the astonished-looking stuffed rabbits, giant plastic eggs and pot plants that surrounded them.

Here she was in May with the summer clothes already well into their season, the next winter collection already launched and she was on her way to see and order the clothes for the next summer. Julia found it a slightly bizarre system, because in London you could never tell what the seasons were anyway.

As she walked along she was pleased to see that Pierre

Marcelle had gone totally overboard with the fuchsia. Their window had been decked out with giant fuchsia blooms and the mannequins were mostly hidden beneath great, wide brimmed, green hats. It looked just like a cheap lampshade store. I really must find out who does their windows, thought Julia – if only so that we never use them.

She reached the Jacquard offices just two minutes early and went in search of Liane.

Liane found her first. 'Hi, Julia darling, the collection is fantastic. You should see the ball gowns for next year – they're simply a dream and they've got this elaborate brown and fluorescent orange embroidery all over them. They're simply and utterly the sweetest and divinest of things. – Actually they look as if they've been upholstered rather than designed,' she added for Julia's ears only.

Julia sighed and asked, 'Madame Boucher?'

'Afraid so.'

Julia groaned. When Madame Boucher's brother had died and she'd inherited his shares, she became the second largest stockholder in Jacquard, and felt this gave her divine right to interfere in the designing and production of all the collections. She was the bane of Jean-Claude's life, not to mention the European buyers. Jean-Claude could not get rid of her because he could not afford to buy her stock, but he couldn't work with her either. In the end he had given her free rein to design three or four items each year in the hope that she would leave his own designs alone. The embarrassing result was that none of the buyers would ever take Madame Boucher's stuff because they didn't like it.

Liane was terrible; she was always enthusing

sarcastically over Madame Boucher's concoctions. The worst one they had ever seen was a horrendous emerald green and scarlet taffeta number that would have gone down well as the centre-piece at the Blackpool illuminations. Julia had bought one, betting Liane a hundred pounds that she couldn't sell it. The whole thing backfired though when Lady Bloomsbury bought it and arrived at an haute couture charity ball wearing it. Julia remembered the evening clearly, she'd spent the whole night trying to camouflage her behind the Christmas tree.

'Have you had a chance to go through the drawings yet, Liane?' asked Julia.

Liane shook her head 'No. You know what a pain Boucher is. As usual she insisted we look at her designs first and pick what we want before we get to see the decent stuff. It's the only way she can sell it. I picked a couple of simple things out, but you might want to check them.'

'That's fine. Let's go for a coffee and croissant and go over it. Do you know where Jean-Claude's designs are?'

'Well, no. Boucher wouldn't let anyone see them. But Jean-Claude has his own set and he's in, I saw him.'

'Okay, I'll have a word. Meet me in *La Coupole* in ten minutes – oh and I'll have a mocha coffee and croissant'.

Liane winked and Julia headed up the stairs to Jean-Claude's office.

There was a rule that all the international staff could have a quick glance at the collection before the show, but had to wait until after its launch to put their buying proposal together. Jacquard's principle, like most of the big Paris names was exclusivity. They made enough of the dresses shown at collections to have a good selection in most of the great 'society' cities, - London, Paris, New York – but never flooded the market. The rule was that there should always be more buyers than garments. People bought the likes of Jacquard because they knew if there were only three dresses in the whole of London they would be unlikely to arrive at a society event and find someone wearing the same thing.

At the Paris show, the European and Americans did their buying from the list on the collection, the first proposals in got honoured and the last had to take whatever was left – usually the progeny of Madame Boucher's unusable creativity. The evening dresses and, if there was one, the wedding dress, were always the most sought after.

It was well know that Jean-Claude had a soft spot for Julia and she invariably ended up getting her proposal together before the collection was even out, although she hadn't left herself much time to get her act together.

She knocked on his door and entered as she heard his brusque reply. The old man's features lit up as she went in.

'Julia, chérie, I was expecting you yesterday; how are you? You look tired and thin, you terrible girl, what have you been up to?'

He kissed her on both cheeks, and gave her a fatherly hug; at the same time passing her a large file of sketches.

'You have two hours, Mademoiselle, and don't tell anyone or I'll be the next grindstone for La Boucher's machete.'

She laughed, kissed him on the cheek and ran off down the stairs to meet Liane.

Julia had no qualms about taking the file. If anything,

she enjoyed getting everybody riled. Madame Boucher would happily stab her in the back just as readily as she got up in the morning and ten times more often. And if the London boutique was making the biggest profit, they deserved a good crack at the collection. The only people who got a look in first were the French buyers themselves. Julia had tried once to get the file before them but the ensuing rows had practically blown the windows out on three floors. Jean-Claude had threatened to let Madame Boucher design the collection for evermore, so the whole company had ganged up on Julia and made her relent.

She met Liane and in half an hour they'd got the whole of the next summer's collection worked through.

The show was held at the Winter Palace. Everyone who was anyone in the fashion world was there, along with a host of celebrities who had become influential through film and television. The main objective of most of the non-business guests was to be seen to be wearing the most outrageous garment ever. This year it consisted of wearing the lowest cut and flimsiest of tops. The whole room gyrated to a two-beat tempo of women shaking themselves back down into boned bodices: first the left, then the right …

For Julia and Liane it was business as usual and they took their seats in the front row between Carla, the Spanish buyer, and Ingrid, who headed up Scandinavia.

The lights dimmed and the rustling of programmes ceased along with the excited whisperings.

The midnight black catwalk extended the full length of the ballroom and a single spotlight tailed the models as they sidled languorously from one end to the other. The contrast of the mixture of platinum blondes and midnight black models showed off the mainly black and white collection to perfection. Evening wear was dramatic – tailored chocolate, deep slate grey or mink coloured satin evening suits cut to the tiny waists of the models. The men were dressed in beautifully tailored dinner suits, the famous Jacquard print waistcoats and silk scarves. The whole performance was an erotic gender neutral wiggling and cocking of hips and heads.

The finale produced a typically cute touch from Jean-Claude. The lights went completely out and the music started softly, built to a crescendo and suddenly stopped. One single child soprano's voice rang out pure as an angel, and there was a unanimous gasp of delight as the single spotlight centred on the bride in the centre of the stage.

Using a delicate Chinese satin, with a sophisticated minimal amount of Bruges lace, Jean-Claude had created a fairy-tale wedding dress. It was cut to the line of the lace across the front of the neck and along the back, revealing the model's creamy white skin. The skirt was cut away at the front to reveal the model's long legs. The sleeves were delicately trimmed to the cut of the lace, as was the veil which was pinned to the model's hair with a diamond tiara.

The single soprano was joined by a choir as the rest of the bridal party joined the bride on stage. Three tiny page boys in silk bolero jackets with scarlet bandanas and white silk shirts unenthusiastically dragged on three bridesmaids dressed in miniature scarlet versions of the bride's dress, which gained Jean-Claude a standing ovation.

There were tears in his eyes as those nearest to him hugged him, and congratulated him warmly. Julia laughed as he secretly threw her a wink, revealing that the tears were just a little added atmosphere on his part.

As they all moved off to the champagne reception, Jean-Claude freed himself and found Julia. He handed her a glass of champagne. 'You like the dress, *chérie*?'

'Jean, it was terrific!' she said hugging him back as he put his arm around her waist. 'That lace was beautiful. Did you design that too?'

'But of course. Everything. The lace is embroidered with the traditional symbols of Provence.'

'It really was beautiful, Jean.'

'Good, *bien, bene*,' he said, satisfied, and wandered off, leaving Julia wondering at the glint in his eye.

As Julia piled her plate up with some of the vast array of delicacies at the buffet, she noticed a heated discussion seemed to have broken out on her left and, as she turned to look, Liane left the group and came over to talk to her.

'Well, that's set the cat among the pigeons.'

'They've all got their claws out already then,' replied Julia, tucking into a large prawn and caviar vol-au-vent. 'I imagine it's over the wedding dress. I don't expect there's much of that lace around so there can't be many dresses up for grabs.'

'It's worse than that,' laughed Liane. 'There aren't any.'

'*What*?' Julia stared in disbelief.

'Jean-Claude has decided that the wedding outfits aren't for general release. He says there's only one and he's keeping it.'

Julia really was laughing now. 'He's such an old devil. Bet he's got it reserved for some celebrity wedding. Can you think of any actresses that are about to tie the knot?'

'No, can't think of anyone.'

'No wonder they're going crazy' laughed Julia. 'Still, I don't think we'll need one do you?'

Liane looked at her suspiciously. 'Well, what about you?'

Julia smiled. 'I suppose I do now. Do you think it's me though?'

'Of course it's you.'

'But Jean-Claude doesn't even know I'm engaged! Whatever you do don't say anything to him. He'll go mad when he finds out I'm marrying an Englishman; he'll never forgive me. He's spent the last two years sending me on blind dates with Frenchmen.'

'I know. He's terrible,' said Liane. 'He believes romance and sensuality are strictly French prerogatives.'

'Wonder what happened to Boucher's share?' asked Julia, taking a large bowl of olives from a passing waitress and beginning to tuck into them. 'She's about as sensual as a dumper truck.'

At that moment Carla stomped over. 'Julia, do something. He is crazy. He is – what do you English say? A soppy sod?'

She was soon joined by Ingrid who, in her perfectly articulated English, said, 'How can you he produce a garment like that for his collection and then not allow us even one each? It is simply not economic. I think he's senile.'

'Boucher's not economic,' said Liane, 'but she's survived.'

At that point the dragon herself appeared across the room, heading straight for Julia. Julia felt she knew just how the infantry felt watching tanks approaching remorselessly over the frontier.

'Julia Connors, I'd like to see you in my office at eight-thirty tomorrow morning.' Madame Boucher had the ultimate look of triumph on her face.

Julia sighed, suddenly feeling exhausted by it all. She couldn't think what she'd done now, but Boucher was looking so confident, she had obviously found some particularly slimy dirt this time.

'Of course, eight-thirty,' said Julia, knowing her brain had told her face muscles to smile, but that nothing had happened.

'And Cassandra Girault is doing live interviews for the Paris Clothes Show over by the catwalk, she'd like to talk to you, though God knows why,' added Madame Boucher, obviously very pleased with herself.

'And be careful what you say to her, we don't want you putting your foot in it.' Julia felt sure she heard Boucher click her heels and tut in synchrony as she turned and stomped off.

Julia excused herself from the group, grabbed another canape and went to find Cassandra Girault. She now very much regretted her behaviour at Alan's dinner party, almost as much as having eaten so many olives. Cassandra was bound to be looking for revenge. But Julia had invited her to the show at Crighton's; she had tried to make amends – well sort of. She sighed; she had an immense sense of impending doom which was made worse by the olives that were now churning around in a sea of nervous stomach acid.

'Hello, Julia,' said Cassandra, shaking her hand formally without even a hint of a smile. She was efficient and totally unflustered. 'Thanks for coming over. I just want to do a short interview; how you think the English

66

will react to the new collection and that sort of thing.' Cassandra looked immaculate in a crisp linen suit. Julia never felt confident enough to wear linen. It was fine for the first ten seconds then it disintegrated into crumples, making it look as if she'd quickly run up a couple of tea towels from the charity shop.

They asked her to sit down in the interview seat and an assistant ran on with a hand iron and sorted out a couple of crumples that had appeared on Cassandra's jacket. So that's how she does it, thought Julia, squinting as a technician pointed the main spot right at her. She couldn't see a thing and she'd eaten far too much, too quickly; the heat was making her nauseous.

Eventually Cassandra took her seat opposite, crossed her long legs and smiled supposedly at Julia but obviously at the camera behind her. Julia smiled back at the camera that was pointing at her over Cassandra's left shoulder, like a sniper.

The heat from the spotlights was stifling and Julia felt a trickle of perspiration run down her forehead into her eye. She wiped it away and looking down was horrified to see a massive black smudge. The sweat had made her mascara blotch and she must have wiped it all over her face. She made a move to ask if they could just hold on for a moment while she rectified things, but the floor manager was already gesticulating wildly that he was ready to roll. The heat of the spotlight was insufferable and Julia began to feel dizzy.

The camera light turned green and Julia knew the interview was rolling.

Her hair was sticking to her forehead and she felt sure she could smell it burning beneath the spotlight. Julia nervously tried to push it back from her face, inadvertently wiping more mascara everywhere. She closed her eyes for a moment, desperate to stop the psychedelic dance that the spotlights and cameras were doing.

'Julia, you have a special relationship with Jean-Claude Vasin and have been very influential at Jacquard over the past few years; how do you think the takeover by Boucher Enterprises will affect the Jacquard designs?'

Julia went completely white with shock. Boucher Enterprises? Boucher had taken over Jacquard?

Cassandra watched Julia for a second, smiling with pleasure at Julia's obvious discomfort.

'Well, I … wasn't … err I didn't …'

'Oh. You didn't know?' Cassandra looked falsely sympathetic. 'This must be quite a shock for you then?'

The camera zoomed in on Julia who felt herself swaying giddily in her chair. *You're fine, you're fine, you're not going to be ill*, she tried to brainwash herself, her voice reverberating around her head hysterically. She'd never felt so sick in her whole life and she could barely hear Cassandra's voice as she continued with the interview.

'It has been said of you in the past that you were the main source of conflict between Jean-Claude Vasin and the Boucher administration, do you think your own position is in any danger through this takeover?'

Julia gulped, the spotlight burned into her head, nausea rose in her throat and she knew her brainwashing had failed. Panic-stricken she dived off the interview set and threw up over camera four.

'Cut! Goddamn it! Cut!' screamed the floor manager.

Julia groaned as she lay in bed. It was the end – it really was. She couldn't have left the Winter Palace quicker if she'd spontaneously combusted. Liane had come running after her and luckily had managed to grab a cab and get her back to the Medici before going off to catch her flight back to London. Julia had never been so embarrassed in her whole life. She'd seen Cassandra laughing as she'd left too. It was a nightmare. Even Jean-Claude had been furious, he'd walked around looking like thunder, refusing to speak to Julia. Now it entered her head that he might not have known about the take-over himself.

Julia got up and got dressed mechanically - what did it matter what she wore? Boucher had so much ammunition on her from last night she could sack her on the spot and, what's more, now that she owned Jacquard, there was nobody to stop her.

Julia pushed a croissant listlessly around her plate – she didn't have an appetite. Then, in a sulk, she imagined it was Madame Boucher and started squashing it so flat that all the jam she'd put in it oozed out onto the plate. There, she felt much better now.

She knew she was going to be late for her meeting but after last night's performance, she was finished anyway. She was sure Cassandra did it on purpose. And why wouldn't she – it was her job as a journalist to make an impact. Don't think the impact on camera four was exactly what she had in mind though.

Julia bent down and picked up the latest *Paris Match* that Jean had delivered to her room and started flicking through the pages. She'd barely got through the first few pages when the telephone went. She dropped the magazine on the table and went to answer it.

'Hello, Julia?' asked a voice that seemed familiar, but that Julia couldn't immediately place.

'Yes, this is Julia Connors,' she replied racking her brains.

'It's Jaimie Girault. How are you?,

'Oh hello,' she said, relieved that it wasn't some over-enthusiastic journalist wanting to know what she thought camera four's chances of recovery were. 'I didn't recognise your voice. I'm fine, how are you?

'Terrific. I hope you didn't get a hangover from all that champagne the other night.'

'No, I didn't, I was very sensible. Thank you so much for the Dom Perignon, it was so sweet of you – and far too generous.'

'Well I actually phoned to invite you to lunch – if you're not doing anything that is.'

Julia smiled relieved. 'No, I'm not doing anything. Well, I do have to go into Jacquard to see Madame Boucher, but she's an old dragon and she's never invited me to lunch yet, I can't imagine she's going to start now.' Unless it's for an express leaving party, thought Julia. 'I'd love to come. Where shall I meet you?'

'Do you know the Café Pompadour? It's not far from the Jacquard offices. I could meet you there about one o'clock. I'll book a table.'

'That would be lovely. I'll see you later then.'

Julia replaced the receiver and sighed to herself. What brilliant timing, she'd need reviving after the kiss of death she was going to get from Boucher. She just knew she was going to get sacked after yesterday. It was all so dreadful, she couldn't afford to get sacked, not until she was finally married. Alan would be furious with her for causing a scandal. And she didn't want to give up her job, even if she was married. She loved her job, she'd worked hard for it.

Julia went back to her coffee and croissant, knowing full well that it was probably after nine o'clock and she was already late for her meeting. The old battleaxe could wait. Who, in their right mind would be stupid enough to arrive early to a slaughterhouse?

Then she noticed that the *Paris Match* had fallen open on the centre page and to her horror a full-length picture of herself with Jaimie Girault, at the airport, his arm wrapped around her, stared her in the face. She quickly read the headline. 'Favourite Jacquard girl bags Girault heir in shotgun engagement. We all know the story behind shotgun engagements. Is there more to this?' They couldn't have been more pointed if they'd superimposed a maternity dress on her. What a cheek. Julia wondered frantically if she could sue. This was terrible; if anything else happened she'd die on the spot. She put the magazine in her bag and grabbed her coat in a complete fury. Things couldn't be going more horribly wrong.

Julia fleetingly wondered if *Paris Match* and Boucher were in cahoots, intending to give her a nervous breakdown, or if the article's appearance was purely coincidental. She took a last look down at the squashed croissant and suddenly felt guilty. It had after all been innocent. She apologised to it and threw it in the bin.

Julia kept her dark *Raybans* on as she entered Madame Boucher's office; she didn't want the old dragon looking her in the eye and having the satisfaction of seeing her annoyed. It was therefore no great surprise to anyone other than herself when she walked straight into Madame Boucher's new filing cabinet.

She cursed, sat down abruptly rubbing her bruised knee and waited for the onslaught.

Madame Boucher was sitting behind her enormous desk and did not find it amusing. Her dyed hair was pulled back from her face into a tight, well-lacquered knot. Julia could just see the grey roots beginning to come through at the front. Her skin was the grey-green colour that usually only occurs when landlubbers accidentally find themselves at sea. Her hollow cheeks were so dramatically highlighted and her lips so thin she could have played the lead in a zombie movie

She smiled a triumphant smile and stood up, for all the world looking like a vulture that's happened upon a mass suicide.

'I have never liked you,' she said, her face rigid, her eyes glinting with triumph.

Julia gulped – well that was to the point.

'For years you have been against me. You have turned Jean-Claude against me, you have brought hatred to this company. You have embezzled funds.'

Julia stood up abruptly. She had never ever taken anything from Jacquard that she was not entitled to.

'That's a damn lie,' she said, her fury evident on her face.

Madame Boucher smiled a victorious smile.

'Please, Please don't go to the trouble of denying it, I have proof. Oh you haven't taken a large amount, admittedly, but I have enough proof. Jean-Claude has been giving you extra salary for a number of years in the form of cash, has he not? Not that the authorities would see it that way; they would see it as you helping yourself. It would make rather a nasty court case, one that you can't possibly afford to contest and that wouldn't enhance your 'society' image overly. Then there's the matter of your rather unfortunate behaviour yesterday. That wasn't any good for your own nor Jacquard's reputation.'

Julia sat down again abruptly. She hadn't ever embezzled funds! But it was true Jean-Claude had given her cash and he probably didn't record it properly, knowing him. The last thing she needed was a scandal which would ruin her. The world of high fashion was very small and the top jobs were few and far between. Also, Lady Bloomsbury would have a field day with it. Madame Boucher had her completely. Her career was ruined. There was nothing even Jean-Claude could do for her now that Madame Boucher owned Jacquard, he was completely powerless.

'All of this of course is most unfortunate,' continued Madame Boucher. 'When someone gets as far as you did, carrying the unshakeable stench of the gutter, it does seem a shame that your greed should betray you.' She stared maliciously at Julia for a second before she delivered her final blow.

'Remember, Julia Connors, I was here the day you arrived and I did a little investigating into exactly where you'd appeared from. You aren't exactly out of the top drawer are you? I wonder how the Bloomsbury family would feel, knowing exactly where you came from and just how much of a little tramp you really are. Rumour has it that you even prostituted yourself in the early days.'

Julia stood up and glared at Boucher. 'That's a bloody

lie and you know it.'

Madame Boucher smiled with pleasure. 'I do, but who do you think people will believe?'

Julia looked at her with complete loathing. She was finished at Jacquard, but enough was enough. She still had her pride and she didn't have to sit here and take whatever dirt Boucher decided to throw at her.

'I wonder how Lady Bloomsbury would feel, knowing the true nature of your lack of heritage? How she would feel visiting your rather disgusting home in the *Rue Pigalle*?'

Julia grabbed hold of the table trying to regain her strength, only just holding back her sobs. She didn't have to take this, really she didn't. Then she remembered the London show, what Karl Fregère had said. She was good at what she did, she didn't need Boucher and Jacquard. She would go and see Fregère.

Madame Boucher moved closer, so that she towered over Julia. She waited for a few seconds before she spoke, giving Julia time to take everything in.

Then she said triumphantly, 'I have decided that you will stay at Jacquard and you will toe the line like nobody has ever toed the line with me before.'

Julia glanced up, not understanding for a moment what she'd said.

'You will continue to run the UK sector,' continued Madame Boucher, 'reporting back to me in Paris once a month with all documentation and up-to-date sales reports, and you will start a UK manufacturing operation as from next month using my designs and fabrics shipped from the Paris office.'

Julia thought she must be hearing things.

'Believe me, Julia Connors, you put one foot wrong

and you will live to rue the day you ever tampered with me.'

Julia recovered her composure and stood every inch of her five-feet-ten. 'On the contrary, Madame Boucher. You can stuff your job up your boney backside and chew on it, it might relieve some of the long-term constipation you've shown towards all new ideas over the past ten years. I wouldn't work on your horrific designs even if the Queen of England wore them.'

Julia flipped her Raybans down over her eyes and strode past a flabbergasted Madame Boucher towards the door, remembering to dodge the new filing cabinet on the way.

CHAPTER 6

'So how was La Dragon Boucher?' asked Jaimie as she flopped into the chair opposite him.

'Oh, she was as horrific as expected,' replied Julia dejectedly. Julia didn't know what she was going to do, but telling Boucher to stuff it had been up there with the best highlights of her life so far. But now she was penniless and jobless – and the thoughts were not having a great effect on her stomach nor her bank balance. As she'd walked to the restaurant she'd been desperately trying to figure out why Boucher hadn't sacked her anyway. She probably just wanted to keep her there so that she could bully her whenever she liked, every day taking her revenge. Well, it didn't matter what her reasons were because Julia wasn't going to stick around and take it. What mattered now was that she tried to get another job. When she got back to the hotel she'd call Karl Fregère.

'I gather the dragon was breathing fire,' said Jaimie, reminding her of his presence.

Julia threw him a rather hesitant smile. 'Sorry, I was

miles away. Yes she was.'

Jaimie leant forward and took her hand in his. 'My poor Julia. So, I find you sacked and destitute…'

'Sacked? No. She didn't sack me. I resigned. I think I can honestly say that I well and truly told her to stuff her job,' she added.

Jaimie laughed. 'She didn't sack you? You resigned?'

'Yes. I definitely resigned.'

'Well what will you do now? Are you okay for money?'

'No, not really. It's something I've got to work on.'

'Julia …' he said, taking her hand in his across the table. 'I can maybe help you out. You remember I told you there are many ways to make money if you are young, beautiful and confident. I told you of my secret new project for Girault wines. Well I will need someone in London. I want you to work with me. You are bi-lingual, you move in the right circles, you love wine. And who would not want to do business with someone as beautiful as you?'

'Jaimie, you are very kind, really but whilst my wine consumption is excellent, I really am more of a quantity than quality girl and I don't know a thing about wine.'

'Listen, you can learn chérie. I know you would be a good partner. Anyway think about it. But now, I have a favour to ask of you.'

Julia looked suspicious. She couldn't imagine what he could possibly want. 'What kind of favour?' she asked, looking at him with suspicion.

'Are you going back to London tomorrow?'

'Yes. Why?'

'Well, I need to get a wine reviewed by a very

prestigious importer in London, and I need a case taking through to be delivered to him as soon as possible. I'd rather not trust it to a courier and I thought maybe you could take it for me. I will pay the excess weight for you of course and I could get it dropped around to the Medici tonight.'

'Sure, no problem. Can I try it?'

Jaimie looked slightly alarmed. 'No you can't drink any, we only have a few bottles at the moment for sales and promotion. Why don't we drink some in London together the next time I'm there. We can celebrate together. Or no. I know, why don't we celebrate now? You, to your new life without *la dragon* Boucher, and me, to the beauty, intelligence and charm of my new friend and assistant. Julia, I am serious. I want you to be my partner. We could do very well together, you and I. I can feel it. And it will be more than that, it will be a marriage of the minds as you might say.'

He smiled his winning smile and signalled for the waiter to bring the champagne.

'By the way, talking of marriage, that reminds me,' she said, fishing in her handbag for the *Paris Match*. 'Those reporters believed you! Just look at this. Honestly, Jaimie, you've got to do something, get them to print that it was a mistake or something. If my real fiancé, or more to the point, his mother, ever finds out, he'll kill me, and I'll be ruined.'

Jaimie leant over the table and looked deep into her eyes, clearly full of mischief.

'Julia, I'm heartbroken! You mean to tell me there's been someone else! I can't believe it, darling, really I can't.' He smiled cheekily and continued to stroke her hand affectionately. 'You'll simply have to get rid of this other person.'

'Jaimie, you're incorrigible, you really are' she said, laughing.

'You're laughing at me,' he said pulling a sad little boy face.

'Now then don't go all sulky on me,' said Julia. 'I've had one hell of a day already…'

'OK. I will stop sulking if you tell me that you will work for me and that I am the only man in the world for you.'

'Well the thing is …'

As she was speaking, Julia noticed Jaimie's face was turning increasingly pale and she realised that he was staring at somebody who had entered the room and was now standing behind her left shoulder. She shivered and erupted in goose pimples all down her back. She knew who it was before she even turned around.

She looked up to find herself staring into the tawny brown eyes of Christophe de Flaubert. She gulped. He must have heard every word. She was so shocked, she barely noticed the statuesque black girl who was with him.

'Well, well, we meet again, Miss Connors,' he said, his voice carrying all the warmth of liquid nitrogen.

'Girault,' said Christophe, acknowledging his presence as if he was some nasty thing lying on the pavement that he'd have to step over.

Jaimie glared at Christophe.

Christophe's emotionless eyes stared back. The atmosphere couldn't have been more loaded if the Russians had pressed the button. Julia began to hunt in the depths of her mind for something to say to ease the situation but it seemed her diplomatic corps were on vacation. Luckily the waiter arrived with the ice bucket and champagne. Well, that should cool things down, thought Julia.

'Celebrating, I see,' said Christophe and his eyes took in the magazine that was resting on the table, open at the centre page. His eyebrows rocketed. 'Congratulations, Miss Connors, I see you're quite the entrepreneur. You have done well, yet again!'

Oh no, thought Julia, life was getting more and more catastrophic by the minute. He was just bound to tell Alan. What was the point of her even trying to explain the truth to Christophe? He didn't look as if he'd believe it for a minute. And who could blame him? What could she say – 'It's all a mistake, that's why Jaimie is here holding my hand over lunch so that we can sort it out'? She didn't like Christophe, but he wasn't a fool. When she looked at him, with no explanation to offer, it was like taking an iced Jacuzzi.

She turned her attention to the black girl who up until now everybody seemed to have ignored. Julia recognised her as one of *St Laurent's* latest models. She was the hottest thing in print at the moment.

'Hello, I don't think we've met, have we? I'm Julia Connors, Jacquard UK.'

'Hello,' the girl nodded and smiled the only natural smile to adorn any of their faces. 'I'm Chantal Tourne. How do you do? Actually I saw your interview last night.' She dissolved into fits of giggles. 'Christophe and I watched it together,' she said, smirking.

Julia blushed bright red. She couldn't look Frenchman in the eye.

Christophe and Chantal went off to their table, luckily right across the other side of the room. Julia gulped her champagne down, choking. Oh hell. Hell, hell, hell. He was *bound* to tell Alan, and it was all Jaimie's fault.

She remembered her hand was still resting in his and snatched it away.

'Christophe de Flaubert thinks he bloody owns Paris and half of France. He's so damn righteous,' said Jaimie looking very ugly in his anger. 'He walks into a room and he thinks he knows everyone, everything and is the most intelligent person in the world and everyone else is an idiot.'

So far as Julia could see, Christophe de Flaubert *was* scoring very high on three of those. But she did agree with Jaimie, it was bloody annoying.

CHAPTER 7

Having passed the afternoon pleasantly trooping around the Bastille area, wondering how the revolutionists could have been so lax as to miss guillotining the de Flaubert family; Julia eventually went back to the Medici to change and meet Jean-Claude.

Julia sat on the bed in her towel and tried to call Karl Fregère for about the tenth time – again there was no reply. She lay back down on the bed and thought things through. If the worst came to the worst, she could still talk to Jaimie about his job. He'd said they were going to expand their operation in London to handle his existing wines and his new top secret project. It was different to the fashion business of course, but she already knew a little about wine, she could learn and as he said, she spoke both languages fluently.

She picked up the telephone again and this time tried Alan's number. Again there was no reply. She bit her lip, she wondered if he'd spoken to Christophe de Flaubert yet. Zero out of ten for this little trip, Julia, she told herself; a disastrous interview, no job and high potential for bigamy all in the space of twenty-four hours - that was going some. She started to towel dry her hair. But at least tonight should be okay. A long relaxing meal with Jean-Claude could not possibly hold any shocks. Surely?

Julia arrived in good time at the restaurant, wearing her favourite midnight blue cocktail dress from the last spring collection.

She was guided towards the table and found Jean-Claude already there waiting for her. She smiled as she approached and was shocked to find that he did not respond. Perhaps he had not seen her?

As she reached the table he said, dramatically, 'Sit down, Julia.'

Oh no. She couldn't cope with Jean-Claude being annoyed with her too. It was just all too much. She knew he'd have seen the interview but she didn't think even that could cause this kind of a reaction. Julia thought back, what the hell had she done wrong lately? On the other hand, what have I done right lately? I'm in one hell of a mess.

She looked closer at Vasin as she sat down. Maybe he was joking? But there was no trace of a glint in his eye, and he'd never spoken to her in that tone of voice before. He sat there silent and unsmiling until she began to feel annoyed and eventually she sighed and said; 'Jean-Claude, please don't you start on me too. What have I done wrong now?'

He took the magazine that was resting beside him and flung it across the table damningly.

'Tell me this is untrue, this ... this atrocity,' he spat the words out, disgusted.

She tentatively picked up the magazine, it was open at the gossip page with the full length picture of Jaimie Girault with his arm around her at Orly airport.

'Tell me this is untrue. This man, he is nothing. He is a dangerous imbecile. Julia, *chérie*, I treasure you like my own daughter, this man he is stupid and too young. He is not for you.'

Julia sighed with relief. Lord! She thought it was going to be something dreadful. She took his hand in hers, 'Oh Jean-Claude it was a mistake. He made it up as a joke for the press and they believed him. I hardly know him.' She decided against telling him about Jaimie's job offer.

'That is terrible. This man, he is uh … a menace. Why did you talk to him?'

Julia sighed to herself. What was all the fuss about? Even Jean at the Hotel Medici had been concerned about her seeing Jaimie.

'Jean-Claude, it was nothing,' she said, looking him straight in the eye. 'He gave me a lift from Orly – and that's all.'

'Humph. He is an imbecile: everything he touches, puff, it's gone! Pounds, dollars, even people – gone!' He raised his hands to the heavens. 'You need to be very careful.'

Julia began to feel irritated. It was all well and good Jean-Claude feeling like her father, but he wasn't and she was perfectly able to look after herself. Besides which, nothing had happened. She wondered what the hell the guy could have done to merit all the bad press he was getting.

Her annoyance must have shown on her face because

Jean-Claude promptly calmed down.

'Ah, okay … okay. We will speak of it no more, but I tell you, Julia, he is not right for you, he is not strong for you and you are too nice for him.'

Julia didn't answer, she dropped her head, seemingly to read the menu. Thank God he hadn't heard about Alan yet – news of her engagement to an Englishman really would be too much for him to cope with.

'Anyway you should stop worrying about me Jean, and worry about yourself. Is it true that Boucher has taken over Jacquard? I can't believe it.'

'You'd better believe it, *chérie*,' sighed Jean-Claude, 'and there's absolutely nothing I can do about it. I don't know where she got that kind of money and who is backing her. Well not at the moment anyway. There is a chance I can get these stocks back or something; I'm waiting to hear from a friend who is talking to all the stockbroker share people. I don't understand a word they tell me these walking calculators.' He threw his arms up in exasperation.

'Can you believe it? She tells me now what to design. *She* tells *me*! And shall I tell you, *chérie*, what I tell her? I tell her she can go to hell, they might buy her grotesque rags there. I will still design for Jacquard, everybody knows it is my genius, she will be nothing without me.

Julia smiled. It was true, Boucher would be nothing without Jean-Claude.

'Did she give you a very bad time, *chérie*?' he asked taking her hand.

Julia grimaced. 'Jean she was hell, I can't begin to tell you. What I couldn't understand was that she didn't sack me. She wanted to keep me on to run the UK operation.'

'Well she's not totally stupid, you are very good at your work.'

'Oh Jean-Claude you are so kind to me,' she took his wrinkled old hand in hers and kissed it.

'Not kind. It is true.'

'Well even so, I really couldn't understand it because she has always hated me so much.'

Jean-Claude smiled 'It is difficult, is it not, for an old crow like her to have so beautiful a swan around, but nevertheless she finds like everyone else she is drawn to it.'

'Well it doesn't matter because I resigned anyway.'

'Yes, she told me. I tell you, I don't know what you said to her, but she didn't look so good.'

Julia laughed. 'I was a bit over the top but so was she, the old cow. Anyway Jean, Karl Fregère came to the show and he wants me to go and see him.'

Jean-Claude raised his eyebrows. 'Well, it would be a good job, if it wasn't for his clothes.' He touched her cheek gently. 'Ah, Julia, what am I to do with you, eh? I worry about you. You look so tired, you need a holiday. So I have told my friend that you will stay in his house in Provence, starting on Monday. He has a beautiful home out in the countryside far from the troubles of the city. He has a wonderful pool and horses, so you can swim and ride and relax and forget about all your troubles and debts for a while. It has been four years since you've been away and you look tired. Too tired.'

Julia looked at him suspiciously. He sounded so forceful, and who was this mysterious 'he' anyway? She hoped it wasn't another of Jean-Claude's matchmaking schemes, her love life was complicated enough as it was.

'Jean-Claude, I hope you aren't trying to match make

again. Who is this friend?' She asked looking him in the eye, much amused by his schemes.

'You don't have to worry, he will be away.'

Vasin didn't look at her and she didn't believe him. But she left it anyway. He was right, she did need a holiday to get herself sorted out; she was between jobs and Alan was probably going to South America, so it was a perfect time for a holiday.

'Here,' he said, passing her an envelope, 'Boucher has not stopped all my pleasures; these are for you to sort yourself out. Call it a four year bonus from Jacquard for all your hard work.'

Julia blushed. How the hell did he know?

'But I don't need money, Jean-Claude,' she tried to lie.

'Julia *chérie*, you are a very bad liar.'

'Oh, Jean. How the hell did you know?'

'The bank called the Paris office looking for you. Julia, much as I understand your maths problem, I think we both know that this is only a part of the trouble. Julia, you have to sort yourself out. And you are not happy. You have been leading this crazy life. What is it with you? Using these poor men who fall in love with you? What has happened to you? And you will not marry this Alan, he is not right for you. He wants a beautiful woman like he wants a beautiful house, a painting and a car. He wants beautiful children and a decoration at dinners for his banking friends. He does not want a talented, beautiful wife like you. You are highly strung, he is not enough for you. He does not understand you and, deep down, you know it.'

Julia choked on her trout and the passing waiter had to pat her on the back to clear the problem.

How the hell … had he found out about Alan?

'How ..?' she began to ask, but her coughing started again.

'Never mind, it is not important. But Julia, this Jaimie Girault *is* important. He is … how can I tell you? I know this family. I will tell you of them.

'I knew their mother, Celeste, she was a beautiful woman, she had the dark, dark looks of all the traditional Provençal women – and some said she had the passion too. I dressed her in the best. She was the inspiration for all I designed. In the early days, just when I was starting out, Celeste *was* Jacquard. She was the toast of Parisian society. She was merely seventeen when she came out and more naïve even than you'd expect such a young girl to be. Then she fell in love. Head over heels for a man much older than her. She fell in love with the Marquis de Flaubert -'

'De Flaubert?' asked Julia interrupting him mid-flow. 'Did you say de *Flaubert*?'

'Of course. Although he was a Marquis he did not like the social life of the gentry. He preferred to live as a quiet country vintner; a nice, kind man. He was strong enough to tame the wildness of Celeste, or so we thought, but Celeste couldn't cope with the life. As he grew older and more serious and she grew more and more beautiful he kept her down in Provence, away from the temptations of Paris. They became estranged and she would come to Paris for a few months and then would return to him, unable to keep away, but unable to stand the seclusion of the estate. Eventually, they had a son – Christophe. He is a lot like the old Marquis in looks, but very different in temperament. He is a good boy. Well, the ladies they think so anyway.' Jean-Claude chuckled.

Julia made a mental calculation: he must be in his mid-to late-thirties. That hardly constituted a boy, and it just had to be the same guy.

'Is he a banker, Jean-Claude? This Christophe?'

'Amongst other things of course, yes he is.'

'I've met him Jean-Claude – at Alan's.'

'This is possible. He deals a lot with the London business world.'

'Well anyway, what happened then, with his mother?'

'Celeste became bored again and left him with the child while she went off to Paris. It was a terrible time. She met Michel Girault – a well-known womaniser who was already married. She became pregnant by him and – *voilá*, Jaimie. Celeste and Michel argued all the time, they were terrible for each other, they had such quick tempers and Michel could not be faithful to his mistress as he could not be faithful to his wife.'

Jean-Claude sighed, 'It is in their blood these Girault. Celeste returned to the Marquis when Jaimie was ...'

He thought for a moment. 'Jaimie was about five at the time. She became pregnant and had a daughter, Simone. It seemed that things would be fine for them, but Michel was a charismatic man and although he had a daughter, Cassandra, with his wife, he did not have a son. He wanted Celeste back and Jaimie with her! It was a terrible, terrible time. I told her not to go, but you could never reason with Celeste. She went back to Michel. It was the final straw for the old Marquis. No longer a young man he lost all desire to carry on. After a year or so he suddenly died. He is probably the only man I have ever known who has truly died of a broken heart. Some ten years later Celeste, having lost her looks, the affection of her oldest child and most of her friends, threw herself off the cliff at Cassis.'

'That's horrible.'

'Yes. It was the saddest day in my life. If only I had been nearer, if only I could have talked to her, I could have stopped her, I'm sure I could.'

Jean-Claude wiped a tear from his eyes with his napkin.

'But it's not your fault, Jean Claude, of course it's not,' Julia held his hand in hers. 'I suppose that explains why Jaimie and Christophe hate each other so much?'

'Of course. Jaimie blames Christophe for the death of their mother. It was partly because Christophe would not see her or talk to her that she committed suicide.'

'And Christophe blames Jaimie for his mother going back to Michel?'

'Partly that, but also because of Simone, his sister. Christophe was left to bring up Simone after Celeste died. She was such a pretty girl, very like Celeste in character too, highly strung and wild. Christophe was a strict but fair surrogate father and they got along very well, they adored each other. Then when she was about thirteen she started to rebel against Christophe's strict rules. She realised she could annoy him by being friendly with Jaimie. She didn't see why she shouldn't go about with him, they were after all half-brother and sister. She used to run off to see Jaimie and his rather dubious friends. Then one day, Jaimie told her that it was Christophe's fault that Celeste killed herself and Simone ran away. She got involved in drugs and died of an overdose. Christophe has never forgiven Jaimie or himself. In fact, if it hadn't been for the intervention of Bernard Chauvenon, a lawyer friend of Christophe's, I believe he would have killed Jaimie.'

Julia shivered and took a sip of her wine. Then, noticing the restaurant had become very quiet, both she and Jean-Claude looked around them and realised the people at the tables surrounding them were leaning forward over their hors d'oeuvres, hanging on Jean-Claude's every word.

There was a second's silence while everyone seemed to realise they were eavesdropping and then a kaleidoscope of embarrassingly loud conversations started up.

It all sounded incredible to Julia. It was no wonder Jaimie and Christophe hated one another. It was all so sad.

'I have some pictures of Celeste somewhere. I will show them to you next time you come. Ah, it was such a waste. Such a dreadful waste. She had so much life and so much to give and she ended as nothing – nothing but a problem to everybody. In the days of the troubadours it would all have been different; then they would have loved her, sung songs about her and worshipped her from afar. And that is why, Julia, I worry about you. You are just like Celeste. You are impulsive, full of life but you have this destructive side to you, too. You think you cannot love; you play games and taunt yourself as much as these ridiculous men you trap. I do not know why you do this, but you will kill yourself just like my Celeste.'

Julia was quiet for a moment.

'Oh Jean-Claude,' she said taking his hand. He was so kind. She didn't tell him that she thought she was totally frigid and therefore it was highly unlikely that she was going to have three children and throw herself off a cliff. He was such an old romantic he'd be horrified.

'Jean-Claude you're such a romantic. Life's not like that. Life's full of practical people running around worrying why their Wifi doesn't work and complaining that the waste disposal's broken.'

'Huh,' he said smiling to himself, 'you can fool yourself, Julia, but you can't fool me. You will like Provence; it is full of romance and history. It is the land of the troubadours. You will love it. You will go.'

His voice brooked no argument and Julia couldn't help but agree. She would go. She needed a holiday so she would go.

'You don't happen to come from Provence, do you, Jean-Claude?' she asked.

'But of course – it is the land of the artist.'

Julia smiled. 'Okay,' she said, 'you win. I'll go to Provence. I'll need a major holiday if I'm going to sort out my disastrous career.' She didn't add that one of the jobs on offer was a partnership with Jaimie Girault; she'd face that if and when she had to. After all the things Jean-Claude had just told her, to say that she suspected he wouldn't approve was an understatement. And as far as Alan was concerned, Jean-Claude would have to come round to her way of thinking. In the end, he usually did.

CHAPTER 8

Julia sighed as the taxi pulled up outside her apartment block and she took a couple of notes from her pocket to pay the driver. The driver smiled at her sympathetically well aware that she had not heard a word of his customary monologue that he used for clients who had a lot on their mind. He knew his monologue off by heart and used his calm monotone voice to pontificate on issues as varied as unemployment, global warming, cost of theatre tickets, racial trouble, and the naming of roses. He didn't need any polite gestures of agreement or murmurs of 'mm' to keep him going because he considered it to be all part of his job and a bit of free relaxation therapy for his clients.

The journey had given Julia time to think. She couldn't have had a worse trip to Paris if she'd crash landed on the Eiffel Tower. She was going to have to sort things out before she went on holiday; she'd have to clear out her stuff from the office and, what was even worse, she was going to have to do some explaining to Alan. She was sure Mr-Righteous-de-Flaubert wouldn't let her accidental indiscretion go lightly. And once Lady B got wind of it, she'd have to charm Alan for days to counteract his mother's well-placed barbs. She wondered if two days were enough to get the whole mess sorted out. It depended how efficient Christophe de Flaubert's texting was she supposed.

Julia dragged her luggage into the lift, slightly regretting the decision to bring back a whole crate of wine for Jaimie Girault.

The lift climbed slowly and strenuously to the fifth floor, allowing the sounds of each floor to drift fleetingly to her ears as it wound its way up.

Julia didn't know many people in the block. She'd seen quite a few of them but they always seemed to be in a hurry and so was she. She vaguely knew the couple in number six. He was a journalist and she was a nutritionist. They were always going away to foreign places for months on end, India and South America were very high on their list. So in fact, she hardly ever saw them, but when she did they always had suntans and not the bottle or sunbed types either, the real authentic ones that had seen a huge yellow solar body. They were actually quite attractive in a new age hippy kind of way, - especially the wife - if she dressed herself properly she could have been stunning. Julia had gone round to dinner once but she'd been a real fish out of water. They were all serious vegans and talked about the state of the planet. Some were even riding bikes home, and they'd had lentils for dinner. Quite an 'out of world' experience for a dedicated, gold digging, steak frites girl like Julia.

She glanced in the lift mirror as it continued to wind its way up. She did look tired.

'Ah!' she screamed out loud. She'd got a wrinkle, a whole one just below her eye and her mascara had seeped into the crease making it stand out like a long black centipede.

The lift creaked to a halt and she pulled back the metal guard door and started lugging her cases out, muttering to herself, 'Wrinkles ... wrinkles at twenty-seven. That's terrible.'

Then she noticed the door next to hers was open. They must finally have let number seven, which had been empty for over a year. Julia had met the couple briefly before they decided to go to Australia and they'd said they were going to rent to finance their travels. The agent hadn't done a very good job for them though.

She wondered what it was like inside. She could just see the wall of the hall, covered with a large brown and beige floral print. It looked dreadful; a trio of green mallards were hovering at various suicidal angles just above the light switch.

It was a shame that somebody was moving into it. It was the only flat that could complain about the noise she made. Number six didn't adjoin hers so they couldn't really hear her but number seven's lounge backed onto hers, she knew that from the raucous laughter that she used to hear greeting her when Australia played in a rugby international.

Maybe she should pop along later and make friends, just in case the new people objected to any of the noise she made.

Julia opened the door to her flat and sunlight flooded through from the large south-facing window, warming her face. She propped the door open with the case of wine, went to get her suitcases and dragged them back to the flat.

The place looked immaculate. Eloisa really was a godsend. She went into the kitchen to put the kettle on. The whole flat had warmed up during the day's sunshine and Julia threw open both the kitchen and lounge windows to get some fresh air into the place. Being clean was one thing, but smelling industrial cleaners was quite another, they held too many bad memories for her. If Julia had her way, cleaning fluids would be scented with the smell of fresh yeasty bread or newly roasted coffee, and bathroom cleaner would be scented with only the most fragrant of French perfumes and would bubble like freshly popped champagne.

The answerphone was flicking away at ten to the dozen so Julia made herself a coffee and set it to playback.

'Hi, Jules, Liane here. Carla and Ingrid have been on the phone solidly since I got back from Paris wanting to know how many of the wedding dresses you've got and whether or not you got the sack. Maybe you should call them and say you've got some, and it'll cost them if they want any. No other crises to report except that Lady Bloomsbury wants to have a word with you. See you tomorrow. Bye.'

On hearing Alan's dulcet tones, Julia stopped what she was doing to listen more carefully.

'Julia, darling, I've missed you. The Gillespies and Sir John Stevens and wife are coming over for dinner tonight. It would be great if you could be here, eight o'clock for eight-thirty. If you're late just give me a call when you get in. I'm probably going to have to take a trip to Brazil on Saturday to sort out this South American funding thing, so if you don't get back in time for dinner tonight, give me a ring tomorrow. I miss you. Bye, darling.' All through the message there was a deep, throaty laugh audible on and off in the background and Julia, being paranoid, was convinced it was Christophe de Flaubert.

'Hoh, Hoh, Hoh,' she mimicked him sarcastically to herself. She didn't think he had a sense of humour. She then missed the end of the messages because she looked up to find a small, slightly portly man standing in the doorway watching her.

'Oh, God – you scared me!' she said clutching her hand to her heart at the same time as he launched into an apology.

'Oh, I am sorry. I did knock, but the door was open and you didn't reply … I've moved in next door and I came to introduce myself. I'm so sorry if I frightened you. Would you like a hand carrying your things in.' He bent down to pick up the crate of wine.

'Oh. Thank you. That's very kind of you. Perhaps you could put that over by the sofa.'

'Pleased to meet you. My name's Carlos, Carlos Garcia'

'How do you do? Julia Connors.'

'I've taken the flat for a few weeks I'm here on business.'

'Spanish, by any chance?' asked Julia. His accent held a slight trace of something but it was barely definable.

'Yes. I heard about the apartment from your cleaner.'

'Oh, right. She's a godsend. Don't know what I'd do without her. His face was very serious with large brown eyes.

'Well I won't keep you,' he said. 'You've just come

back from abroad I see.' His eyes took in the cases and he was still holding the crate of wine.

'Mm, Paris,' nodded Julia. 'The worst bit is the unpacking.'

'Yes, the aftermath,' he said, looking terribly serious as he nodded his agreement.

Slightly dramatic, she thought, I've been to Paris, not a war zone.

She smiled at him as he said goodbye and he shocked her by managing a full blown grin. As he turned to go she noticed he had a thin white scar down the right hand side of his face, running from the side of his temple to the base of his ear.'

Carlos caught her looking at it and he traced his hand along it.

'Don't be alarmed. Just a reckless youth.'

'Oh. Sorry didn't mean to stare', replied Julia

Carlos leaned forward and whispered conspiratorially,' A bit too much bull running in Pamplona'

'Oh?'

'Yes. We all have to do it. It's part of our coming of age.'

'What, the girls too?'

'He looked rather offended.'

'No of course not! It is for our manhood.'

'Oh, my apologies. Well, do call in again once you're more settled,' said Julia seeing him out.

He turned to go and Julia saw he still had the wine in his hands.

'Err, the wine…'

'Ah yes, sorry.' He put it down by the sofa and left.

What an odd little man. Still he looked alright. Didn't look like the type to cause a fuss over a little early morning party or two. Especially not if he was a bull running rebel. Maybe a bit macho though.

CHAPTER 9

Julia got up the next day to be greeted by enough official looking financial post to bring down the stock market. There were letters from her bank manager, irate accounts departments of store cards, cancellation of her spa membership, final demands for electricity and gas bills – and that was only the half she opened. She dumped the rest in the bin. It just wasn't fair, there should be a law banning the sending of post to people with maths dyslexia. She'd found out that she suffered from it far too late to be able to do anything much about it. There was very little help available and the financial companies certainly didn't accept it as an excuse for overspending. She decided her best bet was to escape to work where she could refuse to talk to anybody that called. Then she remembered why she was going into work, to sort out all of her stuff. To move out. She suddenly felt very sad. She'd liked working at Jacquard – it had been her whole life. It was her security, her safety blanket and Jean-Claude and Liane were the nearest thing she had ever had to family. She felt the stinging sensation of tears building behind her eyes. No. Julia, you will not cry over this, you will get your act together and get on with life.

When she got to the boutique it was absolutely packed. She dragged the heavy case of wine along the floor behind her into the back office and collapsed into a chair. She'd be glad to be rid of the stuff, a case of wine was not exactly light luggage. Maybe she should drink it.

'Hi,' said Liane coming into the office and seeing both the wine and Julia dressed in her jeans. 'Oh my God, Ingrid and Carla were right. She did it!' Liane continued, open mouthed. 'Boucher sacked you.'

'She did not,' said Julia frostily. 'I resigned.'

'You what?'

'I told her to stuff it.'

Liane closed the office door so that the clients couldn't hear and sat down abruptly in the other chair.

'But why?'

'She said she wanted me to run the UK operation based around the new form of the company and using her designs, and she is a complete tyrant, so I told her to stuff it.' Julia pushed the case heavily under the desk.

'I can't believe it,' Liane was stunned.

'You'd better believe it, Liane. Anyway don't look so glum,' Julia dropped the keys to the safe into Liane's hands, 'you'll be boss now; and anyway you deserve it.'

'I don't Julia. You know I don't. I'm just a number cruncher, you're the one with the talent.'

'A talent for getting myself into trouble maybe. Honestly, I just don't know how I do it. Every time I seem to get myself on the right track I suddenly get hit by a flying cricket bat from left field.'

'I don't know Julia. You've had a good six years of stability now. What are you going to do? You could always bring the wedding forward and not work anymore.'

'I don't know. I'm just not ready yet, Liane. I love this job. I love working with you and Jean-Claude. I can't imagine not being in the fashion world anymore.'

'I can't imagine Jacquard without you. It will be just awful. I might have to resign myself in solidarity.'

'You are so sweet Liane, but you're crazy, you can't possibly resign. Look I'm going on holiday tomorrow and then I'm going to look for a job. Karl Fregère asked me to go in and have a chat and there's a few other possibilities in the pipeline. That reminds me, you couldn't send that crate of wine over to this address could you?' I said I'd do it for a friend.'

'Sure no problem. Karl Fregère. Julia that would be brilliant.'

'Mmm. Maybe this is the time for a complete change though, marriage, job and who knows what else.'

Liane burst into tears.

'Oh, Liane,' said Julia putting a friendly arm around her shoulders and beginning to cry herself, 'don't cry. You'll start me off. It had to happen sometime, I couldn't have stayed at Jacquard all my life, not with Boucher on my back anyway.'

'Have you told Alan yet?' asked Liane, dabbing a tissue to the rivers of mascara that had begun to decorate her cheeks.

'No,' said Julia sighing. 'I haven't even seen him yet, he's busy working on some Brazilian deal with that French guy.' And he's going to have a lot more to worry about once he gets wind of all that business with Jaimie thought

Julia.

At that moment, the door opened to reveal Lady Bloomsbury's head.

Oh no, here we go, thought Julia.

'Liane, my dear. Whatever is the matter?' asked Lady Bloomsbury rushing over to comfort her.

'Oh really it's nothing,' said Liane embarrassedly. 'I just found out Julia is leaving and well, it's all unexpected and rather sad.' She sniffed back the tears and smiled a brave smile at Julia before rushing off to the loo.

'Oh, dear,' said Lady Bloomsbury turning to Julia. 'And why *are* you leaving, Julia?'

'Well,' Julia took a deep breath, 'Madame Boucher and I have always had our differences and I decided it was time to move on, so I resigned yesterday.'

'Oh, it isn't anything to do with this young man then,' asked Lady Bloomsbury, pulling a *Paris Match* out of her bag, like a witch pulling a hex out of the ether.

Julia gulped. 'No of course not. Those ridiculous reporters got totally the wrong end of the stick. He's just the brother of a friend of Alan's actually; he gave me a lift to my hotel in Paris,' said Julia. Nice one, she thought to herself. Make out Alan already knew Jaimie.

'Well if you are going to marry Alan, Julia, it would really help if you avoided this sort of scandal in future. Have you spoken to Alan about this?'

'Yes of course,' lied Julia. 'He thought it was as ridiculous as I did. I called him the moment I saw it. We had quite a laugh about it actually.'

Julia suddenly felt a stabbing pain in her head, and put her hand up to apply pressure to it. Maybe it's got something to do with the speed with which my Pinocchio nose is growing, she thought to herself.

Lady Bloomsbury looked as if she didn't believe it for a minute.

'Well I'd better be going, I'm meeting Alan for lunch. I'll expect you for tea on Sunday as planned.'

'Actually, Lady Bloomsbury, I'm terribly sorry, I'm going away tomorrow on holiday for a week or two. I won't be able to make it. I *am* sorry.'

Julia walked with Lady Bloomsbury to the door. Sorry? She was over the moon. Lady Bloomsbury always made her feel like a ten-year-old guttersnipe who'd been caught in the drawing room pinching the filling out of the cucumber sandwiches.

The moment Lady Bloomsbury stepped into her cab Julia dived for the telephone, hoping to catch Alan before he left for lunch. She'd got to tell him there was nothing between her and Jaimie before Lady Bloomsbury or Christophe de Flaubert told him there was.

'I'm sorry. Mr Bloomsbury will be out at a meeting until this afternoon. Can I take a message?' asked the glacial voice of Virginia, Alan's robotic secretary who was definitely in cahoots with Lady Bloomsbury.

'No, no it doesn't matter,' said Julia. 'Can you just tell him I called – it's Julia.'

'Does Mr Bloomsbury have your number?' asked the Virgin-Bot as she always did, even though Julia must have spoken to her about a million times.

'I do hope so,' said Julia, 'you see I'm pregnant and he's the father of my child.'

'I'll see he gets the message, Miss Connors,' said Virgin-Bot without a trace of surprise.

You shouldn't have said that, Julia said to herself as

she replaced the receiver. Alan will not think that was funny, especially on top of seeing the picture of her with Jaimie.

Julia spent most of lunch time and the whole afternoon tidying her things out of her desk and briefing Liane on all the projects that she would have to pick up and carry through. It was a miserable afternoon for both of them.

The worst bit was clearing Julia's desk. Julia always knew where everything was because she had a highly efficient visual memory, but there was absolutely no logic to her filing, her drawers, or the bin. The bin was generally used as a plant pot holder; consequently one of the drawers was used as a bin, only she could never remember which one it was so they all ended up with rubbish in them; and the floor generally doubled as filing cabinet.

At the end of the day Julia was left with a pile of items that she didn't want to throw out because she was sure she would want them at some point but that she just didn't know what to do with – one electrical screwdriver; half a packet of tampons; a palette of lipstick that had lost the lid and was covered in bits of chocolate and pencil sharpenings, but that was her favourite colour; the CD of the photos from the Christmas party; an old memo from Jean-Claude which requested that they all wear black armbands for the Chanel show; and a spare photochromic left lens for her glasses. Eventually she threw them all in a carrier bag and decided to take them home.

About five o'clock, a courier arrived with the tickets for her flight and a letter from Jean-Claude telling her how to get to the house in Provence.

She sighed and put the tickets back in the envelope and looked around the office. It had never been so tidy. Julia pulled the last photo from the noticeboard – of her and Liane dressed as clowns at a fancy dress charity ball. They both looked so young. Julia began to sniff, she couldn't believe it, she really *was* leaving. She went to grab a tissue from the side of the plant pot holder, but they'd been tidied up.

The phone rang. It was Alan.

'Julia. What the hell is going on? Mother says you've been having an affair with some guy in Paris and she's got proof, that you're going away on holiday for two weeks and Virginia said congratulations she didn't realise I was going to be a father. Julia, what the hell are you doing?'

'I'm clearing out my desk because I resigned.'

'You what?'

Julia sighed. 'Alan, please don't be mad at me. That's rubbish all that stuff about an affair. I can explain it... And I was just winding Virginia up because she was being so proper.'

There was a loud commotion in the background at Alan's office and his voice faded as he turned to speak to someone. 'No. Don't settle it yet, keep him on the phone, - Julia I've got to go, I've been trying to get hold of this guy all day. I'll come round to your place later this evening, about ten, okay?'

'Yes, okay. I'm going for a drink with Liane after work but I'll be back by ten.'

'And try not to come up with any more shocks between now and then will you? It's taken me a four course lunch and a lot of time that I don't have to pacify mother as it is.'

Julia replaced the receiver and looked up just as Liane came in with both their coats.

'Come on, Jules. Let's go and get well and truly slaughtered down at the Champagne Exchange.'

'You're on,' said Julia picking up her carrier bag of odd bits.

Once in the bar, the first glass of champagne didn't even touch the sides and they were soon well on their way to achieving their main objective.

'I don't know, Liane,' said Julia, letting the champagne do the talking. 'Do you really think there's such a thing as body chemistry and all that? Or do you think it's all a big con? I never get turned on, you know I'm completely frigid, dead as a duck in the water. My sex life is about as successful as a python with lockjaw. And poor old Alan's going to end up as starved as the python if I don't sort it out.'

Liane looked surprised for a second, and then, started fiddling with the champagne glass. 'I don't know,' she said gazing at the bubbles, 'my experience of good sex is pretty limited. I believe in chemistry between two people though. There was this one guy anyway ...'

'Maybe I should try some aphrodisiacs or something. Maybe that's my problem,' said Julia, as the waiter arrived to take their order.

'I'll have the oysters with a dish of celery on the side and if you've got a bottle of Mescal, I'll have the worm at the bottom,' said Julia.

'The worm at the bottom,' repeated the waiter with raised eyebrows.

'Yes. Thanks,' said Julia, smiling as she handed him back the menu.

Liane giggled. 'And I'll have the smoked caviar.'

'I was never really interested in sex before I met this guy,' Liane continued, sighing. 'Julia, I've been so miserable ever since. You see it was just a one night stand for him. He's crazy about this girl I know, and well – we both got drunk one night and it sort of happened.'

'Hell, don't bother about her, Liane; if it worked, go for it.'

'I ... I can't. I like her, a lot. And he ... well. I can't talk to him even now. He says it was all a big mistake. It wasn't for me though, Jules, I know it wasn't. I feel terrible about her, but it just felt so right.'

'Oh, Liane,' said Julia, hugging her, 'so that's why you've been so fed up lately... you should have told me.'

They both sat for a moment thinking.

'Is she madly in love with him, this guy?'

'She seems to be.'

'Well maybe he's not really that in love with her if he found you so irresistible, eh?'

'He says it was the drink.'

Julia smiled. 'Hey. Maybe it'll work for me,' and she ordered another bottle.

CHAPTER 10

Julia giggled as she staggered up the stairs to her apartment, the lift was broken yet again. Aphrodisiacs were one thing but getting this drunk was quite another. She shouldn't have let Liane order that other bottle. She hiccupped. That reminded her, she must remind Liane to ring that importer bloke while she was away and send Jaimie's wine over. Oh dear, what if Liane thought it was freebies and drank it? She giggled, it would serve Jaimie Girry ... Girr-ity-whatsit right, he'd caused her so much trouble.

Girritywhatsit – quite a good name for a wine. Sounded like a very rough red - the kind that gave you a hangover like you'd fallen on your head from three thousand feet without a crash helmet. Flaubert, now that was a good name for a wine - a champagne, all sparkly light and classy. She hiccupped again. How could she pack in this state? How could she straighten things out with Alan in this state? She'd just start to giggle. She waved her finger at no one in particular, saying, 'and it's a very serious matter'. Then she dissolved into fits of giggles again.

Oh well, what the heck, she thought, swinging her bag as she walked up the last flight of stairs. She tripped slightly as she went up – stairs were such a difficult obstacle when you were drunk, they should have moving pavements instead. Come to think of it the pavements had been moving.

She was so excited, tomorrow she was going on holiday. But, at the same time, she felt strangely melancholic and slurred her way up the rest of the stairs singing her favourite Astrud Gilberto tune:- *'he's got a problem if he thinks I need him … I only think about him on alternate Thursdays, when I haven't got anything better to do … dad a … da da da …'*

To her surprise as she reached the top of the stairs she could see that the front door of her apartment was ajar. Maybe she hadn't locked it properly when she'd left? But as she got nearer, she noticed there were wood splinters all over the floor – and a great gaping hole where they'd gouged out the lock. It looked very much as if she'd been burgled.

At first she couldn't believe it.

She pushed open the door and could believe even less what she saw. They'd not just burgled the flat; they'd ransacked the whole place. The carpet had been pulled up, furniture was wrecked and scattered all over the floor and her paperwork was strewn everywhere.

Julia was shocked. All of her things. *They'd ruined her home.* Everything she'd worked for; the only things she'd ever really owned. It was too much. Her hands shook uncontrollably as she walked slowly through the door.

The final straw was when she caught sight of her mother's china doll lying face down in the hall, its skull broken into three large pieces. One of the doll's beautiful bright blue eyes glared at her from beneath a piece of picture glass that magnified it. Her once reassuringly pretty, sweet face now looked as if she belonged in a horror movie.

Julia slumped down on the floor and bawled her eyes out. The doll was the only thing she'd got of her mother's, it was the only thing she'd ever treasured. Each time she'd run away, it was the only thing she'd taken, it was the only constant, the only part of her life that had any hint of normality and love about it.

What was left of the door creaked, making her turn listlessly to stare at the approaching figure of Carlos from next door. He stood staring open mouthed at her.

'Oh dear me,' he said, his deep tones trying to be reassuring. 'I think we'd better get you a drink. Come on, I'll pour you a brandy.'

He helped her up off the floor and walked her slowly to his flat.

'No. No drink,' muttered Julia. Champagne. Had Champagne.'

He passed her a drink and gave her a couple of tablets to take. 'These will calm your nerves,' he said.

Julia swallowed the tablets and sat dejectedly on the sofa. Her life that she'd spent years building so determinedly was being demolished. All this bad luck. Hah, so much for that astrologer, this was supposed to be her best year ever. Her planets must be going backwards or something.

Carlos seemed to be muttering reassuring things to her. The tablets were beginning to work and Julia began to feel more light-headed and relaxed. Thank goodness she was going away tomorrow. What did anything matter anymore? She wished Alan was there.

She finished her brandy and Carlos went to pour her another one. As he wandered over to the drinks cabinet it suddenly hit Julia that Alan wouldn't know where she was and she went out of the door into the corridor. She hesitated for a moment, all the doors looked exactly the same and the whole corridor seemed to be spinning in all directions. Her vision was blurring and everything gradually moved into black and white. Which one was her flat?

She was stumbling along the corridor leaning forward precariously to peer at each of the flat numbers in turn, when Alan arrived with Christophe de Flaubert and two policemen in uniform.

Julia peered at them through heavily-lidded eyes, swaying giddily forward as she did so. She really couldn't understand why they were all looking at her in that very odd fashion.

'Julia?' exclaimed Alan. 'We came by earlier and couldn't find you, but found the mess, so we called the police. Julia, are you okay?'

As she passed out, Christophe de Flaubert, being the nearest, caught her half volley just as she hit the ground.

The policeman suggested that they call in for an ambulance.

'Alan we'd better get a cold cloth and try and bring her round,' said Christophe, carrying her into the flat. When Alan returned with the cloth Julia moaned and started to come round anyway.

'Are you alright, miss?' asked the second police officer

as he appeared, mopping his brow which was sweating profusely due to the long flight of stairs. 'Do we need an ambulance? '

'I'm f … fine, jus … sst fine, doctor,' said Julia, her eyes like saucers and a large, dreamy grin on her face. Then suddenly aware that they were all looking at her oddly again she ducked her head into Christophe de Flaubert's shirt to hide. It smelt expensive, warm and reassuring; it smelt of him and she found she liked it.

Alan didn't think anything of it but Christophe looked a little taken back.

'I think it's just too much to drink,' said Christophe. 'I don't think she needs an ambulance… but… He laid her down on the bed and Alan sat down beside her.

'Julia, what a complete mess you've got yourself into,' he said his voice full of exasperation.

'I know, I know,' said Julia, grinning stupidly at him. Then she suddenly didn't know whether she was coming or going.

'But Alan my flat's been burgled and I … I … I don't know. It just happened. It wasn't me, you know. Haven't you been burgled ever?

'No'

'*No*?'

'No'.

'Well it's not my fault, you know.' Julia drifted off into a dream again.

'Julia. I need this like a hole in the head. I've got to get a plane to South America tomorrow morning and I've got a whole business plan to tie up before then.' He looked at her and, realising it was futile, gave up. 'Julia, the police are here, they need to speak to you.'

'Oh.' She tried to smile flirtatiously up at them but she just fell forwards. 'Well, where's Carlos anyway?' asked Julia, her startled eyes peering into the Frenchman's. He really is very handsome. Christophe, she chided herself as her own brain got the wrong end of the stick – Christophe is very handsome, not Carlos. She couldn't look away. She kept staring at him.

'Carlos?' He asked his eyes not leaving hers. 'Who is Carlos?'

'The man down the corridor,' said Julia sitting up. 'He gave me brandy and … and he gave me some tablets to calm … mm calm mmy nervzz.'

'What kind of tablets?' Christophe asked, taking note of her watery eyes and enlarged pupils.

Julia gave out a sigh that seemed to go on forever. 'Don't know really. Red? No, blue. Maybe yellow? Oh, I don't know, round ones.'

She swayed again and then with her big eyes blinking up at the Frenchman she fell flat on her back on the bed.

'Can't move,' she said. 'Can't move my legs. Do I have any legs? Where have my legs gone?'

Christophe turned to Alan and the policeman. 'I think we should take her to casualty. She's obviously drunk quite a bit, but that mixed with tablets is not a good idea.'

'I'll try and find this Carlos person,' said the first police inspector. 'I don't like the sound of her not being able to move her legs. Call for the ambulance,' he said to the other policemen.

'No, said Christophe,' It's not far and it will be quicker if we take her and it'll save on the emergency services. What do you think, Alan?'

'I suppose it would be best to take her to the hospital,

better safe than sorry, eh.'

They bundled Julia into Christophe's car.

Alan sat in the back cradling Julia's head in his lap. 'Will she be alright, do you think?' he asked Christophe.

'I'm sure she will. She probably just needs to sleep it off.'

Julia slipped in and out of consciousness and began to mutter incomprehensible things. At one time Alan was sure he heard her call out for her father, but then thought he must be mistaken; her father died years ago.

He sighed, his mind going over all the things he had to do before his trip the next day. It wasn't as if he could do the work on the plane either. Damn. He could kill Julia sometimes. When they were married she really was going to have to cut down on the drinking. It was too much.

When they arrived at the hospital Christophe explained everything to the doctor while Alan tried to get some sense out of Julia.

The doctors pumped her stomach just to be on the safe side and ran some tests.

While they were waiting for the results a specialist came in and asked a lot of questions about Julia's moods and how she'd been feeling when Alan had last spoken to her. Had she been depressed lately? Had she had any bad news that they knew of? When Alan said she'd resigned, that she'd said something about being pregnant but he was sure she was messing around and that his mother had accused her of having an affair the doctor was keen to keep her in. Then the test results came back.

'Ketamine,' said the doctor. 'Does she do drugs?' he asked looking at Christophe. Christophe looked at Alan.

'No. Of course not!'

'She said that the neighbour gave her something to calm her nerves,' said Christophe. 'Maybe he gave it to her, but Ketamine is a date rape drug isn't it?'

'Yes it is. And when mixed with alcohol it can be dangerous. I think it's wearing off pretty quickly though so you should be able to take her home soon. She might experience some hallucinations for a short time then she could sleep it off. Don't leave her alone and call an ambulance if you see her deteriorating. Alan and Christophe stood contemplating this prospect in the middle of the casualty ward. 'Christophe, I just have to go back and finish this document, you know it's important. I've got Virginia coming in at breakfast to work overtime on it so that it'll be ready for tomorrow's meeting, well it's today's meeting now …'

His voice trailed off and all sense of hope disappeared as he saw the expression on Christophe's face.

They both stood there silently for a moment.

'Christ,' muttered Christophe under his breath. 'OK. Then I'll take her home and sit with her. Just make sure you've got everything in the document to stitch up that deal Alan, that's all. Make sure you deal from the top like I said. Use any of the names I've given you and get as much information as you can – and if you have any problems call me – whatever time it is, okay? Just don't go over the fifteen million, okay? They aren't worth it; the whole bloody country isn't worth it.'

'Thanks so much, Christophe, for looking after Julia. She can be a bit of a handful really.'

Christophe did not comment. A handful? She was a walking horror movie.

Alan went back to the office and Christophe was left

in a bad humour bundling a still high Julia into his car.

As he tried to strap her in the passenger seat, she kept putting her arms around his neck, kissing him and whispering in a slow deep voice, 'You're very nice, you know, Christophe.'

At first he just pulled her off, cursing to himself, but suddenly he found himself kissing her back.

Julia gradually became aware underneath her haze of drugs and drink that her lips were tingling. It was as if they were attached directly to every other part of her body. She felt a wave of lust seeping through her and, totally uninhibited, she continued to molest him shamelessly.

Christophe suddenly stopped kissing her back and pulled himself away. What the hell was she playing at? What the hell was *he* playing at?

He slammed the passenger door shut and got into the driver's seat, tearing his hands through his hair. He could do without this. This one really was a nightmare.

Julia was giggling in the passenger seat, she couldn't believe it. Her lips – they'd worked! They'd gone all tingly, all the way through. Christophe was so yummy.

'Do you know my lips work now?' said Julia, matter-of-factly and very pleased with herself.

'They certainly do,' muttered Christophe. He decided to drive to his place. She couldn't possibly stay in that mess of hers tonight and God knew what she'd get up to in this state. He remembered what the doctor had said about there being a slight possibility that she was going to get worse. Personally he couldn't imagine how it could get any worse.

Julia had busied herself with staring at the glove compartment and was totally mesmerised.

'Those lights are amazing,' she said incredulously, watching them go on and off as she partially closed the door. 'How on earth do you do it?' she asked, looking at him in wonder.

Christophe had never found the glove compartment light particularly awe-inspiring, but he took her word for it.

'Oh, it's nothing, really,' he said modestly.

By the time they arrived at Eaton Square she was much calmer and had stopped seeing kaleidoscope road signs and flying street lamps. He put her into his bed and sat in the chair with a book, to watch over her.

As she drifted off he took a good look at her. How the hell had Alan got himself mixed up in that! Beautiful certainly, and those eyes. He'd noticed it that day at Alan's dinner party. There was something so mesmerising about them. It wasn't just the amazing turquoise colour, there was something more, that he couldn't quite figure out. You sort of lost yourself in them, like you could feel the hurt. But God what a nightmare she was! Mercenary through and through from what he'd seen so far. And anyone that got mixed up with Jaimie was definitely up to no good.

About forty-five minutes later, Julia moaned, leant across the bed, and he got the bucket to her just in time. The saga went on for another hour or so and eventually she seemed calmer and slept, leaving him to drop off himself.

CHAPTER 11

Julia awoke realising she was in a large, unfamiliar bed. She was lying facing a floor-to-ceiling sash window with tall shutters. She drew a complete blank. Where was she and what had she been doing? She tentatively put out her arm behind her to see if there were any other bodies in the bed. No, nobody. Well that was a relief, but her blank memory wasn't.

She tried very slowly to move her head but found it seemed to have put on a few extra pounds overnight. She had such a hangover she could be anywhere. She looked around hoping to find some clue as to where she was.

It was a beautiful room. Classical yet a sophisticated mix of antique with a subtle touch of modern. It was nice to know she had good taste even when she was in such a diabolical state. A plush, cream carpet covered the whole floor and a richly coloured Persian rug covered the centre. The duvet was crisp and fresh and the bed was a king-size that even Henry VIIIth would have approved of. The mattress seemed to mould itself around her, supporting her and making her feel safe. She snuggled down into it even more. A large painting hung directly opposite the bed; it was abstract but strangely erotic; lush, thick curves hinted at the feminine. Looks a bit too expensive, even for me, thought Julia.

Where the hell was she? And what the hell had she been doing to get there? She began to feel nervous, desperately trying to remember. For a second she felt like she almost had a thread to grasp, a hint of a name, something light and fluffy, f, it began with f, but then it disappeared again. She had a vague feeling she was supposed to be going somewhere. She wondered if Alan knew where she was supposed to be going. Alan! That was it, Alan. Not f, Alan.

Where was Alan? She very gently pushed back the duvet and got out of bed hoping she was leaving her head with its headache on the pillow. Sadly it accompanied her but one pace behind. She swayed slightly and then saw her clothes resting on a chair.

She pulled them on, and then went over to look out of the large window, maybe she'd get a hint of where she was. There were large gardens surrounded by Georgian terraces with a City of Westminster sign for Eaton Square. But she didn't know anyone who lived in Eaton Square.

She wandered over to the bedroom door and as she opened it she bumped smack into a tall dark handsome stranger coming in.

'And where do you think you're going?' he asked.

'Err. I'm not really sure. Look err…. You look as if you might be quite a nice person but how can I put this … I… err… am having a bit of trouble remembering …'

Christophe de Flaubert's face remained deadpan.

'So … err …' Julia was beginning to feel frightened.

120

Who was he and what was she doing there?

'Why don't you sit down,' he suggested, gesturing to a chair.

Julia shook her head. She really was confused. She wanted to know where she was, and what the hell was going on.

'Look, this is all very frightening so can we dispense with the niceties? Can you just tell me straight - did you kidnap me and have you sexually assaulted me?'

He looked quite shocked at that.

'No' he replied.

'No?'

'No'

Julia felt a sudden tingle in her lips. Hang on a minute … 'Err, well, did I … did I sexually assault you?'

Christophe hesitated for a second.

'Not really.'

'Not really?'

'No'

'What does 'not really' mean?'

'Well you did make inappropriate sexual advances to me in my car.'

'What? Look just stop messing about Mr f … fl … whatever your name is and cut to the chase. What the hell am I doing here?'

'I brought you back from the hospital because your fiancée Alan couldn't look after you because he has an important meeting. Somebody drugged you and the doctors said that you couldn't be left alone. Oh, yes and you resigned from your job, your flat has been burgled and you have a fixation with the lights in the glove compartment of my car. You said something about a lip problem, something about them not working before but …

Julia had become more and more wide eyed as Christophe spoke and everything started flooding back to her.

'OK.' She grabbed her jacket. 'I get it! I get it Monsieur de Flaubert. I don't know why you couldn't just say that in the first place.'

'Well I thought it was better to break it to you gently.'

'You call that gently?'

'Where do you think you are going?' he asked, eyeing the jacket.

'Home very probably. I don't know if you noticed but the place was rather a shambles last time I saw it,' she answered tartly. Inwardly she chided herself. That was so unnecessary he'd obviously been very kind looking after her. Why oh why, did he have that effect on her…

'The mess has never bothered you before, by all accounts. And no, you're not going home – not before we've said what needs to be said.'

That's what it is, thought Julia. That! That's exactly what is was that got to her. That school teacher tone of voice. The do as I say, I know best stuff. Red rag to a bull that's what it was.

'Not before we've said what needs to be said,' she mocked in a childish voice. 'Well thank you for having me, Christophe, it's been so nice,' said Julia, grabbing the door handle. 'Will that do?'

Christophe pulled her away from the door saying, 'I didn't have you, you were too ill; so why don't you stay a little longer and I'll see what I can do.'

At that Julia's temper completely snapped and before

she knew what she was doing she'd raised her hand. Thankfully he caught her wrist before it made contact with his face and he directed her back into the bedroom.

'Temper, temper,' he said, the humour belying the anger in his face. 'I'll let that one go. Let's just say for argument's sake that you are not quite yourself after such a terrible ordeal.'

Julia sat down on a chair and put her head in her hands. Oh my God, what was wrong with her? She'd got to get out of there. She stood up and started to say something.

'Sit down,' he said very quietly and very firmly.

She fell abruptly back into the large leather chair.

Christophe started pacing the floor. 'Just what the hell do you think you're playing at? I like Alan, he's become a good friend – and he's too good a business partner for me to see him getting hitched to an aspirational little tart like you. So what the hell are you playing at?'

Julia glared at him. How dare he! Aspirational little tart? Nobody called her a tart and got away with it.

Christophe stopped pacing and glared back then continued.

'What the hell are you playing at? What are you doing hanging around with Jaimie Girault? I heard you talking in the Café Pompadour, remember?'

They stared at each other angrily.

'I didn't realise eavesdropping on other people's conversations was the latest hobby of the international banking world. And what the hell business is it of yours anyway what Alan or Jaimie does? I don't know how they play these things in France, but over here when you're twenty-one you can do what you like.'

'More's the pity,' he said sarcastically. 'In your case they could have done with making it fifty-one, you might have a mature attitude by then.'

'Mature? Like you, you mean? Mature Mr Goody Two Shoes and … and so damn righteous …'

Julia realised she'd gone too far.

'So you think I'm righteous? Well, you didn't think that last night; in fact my interpretation was that you were begging me to be anything but righteous. I wonder just how far you would have gone if I'd let you…'

He moved towards her and suddenly his tone changed completely. He gently trailed his finger across her lips. 'You seemed to have some kind of problem with your lips…'

Julia could smell the warmth of his skin. The gentleness of his touch belied the anger in his eyes and then he held her face gently in his hands.

'Shall we try that again?' he suggested quietly, his eyes no longer angry. 'What do you think?'

'No, I …' Julia's voice was a faint whisper.

He removed his hands from her face but did not move further away from her. 'OK. If that's what you want.'

Julia hesitated. But it wasn't what she wanted. She wanted him to kiss her. It had all come flooding back to her. She wanted him to kiss her, she wanted to feel that sensuality that she'd never had with anyone else. Before she knew what she was doing she had put her hands on his face.

'I've … err … I think I've changed my mind.' She started to kiss him.

Christophe kissed her back passionately. 'I'm so very glad,' he said as his lips moved down to caress her neck and his touch became soft, his lips and tongue teasing hers into an even greater response. Julia's senses were running riot, her head and logic wanted to say no, but her lips and body betrayed them. His hands ran lightly over her whole body making her tingle all over and she found herself moulding her body against him.

Christophe guided her down onto the bed that seemed to have appeared from nowhere and, as she lay beside him, his hands gently slipped beneath her blouse. She sighed and giving in totally, she rolled over on top of him and began kissing him back for all she was worth. Julia was like another person, her hands exploring his body, but already knowing the way.

She wanted to feel him inside her just as adamantly as she had not wanted anyone near her before this. His hand undid the buttons of her blouse and slipped the silk camisole beneath to one side as his lips tasted the warmth of her nipples. Her hands went off on their own trip of exploration, through his hair, over his muscular shoulders and together they rolled over and over so that she was pinned underneath him. Julia felt her legs part to bring him closer to her.

His eyes were full of emotion as they looked deep into hers and his hands caressed her thighs and moved between her legs guiding them further apart. Then the moment was gone.

Suddenly the familiar scene in the streets of Paris that filled her with disgust erupted into her brain, catching in her throat, making her choke and fight for her very breath. The face of the *Rue Pigalle'* landlord flashed into her head and Julia screamed, pushing Christophe away, trying to get away from the things he was doing to her, from him touching her, from the disgust of that time in Paris. Her brain was screaming no, no. Then suddenly she was screaming out loud.

'No! *No! No* never, get away from me.' Julia leapt to her feet and backed away into the corner like a caged animal, sobbing hysterically; her hands tearing her clothes back into place to cover the chill that blew over her nakedness.

Christophe sat up, staring at her in astonishment for a second. Then he moved towards her, put out his arm.

'OK. Calm down.' He said, his voice confused. Julia back away from him even further.

'Look. I'm not going to touch you OK. Just take it easy Julia.'

Julia pulled her clothes into place. She was shaking, and in her panic and fear she turned on him angrily.

'You bastard!' she screamed as she flew at him, her whole being ready to claw him to bits. 'You did that deliberately, you bastard.' He caught her hands and held them rigid as far away from him as he could to defend himself.

'Julia, I didn't I…'

But the fear and terror that the memories had triggered had pushed Julia over the edge. He watched her as she grabbed a towel and started scrubbing at her skin until it was red.

'Julia. I'm sorry. OK. Please stop that. Stop. Just stop. Look at your arms…'

Julia looked down at the bright red welts that had developed.

'I have to go!' She grabbed her coat. 'I have to go and get out of here.'

Julia charged out of the Eaton Square door and stopped a cab by running right into it.

Would she ever forget it? Would she ever be free from the *Rue Pigalle*? She tried frantically to hold back her sobs. She was so disgusted with herself and him. And how dare he? He was vile. How dare he call her a tart. How dare he touch her like that. Tears began to prickle behind her eyes again and she held back a sob as she asked the taxi driver to take her to Kensington. She'd wanted to scream and scream and hit him, but all she could do was sob, choking on her own anger. She was so confused – how could Christophe do that? How could he make her body respond like that? Julia felt sick. Would she ever be able to escape the feeling of disgust and degradation? She didn't know what was worse, feeling her body respond to Christophe, only to feel humiliated and disgusted when her memories came back to haunt her, or feeling like ice when Alan touched her. She had been able to cope with sex because she simply blocked it out. She never engaged herself physically nor emotionally and when she did that she was safe. But Christophe had bypassed that. How had he done that? She hated him, she hated Christophe for all the terrifying feelings he had just aroused in her. She hated him for everything he'd done.

Everything was such a mess. Her flat, her career and everything.

Then it dawned on her, just as she got out of the taxi. She hadn't got any damn insurance. She'd never had enough cash handy to renew it. She couldn't even afford to replace her stuff. She couldn't hold back the sobs any longer. Why did everything go wrong all at once?

As she emerged from the lift she walked straight into

the police sergeant.

'Miss Connors? I'm afraid they've made a right mess in there. You'll have to give us a list of what's missing so that we can circulate it. Anything that's of high value, let us have it by later today if you can.'

Julia nodded at him and entered the flat with him following close behind.

'Not very good these doors, you know. And, well, nice places like this get burgled all the time. We have three or four a night in this area, you know. Cheeky they are round here, finding new ways to get in all the time, they are.'

Julia wandered around the flat. The electronic stuff was all still there and her jewellery and most of her designer clothes. She couldn't think of much else that would be worth taking.

'Well there doesn't seem to be anything missing, sergeant.'

'They must have been scared off by the two gentlemen who came round just before you got back last night.'

'Have the fingerprint people finished?'

'Near enough, miss. If I was you I'd get the locks changed. Sometimes, more often than not, they take a key and come back and do the place over once you've replaced everything.'

'Oh right. Well I'll make sure the locks are changed then when I get back from my holiday. I'm going on holiday this afternoon and I'm late as it is. Have you finished everything you need to see?'

'Yes. We're done and dusted, miss. When will you be back from your holiday, if you don't mind my asking?'

'A couple of weeks or so. I'm going to Provence.'

'Well, so long as we have an address where we can contact you if we need to, then that will be fine.'

Julia nodded and wrote down the address that Jean-Claude had given her. All she wanted to do was get away from it all. Jean-Claude was right bless him. She needed a holiday.

Julia sighed and sat down on the floor amongst the mess. She'd better call Liane maybe she could get the locks changed for her while she was away. She'd better call Alan too. She wondered if Christophe had said anything to him. Come to think of it, she wondered what *she'd* said to him; most of the fiasco at the flat and hospital was still a blur. She had never been so badly in need of a holiday, she was turning into a disaster on legs. Liane's phone was engaged for ages and in the end Julia decided to go round there as it was on the way to the airport anyway. She threw her things into her case and picked up the remains of the china doll. Perhaps it could be mended. She put the pieces carefully into the bag, wrapped the body in a towel and placed it into her case. It was French so yes, it needed to go to France with her. Maybe they could mend it there.

She just couldn't be bothered to tidy up, she didn't have time. Besides which, it didn't need tidying it needed redecorating.

Then she had an idea, Eloisa! She scribbled a note and left all the cash she had left in an envelope on the side hopefully that would cover it. She would just take her stuff and get away from everything.

Julia rang the doorbell to Liane's flat again. Maybe she hadn't heard it the first time. She was just about to turn and go when the door opened.

'Julia. I've been trying to get hold of you all morning. Alan told me what happened.'

Julia stepped inside the door and suddenly found herself smothered in kisses by Alan as he launched himself out of the kitchen and took her in his arms. He looked completely washed out.

'Julia, Liane and I've been calling everywhere looking for you. There was no answer at your place and I couldn't get hold of Christophe. Virginia let me down badly this morning, so I had to get Liane to help out on the documents and anyway I thought Christophe might have brought you here to Liane's.'

'Err. No … no he … err. I slept with him.' Liane and Alan stared at her. 'I mean I slept in his bed. Oh what I really mean is that he looked after me, as you know. I was so ill after all the champagne and you'd disappeared, Alan so …' Her voice trailed off. Why did it all sound so guilty to her ears, when she had nothing to be guilty about? Unless the thought was as bad as the deed of course, in which case she'd hung, drawn and quartered herself.

They all stood there silently for a moment.

'Well you're alright now,' said Alan, 'you look much better than you did last night, I must say.' He looked down at his watch. 'Listen, I'm going to have to go or I'll miss my flight. It's been hell sorting all this bloody business plan out. Thank God Liane could help. I'll call you in Provence.' He picked up his case and headed towards the door.

'But, Alan, I've got to talk to you,' said Julia grabbing his arm as he reached the door, 'about all that stuff in *Paris Match*.'

He pulled her towards him and squeezed her tight. 'Listen, if you say it's okay, I believe you. You just rest and have a good holiday, you must be exhausted. I'll call you.'

Julia went back into the kitchen. 'Ships that pass in the night or what?' she said to Liane.

Liane was leaning over the sink, her hands shaking uncontrollably so that the two coffee mugs she was trying to wash were rattling like a pair of castanets.

'Liane, you're in as bad a state as I was last night. Promise me we'll never ever drink like that again.'

CHAPTER 12

Julia boarded the flight to Marseille and re-read the directions that Jean-Claude had sent to her, along with a map. The house was called Le Castellet but was really an old castle. An old couple called Pierre and Marie looked after it for the owner and they would leave the keys to a car for her to use at the information desk of the airport.

It was so nice to be on holiday. Julia had hardly any money, no job as yet, and a burgled flat at home but at least she was free for a while. She could sunbathe, read and just forget about everything – even the credit card man wouldn't be able to find her in Provence – and he had the determination of a modern-day Herod.

Once they'd landed, Julia went off to find the information desk and see if the keys to the car had been dropped off for her. She couldn't wait to get behind the wheel and hit the open road. She'd hoped there was a satnav, although Jean Claude's map was very pretty with lots of colours, he admitted he'd drawn it mostly by memory. Road numbers were a no go for Julia and if she had to follow those she'd end up God knows where.

The woman behind the desk gave her the keys, the ticket to get out of the car park. And an envelope with a note in it. 'It's in the second car park to the back of the check in terminal,' she said, smiling professionally. 'Enjoy your holiday.'

Julia read the note as she wandered along. The handwriting was very curly as if a spider had woven it onto the page and it took her quite a while to decipher it. In the end she got the gist of it. The little run around was in for service so she had to have a replacement vehicle and it gave the registration number. Excellent, she thought, that usually made it an upgrade.

It took Julia an hour of wandering around the car park checking every car she could find before she finally realised the only one left was a mucky brown little Citroën that looked as if it had come there to die.

She checked the registration number twice. Definitely wasn't a maths dyslexia problem because the letters were correct 'DGT'. There had to be some mistake – surely that thing would never move. They must have given her the wrong note – but it had to be right because it mentioned Jean-Claude. She tried the keys and the lock gave straight away. She wondered why they'd bothered locking it – nobody between here and Nice, going the wrong way round the world, was going to pinch it. Surprisingly it started first time, and she began to warm to it slightly.

Julia drove out of the airport and onto the main road going north and before she knew it she was getting over the embarrassment and starting to feel like a local. She supposed that was how they behaved in the country: pottering along in their clapped-out little heaps, setting off in September to be there for Christmas. At that point a Mercedes sports ran straight past her at about ninety miles an hour. 'Smart-arse,' she said.

She relaxed and sat back to enjoy the rest of the scenery. When you were only going slowly you had plenty of time to do the admiring. The scenery gradually changed from ugly suburbs and industrial estates to a rugged hills interspersed with cypress trees and olive groves.

As Julia neared Cavaillon, the nearest major town to Le Castellet, the countryside seemed to become more and more open. The vineyards clung to the rolling hills, their vines already full of foliage, making waves of bright green against the pale brown earth. Occasionally she could pick out the rich red roof of a farm surrounded by poplars or the dark green leaves of the almond trees. Further on, she began to feel cut off except for the long straight road that could take her on or back. She couldn't believe that the enormous, cosmopolitan city of Marseille was only half an hour back.

The light gradually began to dim and she could see the setting sun in the wing mirror like Haley's comet chasing her down the road. As Julia drove into the centre of Cavaillon it was bustling with activity, and she was tempted to park in the Place du Clos, a quaint square which bustled with cafes on every side but she was already quite late. She drove through a beautiful triumphal arch and then she followed a rough road alongside a large rock embankment, out into Le Petit Luberon.

The road went on for a few miles or so and eventually she came to the tiny village of Menerbes and she stopped to ask the way to Le Castellet as Jean-Claude had suggested. 'Ask anyone in Menerbes,' he'd said, 'they'll all know where it is, might even jump in and take you if you're lucky.'

After about twenty minutes of wandering around, Julia decided the luck lay in finding someone to ask. The place was deserted. Half of the houses on the hill seemed to date from the Middle Ages and weren't even inhabited. The rest were well and truly locked up. She gave up and, re-reading her notes carefully, set off in the direction of the next village. She headed along the road for about a mile and then just as the road swung to the left she found the turning on the right.

Nobody could have prepared her for the sheer magnificence of Le Castellet. Julia whistled loudly with surprise as she drove up the large cobbled track. Considering this wasn't château country, this was one hell of a château. Jean-Claude had said that it was really more of a traditional castle than château but this was amazing. It really was a stone castle, set upon a hill, overlooking a large mountain to the northeast and the village of Menerbes to the South.

The castle had been beautifully restored and had obviously had a very attentive gardener. Large poplars surrounded one side and age old climbing plants trailed all over the front entrance. A neatly tended rose garden sat to the left of the main house in bizarre contrast to the very rambling nature of the large, imposing building.

Julia parked the car in the front and, fearing the sheer austerity of the large wooden door and wrought iron door knocker, went around the back to scout someone out. She very much doubted anyone could open that front door.

Must do wonders keeping travelling salesmen at bay.

To the back she found a row of stables and a small paddock which seemed to slope away over the back of the hill. A large beautiful dark bay stallion stood flicking its tail restlessly under the shade of an almond tree. Julia wandered over to get a better look at him, and he stood rolling the whites of his eyes for a moment, and then crossed over to meet her.

'My, you are beautiful,' whispered Julia into the soft black muzzle.

Learning to ride had been one of the many ruses she'd employed to better herself, to mix in the right society. It was also the only one of them she'd really enjoyed. Since she'd been living in London though she hadn't had much time to ride. She'd been once and had got sick of the plummy instructress making them do a perfect rising trot without stirrups, round and round the park until they got a 'good seat'. A long, reckless hectic gallop, that was more her style. She couldn't wait to try the stallion though, he was beautiful.

She wandered over to the other side of the paddock where there was a large oval swimming pool complete with sculpture-laden sun terrace. The whole place oozed old money, generations and generations of good taste. Julia stood on the terrace drinking in the smell of jasmine and honeysuckle, and letting the setting sun warm her face. This was amazing, almost idyllic. Jean-Claude was a genius.

Suddenly a gruff voice muttered something in French that Julia couldn't understand, making her turn sharply towards the direction of the noise.

An old man stood there rolling his sleeves up. His

face was weathered like an old seafarer and he had a bizarrely shaped black hat perched on his head. Julia thought it must be the Pierre mentioned in the note. She continued to stare at the hat mesmerized. How the hell did they manage to mould it into that shape? It was a miracle.

'Eh?' he said gruffly nodding his head towards her in enquiry.

Julia explained who she was and he stood shaking his head directing her towards the back of the main building. He seemed noncommittal and wandered off muttering to himself. Julia followed. As they reached the back of the house he began to shake his hands and gesticulate wildly, calling for Marie.

An old woman came out and stood staring at Julia for a moment, her brown eyes rolling wildly. She looked as gruff as the old man; weathered and worn, and clearly irritated at the intrusion.

And this must be Marie, the wicked witch of the South, thought Julia, smiling a red herring smile - hoping the witch's talents didn't include mind reading. The woman turned to the old man and asked him something that Julia couldn't understand and the old man just shrugged.

Julia felt very uncomfortable. The signs of a welcome were decidedly absent. The old woman continued to stare, her only movement being a slow and deliberate wiping of her hands on her apron. She then raised them in despair.

Julia was tired and tetchy. Honestly, I've been sacked, burgled and drugged, I just want to rest, tuck myself up in a comfortable bed and forget about everything. She explained this time to the woman in her very careful Parisian French that she was the friend of Monsieur Jean-

Claude who had come to stay; see, she'd come in the brown Citroën.

The woman listened, pouted at her husband who pouted back and then they both went into the house. Julia assumed that she was to follow, and did.

They entered a large kitchen which Julia was amazed to find was fitted out with all the latest luxury gadgets and had a large oak table in the centre, reminiscent of an old farmhouse table. It was surprisingly chic.

She followed Marie through, up half a flight of stone stairs which led to a large stone hall bedecked with an eclectic collection of paintings; traditional landscapes, modern prints and an enormous abstract oil, rich with primary colours, which was the focal point. Julia didn't have time to linger as Marie called from the top of another flight of stairs, beckoning her in a sharp voice that brooked no argument. Julia followed her and they wound their way up a large central stone staircase almost to the top of the building.

The hall and stairs were still stone, but had been carpeted along the centre in a rich royal blue which seemed to take the chill off the place. It didn't take the chill off the wicked witch though, thought Julia.

She tried to take a sneak look through one of the bedroom doors which was ajar as they came up to the third floor, but the old woman's timely guttural cough spurred her upwards.

Eventually they came to the top of the stairs and walked along a long corridor until they must almost have been at the far end of the south wing. Some small rickety wooden stairs wound back over the way they'd come and Julia was aware of a deep musty smell making her cough, as she found herself in a cold blue attic room which must once have been a store room.

Julia smiled a frosty smile at the old woman who just grinned seemingly to herself but she still managed to show Julia her missing canines. I wonder how she lost those, thought Julia morbidly – probably fell over and bashed them on her broomstick.

Julia was amazed; from what she could tell, the whole place was completely luxurious, apart from this one little attic room. She felt like Gretel locked away in the wicked witch's gingerbread house, except she didn't even have Hansel for company.

Marie wandered over to the small dresser, brushed the cobwebs from the top and opened the drawers very slowly, one at a time, smiling proudly as if she was showing Julia around the penthouse suite at the Hilton. She kept muttering something about the monsieur, he wants it so. Julia thanked her and feeling totally unwelcome she turned abruptly to go back down the four floors to get her luggage.

The old couple stood with their arms folded in the hall watching her carry her heavy suitcase and bag in from the car. Thanks a bunch, thought Julia, their intent gaze was doing nothing to spur her bags upstairs – they could have offered to carry one at least. She puffed and panted, red-faced, as she took them one at a time up to the attic room.

She dumped her cases on the floor, and flopped onto the bed realising as she did so that it was rock hard. She'd never felt so alone and unwelcome in her whole life. She sat on the bed and was aware that the musty smell was a familiar one. It played upon her senses drawing memories into her mind.

She felt cold and nauseous as she lay there, she just wanted to cry her heart out. As she gradually fell asleep she realised the musty damp smell was just the same as the smell of the room in the *Rue Pigalle*. As the light dimmed she was soon back there, tossing and turning in her bed, fighting for her sanity.

CHAPTER 13

When Julia awoke, she found she was still fully clothed but someone had thrown a clean duvet over her. She felt exhausted, as if she'd spent the night running a full marathon; she was sweltering, which was not really surprising as she'd slept in her jeans and her shirt. Jean-Claude would be horrified. He didn't even think people should sleep in nightwear let alone their clothes.

'Nightwear is designed with a single purpose, Julia, to entice one's lover to the act of love and then remove it as an act of foreplay.'– she could hear him saying it now.

Julia looked down at her phone and asked lady Google the time. No cover. She wandered out onto the landing and tried again. Still no luck. She wondered if there was wifi. Knowing her luck, probably not. Oh well, so far the day was already going better than yesterday. Today she'd managed to commandeer a clean duvet; yesterday all she could manage was a dirty old Citroën.

Julia pulled on a clean pair of jeans and a t-shirt.

Those old codgers weren't going to get her down. This was the country life and she'd left her make-up, her iron and all her pretensions back in London. It felt great.

Sometimes, continually having to dress up for Jacquard could be a bore, especially when she hadn't done the washing and she had to fish around to find the least dirty of her dirty clothes. There was only one thing she couldn't do without, and that was her Chanel – and this mattress could certainly use some, especially if she was ever going to get a decent night's sleep in it. She splashed it all over the bed and duvet. Then, standing on top of a chair she tried to open the small porthole-like window. It was jammed solid. She pushed and pushed and in the end leapt at it putting all her weight behind it. The whole of the round window frame shot out of the rotten wood and fell clattering onto the roof, scattering a team of voyeuristic pigeons.

'Shit!' Julia said.

She stood on tiptoe and gazed out of the window. She could see for miles: fields of olives and cypresses and large limestone gashes stood out like wounds on the landscape. Grape vines seemed to go on for miles, their patterns making rigid tracks in the fields. On the distant horizon she could see the tall, jagged peaks of Mont Ventoux, casting a sombre conical shadow over the vineyards. Mont Ventoux must be directly to the east decided Julia; its peak was silhouetted against a golden light as the sun strained to climb above it.

Julia decided she'd start her holiday with a spot of sightseeing. She'd bought a good guide book that even the well-travelled lentil eaters at number six would have been proud of. But first, she would just die if she didn't get a *pan chocolat* and a decent cup of coffee.

She ran down the stairs, ignored Marie who was polishing in the hall, climbed into the Citroën and headed for Menerbes.

The landscape seemed so remote and was so scorched it should have been barren, but it wasn't, fields of bright green vines lit up the landscape for as far as the eye could see. A couple of small derelict grey outbuildings signalled the approach of the village, and she was so intent on gazing at the scenery that she didn't anticipate the sharpness of the oncoming bend and screeching the tyres, she frantically steered into it. At the same moment a cream Mercedes sports came around in the opposite direction and she only narrowly missed hitting it. Maniac, she thought, but didn't stop; she was too busy concentrating on righting the car. Anyway, why stop? I mean it wasn't as if she'd hit it, had she? In London and Paris you only had to stop if you hit somebody hard.

The road disappeared off up a steep sharp hill that seemed to have come from nowhere and then she was on the top of the hill with a fantastic view of the village way down below her.

The petrol gauge wasn't working which didn't surprise her in the least; the locals were probably so laid back that such a small thing as a faulty petrol gauge was highly unlikely to bother anyone. She decided to fill up anyway. She didn't fancy getting stranded around here with no petrol. It'd be years before anyone found her and if those two old codgers were anything to go by, even longer before they understood her. She could talk back street French with the best of them, but this Provence dialect was something else entirely.

Julia found a petrol station just a little further on. Well she thought it was a functioning petrol station but it looked more like a movie set from the 1950's. She pulled off the road next to one of the pumps and peered at it. It did seem to have the price in euros so maybe it did work. There was no one in sight so she got out of the car and shouted, '*bonjour, il y a quelqu'un?*' as loudly as she could. No response.

She looked at the pump again, maybe it was self-service but it was difficult to tell and anyway she was not sure she could have worked it out.

A young man appeared from around the corner on the opposite side of the square and casually lolloped over to her. She nodded an acknowledgement as he seemed to be approaching, and received no response except for a very slight increase in his pace. He raised his head in inquiry as he reached her and Julia asked in her politest French if she could have some petrol. He nodded and Julia nearly keeled over as she caught a strong whiff of the raw garlic that he'd been chewing. To her surprise he promptly disappeared behind the garage building again.

Julia sighed and leant against the rusty bonnet of the Citroën. It lamented loudly so she redistributed her weight to a less rusty area. The sun flickered tentatively and then emerged from around the tall water tower behind the garage. Julia basked in the warmth of it, refusing to be riled by the youth's apparent lack of haste as he disappeared around the corner across the other side of the garage. After all, this was a holiday and the Provençal style of life was different; wasn't that what she was beginning to discover?

Five minutes later, after a dozen kamikaze chickens

had charged out from under the garage hut straight for her, the youth emerged again, this time with the moral support of what could have been his father. A large grin spread across the youth's face as he approached her, but that was soon wiped away by a sharp rebuke from the father. Although Julia could hear the remark, she could not hear well enough to decipher the accent. The youth turned quickly, returning to wherever he'd first appeared from, and the old man bent his stocky frame over the pump and started to fill the Citroën's tank.

'Le Castellet?' he asked without smiling.

Julia nodded. 'I'm staying there. Holidays'

He looked surprised but didn't say anything.

She fished in her bag for her credit card and handed it to him. He immediately stopped the petrol flow. Shook his head, tutted. They only took cash.

Paying in cash was Julia's worst nightmare. She started sweating slightly and felt the panic rise. Oh hell. Breathe deeply she told herself as she took out the last of the notes that Jean-Claude had given her, a green Euro note and hoped it was good enough. He shook his head again.

'One hundred too big,' he said, 'probably a forgery. You have to drive into the village to change it in the bank.'

Bank? Bank was the trigger word for her second worst nightmare. Her nausea rose again. She couldn't possibly go in a bank, they would talk money and she'd look stupid.

She asked him if there was a café tabac nearby, she needed a better map and some *pan chocolat* for breakfast. She'd get a map and a *pan chocolat*, pay with her card and ask for cash back.

'Tabac Benail,' he said. 'Don't go to Tabac Grenard.

Le Castellet go to Benail. Come back, get petrol and pay.

'OK,' she said smiling breezily.

She followed his directions but found the café Grenard on the first road. Honestly, it was a free country why shouldn't she go to there, it was nearer.

She pulled up outside and amidst a barrage of curious stares from the locals got out of the Citroën. A sudden silence fell upon the previously bustling café as she entered and Julia felt shivers run down her spine. Woah. Hostile or what!

She asked for a map and got such a cold response that she decided against asking for the *pan chocolat* and quickly got back into the car to go to the café Benail. OK. So Provence lesson number one, listen to petrol station old codger.

When she found the café Benail; once again as with the café Grenard, it was bustling. Only this time when she entered the conversation stopped for just a few seconds. Everybody stared and then the old woman in black behind the counter addressed somebody who was sat at a nearby table and it was as if that was the signal for the conversation to continue.

Julia approached the counter warily and the old woman in black nodded at her. She couldn't be sure but she thought that maybe a slight glint appeared in her eye and then was gone.

'The Le Castellet car?' she asked nodding noncommittally.

'Yes,' said Julia reviving her charm smile from its locker. At this rate, by the end of the holiday it was going to be totally overworked for very little reward.

The old woman smiled and Julia continued, feeling

encouraged.

'Do you have a map of the Vaucluse?' she asked, her voice too sunny for words.

'*Non,*' came the answer with a turned down mouth and pout.

'Oh,' said Julia. 'Well, never mind. Could I have a *pan chocolat* and a coffee please then?'

The woman gestured for Julia to take a chair in the corner and she sat with her guide book in front of her face to disguise the fact that she was scrutinizing the café Benail's regulars. She never could have believed that getting some petrol, a coffee and something to eat could be so traumatic an experience.

Julia glanced up from her book, taking in the group in the corner. There were three men having a lively debate. The elder of the three was gesticulating wildly to express his point and the others listened with apparently daydreaming expressions upon their faces. Two small children played noiselessly around their feet, diving in and out between their chairs, but the men seemed unbothered by them and amazingly managed to avoid treading on them. Another of the men had now taken up the debate and was arguing loudly with the first, pouting and waving his fist damningly and then laughing derisively as the first reiterated his point.

Julia's thoughts were interrupted by the appearance of her coffee and a croissant. She hesitated, opening her mouth to say that she ordered a *pan chocolat*, but one glance at the old woman and she clamped it shut again.

A newcomer arrived and the old woman's face lit up with joy. She kissed him loudly on both cheeks, gripping his face in her hands roughly. He kissed her back and the three men, their arguments immediately forgotten, slapped him on the back affectionately.

He was a tall man, easily over six foot, Julia guessed, and had thick dark curly hair, strong features and a rough dark beard. Then she realised she'd dropped her guidebook, completely blowing her camouflage and consequently the newcomer was staring straight back at her.

She picked up the guidebook and dived for her coffee, inadvertently slurping it loudly behind the safety of the guidebook. The newcomer said something she didn't understand gesturing casually in her direction, making the others burst out laughing and she blushed behind her book. It served her right for being nosy she supposed, but what did they expect when they all ran around treating her as if she was something that had just arrived by meteorite?

Julia finished her coffee and croissant and went to pay. It was then that she noticed the 'No credit cards'. Oh no. She emptied all the coins she'd got on to the counter and smiled nervously, waiting for the old woman to take them. The woman waited for Julia to give them to her. Julia hesitated, smiled and pushing all of the coins towards her said, 'keep the change.' The look of astonishment on the woman's face was a clear indication that Julia had paid far too much. She felt panic rising and rushed out as fast as she could.

'*Attendez,* mademoiselle,' came the voice of the newcomer as she left the café. It was greeted by roars of laughter from the others. Julia was far too ashamed to wait. She couldn't help it. She never knew how much change there was.

She decided to get out of the village, park the car in a

secluded spot to calm herself down. So much for the land of the wandering troubadours.

Just before she got to the village of Lacoste, she found the ideal spot and sat under a huge old olive tree, it looked friendly enough.

'So what do you recommend?' she asked it.

'What about a visit to Oppéde? Looks quite near. It's supposed to be quite pretty and have a castle.'

She looked it up in the guide book.

'Home to Baron Jean Maynier d'Oppéde,' said the guide book. 'The baron led the bloodiest massacre in the Vaudois that France had ever seen. Eventually he was poisoned for revenge.'

'Delightful, I must say,' said Julia continuing to talk to the tree. 'More feuding French'

Next, she looked up Meberbes; maybe she could go back and look around there a bit more. 'Menerbes castle was home to an exiled Danish nobleman who lived with his mistresses and led a debauched life, and spent some time in prison with the Marquis de Sade.'

'Oh fine,' said Julia. 'I bet he was a really charismatic character'.

Surely there had got to be something decent to see around here? Where was all that stuff about the troubadours that Jean-Claude told her about? Where was all the romance and the artists and poets?

The valley between Menerbes and the next village of Lacoste was called the Valmansque, in other words the 'Valley of the Sorcerers', because it was colonised by a bunch of heretics. 'Hum probably good friends with the witch of Le Castellet, thought Julia.'

The final straw was when she read that the castle at

Lacoste, the very next village to Le Castellet had been home to none other than the Marquis de Sade.

She couldn't believe, it, she'd come on holiday to a land of debauchery and sexual perversion. Where in heaven was all the romance???
So far the most romantic thing that had happened was that brief spell of affection she'd had for the Citroën when it had shocked her by starting at the airport. She was going to have strong words with Jean-Claude when she saw him. That does it,' she said looking at the tree, 'and a lot of help you were.'

As she stood up to go, she realised someone had been watching her. A small child like figure ran off across the field. Only it wasn't a child it was a very odd looking man.

She shivered.

CHAPTER 14

As she drove up the drive the battered old Renault had gone and there was no sign of Marie or Pierre. Great, thought Julia, brilliant. I've got the whole castle to myself... and while the cat is away ...'

She went upstairs and changed into her flat boots and then headed off to the stables. A gentle ride would help her calm down. She still hadn't been back and got the petrol but she couldn't until she got the money changed and there was no way she could go into the bank so it would all have to wait until Marie and Pierre got back. The stallion wandered over to meet her. He was such a beautiful animal. He was so sleek, and she bet he was bored and itching to get out as much as she was. It fleetingly crossed her mind that she should have asked first, but Jean-Claude had said there were horses that she could ride, and anyway she was really bored.

She found a bin of oats in the stables with the bridle and saddle and, taking a few in her hand, caught him easily.

He fidgeted impatiently as she tried to tack him up. It was years since she'd ridden such a beautiful animal.

She put her foot in the stirrup and mounted. Even with her long legs it was difficult to get on. He was big for an Arab, at least sixteen hands. He was probably an Arab mix. Julia laughed gleefully as he danced along, impatient to be off.

'Woah. Slow down fella,' she said, stroking him gently on the neck. 'I wouldn't mind a good gallop either.' She found a shady bridle path along the side of the paddock and headed off out into the scrubland. Further along someone had made some jumps from tree trunks, then the path turned down the hill and flattened out across some rugged fields. They took the jumps easily and the horse strained at the bit. Once she was through the last few trees she gave him his head, galloping along the path taking the jumps in both their strides. She could feel the power of him beneath her, he wasn't even trying yet.

The intense and stifling heat had given way to a strong breeze that had built up seemingly from nowhere which blew a whirl of dust around them. The horse shied at a small leafy branch which blew across the bridleway, nearly unseating Julia and she laughed at his antics. She patted him on the neck to reassure him. She was having a job holding him; he was well and truly spooked by the wind now. Her arms were beginning to ache from reining him back and she was tempted to just give him his head and let him go across the open field. But she noticed that further on the field was thick with mud where puddles from earlier rains had sunk into the earth.

As it turned out she had no choice but to let him go.

At the loud clattering of hooves behind her, she

turned to warn whoever was coming that she was on the path. The reins slipped through her fingers and Julia wailed as the horse panicked at the sound of hooves and leapt forward, throwing her to the back of the saddle. He took the bit between his teeth and bolted. The swift approach of the horse behind spurred him on even faster and Julia wailed out loud as she clung on for dear life, her sense of fun rapidly giving way to one of fright.

Her mount galloped, a maddened beast swerving skittishly across the full length of the field, throwing Julia from side to side and splattering through the largest of the muddy puddles. Julia had her eyes firmly shut and all she could tell was that she was getting covered in mud and felt like she was being propelled along at ninety miles an hour.

She tentatively opened an eye and it crossed her mind that she should throw herself over the side of the horse, who then threw in a couple of bucks for good measure launching her onto his neck. Julia gripped for dear life as he continued his mad gallop. She could hear the other rider behind her but dared not look round, for she was trying desperately to recover the reins and try and stop the spooked animal.

As she neared the end of the field she was horrified as she saw a large, five bar gate looming up. What was it she'd been taught – if you can't stop them, ride them into something solid. The gate would have to do. She steered him towards it, offering a little prayer as she did so. The five barred gate loomed nearer and she held on for dear life. She soon realised they were either going through it or over it, but stopping was not on the horse's agenda. They soared high into the sky and Julia promised that if she lived through this she would never ride again.

They landed, the horse's hooves on the ground closely followed by Julia's coccyx on the high pommel of the saddle, she winced in agony, knowing she would never sit down again. Jumping the gate had finally exhausted the horse and dripping with sweat he came to a halt. Julia righted herself in the saddle and turned to see the horse that had been following them clear the gate and catch them up.

'Are you crazy, woman, or what?' said Christophe de Flaubert as he leapt down from his horse and grabbed the bay's reins. He demanded that she get down immediately.

Julia was totally shocked at the sight of him. What in hell's name was he doing here? One look at the black anger in his face and she obeyed him, tears rising to her eyes in pain as she tried to lift her bruised coccyx from the saddle. She fell to the ground sighing, but unable to straighten her back or legs, her body locked solid in a bizarre sculpture of a terrified jockey.

She watched as Christophe's strong, tanned hands moved carefully over her horse's fetlocks, efficiently checking every tendon and bone.

He stood up and said angrily. 'Is nothing sacred to you, Julia? Take, take – that's all you ever do. From Alan, from Jean-Claude – and now you seem to be intent on wrecking my prize Arab too. I don't believe you, I really don't.' He looked livid and Julia stood angrily in front of him; she still couldn't believe it either.

'*Your* horse?' she asked incredulously. 'You mean I'm staying in your house? Le Castellet is yours?'

'Ten out of ten,' replied Christophe dryly. He still looked furious. 'I knew I must be mad to let Jean-Claude talk me into this – mad as a hatter.'

Julia thought he looked mad alright, but nowhere near as amusing as the hatter.

'Christ almighty,' he continued almost talking to himself. 'You're a walking bloody disaster. So far every time I've seen you you've either been drunk, drugged or throwing up; you're not even married yet and you're already organising your next victim. I must have a screw loose somewhere.'

Julia stared back at him coldly.

'Well, you don't have to worry any more Monsieur Smartarse de Flaubert, I am quite capable of looking after myself, and although I've found your hospitality delightfully unwelcoming, I shan't be needing it any longer.' Julia glared at him and turned to storm off.

He grabbed her arm pulling her back. 'You really are spoilt, aren't you? I guess you've always got away with being a spoilt bitch because of your looks. I honestly don't know how Alan puts up with you.'

'An aspirational tart and a spoilt bitch. My, you really are the smooth talker everybody says you are, aren't you? You think you're so bloody right all the time. Christophe de Flaubert can't possibly have got anything wrong. Mr-know-it-all. Well you're wrong about me, I've never been unfaithful to Alan and I'm not having an affair with Jaimie Girault either.'

'Why? Did you find somebody richer? He's going to need to be, the amount you seem to get through. Your poor father, you must be costing him a fortune in half-finished weddings.

'I haven't got a father,' said Julia sharply. 'He died when I was small; both my parents did.' She bit her lip. It was such a well-worn lie. She wondered how much Jean-

Claude had told him about her, but not even Jean-Claude knew that her father was still alive.

'That's a shame, you could have done with one, if only to put you over his knee. Somebody should have.'

'Put me over his knee? I think you're showing your age on that one! They don't do that anymore. It's illegal.'

'Well I'm pretty sure for you they'd make an exception.'

He moved nearer to her, his eyes menacing and for a second she panicked thinking that's just what he was going to do.

She stepped back away from him and found herself pinned against the horse's side. At that point the horse redistributed his weight, placing his inner foreleg on her foot and, in what she was beginning to understand was true perverse local character, it put all its weight on it. Julia shut her eyes wincing at the pain, but refused to cry out. She leant down grabbed the fetlock of the offending foot and leaning her weight against the horse, lifted it off.

She'd been too busy getting the foot up to notice the grin of satisfaction that crossed Christophe's face and when she looked up he was serious again.

'Well, now that you've exhausted Thor and worked him up into a sweat, perhaps you wouldn't mind walking him back to cool off. Otherwise he'll catch a chill.'

'Get on that mad animal? You've got to be joking – I'd ride a man-eating tiger before I got back on that thing.'

'The first thing you should do when you have a fright on a horse, is get straight back on again, otherwise you'll be put off for life.'

'For which I'll be very grateful,' said Julia.

'Julia, just get back on, damn you,' said Christophe

exasperatedly. 'He's been sweating badly and you need to walk him to cool him down.'

'Well, if you wouldn't mind giving me a leg up, I will,' she replied with forced politeness.

Christophe cupped his hands for her and with an enormous sense of satisfaction she refrained from wiping her boot and placed it, thick with mud, into his hands.

It was the sore foot that Thor had just trodden on. Christophe glared at the mud for a moment and then grinned slyly as he gripped it tightly saying, 'Oh I'm sorry, is that your bad foot?' and he launched her so forcefully that she went right over Thor's back and fell in the mud the other side. She lay there, her foot and ego smarting, but not half as much as her bottom.

'Well perhaps you'd better lead him back,' said Christophe. 'If you can't even handle him when he's stationary, it might be better.'

Julia was covered in mud and furious. She had no dignity left and, losing her temper, she went to grab the whip from the saddle but he was too quick for her and grabbed it first.

Julia sank to her knees in shame and humiliation. What the hell was she going to do if she'd managed to get hold of the whip? But he'd made her so mad. She couldn't stay here now, not in the same place as Christophe, she'd kill him. Her world was getting madder and madder by the minute. A holiday in Provence was supposed to make things better not worse.

Christophe sighed, grabbed her hand and pulled her to her feet saying: 'I think it's time we got back to Le Castellet, the Mistral looks about to break.

'The storm,' he said, in answer to Julia's enquiring

look, 'the storm is about to break.'

And that must have been the understatement of the year

CHAPTER 15

Julia sat in her room and fumed. Christophe de Flaubert was just so bloody annoying. 'You must be costing your poor father a fortune in half-finished weddings.' She screwed up her face and mimicked his conceited tones. She'd kill Jean-Claude for this, setting her up in this dump with Attila the Hun for company. And Marie and Pierre were no better. She was so furious she threw the guidebook across the room in a temper. Christophe obviously disliked her intently, but maybe if she played it sweet she could change his mind.

She thought it over for a bit.

No, not a chance in hell. He'd decided she was no good and his mind was about as malleable as a tombstone. She'd just have to play it cool and if she got the opportunity to charm him, give it her all. With both Lady Bloomsbury and Christophe telling Alan she was no good, he might just begin to think there was something in it, if Julia wasn't careful. She decided she'd go and be nice to Christophe and if he wasn't around, she'd do a spot of sightseeing. She wandered downstairs, nonchalantly dragging her coat and bag behind her as if everything was perfectly normal and they hadn't been having their equivalent of the Cuban missile crisis ten minutes before. There was no sign of Christophe.

She pottered around the kitchen and hallway trying to seem casual, so that if she saw him it would look like she'd accidentally bumped into him. The house was very quiet except for the deep hum of the wind outside. Eventually Julia gave up on him and grabbed the keys to the Citroën. Just as she was about to leave, Marie came running out of the kitchen to say there was a call for her from Marseille.

Jean-Claude, thought Julia. She'd give him what for, not telling her that it was Christophe de Flaubert who was hosting her holiday.

She took the phone, suddenly realising how starved of a friendly voice she'd been since she'd arrived there.

'Jean-Claude?' she said, preparing her onslaught.

'Julia? It's me, Jaimie. How are you?'

'Blimey! How did you know I was here?'

'They told me at Jacquard that you were staying here. Listen, *chérie*, I am in Marseille and it is the time of the music festival. Do you want to come tomorrow and meet me? We could watch the festival and go dancing. It would be lovely to see you. We can mix business with pleasure, as I have some more details on that job offer I told you about remember? My secret plans for the Girault in London?'

Julia thought for a moment. Even if she just used Jaimie's offer to fill in time while she looked for another job it would help. She really would need money when she got back. It would be nice to go a bit further afield too.

She couldn't stay holed up with Christophe in this claustrophobic atmosphere any longer.

'That would be lovely. I've been thinking about the job, Jaimie, and I think things might work out quite well. Where shall I meet you?'

'Place du Lezarres about three o'clock. Outside the Hotel Beaulieue, okay?'

'Fine. See you tomorrow.'

Julia was delighted. Stuff Christophe de Flaubert, she was on holiday and she was going to have a good time. Besides if she didn't tell him where she was going he wouldn't find out, would he? But when she turned, she found Marie grinning her toothless grin knowingly. Oh hell, thought Julia, she hoped the old witch didn't know it was Jaimie.

Julia drove along, a sandwich in her left hand, the steering wheel in the right whilst gazing down at the map. She was totally oblivious to the tree branches and general debris that were being blown around her by the mistral.

She drove for a while along the bottom road which was sheltered from the wind but as the car came out on to the top of the Luberon, the full force of the storm threw it to the left, Julia to the right and the sandwich on the floor. 'Oops', she said bending down to look for it and when she looked up again she found she was heading straight for a stone hut. She slammed on the brakes and slid sideways up to the hut door, coming to a halt by hitting it.

'Damn, damn, damn,' Julia cursed, finally noticing that it was rather windy. She sat for moment and listened to the whirling. Christophe hadn't been joking then when he'd said they were in for a storm.

Julia jumped out of her skin as the wind suddenly blew

one of the red tiles off the hut roof and sent it clattering onto the car. There was the sound of slow chugging and clanking, and the car died.

No! Please, please, don't break down on me now, Julia thought, looking around. This place was spooky, and the wind was getting even more ferocious.

She tried to start the car, it spluttered and stammered and then gave up. She looked back down at the map; the nearest place was Lacoste. Maybe she should go there and get some help. Maybe she could telephone back to the house and get Christophe to come and get her. Maybe not – she could be stranded in Timbuktu in the midst of a military coup and he'd still tell her to walk. She grabbed her jacket and handbag and got out, she'd just have to try to get some help in Lacoste; it couldn't be more than a mile or so.

As she stepped out of the shelter of the hut the full force of the wind hit her and sent her reeling back down the road. She finally stopped herself by grabbing a passing tree and then, bracing herself, started out again up the hill. Yikes, she'd never known anything like it. Her jacket blew up like a great bulbous spaceman making it even more difficult to walk and she felt sure her face had contorted and stretched like some bizarre alien out of a Sci Fi movie.

As she approached the top of the hill she realised there was an enormous castle perched just over the rim. Then she remembered what she'd read in the guide book. Lacoste had been the home of the Marquis de Sade. She shivered but continued on anyway. The temperature had dropped suddenly and the wind chilled her through to her very bones. The sun disappeared behind a large cloud, casting her into dark shadow and she shivered again, it was the eeriest place in the world.

Don't be ridiculous, Julia; you've been reading too much into this, she told herself. She gave herself a good talking to. It's simply an old castle where some perverted old aristocrat with dubious sexual habits lived. There's nothing spooky about it. It's perfectly explainable.

The wind whipped up and seemed to throw clouds of coarse gravel into the air and she could feel it biting into the surface of her skin. Everything was totally still and calm apart from the wind. It was as if the earth and the wind were totally disconnected. She shivered again.

No dogs barked. No dustbin lids went flying and clattering to the ground. Everything was silent, apart from the deep persistent whirling.

As she got nearer to the castle entrance she could see the scaffolding at the side where they seemed to have been renovating it, but there was not a soul in sight. The castle was surrounded by huge walls and a large gate. There was no intercom button or bell, so no chance of getting any help there. The wind took on a different note as it licked through the thin stone windows, screeching almost angrily. Julia shivered again. It was as if the castle had taken sides with the wind, and not the earth.

I was stupid to come here, thought Julia, I should have gone back towards Le Castellet. I get frightened so easily. I'm strictly a twenty-first century consumer-goods person. Haunted castles really aren't me.

Suddenly someone's hand touched the back of Julia's shoulder, making her jump with fright. She screamed and screamed with shock, spinning round to give them a piece of her mind.

But there was no one there.

Her eyes scanned the vicinity in a panic. There must have been *someone*. She thought she caught a glimpse of a shadow running back around one of the outbuildings, but she wasn't sure.

Her scream still seemed to be ringing on the wind. She stood rigid, maybe she should go back to the car try one more time to see if it would start or just walk home.

If she was braver she'd have gone and looked out whoever it was by the outbuildings. If she hadn't spooked herself so much she'd have gone and had a look.

Julia's sanity broke and she ran all the way back down the hill to the car, fumbling around in her pocket for the keys. The car had got to start, it had just *got* to start.

She got in shaking and the keys rattled as she tried to force them into the ignition, cursing.

She could have died with relief when she heard it chug into life. She bent down and kissed that darling steering wheel. 'As God is my witness, I'll never say a bad word about you ever again', she said out loud as she backed it out of the shed as fast as she could, cannoning off the wall the other side of the road. Then, as she locked the steering wheel to swing the car around, she looked up and saw a figure standing there staring at her from the wall just above the hut.

It was a close thing as to which screeched more, Julia or the tyres as she put her foot to the floor and careered around the bends all the way to Le Castellet.

She was still shaking and did not hit the brakes until she came right to the door of the house.

Christophe was just walking around the front of the building and looked up as he heard her screech to a halt. She leapt out of the car and ran over to him, hot and flustered; she needed human company but Christophe would have to do.

He raised his eyebrows and stared at the lopsided way she'd dumped the car, at the broken bits of tile that were poking out of the radiator.

'Thank God, we didn't give you a real rally car,' he said meaningfully. 'You look a bit pale,' eyeing her more closely, 'don't tell me your driving frightens even you?'

'Actually, it wasn't my driving, I've just been to the castle at Lacoste.'

Christophe's eyes narrowed slightly.

'What did you go there for?' he demanded. 'Don't tell me, your considerable attributes extend to sexual perversion too?'

Julia's temper completely snapped. She'd near enough had the fright of her life and all he could do was make sarcastic remarks.

'You jumped-up, arrogant pig,' she shouted, watching his eyebrows go up like a barometer as she got ruder. She suddenly burst into tears. He hated her and he was being foul and she couldn't stand it anymore. 'You're hateful,' she screamed and she stormed off towards her room.

'Hang on a minute,' Christophe said, following her and gently taking hold of her arm in the hall. He seemed to regret having riled her. 'So what was it that spooked you?'

Julia sat down in the chair, not that encouraged by this friendlier tone, but desperate not to be alone, she was still shaking.

'Somebody grabbed me by the shoulder and then when … when I turned there was no one there. I know I felt someone touch me. And then when I looked I thought I saw a shadow run off. I ... I was so scared I ran back to the car and then when I started it, there was someone standing on the top of the wall, just staring at me. It was horrible.'

Christophe started laughing his deep throaty laugh. Julia glared at him furious. She should have realised he'd only laugh at her.

'I knew I shouldn't have told you, it's not so damn funny, you know, I damn near died of fright.'

Christophe stopped laughing and eyed her heaving chest. 'You look pretty alive to me.'

She gave him a hate filled look and decided for once to take the high ground and leave with dignity. He didn't deserve any more of her time. He was a waste of valuable energy. She swung around to stomp off.

'Hang on a minute. Look, I'm sorry. What did he look like, this chap? Was he small, bald and sort of child like?'

'Well yes, I suppose he was.'

He nodded reassuringly but Julia still felt she sensed a cynical smile hiding underneath there somewhere. 'That's only Goutal,' continued Christophe. 'He's a bit simple, a special educational needs person. I'm not sure if anybody has ever really found out what's wrong with him. His family worked at the castle when they were alive. He's never been to school, he just hangs around and he's carried on living there'

'But ... why would he do it?' asked Julia still shaking, partly from fright and partly because it had suddenly hit her just how devastatingly attractive Christophe was when he was being nice. He was sitting so close to her she could smell the familiar taint of his aftershave on his shirt. She blushed, remembering in London how she had buried her head in it, and all the incidents that had followed.

Christophe sensed her unease but instead of backing off, he leant slightly nearer to her.

'Marie said Goutal saw you in Menerbes yesterday when you were getting petrol, or not getting petrol as it turns out.'

'What? How does everybody know everything about everyone down here?'

Christophe shrugged. 'It's like that in all small villages. Everyone knows everyone and any newcomers automatically stand out. Goutal is a bit obsessed with you it seems. Your particular type of beauty really is a novelty around here.'

Julia's eyebrows went up in surprise. Wow, a compliment just came in from left field.

'He's an odd little chap, but harmless, he also has an uncanny way of moving totally silently.'

'So why would he follow me like that?'

'How do I know? Maybe he thought you'd run out of petrol...'

'Oh'

'You did.'

'Err ... well probably. The car stopped and then when I went back to the car it started again and ... well ... Now that I come to think of it. He did actually have a petrol can in his hand.'

'Ah.' Christophe was finding it difficult to hide his amusement. He suddenly became serious again when he saw Julia's annoyance. 'I shouldn't worry about it if I were you. He's harmless. I wouldn't go to Lacoste again if I were you. The place does tend to get to people. They say the Marquis left an indelible mark on the place.'

Julia could believe that.

'In fact the Girault family are descendants of his.'

'Oh,' said Julia.

'Yes. Oh,' said Christophe.

'You don't like them, do you?' asked Julia, looking up at him in enquiry, 'why not?'

He hesitated, his eyes holding hers.

They both sat there, eyes locked for a second and then Christophe stood up abruptly.

'I'd keep to the main tourist attractions if I were you, and I'd get a less sensationalist guide book too.' He added, his tone returning to its typical dry note.

Christophe then disappeared into his study.

CHAPTER 16

The Citroën clattered along the motorway to Marseille and Julia glanced in her wing mirror to check that she looked her best. She groaned: she'd gone all red and blotchy, it must be that grit and the damn wind. No matter how much powder she put on to cover up the rash, it still seemed to erupt through it. She looked as if she was suffering from a misplaced dose of nappy rash.

The Mistral was impossible, it had gone on all night and all through the morning. Marie had gleefully told her that it might go on for three weeks, and the whole of Provence seemed to have hibernated because of it. Christophe had made sure the car was filled with petrol and then locked himself away in his study, leaving strict instructions with Pierre that she wasn't to ride Thor under any circumstances. Pierre told her gleefully that Monsieur Christophe had said there was an old pony that they used to pull the manure cart that she could use if she wanted to ride.

At least she was getting away from there for a while.

Christophe ignored her, Marie followed her around grinning inanely and Pierre just had a lecherous look every now and then before coughing up whatever was residing in the more accessible part of his chest and spitting it on the roses. She presumed it made them grow.

As she neared Marseille she turned in towards the centre to look for the Hotel Beaulieue. On her map it said it was in an area called the North African quarter and that Dumas had said Marseille was 'the meeting place of the entire world'. Julia could see it hadn't changed much. As she turned into the next street she realised she was smack in the middle of a street market. People of every conceivable origin haggled for goods outside shops that spilled out onto the street. Pungent spices filled the air, brightly coloured fabrics blew in the breeze and pyramids of exotic fruits teetered on wobbly wooden tables. African music blared out from a record stall – it really was like being in another world. Julia decided there was no point in trying to go any further; she might as well pull up in a space between the stalls; that was what everyone else seemed to have done. She locked the Citroën, noticing that for once it didn't seem out of place and checked her map again. If she took the first right and second left that should be Place du Lezarres. As she set off into the mêlée of people, the beat really got to her and she bopped her way between the stalls.

Thanks to Marie waking her with her noisy hoover, Julia was only a little late as she danced around the corner into the Place du Lezarres. The street, unlike the others, was shaded from the sun and the buildings were crumbling into the dusty gutter. Isolated knots of people stood along the road either chatting or smoking or deep in discussion.

Julia was completely taken aback. She'd known streets like it in Paris. She was wary; in those days she'd known the ropes, known the people, she'd been one of them. This was different. She was hesitant as she walked slowly towards the crumbling hotel. Why the hell had Jaimie arranged to meet her here?

A painfully thin youth in ragged jeans with his eyes all swollen and red stared at her as she walked past. Act like you belong here she told herself, if they think you don't belong you're a walking victim.

She nodded coolly to the youth. Everybody watched her as she walked down the street, their lethargic bodies belying their quick attentive eyes. Wow – nightmare on Lezarres street or what, thought Julia noticing a large hairy guy who was leather clad and covered with rings and studs. He caught her eye and started walking over to her. Shit. Shouldn't have caught his eye, thought Julia. In a place like this you should never look people in the eye. He offered her a cigarette by virtually thrusting it up her nose.

'Cigarette *ma belle*? 'He caressed her cheek with the cigarette.

'No. Thank you.' Julia carried on up the street trying to look as casual as if she did this every day of the week and wasn't scared at all.

She was relieved when a group of African singers came into the street from the other end, and hovered outside the entrance of the Hotel Beaulieue. She immediately hid herself amongst them, trying to keep a look out for Jaimie. Surely there was somewhere more salubrious that they could have met? Most of Marseille must be more salubrious. She kept edging her way into the small crowd.

For a moment, she thought she glimpsed a familiar red head standing on the steps, but as she got closer she realised it was just a red cap. I really should have worn my glasses, she thought – I'll never be able to find him.

She stood around outside the steps and waited, trying not to look too obvious but as if she knew what she was doing. If only she did. People flowed by and a few turned to glance in her direction, but Julia just stood reading the music festival leaflet, occasionally glancing up to look around for Jaimie.

After about ten minutes she began to get impatient and not a little frightened. Where was he? She looked around and her eye caught those of a short dark haired man standing leaning against a lamp-post a couple of yards away. He seemed to be staring straight at her. She looked away quickly. Idiot, Julia. Don't make eye contact. Ten more minutes passed and Julia became furious with Jaimie. How dared he stand her up like this? She became impatient and began to fidget with her bag and kick her feet in the dust. This time she glanced up and her eyes looked straight at the guy with the black leather studs. He'd followed her. Shit. Julia shivered. He reached out and stroked her arm. 'No cigarette. What about something else lady. Something better.'

Julia pulled her arm away and next thing she knew the short man with the dark hair was at her shoulder and the stud guy moved away quickly.

'You waiting for somebody, mademoiselle?' asked the short guy as he lit himself a cigarette.

Julia thought rapidly. If he thought she was waiting for someone he might push off. 'Yes, I'm waiting for a friend.'

'You're not from around here then?'

'No. Paris.' Why am I talking to him thought Julia, this is terrible. I should just leave. Where the hell was Jaimie?

'On holiday?'

'Yes. I'm here with a friend, you know.'

Julia turned to take a close look at him and realised that he looked perfectly okay. Clean-cut, sort of friendly. There was even something reassuring and concerned in the hazel eyes. He didn't look desperate, drunk, or even that bothered about talking to her. She decided he was to be trusted and felt almost relieved to have somebody to talk to.

'If he doesn't turn up soon, I wouldn't wait around here for long if I was you; just a piece of friendly advice,' he said looking serious. 'It's not too nice, you see, around here; just about the roughest part of Marseille, I'd say.'

Julia could believe that. She glanced away down the street, casually and her eyes met those of the tall black-haired man, who seemed to be watching them intently – too intently – and she shivered.

'I think I'll go. I don't think he's going to turn up,' she said looking up and down the street.

'What about this guy coming along now? That him?' Julia looked up to see a tall blond man enter the street.

'No. Jaimie's got red hair, you can't miss him really.' Julia thought she saw a vague flicker of recognition in the man's eyes.

'You don't know him, do you?' she asked.

'No, no I'm afraid not, sorry,' said the man.

'Oh well, I'd better get out of here.'

Julia began to move off and nodded goodbye to the

guy. He nodded back and watched her as she wound her way back up the street, her pace quickening with every step. As she turned the corner at the end of the street she heard someone shouting to her. She looked around in astonishment to find Cassandra running towards her down the street.

'Thank God I caught you,' she said, catching her breath back. 'That idiot brother of mine forgot he'd got to go to Paris tonight, so he called me about half an hour ago to come and meet you and tell you. He's such an imbecile sometimes.' She looked extremely angry. Then she suddenly changed tack. 'I suppose you must be furious with him?'

'Well it's not exactly the Champs Elysées this, is it?'

'No,' Cassandra replied abruptly.

There was a stilted silence for a moment and then Cassandra seemed to relent.

'Come on,' she said, taking Julia's arm, 'where's your car?'

Julia didn't think twice. She felt she'd already outstayed her welcome in Place du Lezarres, and they ran all the way back to the Citroën.

As Julia got into the car, Cassandra passed her a large envelope. 'Jaimie asked me to give you these. He said could you fill them in and file them with the trade people in London for an import licence. He said it doesn't matter if you decided not to take the job in the end, he can always transfer it to someone else but he needs to get the ball rolling. He also said he was sorry about today it was all a complete mess-up. But not half as sorry as he's going to be,' muttered Cassandra under her breath.

Julia sighed. Did she really want to take this job? So

far Jaimie was not proving very reliable. She threw the envelope on the seat. 'Well, thanks for coming and telling me anyway,' she said, itching to leave. She supposed she should offer Cassandra a lift back to her car, but she didn't really want her company any longer than was necessary. Cassandra always seemed to be around when Julia was having a bad time.

'Jaimie said you're staying with Christophe,' said Cassandra, her voice slightly terse. 'Do give him my love, won't you?' She smiled slyly, 'And could you ask him if he's got my gold shell earrings? I can't find them and I think I left them beside his bed,' she sighed to herself as if remembering the exact moment when she'd been compelled to take them off and then continued. 'Oh never mind, he'll probably be coming over to stay soon and if he's got them I'm sure he'll bring them with him.' With that she slinked off, her hips swaying provocatively and her long legs undulating down the street.

She couldn't have said 'hands off' more strongly if she'd chopped mine off, thought Julia.

CHAPTER 17

Julia lay down on her bed at Le Castellet listening to the silence and thinking. It was so quiet here. Nothing ever happened. No wonder Christophe's mother had thrown herself off a cliff. Julia chided herself, that was a terrible thing to think, she'd go straight to hell for thoughts like that – if Christophe's mother didn't come and haunt her first.

The breeze blew through the porthole window and whistled an eerie tune for a moment, as if in response to her thoughts. She wondered if Christophe blamed himself for it. Jean-Claude had said she'd committed suicide because nobody loved her anymore, not even her son. Maybe she'd lain here just like this, planning it and thinking. The whole family was a disaster – father died of a broken heart, mother threw herself off a cliff and his kid sister died of an overdose, so Jean-Claude had said. Poor Christophe, it must have been hell for him.

It was no wonder he was so serious; it couldn't have been much fun being a father so young. For the first time in years, Julia found herself thinking of her own father, wondering where he was and what he was doing. He was bound to be up to no good. He was probably really dead by now anyway, drunk himself to death or maybe he was just a drunken old tramp like those in the Place du Lezarres. She pictured his face as it was the last time she'd seen him. Thin and grey full of agony and anger. Anger at her. He'd hated her so much. She'd never really seen hate before that, not pure hate. He blamed her for everything and she blamed him for everything. If he hadn't hated her she'd never have run away from the orphanage and ended up in the *Rue Pigalle.*

She rolled over and buried her face in the pillow to make the image of him go away. She would never ever forgive him. He could rot in hell.

When Christophe came into the room ten minutes later he found her shouting her muffled thoughts into the pillow. 'Go away go away go away go away ...'

He hesitated for a moment and then said, 'Well, how charming, I must say. I know I haven't been a very good host over the past few days, but telling me to go away in my own home is a bit much.'

Julia looked up and gasped at him, horrified.

'Oh no, not you. I mean. Oh it was just ... something.'

He took in the weepy eyes, great turquoise pools ringed in red. 'Something not very nice?' he asked quietly.

'It was just something, okay,' said Julia staring at him defiantly. She didn't want to talk about it. 'It was just ... something.' Her voice trailed off.

'Of course,' said Christophe as if 'something' was supposed to explain everything.

'I came to tell you to pack some things, we're going off to visit some friends of mine for a couple of days, I think you'll like them. And on Saturday we're going to a masked ball.'

Julia suddenly forgot her weepiness and sat bolt upright, making him jump out of his skin. There it was again. The thing that got her so mad about him.

'You came to tell me to pack some things? To TELL me…'

'Sorry. Yes. Sorry you are quite right. I'm just so used to telling people what to do and sometimes I forget. Let me start again.'

'I came to … ' he hesitated working out how to phrase it.

Julia smiled encouragingly.

'I came to ASK you if you will … err … no … if you would LIKE to come and visit some friends of mine and go to a masked ball.'

'No. Thanks for asking but no thanks.'

'No?'

'No.' The confused look made Julia smile and she had to put her hand over her mouth to hide it. Christophe de Flaubert was certainly not used to people saying no to him.

'But why not?'

'Because I haven't got anything to wear to a masked ball.'

'Oh. Don't worry about that. I've sorted that out with Rochelle, she's already ordered something for you.'

Julia was flabbergasted. 'You've already organised it. You were so certain you could tell me what to do that you already bought an outfit.'

Christophe sat down on the bed beside her. Took her

hand in his and tried to look innocent. 'No Julia. Really. I was hoping … yes … hoping that you'd say yes and I thought to myself it doesn't really matter if we buy the outfit and she says no because, hey it's only money eh?'

Julia shook her head in disbelief.

Christophe jumped up off the bed very pleased with himself.

'So Can you be ready in half an hour?'

'Err … yes I suppose so.'

Christophe watched her for a moment and then left. 'I'll see you downstairs then in half an hour, okay?'

'Okay' Julia looked up to see him disappearing back down the stairs.

She ran over to the basin and washed her face in cold water, poking her tongue out at the blotchy red image that stared back at her. Why was it that some women had a knack of crying delicately, letting one crystal clear tear slide gracefully from bright glassy eyes down their soft pink cheeks, whilst hers let rip like the aftermath of the Dambusters, leaving her eyes propped up by swollen lumps and a complexion like an over-ripened pomegranate? They had hangover cures; they should invent a post-sobbing cure, - something that lets the puff out of your eye bags and reduces the reddening of an over-sniffed nose.

Julia gulped as Christophe led her to a cream Mercedes sports car and opened the passenger door for her. It was him she'd nearly hit the other day. 'Um …' she started to say something.

He just nodded. 'Yes,' he said. 'You nearly wrote off

both of us in one go. That's why we're going to Bernard and Rochelle's. I can't afford you anymore.'

Julia looked up at him quickly. Was he being serious? But she found him grinning to himself cynically as usual.

'Who are these friends?' she asked. Now she came to think of it she didn't know why she hadn't declined the invitation. He didn't like her that much; they argued all the time, why should he want to take her to visit some of his friends?

'Bernard is an old school chum of mine. He's a lawyer, deals mainly in criminal law on the defence side. Rochelle his wife is an artist. In fact I was best man at their wedding and am godfather to their twelve-year-old daughter, Francoise.'

'Oh,' said Julia gazing out of the window as she listened to him. She remembered something Jean-Claude had said about Bernard something or other pulling Christophe off Jaimie when he'd tried to kill him. She was quite relieved he was going to be there, Christophe was scary when he was mad and she scored extra high in the making-Christophe-mad stakes.

'Do they have any other children?' she asked as an afterthought.

He groaned. 'Another four, two boys and two girls, all of them with more energy than an atom bomb. Prepare yourself for the worst.'

Julia smiled, 'I don't mind. I'm used to hordes of rebellious kids from the orphanage.'

'What orphanage?' asked Christophe, sounding surprised.

Julia hesitated and did not look at him. That was a near one.

'Oh, I sometimes help out at an orphanage in London.' Liar, liar she was screaming to herself. She'd only ever been back once and she couldn't stand it. She couldn't stand to see the children staring accusingly at any grown-up who arrived. The anger and pain in their little faces reminded her of too much she would rather forget.

Christophe looked astonished.

'Have you heard from Alan at all?' she asked, quickly changing the subject. 'I tried to call him but couldn't get through. Coverage is virtually non-existent around here. I wondered if there was any news or if he's coming back soon.'

'I did speak to him a few days ago and it was going quite well. In fact he is trying to get a flight to Nice to make the masked ball on Saturday. I came to find you, so that you could have a chat but Marie said you'd had a phone call and gone to Marseille.'

There was a sudden tension in the atmosphere. Julia felt guilty. Guilty about so many things all of a sudden: guilty about the lies, about going to meet Jaimie and being too much of a coward to try and explain it all to Christophe, guilty about lying about the orphanage. Jean-Claude was right. She did have a self-destruct button in her. She thought about what Madame Boucher had said; that she'd bred hate at Jacquard. She thought of Alan; she did miss him, it would be lovely if he made it to the ball. She missed having him there. He was so far away; everything was, the marriage, Jacquard. She felt as if she was sitting in a little specimen jar down in Provence, watching the world all going on at double speed outside. She tried to picture Alan's face. Then she felt even more guilty because she couldn't really see it. She was going to marry him and she couldn't even recall his features. Well she could, but only sort of, it was all like a cartoon of him. She thought about it. He was about the same height as Christophe only not quite so muscular. Alan had much lighter hair and it wasn't so curly, and his face wasn't nearly so sculptured and Alan didn't ooze that unbelievable, let's rip my clothes off sexuality.

She turned to look at Christophe to find he was looking at her. Oh Christ, did I really just think that? He held her gaze for a minute and then she glanced away embarrassed.

'I'll be trying to get hold of Alan again tomorrow if you'd like to speak to him,' said Christophe mistaking the reason for her deepness of though.

'Yes, I'd like that, I'd like to speak to him.'

Julia awoke just as Christophe slowed the car down and pulled into a gravel driveway which led up to a large, split-level modern villa surrounded by a honeycomb of lawns.

Four almost identical-looking freckle-faced brunettes in a steady progression of heights leapt upon Christophe as he got out of the car, screaming their high pitched war cries.

'Geronimo! Get him, get him!'

'Get off! I want to show him the new pool then. I want to!'

'That's not fair you always do. You always do then!'

'Every time you do then. I never do.'

Then – 'Get off, Natasha!' as the smallest girl dived on the pile and began pummelling the life out of a bottom that was sticking out.

'Ow you're hurting,' screamed a voice from the

bottom of the pile as there was a loud crunch, seemingly of bones.

'Okay, that's enough, all of you,' said Christophe heaving the whole lot of them off the top of him so that they landed in a jumbled heap on the grass.

Natasha made to dive for him again but he looked stern and pointed a warning finger at her.

'Behave, will you, for a minute, Natasha. I want you to meet a friend of mine. This is Julia and she knows all about horrible little rebels like you, so you'd best be nice to her. She bites too and very nasty it is so be warned.'

All four children gazed up at her, their little faces a mixture of fear and wonderment. Natasha's gaze seemed to be fixed determinedly on Julia's front canines.

Julia looked away, trying not to laugh.

Her gaze rested on the oldest of the children, a slim pretty girl, who was still standing on the steps to the house, just above them. She did not come down but stayed where she was staring at them for a moment. That must be Françoise, thought Julia, Christophe's goddaughter. Her eyes met the hostile gaze of the girl for a moment and she smiled at her. Françoise glared at her and then ran into the house. One down, four to go, thought Julia.

The rest of the children had stopped their badgering of Christophe and were still staring at her, making no attempt to hide their curiosity. Then the smallest pointed at her and piped up. 'She's got a horrible big scar on her face!'

Christophe burst out laughing and Julia glancing in the car wing mirror realised that as she'd been sleeping against the seat belt, the edge had imprinted an enormous dent across her face.

'Scarface! Scarface! You're a scarface,' screamed the children as they danced around her and prodded her. Julia blushed and rubbed her cheek frantically in embarrassment.

'Alright, that's enough,' said Christophe, deciding to take pity on her. 'Go and get me a gin and tonic, you horrible little tykes, before I die of the wounds you've inflicted upon me.'

'Come on,' he said to Julia taking her arm. 'They're not so bad – once they're asleep.'

They walked up the steps to the house and Bernard and Rochelle came out to meet them. Julia waited for the introductions to be made and took a sneaky assessment of the couple. Bernard was a not overly tall, quite stocky chap with a warm smile and quick intelligent eyes. His smile was all charm and seemed to draw your attention, acting as a decoy while his eyes flitted quickly across the scene, taking in every detail. He gave Christophe a thump across the shoulders and they disappeared in a large bear hug that turned into a wrestling match as they jostled against each other, laughing.

Rochelle was a very petite brunette with a tiny figure of perfect proportions. She was like a little doll. Her eyes were large, warm and brown and seemed to fill the whole of her suntanned face. She smiled wryly at Julia for a moment and then, as if making an instant decision, gave her a big kiss and dragged her into the house, chattering ten to the dozen.

'Oh it's so nice to meet you. We were so delighted when Christophe said he was bringing you to stay. He's so difficult you know – a confirmed bachelor – and he's so fussy as to how you pair him up. This certainly makes a change.'

'Rochelle,' warned Bernard good naturedly. Rochelle bit her lip realising that she was letting her thoughts escape her mouth without any traffic lights as usual.

'Oh, I'm sorry,' continued Rochelle, glancing warily at Christophe.

Julia looked at Christophe too. Somehow Rochelle had got totally the wrong end of the stick about them. The big oaf would be well and truly insulted now. But he just laughed and, sweeping Rochelle off her feet into a big hug, said, 'You'll have me married off more times than Henry VIII, you wicked woman.'

Julia stood thoughtfully for a moment, surprised at Christophe's reaction. He smiled at her slyly. He was definitely up to something decided Julia.

At that point they were interrupted by screams and shouts from the other room, the sound of smashing glass and a loud slap as somebody got hit. There was a second's delay before a loud wail erupted followed by heated whispers as to whose fault it was.

'Oh, no,' sighed Rochelle. 'You'd better come in and have a drink quickly while there's still something left.'

'Where's Françoise, Rochelle?' asked Christophe. 'She came out to the car and then ran off before we could say hello.'

A hesitant smile passed between Bernard and Rochelle.

'She'll probably be up in her room,' said Bernard.

'Oh,' said Christophe. 'Is she alright?'

'Er. Yes. She's er … well we'll talk about it later but adulthood seems to be coming too early and not too easily to your goddaughter.'

'Bernard!' remonstrated Rochelle. 'That's not fair. It's hard, you know, trying to grow up in a household full of children, and it's especially hard for a girl.' She quickly looked to Julia for support.

'I wouldn't ask Julia,' said Christophe smiling to himself. 'She decided to give growing up a miss.'

Rochelle and Bernard laughed and Julia seethed. He thought he was just so smart.

'I'll say it's hard for a girl growing up,' said Julia smiling over sweetly at Christophe. 'Especially if she's surrounded by nasty, evil-minded little boys who spend their time pulling wings off flies and putting them in her hair gel, or connecting the bath taps to the mains supply just as you go to run it. I wonder what your particular speciality was, Christophe? – Lynching innocent Barbie dolls with the lavatory chain perhaps?'

'On the contrary. I was more into what do with the adult variety,' Christophe grinned wickedly.

Julia smiled sarcastically. 'They have even more of my sympathy.'

Rochelle and Bernard just stood watching the banter in amazement, their heads bobbing backwards and forwards as if it was a Wimbledon final.

CHAPTER 18

On Saturday, Christophe and Bernard went off to play golf and Rochelle and Julia lazed by the pool.

The au pair had taken the children out, so they had the house to themselves.

'Shall we open a bottle of wine?' asked Rochelle jumping up and looking mischievous. 'It isn't often I get to sit and have a girly chat in peace by the pool. It will be a treat.'

They sat there sipping their drinks and Rochelle said, 'I do think Christophe likes you, Julia. I've seen the way he looks at you and I've never seen him look at anyone like that before.'

Julia choked. 'Rochelle look you've got it all wrong. I …' she looked at her, smiling hesitantly. She felt the urge to tell Rochelle everything, all about her father and the orphanage, the *rue Pigalle*, Alan… She really would have to be careful, Rochelle was the kind of girl that you found you'd told your whole life story to, by the end of the hors d'oeuvres. And they were obviously all such good friends,

187

Julia felt sure Christophe would be getting it for main course.

'Christophe is just an acquaintance. I … I'm engaged to a friend of his in London. Christophe said Alan might even make it here in time for the ball. He's been in South America, you see.'

'Really? Christophe didn't mention it and that's not like him. Oh well, the more the merrier. You'll love the masked ball, Julia. The men have to go separately from the women, and husbands and wives aren't supposed to know who each other is going as. It's so romantic. Everyone keeps their mask on until midnight and then when the gong sounds they unmask. Last year Christophe went with Cassandra Girault, but she's not good for him. Not like you are, Julia.'

Julia cast her eyes down, unable to look at Rochelle. How embarrassing. 'Really, Rochelle. Christophe is just a friend. I … I'm just staying here for a holiday.'

Rochelle looked determined. 'Well, if you ask me you've made a bad decision. I never saw two people more suited to each other than you and Christophe. He can be such an arrogant old oaf, you know, and women just drool over him. He gets away with absolute murder. He needs someone who can hold their own and you can certainly give him what for.'

'Rochelle please!'

'Christophe has had a terrible life and he just won't settle. I don't think he has ever truly been in love and it just seems to make him even more attractive to women. Oh he's got money, brains and looks, but losing Simone was such a tragedy. He never forgave himself and it's as if he won't let himself love anyone again, he's too scared of being hurt. He could choose from a million women, you know; but none of them are strong enough for him or understand him.'

'Honestly, you shouldn't say these things to me, Rochelle. It's not fair, I'm engaged to someone else.' She was engaged to Alan and she loved him and that was that.

'What's he like then, your fiancé?'

'Oh, you know,' Julia smiled. 'He's terribly nice, terribly English. He's a banker.'

'Um,' said Rochelle twiddling with the stem of her glass thoughtfully. 'What colour are his eyes?'

Julia looked up at her surprised. 'Brown.'

'That's all, just brown?'

'Well yes what else is there to say? Brown is brown…'

'Sorry, Julia *ma cher*. I'm an artist, I paint and for an artist the eyes are more than just the window to the soul, they are the essence of a painting because they are the part of the portrait that everyone will look at.'

'Well Alan's are brown.'

'But eyes change colour according to mood…with the light… sometimes even with the weather. Don't his eyes change?'

'No. Well not that I've noticed. They are so brown they are always the same.'

'Julia. I don't believe it! It is vital for a woman to know the moods of the man she loves. You're telling me that you cannot see the changes in his eyes?' asked Rochelle, wide-eyed in astonishment. 'This is catastrophic!'

'Well, he's been away for a while,' replied Julia rather lamely.

Rochelle didn't look convinced.

'Rochelle, do you believe in body chemistry and all

that? Did you know straight away that Bernard was the one for you, or did he sort of grow on you?' asked Julia.

Rochelle sat up and laughed excitedly. 'I'll say there was chemistry. I didn't have time to think about it then of course, because Bernard sort of swept me off my feet. We spent two days arguing madly, about Lord knows what. Everything he said just seemed to merit an argument, and he's terribly eloquent when he thinks he's right – they say that's why he's such a good lawyer. Anyway we ended up throwing a lot of things at each other, verbally and physically, smashed a lot of crockery and then, suddenly, after a night on the town we ended up in bed together. We had an even bigger row the next morning. I was so shocked at how strongly I felt about him and I was scared that he didn't feel the same about me. It was so silly really; we then proceeded to spend a year avoiding each other and trying to convince ourselves that it had been a really nice one night stand.'

Julia laughed.

'Anyway,' continued Rochelle, 'Bernard came around one day and approached the whole thing as if it were a major lawsuit, putting his case *for* marriage and *against* the miserable year we'd both had. We dived into bed together and got married that afternoon. And here we are now, five children and two sets of crockery later.'

They both sat deep in their thoughts for a moment.

'I must say though,' said Rochelle, 'I'd envy any woman that Christophe loved. That body and those blue eyes.'

'His eyes aren't blue, they're brown,' said Julia. 'Well, until he's angry, which is scarily frequent when I'm around, then they are a bit greener … and except when he's outside in bright light, then they have sort of gold flecks in them ... but when he's relaxed after a few glasses of wine they are kind of tawny like a lazy lion...' Julia's voice tailed off as she realised she had fallen hook line and sinker for Rochelle's trap.

'Really?' said Rochelle smiling smugly

'Rochelle you are most definitely in the wrong job. It's you that should have been the lawyer in the family!' She laughed, then threw the ice out of her drink at Rochelle, shouting, 'You're wrong, wrong, wrong!'

The children, Bernard and Christophe all arrived back at the same time, killing the hazy peace that Julia and Rochelle had managed to surround themselves with by throwing Rochelle in the pool. Christophe made a move towards Julia, but she glared at him and he changed his mind. 'Maybe not,' he said, 'I have no desire to find myself strung up by the lavatory chain or bitten to death.'

'Would Julia really bite you, *Tonton* Christophe?' asked Natasha wide eyed.

He scooped the little girl up into his arms and wandered over to where Julia was lazing on her back on the sun lounger. 'Golly, yes she would. She's English you know and they are very fierce. They have the biggest teeth in the world and during the war they ate all the Germans.'

'She does have very big teeth,' whispered Natasha.

Julia put down the book she was reading and took off her sunglasses to stare at him. 'An afternoon with you is a real education, Christophe. After your expert conditioning, Natasha will make a brilliant Anglophobic dentist.'

Christophe placed Natasha gently down on the ground

saying to her, 'I think I'm going to have to risk those teeth and throw Julia in the pool.'

Before Julia could move, Christophe had scooped her up into his arms and taking a good swing, threw her heavily into the bottom of the deep end.

After she had overcome the initial gasps of shock she swam down to the edge of the shallow end where he'd beaten a retreat, intent on landing him with an armful of swimming pool. It wasn't until she stood up to take aim that she realized her flimsy bikini top had taken off of its own accord and she was completely topless. Blushing a bright red she duck-dived and swam underwater all the way back to the deep end to excavate it. She was fuming and could barely see through the chlorinated water. When she reappeared re-clad, Christophe was nowhere to be seen. Lucky for you, thought Julia, otherwise you'd have been one decidedly deceased de Flaubert.

About five o'clock Julia inadvertently wandered into the lounge, interrupting Bernard having a heated discussion with Françoise.

'You can't go and that's an end to it. You're too young. You can stay in and help Marsha babysit. I told you, you can go to the teenage summer ball in Cannes. This one is strictly for grown-ups which you are not yet. You're thirteen years old, too young, and that's final.

'I'm nearly fourteen and old enough to look after Natasha, Pierre and Phillippe,' replied a tearful Françoise. 'I'm old enough to do all the horrible things but none of the nice things. Why is *she* going anyway? I hate her.' She pointed rudely at Julia, her face full of anger.

'*Tonton* Christophe is my friend, he's my godfather and

I hate her she's ugly.'

Françoise's voice became more and more hysterical. 'I bet Christophe would let me go to the ball with him. I hate you, I hate her and I wish Christophe was my father.' She fell on the sofa sobbing and hid her face in the cushion.

Bernard glared at his daughter. At that moment Christophe appeared beside Julia in the doorway. 'Françoise *chérie*, I wouldn't let you go.'

'You're only saying that because he's here,' she said pointing at her father and because of that, that ...' she thought for a moment '...because of that tart!' Again, she glared at Julia.

Bernard looked anguished for a moment, then his composure broke and he took hold of her and led her to the door. 'Don't you dare talk to a guest in this house like that. Now, apologise to Julia and then go to your room.'

Françoise glared at her father for a second and ran out of the room shouting at the top of her voice 'I won't apologise. I hate you! I hate you I'll run away again, you just see.'

Julia could not look at the two men. She walked out and went up to her room. How familiar the scene was. Françoise's words rang in her ears: I hate you, I hate you.

She sat down on her bed and thought for a moment. There was a knock on the door and Christophe came in, looking white as a sheet.

'Hello,' he said. 'Sorry about that. Bernard's been having a few problems with Françoise, it seems. She's run away twice so far – the last time she got as far as the Italian border. God knows where she was going but it terrified the life out of him.' He sat down on the bed for a moment.

Poor Christophe thought Julia. If Françoise's behaviour brought back bad memories for her; God knew what it was doing to Christophe, after all the terrible things that happened with his sister Simone.

Christophe ran his hands through his hair in despair. 'It's difficult for her, you being here. I suppose, being her godfather, she's always looked up to me and well – this is the first time she's ever come across anyone who she thinks is competition. Ironic, isn't it?' he added dryly.

Julia smiled, for once ignoring the bait. 'It doesn't matter. In a way I know how she feels; some girls find it harder growing up than others. She has a lot of responsibility and she just wants some fun that's all, a bit of attention.'

Christophe's surprise was written all over his face. 'Well it's nice of you to take it that way. I'm sure she'll apologise to you when she's calmed down a bit.'

'Oh, it doesn't matter. Christophe … I have a bit of a headache, err … do you mind?' Suddenly she didn't want to be having such an intimate chat with him. She didn't want him sitting so near her on the bed. She wanted him to be his normal arrogant self.

'Oh … of course. Have you taken anything for it?'

He leant across and placed his hand on her brow to see if she was hot. Julia gulped, this was even worse.

'I'll get you some tablets,' he said and left the room.

She waited for a few seconds and then she decided. She crept along the corridor to Françoise's room and, unlocking the door, stepped inside. The girl was staring determinedly out of the window, her tear-stained face rigid with defiance, anger and frustration.

'You can bloody get lost. I'm not sorry about what I said to you or my father, I hate you both,' she said turning to outstare Julia.

Julia steeled herself and tried to smile casually. 'I just came to have a chat, that's if you want to talk. If you don't, I'll go.'

Françoise assessed her for a moment. 'What is there to talk about? You're all against me. You're just the same as my father.'

Julia sat down on the bed beside her. Françoise turned her back on her and continued to stare out of the window.

'You don't have to listen to me if you don't want to. But believe me, running away is not the answer, you know.'

'What do you know about it? Shouldn't think you know much about it at all.'

Julia was so intent on her own thoughts and on watching Françoise, she did not hear the steps outside the door stop and wait.

'Running away would get me away from *him*,' said Françoise turning to look at Julia.

'Say you did run away. Where would you go?'

'Italy. Or maybe I'd go to Paris.'

Julia sighed. She only just stopped herself from laughing out loud. Good old Paris, the answer to every young girl's dreams.

'I ran away to Paris once when I was about your age, and twice when I was older. They brought me back twice and then gave up on me.'

Françoise looked at her in surprise. 'Why did you run away?'

'Oh, because like you I wanted to get away from all the children, to have some peace, be treated like a grown-up. I wanted to go to parties and dance and have nice clothes and meet a nice boy. And I ran away because my father didn't love me.'

'Why didn't he love you?'

'Because … because …' Julia choked on the words. She took in Françoise's look of amazement. 'Because my mother died having another baby and he loved her and I reminded him too much of her I think. The baby died too and he didn't want me around anymore.'

'What happened when you ran away?'

'It was dreadful. The first time I ran away, I got hungry and cold and I was very unhappy, I didn't have anywhere to go or stay and I had to beg to get food. In the end I went back to the orphanage.'

'Did your father love you when he got you back?'

Julia sighed. 'No he didn't.'

Françoise stared at her mesmerised. 'He didn't love you when you got back?'

'No he didn't, he wasn't there anymore. He hadn't been around for a long time.'

Julia smiled sadly. This conversation wasn't going at all the way she'd planned. 'Look, Françoise, if you ran away it would be horrible for you. Your father loves you very much, he wants to look after you until you're able to look after yourself. He only does these things because he loves you. You're a very lucky girl; not everybody's mother and father loves them and looks after them. When he gets angry it's only because he wants what's best for you.'

'Does your father love you now?' asked Françoise, still

staring in amazement.

'No. I don't know where he is; he might even be dead now.'

Françoise bit her lip thoughtfully. 'Do you think father would let me come downstairs now?' she asked.

'I don't know,' said Julia smiling, 'maybe you'd better go and ask him.'

'Could I come and see where you work and see the clothes and things one day in Paris? I'm a size six now and as soon as I'm a size eight I'm going to buy a whole new wardrobe of clothes, and make-up and high shoes.'

'Of course you can come,' said Julia, 'so long as your mother doesn't mind. Well, you can, just so long as you promise not to run away again.'

Julia was astonished as Françoise gave her a big hug. 'I promise.'

As Julia stepped out of the room, she walked straight into Christophe who was standing, mouth agape, grasping a packet of paracetamol in one hand and a glass of water in the other.

'Are you alright?' he asked.

'Yes, I'll be okay in a minute. Thank you for the tablets.' He still looked pale. For a moment Julia debated giving them back to him, he looked as if he needed them more than she did.

'Christophe, is anything the matter?' she asked.

'No. Nothing. I think I need to ... err ... not sure. No fine. I'm fine.'

CHAPTER 19

Julia checked her powdered wig in the mirror. As she suspected it was wildly askew. She dabbed on the final black beauty spot and she was ready. She could have done with a size bigger really, the neckline of the dress was pretty uncomfortable. She didn't know how they stood it in the eighteenth century. It might have been alright for Madame de Pompadour but her boobs were squashed in like a couple of bruised mangoes. She supposed it was alright to show this much cleavage, and she hadn't really got much choice now, had she?

Rochelle knocked tentatively on the door and came in.

'Oh Julia, just look at you, you look beautiful. Does it fit alright? I wasn't really sure of the size; Christophe told me he thought you were a twelve but he didn't say much else and I wasn't sure about the bodice and, well,' she started giggling, 'I couldn't really ask because it might have given the game away.'

'Okay I think, but do you think it's alright to show this much cleavage?' Julia asked hesitantly. For some reason down here in Provence, away from her London life she felt extraordinarily vulnerable with such a lot of herself on very public display.

'Maybe I could wear a scarf around it, what do you think?'

'Oh, Julia, don't be silly. It looks fantastic – and if you've got it flaunt it that's what I say,' answered Rochelle. 'If I had such a wonderful cleavage as yours, I wouldn't think twice.'

Julia wasn't convinced, the bodice was pushing her up so much she was sure one of her boobs was going to pop out at any moment. 'Well listen, if you see me with my boobs in the punch, for God's sake tell me, Rochelle.'

'If they are, I should think there'll be a lot more interesting people than me making a note of it,' grinned Rochelle. 'Well tell me what do you think of my dress? I feel like Peter Pan's poor old Wendy. I'll never be sophisticated like you,' sighed Rochelle.

Julia turned and looked her over. Rochelle looked so lovely, her cheeks had a rosy glow and the clinging, flimsy, Empire style dress was perfect on her petite figure.

'Rochelle, you do talk nonsense, you look wonderful. You're the most feminine woman I've ever met. You'll be the belle of the ball.'

The two girls grinned, their eyes alive with excitement at the thought of the impending evening.

'What about the masks?' asked Julia.

'I have them here in their boxes,' said Rochelle. She passed one to Julia and took the lid off her own. 'If it's too tight I can adjust the fixing at the back.'

Julia took the lid off and gave a squeal of delight. Inside was a stunning gold and black satin and lace mask that covered half of the face. The eye slots to see through were cut in a slanted almond shape and surrounded by diamante.

'Oh my God, it's beautiful!' said Julia lifting it out of the box and rushing over to the mirror to put it on.

She turned to show Rochelle.

'Perfect, Julia. It's just perfect.' said Rochelle.

Julia could just see Rochelle's eyes twinkling out from her own snow white and diamante cat shaped mask.

'Oh Rochelle, you look amazing.'

'All that we need now are the cloaks,' said Rochelle and she threw a large dark cloak over Julia and pulled her own around her shoulders.

'It's just like being Cinderella,' laughed Julia.

'Gosh I'm so excited,' said Rochelle. 'Some people go to extraordinary lengths to disguise themselves with wigs, contact lenses and even prosthetics! Last year a friend of ours went to a proper stage makeup company and spent hours getting himself turned into the Elephant Man!'

'Unbelievable,' said Julia, 'Did he stay like that all night?'

'Yes. He won the first prize too.'

'You don't think Bernard and Christophe will be doing anything that complicated do you? We'd never find them!'

'No I don't think so. Do you know I spent the whole afternoon the day before you arrived trying to find Bernard's costume, and he was so sneaky as to keep it at his office; honestly he's so distrustful. It will be so exciting trying to find them when we get there. And remember, no telling and no taking off your mask until midnight!'

'I wonder if Alan will make it? Christophe couldn't get hold of him yesterday when he tried,' said Julia.

'Well if he does make it, I'm sure Christophe will have sorted out a costume for him. I couldn't do it obviously because I'm not allowed to know what they are going as.'

The ball was bustling as they arrived and a tall, loud voiced impresario stood at the top of a large double staircase, announcing each guest as they passed him their cards. 'Madame Josephine Bonaparte and Madame de Pompadour.'

Eyes followed them as they descended the long staircase into the reception hall. The air was full of excitement as eyes darted to and fro peering into masked faces trying to discover who was who.

They took a glass of champagne from a waiter dressed in traditional French livery of the seventeenth century and glanced around. Acrobats dressed as Harlequins were moving amongst the guests balancing on their legs and hands whilst offering their platters of canapes. The musicians dressed in black and white with powdered wigs played a gavotte and out on the terrace a fire eater and circus troop juggled and did tricks.

Julia had been sure that they would recognise Christophe and Bernard easily but, seeing the expertise of the make-up, the wigs and the costumes around, she wasn't so sure now. It was like standing in the middle of a film set – *Dangerous Liaisons* most likely, thought Julia as she watched a blue-stockinged rake slip a note into the cleavage of a Marie Antoinette. As she looked around the room she noticed three musketeers rolling around by the bar. The dark one, D'Artagnan, looked as if he might be Christophe and the slightly shorter, stouter one – Aramis – could have been Bernard. She whispered to Rochelle behind her fan and they made their way over, hovering behind them hoping to catch some of their conversation.

Across the room the impresario's voice boomed out, announcing further guests.

'The Marquis de Sade, Milady de Winter, Joan of Arc.' Julia looked across and watched the trio descent into the melee of the hall. There was something familiar in the slightly cocky gait of the Marquis de Sade.

'Oh dear,' said Rochelle. 'That spells trouble.'

'Why?'

'If I'm not mistaken that's Jaimie Girault, he's the only one who can't be bothered to play the game properly, he always comes as de Sade, he never wears a wig and you can't miss that red hair. That's probably Cassandra with him. Milady de Winter suits her just fine. There will be hell to pay if Christophe and Jaimie see each other, and there will be even more hell if Cassandra sees Christophe with you. She's still besotted with him.'

'Well, she's unlikely to find me with him because I can't even find him myself.'

Rochelle giggled. 'It's a lot harder than you imagined it was going to be, isn't it.'

'Cassandra came to our dinner party in London with Christophe a few weeks ago,' said Julia.

'Really?' Rochelle was surprised. 'I didn't think Christophe was seeing her any more. They did have an on-going thing for a couple of years and she even went away on business with Christophe a couple of times when she could get away, but Christophe never saw anything permanent in it, I don't think.' Rochelle smiled cheekily at Julia. 'I think he only went out with her to annoy Jaimie, as Christophe is by no means the righteous angel that he and everyone else likes to make out.'

Julia realised that, and she blushed a bright red as she remembered her own experience of Christophe that day in Eton Square.

By ten o'clock all of the guests had arrived and the dancing began. The costumes were tremendous and some of the weirdest combinations of couples were developing. The subtle lighting and elegant surroundings only added to the mysterious atmosphere of the ball.

Julia turned around to find Asterix taking another Marie Antoinette for a twirl around the room while the Man in the Iron Mask was getting amazingly close to Esmerelda, despite the handicap of his all-too-solid mask. Two Avignon popes had disappeared backstage, having last been seen molesting two can-can girls and three girls in the guise of Liberté, Egalité and Fraternité were trying to bring out the poly-sexual tendencies of Van Gogh.

Julia and Rochelle had decided Christophe and Bernard were either D'Artagnan and Aramis, or Napoleon and the Count of Monte Cristo. They sipped their drinks and watched and waited excitedly, knowing that sooner or later Bernard and Christophe would make a move. Both girls were sipping their champagne for Dutch courage, and soon the two of them were feeling bold enough to go and accost a musketeer each.

There was a slight quietening of the atmosphere as the impresario announced a late arrival and everyone turned to look.

'Sir Percy Blakeney.'

For a moment there was surprise as everyone wondered why anyone should come as an Englishman and then, seeing the tiny scarlet pimpernel attached to his lapel, some who knew the famous book by Baroness Orczy clicked on, the rest just didn't understand what the English fop was going on about.

'Sink me, if there ain't a fine bevy of aristos here need rescuing from madame la guillotine,' said Sir Percy, very loudly, playing straight into his role. He really did have the most perfect foppish English accent. Julia watched him for a moment before he disappeared into the crowd.

When she looked round again, Rochelle had been spirited away by Cyrano de Bergerac and was having a heavy conversation with him whilst dodging his over-enthusiastic main prop.

Julia hesitated, then took another glass of champagne, content to remain for a moment in her own company.

It didn't look as if Alan had made it. She supposed he'd get around to calling her eventually. She really had so much to say to him.

Julia obligingly moved up the sofa where she was sitting so that Getafix could sit down and re-adjust Quasimodo's hump more effectively. Quasimodo was in a bad way, complaining that Esmerelda had no right to run off with the Man in the Iron Mask.

Getafix replied that, first of all, they shouldn't have come as a pair; it was against the rules and secondly, he thought it wasn't surprising, he would run off with the Man in the Iron Mask in preference to spending the evening with anyone who was stupid enough to come as someone as unattractive as Quasimodo.

Quasimodo replied that Esmerelda should love him for himself, hump and all.

Absolutely, agreed Julia, hump and all. They should add that into the marriage vows, she thought – *do you take this man, for better, for worse, hump and all?* Her attention was diverted by a voice whispering in her ear.

She swung round to find herself gazing into the eyes of the Marquis de Sade.

'Jaimie, what the hell are you doing here?'

'Looking for you, *chérie*.'

'Well, you are only five days late. We had a date in Marseille, remember? I don't know what you were playing at, but it was a dreadful place, I damn near had the fright of my life.'

'Julia, *chérie*. I'm sorry, terribly sorry. Can you ever forgive me? ' He took her hand in his and bowing to her, he kissed it. And the mouth beneath the mask broke into his very charming boyish smile.

Julia sighed. 'I'm not sure Jaimie. I'm really not sure because frankly that place was awful.'

'I know. Cassandra was furious with me. I only chose it because during the carnival it is so difficult to park and I knew you'd be able to park there because nobody ever wants to park there, it's too dangerous.'

'Jaimie, that's a very weird and dangerous kind of logic.'

'Don't you like to live dangerously..?'

'No.'

'I don't believe you.'

'Well you'd better. I've had enough of danger,'

Jaimie sighed. 'That's such a shame. How can I make it up to you my darling?'

'You can't Jaimie. I'm sulking.'

'Sulking? What's that?'

'Sort of passively aggressively annoyed with you and don't want to talk to you anymore.'

Jaimie took her hand in his again and like a schoolboy who has just had a brilliant thought, he spun her around and lifted her off the floor.'

'I have a fantastic idea. What if I pay you in advance for the work you are going to do for me? Cassandra gave you the papers didn't she?'

'Yes but I haven't had time to sort them out yet.'

'Jaimie pulled a paper and pen out of his pocket. Give me your account number and I will make a transfer to your account immediately, this very second.'

'I don't know Jaimie. What if I decide to go back into the fashion business and don't want to do the job.'

'Well I'll pay you for doing the papers for me and then you can decide.'

'OK. But I'm not promising.'

'So… your account number?'

'It's ABC123456789'

Jaimie shook his head. 'Julia why are you messing me about? That is obviously a false number. If you don't want me to pay you just say so.'

'It's not a false number. Really it's not. I have dyscalculia'

'You have what?'

'It's like dyslexia but with numbers. So the bank gave me an account number that was easy to use.'

'Oh. How kind of them. So how do you manage to do your job?'

'I have a brilliant assistant who does all the figures. She is extremely trustworthy.'

'Oh. Well you wouldn't have an assistant initially Julia you would have to do it all yourself.'

'Well you'd have to check it all then Jaimie, wouldn't

you, to make sure I haven't spent a million on a wine rack!'

'Are you telling me that you wouldn't know the difference between paying ten euros and a million?'

Julia smiled cheekily, winding him up. 'I'm not that bad Jaimie. I know that one million is a much longer number than ten euros for goodness sake.'

'Oh. You're joking with me. How naughty you are!' he stroked her cheek affectionately. 'By the way what happened to the bottles I gave you to take over to England Julia?'

'I got them sent over to the address you gave me.'

'Well sadly they didn't arrive and my business partner is a little worried about it.'

'Sink me if that ain't the demn finest party piece,' came a familiar very British voice from behind Julia.

'Alan?' asked Julia peering into the masked face beneath the powdered wig with complete surprise. 'I … I didn't think you'd make it on time. Christophe said he wasn't sure.'

'Well I nearly didn't. You've led me a dance, I must say. I've been peering into all sorts of masks and horrible eyes looking for you. You 'ain't seen an English filly with a pair of blue ones I asked 'em and they pointed me over here.'

'Alan. Do you? … Have you met?' mumbled Julia, now thoroughly confused. She was pleased to see him but he'd caught her flirting with Jaimie and… it was all so unexpected because Christophe was being so nice to her too and oh my God she was just so confused.'

'Tch, Madame de Pompadour, m'dear, don't you know better? This is a masked ball and it ain't the done thing, sink me if it ain't to go introducing people.'

Julia giggled, suddenly enjoying this rather odd side to his character. She couldn't stop laughing, she'd never seen him in such a ridiculous mood before and she couldn't imagine anyone who fitted the part of the Scarlet Pimpernel better. She looked up into his eyes shadowed by the mask and smiled warmly. He looked so different in his make-up and costume.

He took her hand and, leading her off, apologised to Jaimie.

'Sorry, de Sade, old boy. Priority booking and all that.' Julia giggled as they ran off to the dance floor.

Alan pulled her close and they moved around the room in time to the music. The champagne had removed all Julia's inhibitions and as she relaxed in his arms she found she was really pleased he was there.

'Alan, you just wouldn't believe all the dreadful things that have been happening to me. Staying at Christophe's was awful. He made his housekeeper put me in this horrid attic room with musty sheets and no curtains. I know you like him but he really has been horrid. Well actually that's not completely accurate because he's been a lot nicer since we came here to Bernard and Rochelle's. You know how Jean-Claude thinks I should get hitched to a Frenchman, well I think he was trying to do another match-making job on me, sending me to stay with Christophe. Honestly, this time he really did come up with a misfit.'

At that point Alan stumbled slightly, treading on her left foot. She laughed; he never was too good a dancer.

'I see South America didn't improve your dancing.'

He smiled dryly. 'My dearest Julia, South America was simply dreary and I couldn't wait to return to you.'

She didn't answer. They twirled around in time to the

music. It was so rare that they had ever shared this relaxed mood. Julia found herself thinking he should go away more often; absence makes the heart grow fonder.

'Christophe does have some nice friends, though,' said Julia. 'Rochelle is just wonderful; you'll simply have to meet her, and Bernard her husband is sweet too, he's a lawyer. It's amazing how someone as stuffy as Christophe can have such nice people as friends. Have you managed to find which one is Christophe yet?' she asked. 'Rochelle and I thought it was either D'Artagnan or the Count of Monte Cristo.'

'Be gad, I think you're right m'lady, demn me if you ain't.'

Julia laughed. 'Alan, stop it, stop being so ridiculous. Which one?'

'Ah, there you have me, demn me if you don't.'

'Alan, have you been drinking?' asked Julia.

'Well a man needs his courage, demn me if he don't, when confronted with such a beauty as yours, ma'am.'

Julia realised she was going to get no more sense from him this evening and when the music stopped excused herself to go to the loo, telling him to go and talk to the Count of Monte Cristo and see if she was right.

Julia went into the loo and gazed at herself in the mirror for a moment. Her eyes were all aglow; she really did look like a woman in love. Maybe everything was going to be alright. Maybe she and Alan could make it work. She sighed. Maybe she was going to tell Alan everything. Taking a gulp from a nearby champagne glass, she went into one of the cubicles.

There was a banging of the door and two women came in, chattering rather heatedly.

'Well my money's on Madame de Pompadour. Did you ever see such squashed tits outside of a mammogram?'

'You're just jealous. Because even silicone implants and a bout of triplets wouldn't make you that well-endowed. If you ask me you've been taking far too much of an interest in her. It's an insult to the female of the species running around displaying your wares like that.'

'You've been taking quite an interest in her yourself.'

Julia sat rigid, she couldn't help but listen. Who the hell …?

Then she recognised Cassandra's clipped tones.

'Yes well, my interest is purely due to a family matter. I said I'd help Jaimie out.'

'And where is the lusty Marquis de Sade?'

'God knows. He said he had some business to attend to.'

'Well my money is still on the Pompadour.'

'No way, and anyway, even if she does fall out of her dress, you'll not be able to see to win the bet the way she's been dancing groin to groin with that Scarlet Pimpernel.'

'Who is he anyway?'

'Somebody said it was an English friend of Bernard Chavenon's.' The voices faded and Julia was left feeling annoyed. So they'd got a bet on her falling out of her dress had they? She looked down at her boobs that were just so uncomfortable in the bodice. Actually if they did pop out of the bodice, it would be a great relief.

She came out of the cubicle, re-adjusted her beauty spot and headed off back towards Alan. Halfway across the dance floor she was suddenly twirled into the arms of a new partner for the waltz. Jaimie lifted her arm up onto his shoulder and expertly manoeuvred her around the floor.

'Julia *chérie*. I've missed you. Stop dancing with that stupid Englishman and dance with me.' He started twirling her around and around until she was dizzy and before she knew it he'd manoeuvred her off the dancefloor out into a corridor.

'Jaimie what are you doing?' she asked turning to go back.

'I'm calling our first business meeting.' He opened the door to a small sitting room and led her through. 'And the first item of business is getting you to forgive me for Marseille.'

'OK but you'd better not do that to me again. Now let's go back to the party.'

'Not yet because I don't believe you've forgiven me. And I won't believe you until you kiss me and make up.'

He pulled her roughly up against him and started kissing her.

'No. Jaimie. No, I …' she tried to push him away but he held her more tightly.

'Stop Jaimie! You're hurting me.'

His hands started running all over her and she felt sick. The horrors of the landlord in the *Rue Pigalle* came rushing in.'

'Get off me. Get off me.' She started shouting.

'Heavens, de Sade, have you no manners? Don't you think you're overplaying your role slightly?'

There was silence as Julia and Jaimie both stared at the Scarlet Pimpernel's motionless figure that had appeared in the doorway

'That, by the way, is my fiancée,' he added, as an afterthought.

Jaimie's face looked like thunder and he stormed out

of the room.

'Oh Alan,' cried Julia as she flung herself into his arms, laughing. 'You were marvellous.'

'What was all that about anyway, Julia?'

'Oh I don't know. I think he must have drunk too much.'

'I can see that I am going to have to keep an eye on you Julia Connors,' he said, his voice much more husky than usual. He pulled her into his arms.

Suddenly, the relief at him being there overwhelmed her and Julia found herself collapsing into his arms, sobbing. It didn't help matters when he gently stroked her hair. He let her go slightly and gazed into her eyes, through the mask Julia's sobs quietened. What was wrong with her? She was trembling all over. She felt like a great lump of jelly. He bent over and turned out the lamp so that the only dim light in the room was from the embers of the fire. Julia closed her eyes and he gently removed her mask, then kissed her deeply. All her previous thoughts disappeared as lust took over.

Suddenly she turned away. She had to tell him everything. She'd got to say all the things she'd never said to him before.

'Oh God Alan. I know it's never been right between us before but somehow I feel different now. Before I could never bring myself to … to … because I was frigid, you see I had a terrible experience and …'

She couldn't go on; somewhere back in the sober part of her brain the warning bells were sounding. She could not tell him about *Rue Pigalle* and what happened. He would never understand, *never*. He wanted something beautiful and perfect, that he could appreciate for its perfection. He didn't want Julia Connors, a frigid, screwed-up tramp. She pulled away from him violently. She'd got to find Rochelle, she'd got to get out of there.

'Julia, go on,' he said.

'No I can't. I ...' and she rushed out of the room.

Not caring that she was unmasked, Julia rushed into the main ballroom and darted to and fro, looking for Rochelle. Luckily she did not see Jaimie anywhere. The rooms seemed to be spinning and her arms felt weak and her head light. She gripped the imitation Roman pillar for support, thinking that she was going to faint.

Rochelle came over with Bernard who she had discovered was Napolean and found Julia stuck to the pillar like a Pompeii lava form. That must mean that Christophe was the Count of Monte Cristo after all, thought Julia, trying to think of anything to stop herself passing out.

'Julia, are you alright?' asked Rochelle.

Julia's eyes caught sight of the Scarlet Pimpernel coming over to them with the Count of Monte Cristo. The gong sounded, it was midnight and time to unmask. The ballroom was suddenly a blaze of chandeliers making everyone blink for a moment as their eyes re-adjusted to the light. The Count of Monte Cristo and the Scarlet Pimpernel approached, pulling off their masks, just as Julia felt strong enough to let go of the pillar. She looked up and saw Christophe's face emerge from behind the Pimpernel's mask.

'Julia, you look very pale,' said Rochelle, seeing her grip the pillar again. 'Did you know Christophe was the Scarlet Pimpernel?'

'No I bloody well didn't,' said Julia.

CHAPTER 20

Julia threw her case into the back of the car, slammed the door shut and glared at Christophe through her dark sun glasses.

'Believe me, Christophe, if there was a decent train or bus, I'd get one,' said Julia her tones low so that Bernard couldn't hear.

'Believe me, if there was – you would,' Christophe whispered back.

Rochelle came charging out through the front door and smiled at them both hesitantly. They both turned to her and gave broad, mirthless grins.

'Julia, you look exhausted. Are you sure you're alright?'

'I'm fine really, Rochelle, just tired that's all.' replied Julia trying to look more alive. 'And I miss Alan,' she continued defiantly.

'It's a pity he could not come, but I really am sad you're going,' continued Rochelle 'You really must come again soon. Whenever you like you'll always be welcome, you know that, even if Christophe isn't going to be coming down.'

Especially if Christophe isn't coming down thought Julia, seething inside.

'Rochelle, it really has been wonderful,' Julia replied, 'and you must come and see me once I start my new job and am more settled. You'll always be welcome also. And don't forget to bring Françoise with you,' said Julia, smiling with a little sadness. She really did like Rochelle, but it was unlikely she'd see them again after last night's little fiasco.

They gave each other a last hug and Julia got into the car, slamming the passenger door after her. She winced as the vibrations reverberated around her headache. If drink gave you a headache, crying all night must give you a brain tumour.

Christophe said his goodbyes, got into the car and in a stony silence they drove out of the driveway.

Christophe broke the silence after a moment, when he realised the passenger side mirror was badly set.'

'Could you just, move the mirror out a bit and up a bit please,' he asked, his voice still cold.

The tears brimmed over again and she launched into him as she let down the window. 'So what was the game then? I hope you enjoyed your little laugh last night at my expense. With your ability for impersonation you should go on the stage, you really should – as a snake.'

'Damn it I didn't expect the evening to go the way it did; just take my word for it that I had reasons for doing what I did. And don't come the avenging angel with me. You weren't exactly Miss Innocence last night yourself. If you'll remember, I caught you having a more than intimate chat with Jaimie.'

'That's none of your damn business. At least he didn't have me half seduced, like you did.'

'Well, better luck next time!' said Christophe. 'And don't blame me for your decided lack of judgement whilst under the influence either,' he continued. 'It wasn't me who was pouring out my heart to the nearest piece of human upholstery.'

'What? I thought I was pouring my heart out to my fiancée, not a big shit in sheep's clothing. I could kill you right here and now, if you weren't driving. ' swore Julia and yanked the side mirror so hard it broke off.

Christophe pulled off the road. 'You don't have to take it out on the car!'

Now that the car was stationary, she leapt upon him screaming and shouting at him for all her worth. 'You are hateful, I'll never forgive you! I hate you, do you hear? I hate you for what you've done to me!'

Neither of them gave a second thought to the car that pulled up beside them, they were too busy flinging barbs across the car bonnet. Julia still had the mirror in her hand.

'Julia, put the mirror down,' said Christophe, suddenly very calm. 'Please put the mirror down.'

Julia hesitated and then threw it hard onto the ground.'

Christophe had had enough. 'That's enough, Julia! For God's sake, grow up. Nobody has to know anything about it. So your pride's hurt now; soon it won't matter. Only you and I know about it and that's the way it'll stay.'

'Ahem,' came a polite cough. They both turned around to see a young couple standing there. 'We wondered if you were alright,' said the husband looking like he wished to God they hadn't stopped at all. A neat row of three astonished young faces peered out of the back window of their car.

'We're fine really,' said Christophe stonily. 'Julia was just giving a rendition of World War Three. As you can see I'm playing the Russians.'

There was a long embarrassed silence, after which Christophe insisted that really they were fine and they got into their respective cars and drove off.

Back at Le Castellet Julia went to her room and furiously threw everything into her case. Tomorrow she was going to get the first flight back to London. She'd had enough of Christophe de Flaubert, Jaimie Girault and their stupid games.

Christophe had ignored her and once again disappeared into his study to make some phone calls. He'd told her in rather clipped tones that he was going to call Alan later and if she wanted to speak to him she was quite welcome to, at which point she had dissolved into floods of tears remembering the humiliation she had suffered due to Christophe's all-too-effective impersonation.

She sat on her bed with a book she'd found in Christophe's study. It was a mystery with a massively complicated plot and she managed to miss the crucial clues in chapter five because she couldn't read them through the sea of spontaneous tears. When the pet Labrador died in chapter six, because some evil woman had fed it drugs in condoms Julia gave up and sobbed wholeheartedly into her duvet.

It was well past six o'clock by the time she managed to

finally put an emotional tourniquet on her tear ducts and she found she was ravenous. She crept down the stairs, taking her shoes off as she went past Christophe's study, so that he wouldn't hear her. One look at him and she'd dissolve again.

She bumped into Pierre at the kitchen door as she was hopping on one leg trying to get her other shoe back on.

He had a case in his hand. They had to go to Nantes, Marie's mother was very sick he said. She was to tell Monsieur Christophe. It was important. He'd gone out and wouldn't be back until later. Maybe not until tomorrow. She was to remember to tell him when he came back. And she was to remember to put the security alarm on when she went to bed. He wrote the code down for her and pushed it into her hand. It was very important.

Julia nodded, looking sympathetic as Marie came out in tears. She suddenly felt guilty for having been so mean about her. The old woman was clearly very distressed. Julia then shocked herself and Marie and Pierre by suddenly giving Marie a hug. She said they weren't to worry, she would tell Monsieur Christophe, just as soon as he came back and she hoped that Marie's mother was going to be alright. Marie smiled a hesitant smile back at Julia and they left.

Julia waved goodbye from the door. There was definitely something wrong in the Julia Connors State of Denmark. Spontaneous hugs? What the hell was wrong with her?

Julia decided a raid on the kitchen would get her back to her normal self. She'd done so much crying she hadn't eaten anything all day and she suddenly found she was famished.

She found the music system control and set it to full blast. Music - that would cheer her up. Marie had kindly left her fresh trout for her dinner and she found an omelette which presumably was for breakfast. Julia didn't feel like a whole trout so she threw the omelette into a pan with some butter to heat up and found some French weird green grass stuff that Marie said were herbs, and chucked them in too. It smelt delectable. She really was hungry. She knew she shouldn't cook anything too adventurous when she was hungry, just like she shouldn't go shopping when she was hungry; it always led to her buying all sorts of things that she craved but didn't go together. It was this mentality that led her to throwing chutney and cheese into the pan, hopeful of it turning into some kind of sauce. It all looked so easy when Jean-Claude did it. He just threw it in and it smelt and tasted amazing.

She decided it needed some wine so, turning the flame down, she went off in search of some. There was none handy in any of the fridges nor were there any stray bottles lying around, so she went down some back stairs she'd seen which led into a long dark damp smelling corridor. She fumbled around feeling for a light switch and eventually found one and flipped it on and lit up a huge dusty old room with smaller rooms off to each side, like side altars in a church. Or more like cells in a dungeon, thought Julia. This must be where Christophe incarcerates the people who don't live up to his very exacting righteous standards.

At the very end of the room she came across a sectioned off area that contained rows and rows of old bottles from floor to ceiling. She pulled a bottle out of the rack and read the label. Chateauneuf du Pape, looked pretty old so that would do. She took the bottle upstairs and hunted for a corkscrew. Surely they'd have a corkscrew? I mean the kitchen was so well decked out, there must be a cork screw somewhere. After a good ten minutes she hadn't found one, so gave up and pushed the cork in with the end of a fork. The cork smelt a bit old but the wine smelt pretty good to her.

She'd forgotten that she'd left the omelette sautéing in the cheese and chutney which had melted and burnt itself into a splodged mass with craters that looked like they might have been made by Martians. Julia decided to try adding the wine anyway; it might rescue it. The wine slid around the burnt cheese mess like seawater over a big jellyfish and, try as she might, she couldn't get it to mix in. The whole thing looked positively revolting, so she threw it into the bin. She really was disappointed – she was sure she'd been channelling her inner Master Chef. She contented herself with a large piece of baguette and chunk of cheese, washing it down with the rest of the red wine.

The music had now launched into the Marseillaise. God she loved the Marseillaise. When she did her 'improve herself' piano lessons it was her favourite thing to play. It was simply the best piece of music ever. Shame about the words though. All that vile despots stuff and cutting the throats of your sons and consorts. Definitely needed updating.

Julia stayed in the kitchen drinking her wine, taking stock of her current situation. Finances - broke and unemployed, but some cash coming in from Jaimie's project, so not a complete disaster. Career – good at her job, interest from Karl Fregère and back up of switching

to a wine career with Jaimie, so not too bad. Love life –
engaged to a man she doesn't fancy. Fancies a man she
doesn't like. The man she fancies but doesn't like, thinks
she's having an affair with a man he doesn't like, and is
about to spill the beans to the man she likes but doesn't
fancy, who she wants to marry – disaster! Not so much a
love triangle as a dodecahedron. How the hell was she
going to sort the mess out? Maybe she should just tell
Alan everything when she got back. She could come clean
about her whole life being a bit of a porky pie. Porky pie?
That was definitely an understatement, was more like a
huge hog roast.

Her body was so fickle too, responding to Christophe
of all people. Why did it betray her like that? It really
wasn't good enough. All Christophe had to do was touch
her and she came over like a great lump of biological agar,
all limp and oozing. It was so ironic it was untrue; the one
man in the world who could prove she wasn't frigid, was a
loathsome frog – so in fact, that probably made him a
toad. On the other hand, when you kissed frogs, more to
the point when she kissed the Christophe frog ...

You're stupid Julia, you're engaged to Alan, she chided
herself. It's your life plan. Hum, probably not best to dwell
on it and it'll all go away on its own. Leaping up
determinedly, she decided to have a prowl around the
house. She wandered along to the room at the end of the
ground floor main corridor. The big oak door was solid
and heavy but opened when she pushed against it.

Inside she found a traditional country room that could
have featured in the top interiors magazines. There was a
large medieval stone fireplace and rich thick carpets and
curtains. The sides of the stone bay window were covered

in pictures of horses and the rest of the walls were obscured by shelves of leather bound books. Some of them appeared to be first editions. There was everything from Balzac to Sartre, Shakespeare to Henry James. This just had to be Christophe's study. My, thought Julia, the veritable intellectual man from international banking. On the desk there was a large photograph of a teenage girl, caught in mid-giggle. That must be Simone, thought Julia. She picked the photograph up to have a better look. She was a beautiful-looking girl and Julia could see the resemblance to Christophe immediately, the strong jaw and dark curls.

She put back the picture.

The room had a cosy timeless feeling. Unlike the other rooms that mixed contemporary with antique, this was pure antique. A blue and white porcelain vase stood on a table in the corner. It didn't look much but from what she knew about Christophe it was far more likely to be a Ming than a Jackie Chan takeaway. Julia could imagine Christophe spending a lot of time in here. It suited him. Here time stopped, along with all its problematic hangers on, leaving you to quietly read your book in peace. Above the fireplace there was a stunning painting of Provence that Julia recognised. She went in closer and looked at the signature. Cezanne. Oh my God! He'd got a real *Cezanne*. She was tempted to pry further, but a sudden sense of guilt overtook her and she closed the door quietly and came out.

Julia wandered down the corridor, and through the large double doors at the end she found an enormous formal drawing room covered with dust-covers. Underneath the far one, to her glee, she found a grand piano. She dragged off the cover and started playing the Marseillaise. She laughed out loud, remembering how her teacher Monsieur Moreau had regaled her daily with the words, *'moins de gusto Julia et plus de dignité'*. Rubbish thought Julia, the Marseillaise has to be played with gusto, that's the whole point of it, and she played it over and over again. Eventually she felt exhausted and went up to bed. It was midnight and Christophe still hadn't returned.

She slept fitfully; somehow just as she was dropping off, Christophe would barge into her half-dream, kissing her wildly and she'd wake up annoyed that it wasn't true and then be even more annoyed with herself for wishing it was.

Christophe had just left her in the middle of a soft and tantalizing reciprocal lip massage with melting chocolate undercurrents, when Julia was woken by a loud noise downstairs. She found herself upside down in the duvet cover and knocked her mobile over finding her way out.

She struggled to get out and listened for another noise. It seemed to be coming from one of the rooms below. It must be Christophe arriving back.

She knew she was being reckless but she was going home tomorrow and well … she just wanted to check up on this chemistry thing that Liane and Rochelle both swore by. She just wanted to see if Christophe could turn her on all the time.

Oh my God I am so fickle, she thought and jumped back into bed again. Julia you have to stop this. Your love life is complicated enough.

Then she jumped out again. She owed it to herself to check. I mean what if something happened to her and she died not knowing? That would be a tragedy.

She made her way quietly down the stairs. The noise seemed to be coming from his study. She pushed open the door, and a cold chill encompassed her whole body.

It wasn't Christophe.

A tall man was standing over by the bay window. He turned around, shocked, as she entered. Julia was rigid with fright and for a moment they both stood there, as if held, suspended in time. She thought of screaming but there was no one to hear.

He pulled something out of his jacket and gestured for her to move away from the door. His gun gleamed in the dim light of the moon.

Julia panicked. What did he want? She moved towards the fireplace and her eyes whisked across the room, looking for anything to grab.

Her hand fixed on the porcelain vase and she grabbed it, swinging round and launching it at him all in one go. The vase missed him but it caught him by surprise as it smashed against the bookcase, sending shards into his face, cutting into his flesh and making him drop the gun. Julia acted on pure instinct and dived for the gun but he pulled out a knife and launched himself at her as she reached for it. Julia had the gun but he caught her across her left arm and the blade sunk into her flesh. She screamed in pain and the rush of adrenaline gave her the strength to leap up. In a terrified panic, she started whirling around in circles in the middle of the room holding the trigger down so it fired nonstop. Bullets were flying everywhere. She didn't even try to aim she was just hoping the bullets would keep him away from her. One bullet did get quite near to his head but ricocheted off the stone fireplace into the complete works of Shakespeare, making him dive for cover behind a chair. He crawled back into the corner using the chair as a shield. Julia stopped running round in circles and stood facing him, and she kept the gun firmly pointed at the chair

Her left arm was bleeding and her whole body was taut. If he even moved an inch she knew she had to let loose again. Where the hell was Christophe? She couldn't think: all she knew was she had to keep the gun on him to keep this horrible man away from her.

Julia was terrified. He raised his head slightly above the chair and she saw the cuts on his face and hands were bleeding heavily and still he didn't speak. He sat there, watching her over the top of the chair, his eyes gleaming in the darkness. They never left her face. He gradually edged his face higher over the chair, more confident that now that she was calmer, she was less capable of hitting him even by accident.

As his head appeared even further above the chair, Julia realised he was going to go for her. Her sanity broke and she decided to run in a mad panic. She backed out of the room slamming the door behind her and ran out of the front door screaming for all her worth, just as a car pulled into the driveway, its headlights dazzling her. Julia couldn't think straight and her screams rang out and seemed to go on forever as she ran around in circles firing the gun madly.

A man got out of the car and started to speak

'What in heaven's!' He ducked down behind his car to avoid a bullet flying over his head.

'Julia, Julia it's me. He shouted. 'It's me, Christophe.'

Julia couldn't see and she wasn't listening, she couldn't hear properly for the sound of the gunshots and loss of blood was making her feel faint. All sense of reason had disappeared. All she knew was she had to protect herself.

'It's me, Julia!'

Julia stopped and stared at the car. She hesitated and pointed the gun at where the voice was coming from. She was trembling and her hands were shaking uncontrollably.

'OK Julia, sweetheart. It's me. Everything is going to be OK. I want you to put the gun down, and I am going to stand up, OK?'

Julia stared at the shadow near the car and aimed more carefully. No it couldn't be him. He'd gone away. It must be an accomplice. And he would never call her sweetheart, never.

'No. No. It's not you. It's not. It can't be. You are a liar! Liar! Liar. You are not Christophe because Christophe would never call me sweetheart!' and she started firing at the car and running around in mad circles again pulling the trigger so fast it sounded like a machine gun.

Shit, thought Christophe as he dived into a space between his car and a huge plant pot. Really should have been nicer to her. OK. There was only one thing for it.

'Julia! You're a bloody walking nightmare! Drop the gun you stupid bloody cow.' He winced inwardly as he said it. 'For Christ's sake drop the gun you crazy idiot!' he shouted again. 'You're going to kill us both!'

Julia stopped. And Christophe hesitated and then said in a very firm voice.

'Put the bloody gun down!'

Julia lowered her hand but didn't put the gun down so he carried on in the same vein. 'Julia you are a bloody imbecile! Now I am going to stand up and don't you dare bloody shoot me you crazy cow!'

He stood up so that she could see him and he slowly started walking towards her.

'Julia. Put the gun down.'

She stared at him trying to concentrate as her vision became more and more blurred. Something in the way he moved, tall and confident, finally convinced her.

'Oh it is you,' she said and passed out.

He caught her as she fell and she didn't hear him when he quietly said:

'Yes it's me sweetheart. It's me. And I do call you sweetheart, I really do.

CHAPTER 21

Julia woke in an enormous deep bed in a large room with polished oak floors and large Persian rugs. Her arm was still hurting as she moved her body to try and sit up. As she turned, she saw Christophe sitting in a wicker chair by the window reading a book that was so thick it was cubic. It had a large hole in the middle.

He glanced up on hearing her move.

'So you're awake at last. How do you feel?' He moved over to sit beside her on the bed. Unshaven and dressed casually in a white shirt and jeans, he looked amazingly attractive.

'Are you hungry?' There's not much in the house, but I could rustle you up an omelette and some English tea if you like.'

'Just a cup of tea would be lovely, thank you,' replied Julia quietly.

Christophe held up the book.

'Shakespeare took one for the team I see.'

Julia shivered, remembering those black eyes, then looked at Christophe and was suddenly overcome with embarrassment. She tried to hold back the tears but she couldn't cope with anything anymore: she was still in a great state of shock.

'I'm sorry. I'm so sorry about Shakespeare. I panicked. I was trying to shoot the burglar not Shakespeare.' She sobbed even more.

'Hey,' he said pulling back the covers and holding her to him. His strong hand caressed her hair. 'Don't cry, Julia. It's all over now.'

His strong, comforting arms were like the keys to the sluice gates and next thing she was shaking and sobbing uncontrollably.

Christophe held her to him, stroking her head until her sobs subsided.

'Oh God, Christophe, I'm such a mess. My whole life.'

'Come on, it's not so bad. You're getting married. You seem to have been a bit misguided occasionally but ...' He pulled her round to look at him. 'Listen to me, you were a bloody star last night. You've got everything going for you, and Alan's a damn lucky guy.'

Julia blinked at him in astonishment through her tears. Did he really mean that? She sighed. She was so confused about everything. She slumped back down on the pillow. It must all be one of those Christophe-laden dreams again.

Christophe sat watching her thoughtfully for a minute and then asked 'By the way, where are Pierre and Marie?'

'Oh, they had to go off as Marie's mother is very ill. I'm sorry, I should have told you.'

Christophe still looked thoughtful. 'That's okay. Now I suggest you get some more sleep while I make breakfast, then I'm going to have to drag you off to Marseille to see

Jacques, the police chief. He wants you to look through some identification shots. Do you think you're up to it?'

'Mm, I think so. But, Christophe, what did he want? Why did he break in?'

'We think he was just a burglar. There's quite a lot of decent art in the place and books too, he was probably after that. Don't worry about it. Now get some sleep.'

Just as he reached the door, Julia asked, 'Why aren't I in my own room? Whose room is this?'

'It's mine,' said Christophe and quietly closed the door behind him.

Julia rolled over to try and get some sleep. The faint familiar smell of Christophe's aftershave lingered on the pillow and she found herself sighing. She had discovered something that went totally against all of her previous convictions. Somebody being nice to her can be quite an aphrodisiac.

A couple of hours later Christophe woke her with a cup of tea and the telephone.

She sat up in bed trying to blink her eyes awake and took the phone looking at Christophe in enquiry.

'It's Alan,' he said, making no move to go, and sat down on the edge of the bed beside the table to pour the tea.

'Julia darling, listen I'm coming straight down to Provence. Are you alright, darling?'

It was so odd hearing his voice: he wasn't just in another country – he was in another world.

'No, Alan. Please, please don't do that.' Julia's voice was unnecessarily sharp. 'I mean, it's alright really, I'm alright and I'll be back in London in a couple of days.

There's no need. I'm fine.' Somehow she didn't want to see him now, not here in Provence. He didn't belong here.

There was a clinking sound as Christophe stirred a little sugar into her tea. He handed it to her and smiled.

Julia felt very uncomfortable. She couldn't possibly talk to Alan with Christophe sitting so close to her.

'Alan really, I'm fine.'

'Well, is Christophe taking care of you?' Alan asked sounding ill at ease.

Julia gulped. 'Yes, yes, of course he is.'

'I spoke to Liane yesterday,' said Alan 'She sounded well. She's missing you I think, although she's enjoying running the show for a while.'

'Yes,' said Julia trembling as, for no apparent reason, the tears suddenly brimmed up into her eyes.

She wished she'd never come to Provence.

'Well I'll see you soon then. Take care of yourself, darling Julia,' said Alan 'I've got to go.'

'Yes,' muttered Julia 'Bye.'

Christophe took the phone from her hands.

'Okay?' he asked, and he walked out of the room.

CHAPTER 22

By the two hundredth mug shot at the police station, Julia was feeling totally confused and depressed. She'd never realised there were so many sinister-looking people in just France alone.

She'd think she'd found the burglar when the policeman showed her one shot, but then the eyes wouldn't be right. The next would have the right nose but the wrong hair. Christophe was being very patient with her, coaxing her through them and telling her to take her time. It was alright for him to say that but, judging by the enormous pile she still had to go through, she could end up spending the rest of her life eyeing the ill-boding citizens of France. She couldn't help looking at each of them and wondering what dreadful things they might have done.

Eventually the pile was finished and she'd found two that might vaguely have been right but she wasn't at all convinced and she was usually quite good with faces. What she lacked in mathematical ability she more than made up for in visual acuity.

The policeman picked them up and said he would show them to Jacques.

'Neither of them are him,' said Julia.

'You're sure?' He looked surprised.

'Yes. I have a really good head for faces.'

Christophe looked surprised.

'I do Christophe - when I'm sober and the person in front of me is not wearing a mask and is not deliberately trying to pretend that they are somebody else!'

'Fair point,' replied Christophe, magnanimously.

'Then why did you pick them out? 'asked the policeman

'I picked them because they have something similar to him. But it's not him.'

Christophe decided he wanted to see Jacques alone for ten minutes so the policeman showed Christophe the way and asked Julia to wait for him there.

An hour later, after Julia had practically drummed her fingernails through the table top, and had given herself a headache with the machinations of her own brain, she stood up and decided to go and look for Christophe. She was tired and she just wanted to go home.

She wandered down the corridor looking for him, tentatively knocking on office doors and then opening them only to have to smile and mutter apologies when he wasn't there. Eventually she came to the last door in the corridor and knocked and opened it. She found him sitting opposite a familiar figure.

'You're the Count of Monte Cristo,' she said in astonishment to the dark-haired man who was sitting behind the desk.

The man smiled, his face somewhat guarded as he said, 'Well not quite, not today, Miss Connors.'

'And you were in the bar in Menerbes when I had breakfast.'

He looked surprised that she remembered, and smiled wryly. 'Ah yes. The day you paid eighteen euros in small coins for a coffee and croissant and left before we could give you most of the money back.'

'I can explain that sort of …'

'Julia this is Jacques Morell, the police chief,' said Christophe reminding them of why they were there.

'I'm sorry, Christophe I didn't mean to interrupt.'

Which of course is a big lie, she thought to herself. Everybody who says that, is interrupting somebody, and so they do mean to interrupt, in fact.

Both Christophe and the police chief were waiting for an explanation.

'It's just that my arm is killing me and I wondered … I …' She hesitated and then stopped abruptly. There, lying on Jacques' desk, was a photograph of the burglar. She'd recognise those hooded black eyes anywhere.

'That's him,' she said, gazing at Christophe in astonishment, 'that's the burglar.'

'Are you sure, Julia?' asked Christophe sitting her down in a chair.

'Of course I'm sure, dead sure. I spent nearly a lifetime staring at him didn't I? That's him.'

Christophe and Jacques gave each other a knowing look.

'Who is he?' asked Julia.

At that moment another officer came in to talk to Jacques. Julia was suddenly aware that he was staring at her in a rather odd fashion.

As he stared, she realised that he was familiar to her too. It was the short man who had spoken to her in the Place du Lezarres, when she was waiting for Jaimie.

'Hello again,' she said, 'I didn't realise you were a policeman.' Julia glanced round at Christophe. Why were they all staring at her?

'What's wrong?' she asked, looking at Christophe.

He pulled his hands through his hair, he looked tense and tired.

'Why did you meet Jaimie in Marseille?' asked Christophe.

Julia sat down in the chair abruptly. She looked at Christophe hesitantly. 'He's offered me a job and he wanted me to meet him and talk about it. I don't have a job so …'

Jacques stood up and dismissed the two other police staff who were in the room.

'It seems as if you are right, Christophe.' He came around the desk and sat on a chair next to Julia, smiling reassuringly at her.

'What's this all about?' She asked nervously. She felt guilty. Why should she feel guilty? She'd just met Jaimie to find out about a job. OK so he was Christophe de Flaubert's arch enemy number one but that shouldn't make her feel guilty. It wasn't as if she owed Christophe anything.

Julia hesitated.

'Julia, if you're in trouble, you've got to sort it out,' said Christophe.

'Why would I be in trouble? Hang on a minute!' Julia folded her arms defensively and raised her voice slightly, beginning to feel very annoyed.

'What are you talking about? Am I in trouble? Have you both forgotten that I'm the victim here? There I was, happily going about my business as usual, organising a fashion show, drinking a bit of champagne and clocking up a few credit card debts, and next thing I know my flat gets burgled, somebody drugs me, and then some mad burglar tries to shoot me and stabs me with a knife! While he is trying to rob <u>your</u> house, I might add, Christophe. I really do think that makes me the victim, not the person in trouble. Don't you?'

Jacques Morell nodded, almost to himself.

'Yes. I can see that, Miss Connors. My apologies.'

'Right. Good. I'm glad we've got that settled.' She turned to Christophe. 'Do you think we can go now Christophe? I'm so tired. I think I just want to go home back to England.'

'Before you go, just one more thing, Miss Connors. Our people have picked up on a transfer that has been made to your account from an offshore bank account in the Cayman Islands. Do you know anything about it?'

Julia shrugged her shoulders. 'I suppose it's from Jaimie Girault. He said he'd pay me in advance for doing the paperwork for his new business in London.'

'Yes. I see' replied Jacques nodding. 'How much do you usually charge for consultancy work Miss Connors?'

'Well I don't know because I've never done it before and we didn't talk about it. He just said he'd send an advance payment…'

'3.2 million is rather a lot for a bit of consultancy don't you think?'

'What????' Julia just couldn't help herself, her eyes lit

up. Then she quickly told herself to be sensible. 'Why would he do that?'

'I was hoping that you could tell us Miss Connors.'

'Well no. He just said he'd pay an advance into my account.'

'That's near enough what I overheard at the ball, Jacques,' said Christophe sighing.

Julia looked at him stunned. 'So not only did you trick me by pretending to be Alan, you were also spying on me?'

Christophe smiled, wryly. 'Well not exactly. I was there to help out Jacques. And technically, if I was spying on anyone, it was Jaimie.'

Julia shook her head disparagingly. 'So you think that makes it OK. Mr Righteous de Flaubert.'

'No I don't but…'

Jacques Morell, seeing an argument was about to ensue, interjected.

'Miss Connors. We knew that Jaimie had befriended you and we also knew that if he thought Christophe was hanging around you, he wouldn't have said anything. As it is he didn't say much, but the little that he did say and with Christophe's assurances, it could be enough for us to accept that you are not knowingly part of the money laundering.'

'Money laundering?' Julia was horrified.

'Yes there can be no other explanation for Jaimie Girault transferring that kind of money. We've had our suspicions for a while. Jaimie Girault is a playboy who has lived way beyond his means for most of his life but over the past year he seems to have amassed a considerable fortune and it is not clear where it has come from.'

Jacques and Christophe looked at each other.

237

'So what do we do now?' said Christophe.

Julia's eyes strayed to the picture still on the inspector's desk.

'So who was the burglar then? And what has that got to do with it?' she asked.

'His name is Giorgio Hernandez.' He is a fairly lightweight crook but we do know he has been involved with Jaimie Girault on occasion. We are not sure why he was at Le Castellet, but we did suspect that Jaimie might have been accruing his cash through art theft at one point.'

'The Cezanne.'

'Yes. Somebody sent Christophe off on a wild goose chase. He went to help Bernard Chauvenon find his daughter, who in fact hadn't run away at all and was tucked up in bed. That person also rang and said Marie's mother was ill in order to get her and Pierre out of the house.

'They probably had no idea you were in the house,' said Christophe.

Jacques stood up and went over to a large filing cabinet and pulled out a photograph. 'Have you ever seen this man at all?' He passed it across to her.

The round, suntanned face of Carlos was unmistakable.

'Oh my God! Yes. His name's Carlos, he moved into the next door flat to me in London. He gave me some tablets to calm my nerves when my … flat was burgled. It was him that drugged me.'

Jacques sighed. 'Yes Carlos Garcia. He's another low key crook that we've seen with Jaimie Girault. Well, he was a low key crook. He is now a dead low key crook. He turned up beaten to a pulp in the backstreets of a London suburb three days ago.'

'Oh my God, that's terrible.'

'Indeed. And his finger prints were all over your apartment. Is there anything more you can tell us Miss Connors?'

'Well no. I only met him at the apartment and he said that he knew my cleaner Eloisa and she told him about the next door flat'

'The London Police asked Eloisa about him and she said she didn't know him.'

'So he lied' said Julia

'Yes and we have two burglaries by two associates of Jaimie Girault, one in your flat and one while you were in Christophe's house Miss Connors.'

Christophe looked extremely worried. 'One in London and one in Provence. That's no coincidence.' said Christophe.

'No.' said Jacques. 'It is not. And this makes a huge difference.'

'You'd better make yourself comfortable Miss Connors.' said Jacques. 'This is now a formal interview.

'Jacques. What the hell do you mean a formal interview?' interjected Christophe. 'You can't seriously think Julia's involved.'

'Christophe. I do not know but I am going to find out. You know as well as I do that money is the main motive for crime. Listen, if you are going to let your personal feelings affect you then I suggest you leave the room while we interview Miss Connors.'

'No. I'll stay thank you. Julia has the right to have a lawyer present doesn't she?'

Jacques sighed. 'She does but perhaps a criminal lawyer would be more useful to her than a financial lawyer.'

'Actually, no Jacques you're wrong.' He pulled up a chair and sat down determinedly. 'I am very well placed to defend Julia. I can give you all the evidence as to why my client Miss Connors is not involved in money laundering. And do not forget that my client is a victim of two crimes, not the perpetrator.'

Julia felt a sudden warmth go through her. Her arm was killing her. Before, she'd just wanted to get out of there but now she didn't care. She just wanted to curl into a ball like a contented cat and snuggle under the protective arm of Christophe and let him look after her forever.

She looked at Jacques and smiled contentedly. He looked slightly nervous. And so you should be, thought Julia. Christophe de Flaubert is batting for me and that means you are in deep shit.

Jacques called through to the main desk and a female officer came into the room to be present while the official interview took place. He nodded to her and she started the recording system. After the official formalities of stating the date, time, place and those present, Jacques started his questioning.

'Do you know Jaimie Girault Miss Connors?'

'Well yes. You know I do.'

'Julia, just answer yes or no for the moment,' said Christophe.

Jacques threw Christophe a despairing look.

'Where and when did you first meet Mr Girault?'

'At Heathrow airport about a week ago.'

'And are you are engaged to Jaimie Girault?'

'No.'

'So can you explain this please?

Jacques pushed a copy of the *Paris Match* article over to Julia.

'Yes.'

There was a pause and then Christophe and Jacques both looked at Julia expectantly.

'What?' she asked.

'So…' hinted Jacques Morell

'Christophe said to just answer yes or no.'

Christophe couldn't help grinning slightly. This was a new one, Julia Connors actually doing as she was asked.

Jacques Morell sighed with no small amount of exasperation. 'Please explain this article in *Paris Match*, Miss Connors.'

'Well…' Julia looked at Christophe for confirmation and he nodded. 'I was talking to Jaimie at the airport when our flight was delayed so we chatted and when we left he offered to give me a lift to the hotel. As we were walking out the paparazzi started doing their thing, in our faces, taking pictures, and Jaimie got annoyed. He pushed them away but they kept on coming so then he changed his mind and decided to wind them up about me being his fiancée. That's it and the next day it was in the magazine.'

Jacques Morell nodded understandingly. 'OK. Thank you Miss Connors.'

'Great.' said Julia, standing up. 'So can we go now?'

'Jacques was just saying thank you for answering that question, Julia. The interview is nowhere near finished.

'Oh'

'Are you having a sexual relationship or have you ever had a physical relationship with Jaimie Girault?'

'No!' she glared at Christophe.

'Have you ever received any money from Monsieur Girault?'

'No. Well not until you just told me about the money he put in my account.'

'Have you ever received any presents from Monsieur Girault – jewellery, paintings, antiques, diamonds, fine wine?'

'No.'

'Has Monsieur Girault ever asked you to buy anything for him, property, bid for paintings or works of art, antiques, jewellery or wine?'

'No.'

'Has Monsieur Girault ever asked you to carry out any work or business deals on his behalf?'

'Yes.'

'What is the nature of that business arrangement?'

'He said that I could make a lot of money working with him in his new wine business and he asked me to take a case of wine back to London for him and get it sent over to his importer friend.'

'Do you have the details of this importer, Miss Connors?'

'No but I can ask Liane at work for the address. I left the case of wine in the Jacquard offices and she was supposed to send it over to the importer'

'Supposed to?'

'Yes but I think she forgot because Jaimie asked me at the masked ball what had happened to it.'

'Do you know where the wine is now?'

'No. Why? Do you think this has something to do with the wine?'

'Possibly'

'But it was only one case of bottles, that can't be worth much?'

'Depends what it was' said Christophe. 'A bottle of 1945 Chateau Mouton Rothschild sold for 320,000 last year.'

'Indeed,' said Jacques Morell. 'It has become a lucrative new area for money laundering.'

'Investment in fine wine outstripped cars and works of art last year for the first time,' said Christophe. 'Prices have gone through the roof. Even a relatively young *Chateauneuf du Pape* is fetching ten thousand dollars a case.

'Shit!' said Julia horrified. Then seeing their shocked faces she quickly recovered. 'I mean wow, that's a lot.' Oh Christ, she was thinking to herself. I sloshed half of one of those over my disastrous Master Chef effort.

'I guess that could be what Jaimie is up to,' suggested Christophe.

'Yes. And fronting it with the official Girault vineyard business.'

'Err. Chateauneuf du Pape. Is that the one with the big red seal on the label?' asked Julia, just wondering if it really was that wine.

'Yes that's it. Is that what Jaimie gave you in the case?' asked Jacques.

'No. No. I just thought I'd seen it somewhere before. Or well maybe it might have been. I didn't really look.'

'OK, so you don't know what the wine was, Miss Connors?'

'No. Err, well Yes. It was red, I think. Jaimie said something about it being red'

'But you didn't see the labels?'

'No.'

'Did you even look inside the case?'

'No.'

'So it might not even have been wine,' suggested Christophe.

'True.' said Jacques 'It could have been anything heavy. Stolen artwork, a sculpture, a vase. I'll check with our antiquities department on any recent thefts. Were there any markings on the case?'

'Yes. *Famille Girault.*'

'Just the old family wine business,' said Christophe

Jacques nodded. 'What exactly does Jaimie want you to do for this new business Miss Connors?'

'He wants me to set up the London branch of his fine wine company. He said the papers Cassandra gave to me were to register as an importer and exporter.'

Jacques Morell was thoughtful for a moment then he changed tack.

'And you'd never met Carlos Garcia before?'

'Not before he moved in to the apartment next to me and drugged me, no.'

'Ketamine.' Christophe explained. 'When we got there he had disappeared.'

'Had you ever seen Giorgio Hernandez before today?'

'No.' said Julia

'Do you think Garcia and Hernandez are in this together, Jacques?' asked Christophe.

'They may be,' said Jacques.

'It must have something to do with the wine,' said Christophe. 'Surely?'

'Maybe that's what they were looking for. Was the wine in your apartment when Garcia burgled it Julia?'

'No, I'd already taken it into Jacquard. But it was

there when he first came and introduced himself because I remember propping the door open with it when I took my suitcase in.'

'But why would they want to steal it if they are working for Jaimie?' asked Christophe.

'An insurance scam, maybe.' Suggested Jacques

'But Jaimie knew the wine was in London didn't he Julia? Asked Christophe. 'So why would he send Hernandez to look for it at Le Castellet?'

'Maybe he didn't send him.' suggested Jacques. 'Maybe they've gone rogue,' 'Maybe they've decided to take a cut for themselves. Maybe Garcia and Hernandez have fallen out. Or maybe he was there for another reason…'

Jacques paused and both Christophe and Julia looked at him expectantly.

'Miss Connors. Can you explain why the glass in the bay window of Christophe's study was broken from the inside?'

'What??!!' cried Christophe and Julia in unison.

'There is no sign of a break in. The glass had been smashed to make it look like a break in but in actual fact the glass shattered outwards.'

'Which means Hernanadez got in another way,' suggested Christophe.

'Yes. It means either he had a key or somebody on the inside left the door open or let him in.'

'Look. I don't know what the hell is going on, but I have nothing to do with this.' said Julia looking at Christophe. 'You've got to believe me, Christophe for God's sake. You know what I'm like Christophe I'm scatty as hell. Maybe I didn't even lock the door and I certainly didn't put the alarm on, too many numbers. I swear to God, this has nothing to do with me.' She held Christophe's gaze pleadingly. They sat there in silence for a moment.

'I promise you, Christophe I am telling the truth.'

'I believe you,' said Christophe and he turned to Jacques expectantly.

'We shall see,' replied Jacques noncommittally.

'Look. Do you know what? I've had enough, really. My arm is killing me. My perfectly normal life has been turned upside down. I just want to go home.'

'Can't we finish this for now Jacques? Julia is exhausted.' said Christophe.

'And what's more,' said Julia. 'Why don't you just arrest this Hernandez bloke and ask him about the window and while you're at it you can charge him for stabbing me and trying to shoot me!'

'Please sit down Miss Connors. I do understand that you're tired. I only have a couple more questions. And of course we will be looking for Hernandez.'

'Well why haven't you got him if you know all about him?' asked Julia.

'We don't want the likes of Garcia and Hernandez, Miss Connors, we want Jaimie Girault, his contacts, the source of the cash and the people who are at the top. We want to know exactly what kind of criminal activity is creating the cash and exactly where it is coming from. There will always be millions of Garcias and Hernandez, they are dispensable.'

Jacques looked her straight in the eye, and she could see that behind his earlier friendly attitude he'd been plotting all along.

'The proof is the problem, Miss Connors. Getting the proof and getting witnesses. You could help us get that proof. You could agree to Jaimie's proposal and by listening to his conversations and copying documents. Just by being close to Jaimie, you can get us that evidence. Is he working with anyone else? Is he dealing in fraud? Is he stealing art and then buying fine wine to launder the money? Or is he laundering it for somebody else by dealing in fine wine? You are an attractive woman, Miss Connors, Jaimie is not averse to that. And he has already shown considerable interest in you.'

She felt Christophe go tense next to her.

'It's too risky, Jacques.' Christophe stood up and began to pace the floor. 'Julia hasn't ever done anything like it before. Jaimie is smart, and just think what would happen to her if she got caught. They've already tried to drug her and taken a pot shot at her. I don't like this one little bit.'

Jacques looked annoyed. 'Christophe, it's the only chance I've got, I'll never get this opportunity again. You want it stopped more than anybody, you've taken enough risks yourself helping us get this far.'

'Well that's me, Jacques, and that's different. I've just got an inherent death wish. How the hell are you going to be able to protect Julia? The truth is that you won't be able to.'

Jacques faced Julia. 'Why do we not let her decide for herself?'

CHAPTER 23

They got back to Le Castellet and Julia was so exhausted that Christophe made her go straight to bed for a siesta – in his bed.

Marie, having gone through a major transformation from Julia-hating witch to adoring surrogate mother, came into the room and fussed over her. She fluffed up the pillows and duvet and decided to redo the bandage on Julia's arm. She went off and came back with some weird smelling gunge and tutted and pouted as she worked. She was clearly not impressed with the work done at the hospital. The gunge smelt bizarre and although it was pungent it was not unpleasant. She shut the shutters and made Julia drink a cup of hot milk and take some painkillers to help her sleep.

Wow! Things really have changed around here, thought Julia. Christophe de Flaubert has become a knight in shining armour, Marie has become my adoring personal carer and I'm about to become an undercover detective.

Or am I?

She didn't know. She just didn't know what to do. She didn't know which way she should jump. She nuzzled into the pillow, but it was no use, the pungent gunge smell had cancelled out all trace of her knight in shining armour.

As Julia drifted off to sleep she suddenly found herself standing on top of the Eiffel Tower in the middle of the English Channel on a stormy night. She looked down and to the left she could see Christophe dressed as Napoleon on a big white stallion, leaping over the huge waves.

'Jump! Julia jump!' He shouted. 'Jump for your life. I will save you and make you a truly righteous person.' Jacques Morell dressed as the Count of Monte Cristo followed him with a huge army of French Gendarmes.

To the right Jaimie Girault was advancing on her in Redbeard's pirate ship. His russet curls were blowing wildly in the wind and he was wielding a cutlass.

'Jump! Julia Jump for the time of your life. A life of devious debauchery, rampant ravishing and highly profitable pillage!' Then he started shooting cannonballs at Christophe.

The wind and salty sea spray was stinging her eyes. She looked down in front of her and could see something else. It was moving very slowly and gradually out of the mist, Alan appeared in a tiny dingy. He was being thrown about dangerously on the waves.

'Alan?' she shouted. 'Is that you?'

'Yes Julia I'm coming. I'm on my way!'

She wiped away the salt from her eyes and shouted back. 'Honestly Alan! That dingy is totally unsuitable for these heavy seas.'

'Julia. I'm not a very good sailor but I'll try very hard and save you.' Then a big wave hit him at the same time as one of Jaimie Girault's cannon balls and he disappeared.

Oh no. Alan. Oh no. Poor Alan. It's all my fault! Then she could hear her father's voice. 'It is all your fault. It's always been your fault. It never ever stops being your fault.'

'No Dad. Daddy, please. Please don't leave me. Please.' She called out, but he left and suddenly she was back in the *Rue Pigalle*. She was alone in the dark basement and she knew what happens next, the door opens and she smells him, his foul alcohol breath before he enters, the bulbous form, the landlord heading towards her and she screamed before disappearing into blackness.

She was woken by Christophe after a few hours. He sat down on the bed.

'Wow that was a pretty good siesta. You must have needed that,' he said. 'Here.' He passed a cup. 'I'm guessing you are a tea person not a coffee person when you first wake up.'

'Yes,' said Julia. Despite having slept, she felt exhausted.

'Do you know you talk a lot in your sleep, Julia?'

'Do I?' Julia looked up surprised.

'Well, you do when you've been drugged or taken strong painkillers. Obviously I can't vouch for the rest of the time.

'I know I dream a lot; some good things and some not-so-good things, but I didn't realise I talked to myself. They say it's the first sign of madness, you know.'

Christophe smiled for a second and then passed her a glass of water. She took a large mouthful, her mouth was dry and she felt suddenly very nervous.

'You're not totally mad. You converse with yourself

and other people. You talk to your father.'

The glass began to shake in Julia's hand.

'Oh. Christophe what am I going to do? It's all such a mess and I'm scared. I'm scared to not do what Jacques wants, but I'm scared to do it as well. My life is a disaster.'

Christophe took her hand in his. 'No it's not, not anymore. I think you're beginning to sort yourself out.'

Julia began to tingle all over. She didn't know if it was due to Christophe touching her or the after effects of the pain killers.

'Julia I want you to tell me what happened in the *Rue Pigalle* and I want you to tell me about your father.'

Julia went pale. 'How did you...?'

'As I said, you talk in your sleep, but I also heard you talking to Françoise when we were at Bernard and Rochelle's'

Julia was silent for a moment. She *did* want to tell him but it had been bottled up for so long. She took another gulp of tea. The British always made tea in a crisis to calm things down but for her there was much more to it than that. Even when she was small whenever her mother made tea for her father she always made a little cup for Julia, always putting a little honey in it. I was one of her most treasured memories, along with her china doll.

Christophe leant forward and gently cupped her face in his hands and turned her face so that she had to look at him.

'You will never get it out of your system and get on with what you really want out of life until you face it.'

Julia half-smiled. 'What is this, Christophe? Christophe de Flaubert, the man of many roles, impersonator, criminal lawyer, part time investigator, and now doctor?'

Christophe's face clouded over. 'If I'd been any good at any of those, my sister Simone would not be dead, and nor would my parents.'

'Oh God, I'm sorry, Christophe.'

Julia took a deep breath. 'It started when my mother died. I ran away.'

'You ran away. Who did you run away from?'

'From the orphanage where my father put me. I … I lived on the streets and then I went … I went to *Rue Pigalle*.' Her hand clutched the tea cup. Now that it was all coming out she could barely keep the words coherent as she stumbled over them.

'When … when Mum died, father tried at first but he couldn't cope. I think every time he looked at me, he saw my mother and it was too much for him. He turned to drink and things got worse and worse. He blamed me because I wanted a brother or sister. I would talk about it all the time and so in the end they tried for another child. I know it was dangerous for my mother because I used to hear them talking about it but I never found out why. My mother died having my sister and my father just never could forgive me. We were in Paris then but father took me back to England. For both of us Paris was always associated with my mother. We ended up in a flat in the London suburbs first, then somewhere else, then another…As we moved the places became smaller and smaller and more and more damp in line with how much my father was drinking. We kept moving because he kept losing jobs.'

'I wanted to help him and look after him and make it better but I was scared too. My Daddy who looked after us was gone and in his place was this strange man who shouted all the time and smelt horrible and he was a sort of grey colour. I remember trying to cook something because he couldn't even manage that. I think it was rice. Anyway I dropped a bowl and it smashed on the floor. He just lost it and started hurling plates around the room. The drinking became worse and worse and he became more and more violent and in the end they took me away from him into care. He didn't even fight to keep me. He just told them to take me away.

I hated the care home. They tried with us but they just thought I was stupid because nobody understood dyscalculia back then. Well most of them were awful but Carol wasn't. She tried to help me. She would bring me books in French and copies of Paris Match to make me feel better. In the end it just fuelled my need to get back to France, until I had just one thought, get to Paris get back to Paris where my mother came from. That was where we'd been happy. That's where everything was good and everything went right. I thought maybe I would find people who knew her and they would take me in but they kept sending me back.'

Christophe listened, gently brushing her hair back from her face.

'Go on, chérie.'

'So the last time I ran away I met another girl, Chloe who was going to meet a cousin in the *Rue Pigalle*, she said we could live there and work in the kitchens of her cousin's restaurant. I found a job washing up where they didn't care about my papers. I so wanted to be better and get a good job, to become somebody that my mother would be proud of. My mother was so beautiful and elegant. I wanted to work on Avenue Montaigne I wanted to work in fashion and be as beautiful and elegant as my mother. An old English lady, Mrs Gladstone would come into the restaurant regularly and she found out I was English too. She was a bit lonely and after a while she asked me to visit her so she could speak English. In return she gave me music lessons and paid for me to learn to ride. She smoothed out the rough edges of the various accents I'd picked up along the way. Then one day she suggested that I might like to move in with her instead of staying in the rue d'escalves.

I remember running back to work and telling the Landlord that I was moving out. I was fifteen then. That's when it happened. The next day when I came home to collect my things, the landlord, he ... he' Julia stumbled over the words and pulled at the sheet.

'It's okay, darling. It's alright.' He gave her some more water. 'Go on, what happened?'

'He ... he lit a match under some silver paper. I didn't know what it was. He made me breathe in the smoke, saying it would make me feel good. And then he touched me and then ... and I couldn't st ... stop him. I tried, I screamed and screamed and ... oh God.'

Christophe pulled her into his arms, cursing under his breath. 'It's alright, Julia, it'll be alright you'll see. What happened after that?'

'I felt sick and dirty. I wanted to get clean so I ran to Mrs Gladstone's, I knew she'd help, but ...'

'Go, on.'

'She wasn't there. She'd gone. They'd taken her away. The neighbour said she'd fallen ill and they'd taken her.'

She looked at Christophe and could see the pain in his

eyes, pain for her and she threw herself into his arms and sobbed. He held her tightly as twelve years of pain burst from her.

After a few moments, when her sobbing began to subside, he released her and gently stroked her damp hair.

'Julia I know I've not been very kind at times and I'm very sorry for that. I just didn't know and didn't understand. I tend to judge people too harshly and I'm not very good at understanding people... I...'

'I think you might be better than you think,' said Julia still sniffing into her handkerchief.

He took her next dose of painkillers from the side of the bed and held a glass of water to her mouth for her to take them.

'Here take these, they'll help you sleep. You must be physically and emotionally exhausted.'

Only when he was sure she was sound asleep did he gently pull the duvet over her.

Julia did not wake until gone one the following afternoon. The sun streamed through the tall windows of Christophe's bedroom making criss-cross patterns all over the Persian rugs and a flock of house martins swapped gossip over the stone balustrade.

She decided to get up. She wanted to go for a long cool swim and then she would seek out Christophe and decide what she was going to do.

She took a towel from the end of the bed and wound it around her body and made her way down to the pool. As she passed the study she could hear Christophe on the phone. He sounded very annoyed.

'I'm telling you, Jacques, she's not strong enough.

She's had a shitty enough life without this, for Christ's sake; don't ask her to do it. You know damn well she would probably have to have an affair with Jamie and what if she doesn't want to? You don't understand what she has been through!'

There was silence for a moment while Jacques replied.

Christophe's voice was very angry when he finally spoke. 'I am not jealous and she is free to do as she likes. If she wants to sleep with Jaimie Girault it's up to her. But I know she is not as strong as you think she is. And I can't do any more for Simone and it won't bring her back, but I can help Julia!' He slammed down the receiver.

In that moment Julia made her decision. She would *have* to do it. It was time she stopped living a life where she used people for her own benefit. Perhaps she could make a difference. Maybe the money was drug money and Jacques Morell could shut it down. She would have to do it because of what happened to her, because of Simone and because of Christophe.

She went down to the pool feeling better at least for having decided and realising that she'd forgotten to go and get her swimsuit, she sat in the sun instead. The Provençal countryside looked beautiful spread out across the valley behind the Mediterranean blue of the infinity pool, and the sun warmed her face. After about ten minutes she began to feel quite hot. Her skin had turned a golden brown from the few days at Rochelle and Bernards'. She looked extremely healthy, inspite of her ordeal with Giorgio. The wound on her arm was healing well. She probably shouldn't get it wet but it was so tempting.

The pool looked so inviting and Julia gazed into the depths thoughtfully. She couldn't be bothered to go all the way inside and back up to her attic room to get her swimming costume. Eventually she couldn't stand it and throwing decorum to the wind she pulled off the bandage from her arm and dived into the pool, nude. The cool water flowing over her body relaxed her. She thought about Christophe. Somewhere in the middle of all this muddle she had come to like him.

She duck-dived deep into the water swimming around the bottom and letting her long hair flow freely around her body. There was something extra refreshing about swimming in the nude. She dived again, deliberately holding her breath longer and longer, as long as she could bear, until when she surfaced she was gasping for air.

'I thought you were never coming up,' said Christophe. He wandered over to the side of the pool, his tall dark figure casting its shadow over her. He was dressed only in his swimming shorts and Julia couldn't help staring at his muscular tanned torso with its smattering of dark curly hair.

'How long have you been there?' she gasped hoping the water wasn't too clear.

'Long enough,' he said casting her a cynical smile. He held the towel in his hands 'I suppose I could come in and give this to you, but then it would probably get wet which would rather defeat the object of bringing it over. The only other alternative is for you to come out and get it.'

Julia blushed. 'I'm not getting out unless you turn your back.'

'You English, you're so prudish, he said, turning his back on her.

As she leapt out of the pool grabbing the towel from his hand and pulling it round her, she caught her full, crystal clear reflection in the conservatory window and realised he'd had the benefit of exactly the same view.

'Beast!' she said.

He laughed and then took hold of her hand and led her over towards the bench.

'Come here, I want to talk to you.'

His tone was gentle if a little exasperated and Julia felt a warmth flood through her body.

Christophe sat down on the bench beside her and then, hearing a movement, he glanced over across the other side of the pool.

'It seems we have a visitor,' he said nodding towards a small figure who had crept around the side of the paddock and was staring at them. He stood up and shouted good naturedly but firmly, 'Goutal! Come here.'

Julia went cold – it was the scary little man from Chateau Lacoste.

'Goutal, come here and meet Julia.'

Julia caught Christophe's eye imploringly. 'No, Christophe,' she muttered, jumping up and trying to hide behind him. Goutal might only be small and simple, but he freaked her out.

'It's okay,' said Christophe. 'He's harmless and it's the only way to stop him following you around, as he's obsessed with you. Seems to be a common failing,' he said smiling down at her.

Julia's heart lurched full throttle into her mouth.

Goutal came nearer, obviously still wary.

'This is Julia,' said Christophe carefully and deliberately. 'She's a friend and you must be very nice to her.'

Goutal looked sheepish, but at the mention of Julia he

smiled and nodded, pointing to her.

'You must be very nice to her,' repeated Christophe. 'You mustn't follow her around and when you meet her you must say hello as you do to me and Pierre, okay?'

Goutal nodded, still staring at Julia.

He was a curious little man: short and squat with a very tanned face and enormous blue eyes. He had a childlike quality about him but was obviously quite old to judge by his wrinkled skin and his short, receding hair.

'Now you must go back to Lacoste,' said Christophe. 'Say goodbye to Julia.'

Goutal nodded gently, making no move to go, but suddenly there was a shrill voice as Marie spotted Goutal and came running out. She started to shoo him away, screaming and waving wildly at him. He charged off yelping jokingly at Marie, and Christophe laughed.

Marie muttered, shaking her head to Julia. He was an idiot, she said tutting, and a nuisance. Marie continued to talk to them whilst she tutted at Julia as she replaced the bandage. Was there anything Julia wanted, a drink perhaps or something to eat; was her arm feeling better?

Christophe interrupted, smiling cynically to himself, 'I'm sure Julia's arm is fine, Marie. Now we're trying to have a discussion here, do you mind?'

Marie looked disapproving.

'Alone, Marie,' said Christophe steering her back towards the kitchen. 'We would like to have our discussion alone.'

Marie departed in a huff and when Christophe came back to talk to Julia he was very serious.

'Julia, Jacques will be here in a minute to talk to you. I'm not sure you realise what will happen if you do what he wants. For a start you will not be able to tell Alan about any of this. It probably is not even a good idea to get married yet; in fact you won't be able to marry him until the whole thing is over, which means he is going to think you are behaving rather oddly for someone who is in love with him. You will have to spend an awful lot of time with Jaimie Girault in order to get the information Jacques needs. You may even be in a position where you cannot avoid sleeping with Jaimie. We have no idea who the people are that he is working with. They could be anything from low key crooks to major international gangs.' Christophe spoke quickly and quietly as if he expected Jaimie to appear out of thin air any second. He paced up and down, not looking at Julia and reeling his thoughts off dispassionately, like a lawyer.

'No matter how much Jaimie is attracted to you, you will always be dispensable to him. And do not make the mistake of thinking that Jaimie is just a bit of a rogue and a playboy, he has a nasty side to him if you cross him. I'll be honest, I don't like it one bit.'

Julia bit her lip. She had already decided that she couldn't marry Alan. For the first time in her life she was being totally honest with herself. She was not in love with Alan; he would never have understood all the things that she'd been able to tell Christophe last night. Jean-Claude had been right when he'd said Alan wanted a wife like he wanted a car or a house or a beautiful painting. That side of her life was done with. She had to move forwards from this point.

Christophe continued. 'As you've already pointed out, everybody knows everybody's business around here so we would have to stage a sort of row between us, something that makes you go hot-footing it to Jaimie needing his job and his help - and hating me.' At which point he smiled to himself and said more quietly, 'That shouldn't be too hard for you.' He continued in his lawyer's voice. 'People around here gossip and Jaimie must have no suspicions at all that you've told me or Jacques what happened. You can explain going to the police station with the burglar incident.'

Julia smiled. 'Well, a row between us two will be the easy bit. Which one would you prefer? Take your pick.'

'I rather liked the one in my apartment in Eaton Square,' said Christophe smiling wickedly.

'We can hardly stage that one in front of witnesses,' said Julia blushing.

They were both silent as they both thought over the incident. Christophe eventually broke the silence. 'Look, Julia what goes on between you and Alan is none of my business. If you do love him, don't do this; don't ruin everything to help Jacques.'

Julia sighed. 'I don't love him. I mean I love him as a friend, but I'm not *in* love with him. I've been kidding myself for so long I nearly made myself believe it.'

'Julia, I still don't think you should do what Jacques wants, it's far too risky.' He looked at her beseechingly. 'Julia ...'

'Christophe, I thought we'd agreed that we would let Julia decide for herself,' said Jacques angrily, as he walked across the patio.

Christophe ignored him. 'Julia, please don't do it.'

You could have cut the atmosphere with a knife.

Julia looked up at Christophe. 'I've got to do it,' she said. 'It's probably the only totally unselfish thing I'll ever do in my life.'

CHAPTER 24

It was the most gorgeous day as Julia drove to Menerbes. The sky was as blue as Van Gogh could have wished and the Mistral had mellowed to a gentle breeze that spread the pollens and cooled the grapes. It's far too nice a day for a row, thought Julia.

She drove the Citroën into the Place du Clos, noticing that Christophe's Mercedes was already there and she began to back into the space beside it. They had agreed that she would arrive having spent rather too much money and she would ask Christophe for a loan to start the row off. Julia hadn't been that enamoured of the idea, thinking that it was going to be hard to make it look authentic but it was the best that they had been able to come up with.

As she backed out of the space slightly, to straighten up, Julia suddenly had a brainwave; she reversed out a bit further, put the Citroën into first gear, let the clutch out too suddenly and shot into the driver's side of Christophe's car.

The force with which she hit it made even her jump –

and she was expecting it. She quickly backed out again and got out to look at the damage which was definitely authentic and far more extensive than she'd intended.

Christophe's face realistically looked like thunder as he stormed out of a nearby café.

'For Christ's sake what the bloody hell are you playing at?' he said – and he meant it.

I either laugh hysterically or take this seriously thought Julia. If I don't want to do this, now is the time to back out. She took another look at Christophe's furious face and decided now was already too late.

'Look, I'm bloody sorry, okay,' she said. 'It's this stupid cranky old Citroën, the clutch is always slipping. You should have got the heap fixed ages ago.'

'You're a complete bloody imbecile. Look what you've done to my car – *both* my bloody cars.'

By this stage quite a large crowd had gathered around them to observe the excitement.

'It's not my fault, you should've got the Citroën fixed. I hate driving around in the little heap anyway, it's so bloody embarrassing.'

'You're so damn ungrateful. All you ever do is take from people. That's all you care about, getting whatever you can out of people. Well I've had it with you. You can move your stuff out by this afternoon. I don't care where you go but just piss off out of my life. You're mercenary through and through.'

'Leaving you will be a pleasure, you're about as exciting as … as the cricket scores when it's been raining. And what's more sex with you was crap too.'

Christophe looked more than startled at that.

'Well you should try quality rather than quantity. If

you didn't open your legs to every Tom, Dick and Harry, you might find you enjoyed it when you eventually played at home.'

Julia went bright red. This is not real she told herself. I did not mean that. He did not mean that. She frantically pulled her shopping bags out of the Citroën and, turning to Christophe, she flung the car keys on the ground in front of him.

'You can drive your own bloody car home – both of them!' She stormed off to find a telephone.

She was trembling as she asked the operator to put her through to Jaimie Girault.

'Jaimie, it's Julia. I ... I'm in a spot of bother. Christophe de Flaubert is a complete righteous git and a bastard. He's thrown me out and ... and I've got no money.'

Jaimie's voice was serious.

'That's not true, Julia.'

Julia gulped. What? How the hell did he know it wasn't true?

'What do you mean? Look I'm desperate Jaimie.'

He started laughing. 'Julia, Cherie. Have you checked your bank account lately?'

Julia gave a sigh of relief. That's the bit he meant was not true.

'Well no. I don't check it very often because of my maths problem. Usually I just get my assistant Liane to tell me if it looks good or bad.'

'Well I think you will find that it looks very good! I transferred some money into it.'

'Oh Jaimie. Thank you so much. You are an absolute darling!'

'You're very welcome, *chérie*. Where are you? I'll come and pick you up and you can thank me in person.'

Julia sat sipping a coffee whilst waiting for Jaimie. She kept going over and over the telephone numbers that Jacques had made her memorise in case of emergencies. He'd put them in her mobile phone but pointed out that the coverage all around the area was pretty bad and Jaimie used some kind of blocking device, and changed his phones regularly. They'd been trying to hack into his conversations but hadn't been able to. Not being good with numbers meant that Julia had to be given a number to use that had a visual trigger for her, so Boo Boo it was, the one and three looked like a capital B and the rest was simple, zero zero.

She muttered to herself, boo boo, boo boo over and over again.

Jacques had not given her any more information about where they'd placed the bugs so that she would not be tempted to keep checking that it was okay. They said if it got lost it was better than if it was found, and if it did get found it would be easier for her to be surprised. They were going to be listening in while she was in France but they couldn't do any surveillance once she was back in London because they didn't have time to set up the legal warrants and they didn't know the location yet. It turned out the 'importer' friend of Jaimie's was just a box number in the city.

Why in Hell's name am I doing this? Julia asked herself. I'm so bloody scared.

You're doing it because you love Christophe that's why, she told herself. So she'd finally admitted it to herself and look where it had got her. And you think if you do this he might respect you and love you back. And what's more you're stupid. You know women in love are stupid and you are the stupidest because you've never been in love before. At least we agree on something, she told herself.

Jaimie finally appeared, striding confidently the length of the café and Julia stood up to say hello, whilst her brain asked her knees to stop knocking themselves together.

He took her face in his hands and gave her a long kiss on the lips. Julia tried not to resemble the latest in high tech refrigeration systems; her head was willing but her body wasn't. That was all Christophe's fault. She used to be really good at blocking out any kind of feelings or reactions until he came along and got her chemicals all confused.

'Oh, Jaimie, I'm so glad to see you. I can't believe Christophe de Flaubert. He was so horrible to me.' She pulled Jaimie across to sit in the seat beside her. 'Do you know what he did?'

Jaimie shook his head.

'Well this burglar broke into his house in the night, and I went downstairs to see what was going on and he attacked me.'

Julia pulled up the sleeve of her shirt and showed Jaimie. 'He even tried to stab me, see he cut my arm.'

'Christophe de Flaubert attacked you?'

'No! The burglar attacked me!'

'Oh,' laughed Jaimie. 'You had me worried, *chérie*. Christophe de Flaubert is known for his temper but he's not usually violent with women. In fact he's got quite the opposite reputation to be honest. That's probably why my sister likes him so much.'

'Mm. Yes I saw that in London. She did look pretty smitten.'

'Yes.' Jaimie's face clouded over. 'I don't like it one little bit. How can she be in love with the man who tried to kill me?'

'He tried to kill you?'

'Yes. It's a long story to do with his sister. He blamed me for her drug problem but frankly she was as screwed up as the rest of the de Flaubert side of the family.' He caressed her hand and looked at her arm. 'Enough of that. Look at you, you poor thing. You have been in the wars. Haven't you?'

'Yes,' sighed Julia. 'And do you know what smartarse Monsieur de Flaubert did when he got back? All he could do was complain about the mess in the place as if it was my fault or something.'

'How mean of him'

'Yes and then he got really furious because I'd smashed a Ming vase.'

'Did you really?' Jaimie laughed without humour. 'How wonderful. I'd heard he'd got one but I couldn't quite believe it.'

'Do you think that's what the burglar was after?' asked Julia

'Possibly. Or maybe his Cezanne. I hear he also has a Cezanne at Le Castellet'

'He made me go to the police station and go through loads of pictures to identify the guy. Not a word of thanks …'

Julia's voice tailed off as she realised she was rambling. You can always tell a liar, Jacques had said - they talk too much.

She looked at Jaimie who was looking at her, amused.

Jacques had also said the most important thing of all was to convince Jaimie that she was mercenary and in it purely for the money. At that point Christophe had started to speak and it had sounded very much as if he was saying, 'that should be eas...' and had quickly transformed into, 'that should be eas...ily achieved if you just focus on the moment and don't think too much on the bigger picture of why you are doing it.' Thinking about it made her smile. Christophe was already changing his opinion of her.

Jaimie took Julia's hand in his, and stroked it with the long white nail of the index finger, wrongly interpreting the reason for her smile.

'I amuse you *chérie*? I like that. You amuse me too.'

'Oh yes? In what way Jaimie?'

'Your funny smile when you have completely missed the point, your uninhibited love of money, and your rather endearing intense dislike of Christophe de Flaubert.'

Julia smiled at him.' I see you have me all summed up Jaimie. So to get to the point. How much cash will I be getting for me and what will I be doing in the new job?'

'Very direct, Julia. Although I think a café full of nosy locals is not the place to talk about it.' He stood up and indicated that they were leaving.

Jaimie opened the passenger door of his Porsche for Julia to get in. He had the roof down, and Julia thought how wonderful it would have been driving through Provence in the sun under any other circumstances.

Jaimie got in beside her and started the car. 'We'll go to my villa first, I think; it's just the other side of Lacoste. Did you leave the rest of your things at Le Casellet, Julia?

Do you want me to get someone sent over to collect them?'

'I did leave quite a few things there; that would be great, thanks, Jaimie.' In her head she was thinking, I left the most important thing in my life there, the only man I've ever loved. As Jaimie took the next turning out towards Lacoste, Julia realised they were going to drive right past the entrance to Le Castellet. God, stop the world I want to get off here, she thought.

'Jaimie, 'em …' Julia dropped her voice slightly, hoping it was a bit more sultry. 'Could I perhaps have an advance on … well on the money. The thing is I'm a bit broke, and well it's going to be a while before the import licence comes through, isn't it, and I really will need some cash.'

Jaimie laughed. 'Julia, how greedy you already are. I'll give you some cash when you are ready to go back to London. I want us to speed up the process for the licence too. Can't that Englishman of yours do something – he's well connected isn't he? Especially with banks. Where is he by the way?'

'Oh he's in London. I was going to write to him …'

Julia slipped her arm through Jaimie's. 'Now that we are … how did you put it? – a marriage of minds – I thought you'd want me to give him the push.' The least she could do for Alan was not get him involved in all this mess.

Jaimie turned to smile at her. 'On the contrary, Julia, much as I adore you, I think it is very important that you continue to see him. He is very influential, is he not? '

'Oh, but …'

'He does a lot of deals with South America and we

need those contacts to easily run the finances. I think you should ring him, Julia, and see if he can get this licence through a bit quicker. And you and I, *chérie*, will just have to be a little more discreet in our affairs, eh?' His left hand rested on her thigh and began to caress it, indicating that it wasn't just business affairs that he was talking about.

Poor Alan, thought Julia. She'd wanted to send him a letter breaking the engagement and letting him down gently with the real reasons, their lack of compatibility, her difficult past and the truth of her background but Christophe and Jacques wouldn't let her. They said that if Jaimie heard he would get suspicious.

Jaimie pulled up in front of a large iron gate and using a remote control, electronically opened it. It slid closed behind them and Jaimie drove along a gravel road up to a large modern villa which reminded Julia more of a doctor's surgery than a private house.

'There are guard dogs in the grounds and all manner of cameras just in case we have unwelcome visitors,' said Jaimie. 'Now, there's no cover here so just let me find you a landline and you can call your Englishman.'

Julia dialled Alan's office number, and hearing Virginia's calm, cool voice made her collect herself together, and act more matter-of-factly. She was put straight through to Alan.

'Julia, where the hell have you been? I've been trying to get hold of you. I thought you'd be coming back soon darling.'

'I was, Alan. But …' Jaimie sat down beside her and kissed her hand. She snatched it away and stood up abruptly. Jaimie laughed and sat watching her.

'Alan, I've decided to go into business on my own and

so I'm going to be staying down here for a few days to set things up. It's a wine importing business and I've already made some good contacts here. One of them is Cassandra Girault's brother actually.' Julia paced up and down as she spoke, avoiding looking at Jaimie.

'What? Julia, you don't know a thing about wine.'

'I know, but I'm learning, that's why I've got to stay a bit longer.'

'But you haven't even done a business plan, you don't know anything about running a business and your problem with figures makes this a ridiculous idea.'

Julia took genuine affront at that. 'Some people would say I ran a very successful business at Jacquard, Alan.'

'Sorry darling, I know that but you did have Liane to help you on the mathematical side and the whole thing was overseen by Jacquard in Paris.'

'Yes but I still ran a business Alan.'

'I know darling, but I wish you'd talked to me about this first. I could have helped you. And anyway, what's the point? We'll be getting married soon and you'll want children. It takes years to get a good business going.'

'Well, I'm not sure I want children just yet, actually. Look, Alan, believe me it's going to be great. Listen, I'm sending the papers off for the trade office and I wondered if you could pull a few strings and get the whole thing pushed through quicker. The quicker that's done, the quicker I'll be able to get back to London.'

'Alright,' said Alan and Julia could hear Virginia in the background telling Alan he had three calls holding. 'Julia, call me tomorrow, I've got to go.' The line went dead. All contact with safety, home and sanity is totally dead, thought Julia.

Jaimie pulled Julia roughly into his arms and gave her a long lingering kiss. If it hadn't been for the blistering heat of Provence, she was sure he would have noticed that she had turned into an ice sculpture. As it was, he picked up on the fact that she was as stiff as a Jacquard dressmaker's dummy.

He broke away from her and started to massage her shoulders roughly. 'My, oh my, Julia. Such tension.'

Julia smiled hesitantly. 'Well, you know it's been quite a stressful few days.'

'Of course, *chérie*. Christophe de Flaubert has been quite beastly to you. I understand completely. That man could turn anyone to stone.' Julia couldn't help laughing. How ironic. The one man in the Universe who didn't turn her to stone. She wondered if Jacques and Christophe were listening in.

CHAPTER 25

After a very nervous lunch at which she talked too much and ate too little, Julia was left in her own company for the afternoon while Jaimie went over to Château Lacoste. He'd said he wanted to see how the renovation work was going and that, when he got back, he would sort out a return ticket to London for her and some cash for her to be going on with.

Leaving Julia in her own company was always a bad move; it usually led to her getting bored, then setting out on some disastrous move of impulse. She lazed by the pool at first, pondering over a book on wine that Jaimie had given to her. She found herself flicking through the pages on the Provence area and settling down to read all about the de Flaubert vineyards. There was even a picture of Le Castellet and Julia was soon daydreaming about being back there – of a future where she was sitting in Christophe's study at Christmas with their children around their feet, and Christophe dishing out the presents. A crazy completely unattainable dream. She'd been well on her way to reaching her original dream - the top of her career and marrying into the British aristocracy - and look at her now, completely veered off course by Christophe de Flaubert charging in from left field.

Julia turned her attention back to the book. She supposed she ought to get clued up a bit if she was going to make this look authentic. The first page she turned to was all about Chateauneuf de Pape, and there was a two page article about how it was one of the most profitable wines for collectors. Oh shit. That made her feel so bad.

On hearing the engine of Jaimie's car start up, she put the book down under the sun lounger and listened until the sound drifted away to nothing, then she leapt up and went to have a snoop around.

The villa was built on two levels around three sides of a central swimming pool. In fact, if you were energetic and had a good aim you could've used the bedroom balcony as a diving board. So far Julia hadn't met or seen any staff – no housekeepers to keep Jaimie's cupboards clean, no gardeners to tend the lawns and no one to keep watch over the dogs and security cameras either. Come to think of it, she hadn't seen hide nor hair of any dogs.

She wandered through the patio doors into the large sitting room. Jaimie had very modern, minimal taste; a couple of pieces of sculpture and furniture stood symbolically on a long bright red carpet. There was a straight-backed, wrought iron chair that if it had a few spikes added to it would have been perfect as an instrument of torture. There was also a chrome and leather dentist's chair complete with the mouth wash dish on one side. Very bizarre.

The other door in the sitting room led to the hallway

of the villa and Julia continued on, looking for some kind of study or workroom. Jaimie must have a study, surely. She found a door at the end of the corridor that was locked and went back out by the patio to see if the window to it was open. She was in luck.

She hovered for a minute next to the window. It was quite small but she was sure she could get in, if she went through one leg at a time and sort of straddled it, then bent her back very low. She knew she was taking a risk but she couldn't bear to just sit there and do nothing. Evidence wasn't going to come running up to her and introduce itself, now was it? She was hovering with one leg in mid-air when a voice behind her made her jump out of her skin.

'What in heaven's name are you doing here?' Cassandra's smile did not reach her eyes. Julia put her leg swiftly down and turned around, looking as guilty as a car thief caught with a can of respray in his hand. She wasn't sure how much Cassandra knew of Jaimie's wheeling and dealing.

'I'm staying with Jaimie for a couple of days,' she said and started rubbing her ankle. 'I fell asleep on the sun lounger and I've got cramp in my leg.'

They both stood in silence for a moment, looking down at the offending leg as if they were the prosecution and defence lawyers waiting for the key witness's statement – but none was forthcoming.

Cassandra smiled cynically at Julia. 'My, you do get around, don't you. Alan Bloomsbury, Christophe de Flaubert and now Jaimie.' She removed her towelling robe to reveal a high-cut designer swimsuit and an equally impressive tan, then lay down on a sun lounger, stretched out her body in the sun and yawned.

Beside her Julia felt like some matriarchal frump in her shorts and baggy t-shirt.

'So what brought you down here, besides Jaimie's obvious charms?' asked Cassandra, not looking at Julia but looking up towards the sun. 'I'm guessing those papers I gave you were for his latest crazy scheme, the importation business.'

'Yes, as a matter of fact, Jaimie's gearing me up for the wine business; we're going into partnership.' Julia indicated the book she had been reading. Cassandra glanced at it and smiled cynically. 'Honestly, his schemes are so hair-brained. I don't see why he can't just settle down to one thing like the rest of us. Still, he seems to make ends meet well enough, more than well enough in fact.' She stood up abruptly, not waiting for a reply, and dived into the deep end of the pool, cutting the water cleanly.

'Are you coming in?' she asked as she resurfaced. 'You shouldn't sit in the sun for so long, you are after all British and you're looking like a lobster.'

Bitchy, bitchy thought Julia.

'No, I think I'll get on with some more reading thanks,' she said, dropping her sunglasses back over her eyes.

'Well don't put too much effort into it. Jaimie's schemes usually only last about a week. If I was you I'd go back to the rag trade. At least there you get free clothes – even if they are appalling.'

Cassandra swam over to the side of the pool where Julia was sitting and lifted herself out to lie on the edge. 'By the way, did I tell you that Madame Boucher offered me a job?'

Julia froze slightly. Why should she care, she hated Boucher and had resigned anyway. But she did – it was professional pride she supposed.

'No. You didn't,' she said frostily.

'She wants me to head up the international network and develop the States and South America. It's very high-powered. I'm quite tempted actually, except that Jean-Claude Vasin is so temperamental and, to be honest, I've always thought his clothes were hideous. I hear he is impossible to work with.'

It took all Julia's strength not to rise to the bait. 'Jean-Claude is fine if he's handled right. With your powers of tact and diplomacy, Cassandra, you should go down a treat.'

'So how are my two favourite women getting on?' asked Jaimie as he suddenly appeared from the lounge. He kissed Julia on the lips, and then hovered over Cassandra.

'I didn't know you were back,' said Julia, 'I didn't hear your car.'

Jaimie was not smiling when he replied. 'We were going past so I got dropped off at the gates and then walked.'

'Oh' said Julia. Thank God she hadn't been snooping in his study.

'I've got to go back to the château later this evening, and I thought you might like to come with me and have a look around,' said Jaimie. 'Cassandra could drop us there and I can pick my car up. What do you think, Cassy?'

Cassandra and Jaimie looked at one another meaningfully. 'I think it'll be alright.'

'Good,' said Jaimie, turning to give Julia a beaming

smile.

Cassandra disappeared for the afternoon so Julia set about getting Jaimie to talk more about the wine operation, while they lazed by the pool. She hoped that Jacques bug was working in case Jaimie did say anything. The only good thing about the escapade was that if she did have to make a run for it, she was so well greased with suntan lotion that not even the dogs would be able to keep a grip on her.

The afternoon heat was scorching and Julia kept diving into the pool to cool off, and to get away from Jaimie's roaming hands. The only trouble was that she washed all the lotion off which meant Jaimie had a good excuse for re-greasing her.

By the end of the afternoon, Cassandra returned and, although Julia was turning a pleasant enough colour, the red and gold measles that darted across her eyes when she blinked told her she had had enough sun for the day. She excused herself, leaving Cassandra showing Jaimie all the things that she had bought in Cavaillon, and went upstairs to shower and change.

The warm water brought out the heat of the sun that had been infiltrating her skin all afternoon but she didn't have time to worry about that. Pulling out a shirt and leggings, she got dressed so quickly that they clung to her still damp body. She'd already decided to go and have a look in Jaimie's bedroom to see if she could find anything of interest.

The room was as spartan and modern as the sitting room had been. A huge futon doubled as a bed and the whole room had an oriental feel. There was an adjoining bathroom and dressing room with a large wardrobe at one end. Everything was immaculate; there was not a thing out of place and the room looked more like a show house than somebody's home. To the other side of the room there was a large study which, in contrast, contained a messy desk strewn with papers. Julia picked up a fistful to have a look and took some photos on her phone. She had no cover but maybe they could pick them up from her phone once she got somewhere with cover. Underneath the last pile she found a small black address book and began to read out some of the names and numbers, concentrating on the international ones first, in case they could hear her. She continued snooping under the papers on the desktop, and then started on the drawers.

Suddenly she heard footsteps outside, and she froze. She'd got to think of a good excuse for being there. Swiftly she went back into the bedroom and lay down on the futon, opening the buttons of her shirt slightly. She didn't know what she'd do if Jaimie took her up on the offer, but at least he might not suspect what she'd really been up to. As she heard the door handle turn she looked up and smiled enticingly.

'I thought you were never coming,' she said to a surprised Cassandra who stood in the doorway.

'I take it you were waiting for Jaimie,' said Cassandra. 'His rooms are further along the corridor,' she said, smirking, as she grabbed a towel and disappeared into the bathroom.

I used to be much better at this deception lark, when I was trying to get Alan to marry me, thought Julia.

About an hour later they set off for Lacoste and Julia

hoped that one of her pet bugs was tagging along. She supposed they were out of Jaimie's blocking area and they might be able to pick up some of the conversation. She was squashed into the back ledge of Cassandra's Porsche, closely resembling Houdini at a yoga class. Jaimie sat in the passenger seat and frowned as Cassandra made him put 'Bat out of Hell' on the cassette player. She turned the volume up full blast (the speakers were in the back next to Julia's left ear) and proceeded to drive in time to the music. Conversation was therefore kept to a minimum as they rocketed around the bends. Julia wondered what the man on the other end of the bug was thinking, if he was capable of thinking anything at all, given the volume of sound that must be deafening him.

Cassandra pulled up outside the castle, which seemed a lot friendlier in the warm evening sunshine than it had been when Julia had paid her previous visit. The scaffolding was still up and, as before, there didn't seem to be anyone around to work on it.

Jaimie helped Julia out of the car and Cassandra drove off without saying goodbye, leaving skid marks in the gravel.

With Cassandra out of the way Jaimie seemed to relax much more.

'Come on', he said, 'the inside of the castle is amazing. We keep all the wine and bottles in the cellars obviously. The wine is produced north of here, further up the Rhône Valley and it is delivered in bulk and then we bottle it ourselves. There are a number of vineyards that will supply us. We've also started making a generic house red that we want to sell to supermarket chains as their own label wine. That's why I sent a case over to the UK with you. Did you taste it?'

'Well no. You told me not to.'

'Good girl.'

'Has it arrived at the importer then?'

'Yes, thank you. It arrived safely, in the end.'

'You had me worried when you said it hadn't arrived.'

'Things have been going so well, that we now have a problem that we don't have enough red grapes. So we have to bring in a lot of red wine concentrate from other places, like California, Argentina and Chile.'

'Really? But then the wine won't be able to have an *Appellation d'Origine Contrôlée* will it?'

'My, my Chérie . You have been doing your homework!'

'Well I really want this to work and earn tons of money Jaimie'

'Ha ha. It always comes back to money with you, Julia doesn't it.

'Well what else is there in life?'

'Indeed. Well, in theory, you are right about the *Appellation d'Origine Contrôlée* but we have a little plan that will get us around the problem. In fact we are going to be buying a bottling plant so that we can blend and bottle wine in the UK. That's why I put over three million into your account.'

'Oh, thanks.' said Julia.

'You don't sound surprised, Julia?'

'About what?'

'About the amount of money I put into your account.'

Christ. You idiot Julia, she thought to herself. You only know that because Jacques told you!

She hugged Jaimie enthusiastically.

'Thank you. Thank you Jaimie. That's the nicest thing that anyone has ever done for me. But you know me, I have maths dyslexia and the minute anybody mentions numbers to me, I just block.'

He laughed. 'Well it isn't all for you, Julia.' In fact, none of it is for you.'

'Oh.' Julia looked crestfallen.

'I think, given all your disastrous problems with money, it is best, for the moment., that you give me the codes to access your account and then I'll just give you a little pocket money every now and then in cash when you need it.' He patted her hand condescendingly.

Jaimie led her through a dark passage down into the basement where there were huge vats of wine and boxes of empty bottles were all stacked ready to be filled.

'We're working at maximum capacity here at Lacoste. So we're extending here, that's why I have the scaffolding and that's also why I want to set up a sister operation in London, as the British are one of our biggest customer's. We'll get the wine concentrate sent over there and then blend it and bottle it, for the supermarkets, whilst also dealing in our high quality fine wines of course.'

'Of course,' said Julia. 'Big money. I read that a case of Chateauneuf du Pape went for ten thousand dollars recently.'

Jaimie looked surprised. 'Where did you read that?'

'In the book you gave me...'

'Really? I thought you couldn't read figures and there are no prices in the book...'

Jesus. I am so rubbish at this, thought Julia. I have got

to get a grip.

'Oh. Well I must have dreamt it then when I fell asleep in the sun. You must have realised that I dream about money all the time Jaimie.'

He looked at her in disbelief.

'Seriously. I can clock up a few grand with just a short power nap.'

He burst out laughing. 'You really are adorable.'

'So,' said Julia 'Let's get down to business. With all this money you'll be making - how much of it will be mine?'

'Well that all depends on you and what you are prepared to do for your cash?'

'What? You mean, like become a kept woman?' Julia smiled warily

'No. Julia much as your body is incredibly desirable, I will not be paying you for sex. I thought I'd just throw that in as an added bonus for you.'

'How generous of you,' Julia laughed, cringing inside.

'First let me show you around the castle and then we'll go to my office and discuss it,' Jaimie suggested. 'We'll be more comfortable there.'

Julia smiled in agreement. Although, truthfully, she thought not. Not if the torturous seating arrangements in his villa were anything to go by.

They wound their way up a narrow stone staircase into a small, dimly lit room on the first floor. It was cold and damp and the atmosphere was almost medieval. Tapestries depicting various orgies and couples in all states of undress and erotic positions, hung from the stone walls. Incense burned in a dish in the corner of the room and candles flamed in sconces on two of the walls. In the centre was a large wooden bed, covered in red and black silk sheets.

'I'm trying to get it back to how it was in the time of the Marquis,' said Jaimie, laughing at her shocked face. 'He was an incredible character, one of the few aristocrats to survive the revolution. They say he had a fixation with his mother and that he fell in love with a girl who resembled her in her youth. The girl rejected him and refused to marry him, and so from then on he dedicated his life to debauchery. He was an accomplished author and playwright. In fact, our family are descendants of his, you know.'

Julia did know, because Christophe had told her, but it was something she hadn't wanted to dwell on, particularly under the present circumstances.

'Really?' she said, not liking the look on Jaimie's face at all.

'Yes.' His eyes wore a glazed, mesmerized expression. 'Perhaps we inherited some of his preferences. What do you think, Julia?'

'What sort of preference do you mean?'

'A touch of sado-masochism perhaps?'

'As long as I get to be the sadist,' said Julia trying to laugh it off.

Jaimie was smiling, but his eyes still had a glazed look as he pulled her onto the bed beside him. He fished in his pocket and pulled out a small packet of white powder.

'How about we have a bit of fun first Julia? This should get us in the mood.'

Julia stared at it, horrified, and backed away from him. She'd lived the scene before, smelt the dampness and sat in a similar cold, dim room. Jaimie lit a match beneath the silver foil and the reflections of the flame flickered around like little fireflies.

Julia leapt off the bed and darted into the corner, backing as far away from him as she could. The memory of the *Rue Pigalle* had now completely taken over; she was replaying the horrific scene with Jaimie as the landlord.

'Julia?' he asked quietly as he moved towards her, the silver foil smoking in his hands. 'Julia *chérie*, there is nothing to worry about. It's only crack. It will make you feel good, *chérie*.'

He touched her arm as Julia broke away and ran out of the room and down the stairs, leaving Jaimie shocked at her reaction. She was sweating with fear and ran wildly round and round the maze of stairs and hallways. She just had to get away from the room and Jaimie, and what he was trying to do to her. Eventually she came to the end of the corridor and the only way forward was through a large white door. Panting, she charged through it into a huge windowless laboratory. It was sterile and artificially lit and the contrast with the dingy room of the Marquis snapped her out of the trance-like memories that had been driving her.

She stood still in the corner of the room and gradually stopped shaking, her hands were no longer clammy and she could think sensibly again. She took a deep breath and sat on the nearest available stool, and wiped her brow. Her hair was sticking to her face and she pulled off her sunglasses from the top of her head and put them on a desk to retie her chignon. What was this place? Everything looked brand new, with most of the flasks and bottles still in sterile bags. On one of the desks there were large containers of the different wine concentrates along with some bottles of wine one of which was half opened.

God I need a drink. I'll just have a sip. I need some Dutch courage to get through this. I can't do the crack, I just can't. What the hell am I going to do? She took a slurp from the bottle and nearly threw up. Christ. Surely he didn't expect to sell that! She spat it into the sink. Her lips started going numb. Bloody hell, it tasted more like anaesthetic than wine.

Julia sighed to herself. What was she going to do? She really shouldn't have got involved with this. She was no good to anyone. What a huge mistake she'd made. What the hell was she thinking? She was just going to have to get as much information as she could as quickly as possible and then leave. If she could get back to London, she'd be away from Jaimie and maybe Jacques Morell could get on with it all without her involvement. Yes that's what she'd do. As she stood up and went over and headed for the door, she took a deep breath and walked into Jaimie coming in.

'Ah there you are. I see you've found our new high tech blending laboratory,' said Jaimie, acting as if nothing had happened.

'Yes. It's amazing.'

'I have to say that I am rather pleased with it. We have all the latest techniques for testing the acid, tannins and sugar content. We have gas chromatography, mass spectrometry, sorbent extraction, identification of volatile and non-volatile components. This way we can ensure that all our brands of house wine always taste the same, and there are no nasty surprises for the purchaser.'

Julia was starting to feel quite a lot better, even if it was only Dutch courage. She debated mentioning that she'd tried it but thought twice. No, she was supposed to be charming him and getting information.

'I didn't realise making wine was so scientific, Jaimie.'

He smiled and took her hand. 'Did you think we still worked with a little old man grumpily checking his grapes?'

'Well yes, I suppose I did.'

Jaimie laughed. 'No, no my sweet. The days of the eccentric *vigneron* with his perfect tasting palate are long gone. In fact I don't think there is a better laboratory anywhere else in Europe.'

'I'm sure there isn't,' said Julia, adding to herself, nor a worse tasting wine. But it did kind of have a kick to it. She really was feeling much better. So much so that she decided to explain why she ran away just now. Jacques had said that if she has to lie about something to try and make it as near the truth as possible because it sounded and felt less like a lie.

'Look I'm so sorry I ran away like that Jaimie, I panicked.'

'So I saw.'

'It's just that something dreadful happened to me when I was young and the sight of you with the drugs just made me freak out.'

'Ah. So you've tried it before?'

'Yes. No. Well not voluntarily.'

'And you didn't like it?'

'No, it's not that. It's that it triggers a really bad memory and …'

Jaimie took hold of her hand. 'Poor you. You should have told me. Well I have a wonderful idea. Why don't you and I go and have some fun, and get rid of that memory once and for all.' And he led her out through the door and up the stairs.

Oh Christ, thought Julia. What the bloody hell am I going to do now? Oh, what the hell, I'll think of something. She started rubbing her lips, they really were numb, like she'd been to the dentist or something but my God she was starting to feel seriously fantastic.

Jaimie led her up the stairs to a large sitting room that had huge windows that filled the room with sunlight.

'What a bloody fantastic room,' said Julia over enthusiastically.

Jaimie looked a little startled at her swearing like that. 'This is the business office for Girault wines. It's not really my taste but it's what the clients expect, especially the Americans.'

The old wooden floor had been stained and polished, and three huge sofas covered the other three sides of the room and a large Picasso hung on the wall.

'Oh my God!' Exclaimed Julia rushing over to it. 'Is it real?' Is it a real Picasso? Wow!'

'Of course. Christophe de Flaubert isn't the only wealthy art collector here about Julia.'

There were a couple of small wooden boxes on the large desk in the corner of the room. Julia rushed over to them.

'What's in the boxes? Can I look? She asked diving into them like a hyperactive child at Christmas. He grabbed her hand to stop her.

'Julia my darling, you are so nosey. What's got into you all of a sudden?'

'Dunno. I'm just feeling really good.'

He took a bottle from a cupboard and poured them

both a glass of wine.

'Well that's a great improvement from mad panic Julia I must say. Here take this, now you're in such a good mood we can celebrate.'

She looked at it, suspiciously, then suddenly necked it down in one, to his astonishment.

'Wow! Bloody good. I was really worried that it was gonna be that awful shite that I found in your lab! Fuck that was awful, tasted like anaesthetic!'

Jaimie looked shocked. 'You drank some of that?'

'Yes. Well no. I took a slurp and spat it out in the sink. Fuck it was awful. Only drank it because I needed Dutch courage and all that.' She sniffed the wine in the glass he'd given her. 'Yep this is much better'. She grabbed the bottle and poured herself another glass, necked that one, then started pacing around the room. 'So what's the plan Jaimie? You must have a business plan. Alan always says you have to have a good business plan for anything to work, and let me tell you Alan is fucking brilliant at business.'

Jaimie watched her slightly amused by her increasing use of the vernacular.

'Well the first job you have is to find a location from which we can work. The best thing would be an industrial building, near an airport. Preferably in the South of England. You will then need to get the licences for wine blending and bottling. You'll import the wine concentrate directly from us. Our blending expert will come over to do the blending but you'll have to interview and employ a plant manager and all the bottling staff.

'Yeah. Yeah, yeah, Jaimie. Forget all that crap. Just tell me how many millionsy, billionsy, squillionsy money thingies I'm going to make. This is so much fun. It is going to be so great. Fucking fantastic. I've never felt so good in my whole life!'

He started laughing. 'Err Julia are you sure you didn't drink a lot of the wine in the lab?'

'That shite? You've got to be kidding! No, like I said, I spat most of it in the sink.'

He laughed again. 'Well that's a relief! If you had, I'd have to get you to a doctor. It's a very special concentrate and it's not really for drinking. It's a rather different product we've been developing. Let's call it a kind of wine flavoured pick me up for parties.'

'Well you really do need to work on the taste. It was bloody awful.'

Julia started pacing around the room. Picking things up and looking at them and Jaimie followed her calmly taking them out of her hands before she dropped them.

She suddenly turned around and stared at him, her pupils hugely dilated.

'You know something Jaimie, a lot of people think you are cute.'

'Well that's so nice of you to say so Julia.'

'No, no. Some other people. Not me. I don't.'

'No?'

'No.'

'Oh.'

'No. Me I like Christophe. If he was here I'd shag him.'

'Really?'

'Yes. Abso-fucking-lutely! I nearly did once. In his flat in London. You see my lips don't work, never have, but then he snogs me and fuck me if I didn't do that whole melting chocolate thing and want to rip his clothes off and shag him.'

Jaimie watched her, torn between annoyance and fascination.

She walked over to the Picasso.

'Love this though. Did you steal it?'

Jaimie gave a false laugh. 'No.'

'Are you sure?' asked Julia trying to take it off the wall 'Are you sure you didn't steal it?'

'No I didn't' said Jaimie smacking her hand and straightening the picture.

'Well OK if you say so but I don't believe you.'

'You don't?'

'No.'

'Why not?'

'Because Christophe and Jacques said you steal things'

'Did they now?'

'Oh Yes!' nodded Julia wagging her finger at him.

'Interesting Julia, very interesting. And what else do they say?'

'Lots and lots. They think you steal antiques and sell them for money.'

Jaimie raised his eyebrows. 'Do go on. This is fascinating.'

'And me I think they must be right because they are both so much sexier than you.

'Really?'

'Yep.' She leant forward and put her finger to her lips and whispered, 'shhh, don't tell anyone.'

'No. No I wouldn't dream of it.'

'Because I'm a spy you see but it's got to be a secret.'

CHAPTER 26

Julia was lying down on a bed in a basement room with no windows, not too sure how she got there. Her head was killing her. Hangover from hell was definitely on its way. She hesitated, the last thing she remembered was a Picasso and Jaimie in his office. Oh my God! She'd drunk that stuff in the lab and then started talking. Christ. She'd got to get out of there. She ran over to try the door but it was locked from the other side. Then she heard a key turn.

Jaimie came in, his face like thunder, and he pulled her inside the room by her hair, but did not say a word. In silence he started scanning all the buttons on her shirt with some kind of rod, examining each one before tearing them off the fabric and throwing them on the floor. Then he took her locket off and started looking for something on the back' eventually he prised out a small thing that looked like a battery. He then pulled at her stud earrings trying to rip them out. Julia refused to scream, even though the pain was excruciating.

'Take them out!' shouted Jaimie. He locked the door

behind him, then walked over to Julia and slapped her viciously across the face.

'You are a stupid bitch,' he said quietly.

Julia's face stung from the blow, but she just stood still, unable to believe what was happening.

Jaimie paced up and down the floor. 'A locket and some earrings. Not very inventive places for a bug. Not that it matters because everything is blocked here and at my villa. Jacques Morell really is rather amateur. And you were the best they could come up with. What a joke. A gold digging tramp as their top spy.'

There was a knock at the door. Jaimie moved over to open it and Hernandez stood there, waiting.

Jaimie turned back into the room and glared at Julia.

'I believe you two know each other.'

'You sent him to Le Castellet.'

'Yes I confess. I did. You see I was a little concerned that your relationship with Christophe de Flaubert was getting rather too comfortable and that you would not take my little job offer. So I sent Giorgio to frame you for attempting to steal the Ming vase. It did rather backfire and tragically quite a lot of the Ming vase has ended up in Giorgio's face. I expect he'd like to return the favour at some point. A shame, such a beautiful face. But of course it won't really matter after we've finished with you.'

Julia stared at the stitched cuts that were still standing out red raw on Hernandez face.

Jaimie whirled around and raised his hand as if he was going to strike her again, but instead he punched the table in his anger.

'Take her away – out of my damn sight.'

Hernandez led Julia out of the room and down the back stairs into the courtyard where he pushed her into the back of a waiting van and locked her in. Julia was so shocked that she didn't even put up a fight, she sat rigid and zombie-like. The engine started and for a while the van wound its way around several hairpin bends and it felt like they were going downhill. There were no windows and, after a while, Julia had completely lost her sense of direction. Eventually they came to a halt and Hernandez dragged her from the back, making sure she got a good view of the gun in his left hand, but giving her no chance to see the building looming over them.

He did not speak to her but pushed her ahead of him down some stone steps into a damp, musty basement. What little Julia had glimpsed of the countryside before she'd got too far down the steps to see, had been only barren and rocky isolation.

Hernandez pushed her into a cold stone room, which smelt like a sewer. He slammed the iron gate shut and locked it behind him and Julia was left to contemplate the walls of her cell. There was no possible way out – the room was hewn from solid rock, on three sides with no windows. The only door was the one he had brought her in. It was dark and damp, the only light that came in, came down the stairway. She was in the perfect dungeon.

Julia sighed and sat with her eyes shut, hoping it would all go away. It was the end of her life unless she could find a way out. She was freezing, her shirt was thin and still ripped open, in tatters from where Jaimie had torn it. She had never been more desperate and frightened. She had known this might happen, but deep down she hadn't really believed it. Jean-Claude said she had a self-destructive streak; well this was her best effort yet.

She sat down in the corner and pulled the tatters of the shirt around her to try and keep warm. She wondered what Christophe and Jacques were doing; if they'd heard anything through the bug. If they hadn't they wouldn't know she was in trouble and come and look for her. And without the bug to home in on, they wouldn't know where to find her.

She stood up, realising that her only chance was to get herself out of this mess. Maybe if she used a little charm on Hernandez … She thought about it for a moment. No there was no way. If anything he looked vicious and out for revenge, the Ming vase shards had done nothing to improve his looks. She wondered if anyone could hear her.

Julia went to the iron gate and started to scream loudly. 'Help! Help let me out. Help.' It was futile. She must be miles away from anywhere.

She tried one more time. Giving it her all. 'He … elp!'

She stopped when she heard footsteps coming down the stairway.

Hernandez opened the gate, grabbed her by the arm and slapped her hard across the face, his ring cutting into her cheek.

'Shut up,' he said brusquely and threw her on the floor in the corner before locking her in again and disappearing once more up the stairs.

Julia sat in the corner, shaking. She put her hand up to her cheek, it stung like anything and was bleeding slightly. She half-dozed the night away and then realised there was a dim light coming down from the top of the stairway. It must be sunrise.

She ached all over and her face felt swollen around the cut where Hernandez had hit her. Everything hurt, from the very depths of her bones; her head ached and she felt hot and shivery, she must have caught a chill in the night. She was so hungry and desperate for something to drink. Oh, God, don't let me die here now, please. She prayed that Christophe and Jacques were looking for her – they'd got to be, surely?

Eventually she dozed off again, taking refuge in the blissful time just into her dreams before she was fully asleep. Christophe was there hugging her and telling her it was alright and her father was there telling her to come home. That was when she woke up, knowing it wasn't true.

As she became more fully awake she heard the sound of something being placed on the ground, and when she turned her stiffened body over to look she found a cup of coffee resting by the gate. A shadow disappeared up the stairs and she was fairly certain it wasn't Hernandez, the shadow wasn't tall enough. Julia looked disbelievingly down at the coffee. She wasn't dreaming – it was there alright. She began to laugh hysterically. She'd got a fairy godmother. She warmed her hands on the steaming coffee cup and gulped down the sweet hot liquid. It tasted like nectar.

A couple of hours later, the sound of determined footsteps beat their way down to her cell and both Cassandra and Jaimie appeared in the doorway.

Cassandra stood at the gate, looking immaculate in a Chanel suit, her hair drawn back into a chignon, and lips painted a dark blood red. She paced the floor outside the gate, regarding Julia with a thoughtful but determined gaze.

'How many bugs did Jacques Morell plant on you?' she demanded.

There was something in her controlled, commanding manner that made Julia realise that *she was not all she seemed.* It all made sense now. Jaimie had been so relaxed at Lacoste only after she'd gone. All that business in Marseille was a red herring. That time on the patio was Cassandra just checking up on Julia. *Cassandra* was the real brains behind it, not Jaimie.

Julia sighed. 'Why should I tell you, Cassandra? I don't expect you are here for us to kiss and make up?'

'Very true and quite sensible. It was a shame you weren't sensible earlier. I'm just trying to decide on exactly the best way of dealing with this. On the one hand, we could keep you, use you to run a red herring or two sending Jacques Morell off on a wild goose chase. On the other we could just dispose of you.'

'And you don't think Jacques and Christophe will know that it's you?

'Christophe?' Cassandra started laughing. 'You think Christophe cares about you?' 'Oh dear me,' she said shaking her head. 'You really have got it bad. Tell me, Julia. Why did you agree to do this? It wasn't for the love and appreciation of Jacques Morell I'm sure…'

'No.'

'So it was Christophe that charmed you into it.'

'No. He didn't want me to do it. He told me not to… he …'

'And you believed him?'

'I …'

'Christophe is an expert charlatan, you have no idea. If you think Jaimie's good, he's got nothing on Christophe.

Christophe will do anything he can to get what he wants. You really are very naive. I guess that's what Alan Bloomsbury likes about you.'

Cassandra must have seen something in Julia's face at the mention of Christophe.

'I don't believe it!' she said, laughing sarcastically. 'It *was* Christophe's charm. You're in love with him.' Her laugh echoed even louder around Julia's cell. 'You stupid, stupid bitch. Christophe doesn't love you. Christophe will never love anyone. Christophe is incapable of love; he will use his charms to get anything out of any woman, but he will never love anyone.'

'You're not so averse to his charms yourself, from what I hear,' said Julia before she could stop herself.

Cassandra laughed. 'Goodness you are so much dumber than I thought. Christophe has provided me with all the most important financial contacts all over South America and he always knows what Jacques Morell is up to. I really have to take my hat off to him this time though, managing to convince you that he cared even though he detests you for a gold digging bitch.' continued Cassandra smoothly, 'What did you tell Jacques Morell?'

'Like I said. Why should I tell you?'

'It doesn't matter. Christophe will tell me I'm sure.'

'Why would he do that?'

'Well let's put it this way, he's not the knight in shining armour that you think.'

'So why do you care what I say?'

'Well it's all part of the fun. You see you can tell and die quickly and quietly without any nasty side effects – other than death of course – or you can suffer miserably. Jaimie tells me you have quite a few insecurities. We could get Hernandez to work on those. We have a nice drug cocktail that is guaranteed to get you gabbing – you've obviously tried a bit of the concentrate of that one already. Or we could simply put you through a lot of pain and mental anguish until you tell us the truth. I want to know what information has been sent to Jacques Morrell. I want to know who your contacts are supposed to be and where you meet them. I'm not sure where Christophe is and I can't afford to sit around and wait.'

'Well you are going to have to. I don't know who the contacts are. The only ones I know are Jacques Morell and Christophe. You've found the bugs so just let me go.'

'No. That's just not going to happen. We've invested too much in you to waste it now. There's the three million in your account not to mention paying to block your calls to Fregère and funding the Boucher buyout.'

'You did that?'

'Yes. Christophe mentioned that you were a gold digger who was in financial difficulties with a fiancé in international finance, an excellent candidate for a bit of money laundering and to expand our drugs operation to London. We financed Boucher expecting her to sack you.'

'You must have been so pissed off when she didn't.'

'Yes although it was wonderful to see you shoot yourself in the foot by resigning. In fact you really have been a thorn in my side. You were supposed to go hot footing it to Jaimie but you didn't, you started playing happy families with Christophe. That was when Jaimie came up with one of his better ideas. Get everyone out of the house and send Hernandez round to steal the Ming vase. Christophe accuses you but plays the gentleman and lets you go with a few vicious words and warnings of what could happen to you, and you go running to Jaimie. Christ we've wasted so much time and energy on this, my God we've shot you, bankrupted you, ruined your reputation but you still seem to come up smelling of roses. You're incredibly resilient for a disaster on legs.'

'You've forgotten drugging me.'

'Oh that business in London? No that wasn't us.'

'But Carlos Garcia is one of Jaimie's men?'

'No. Carlos decided to go it alone and take the drug concentrate. He drugged you so he could take it and sell it to another drug ring.'

'So how did you know he drugged me?'

'You still think Christophe is a hero? Really? There's something sadly quaint about it. He told us. He's in it with us, you stupid cow. What to do now, that's the problem...'

'We could deal with you the same way that we dealt with Garcia, I suppose...'

Cassandra paced up and down outside the cell whilst she was thinking.

'I think I'll let Hernandez have a go at you and then we'll see whether your desire to live is enough to make you co-operate. This new drug we've made is really rather excellent. It combines increased sexual desire with a truth drug, that's the one you tasted but I think it will be far too nice for you. What you really need is reminding of the horrors of your time in Paris... crack wasn't it? I'm going to let Hernandez and Jaimie have their way, they can play with you a little before I get rid of you.'

Cassandra turned on her heel and nodded to Hernandez. Jaimie stood by the gate leaning against the wall, watching her with an unblinking gaze, as he had all the time that

Cassandra had been delivering her ultimatum.

Hernandez unlocked the gate and Julia crawled into the corner to get away from him. In his left hand he held a knife. In his right he held the silver paper of smoking crack. He dived at her and threw her to the ground, lying on top of her, holding the knife at her throat. Julia ceased to struggle, she could feel the point digging into her neck. He used his other hand to pull what was left of the shirt off her, his hands wandering all over her exposed skin fondling her. Julia could smell the heavy, acidic odour of his skin beneath her nostrils and she screamed out. She could hear Jaimie laughing loudly as he watched Hernandez. Julia closed her eyes praying that she could just pass out.

Then suddenly like a well-trained dog, he released her and stood up. He did not even glance down at her, he just left the cell and locked the gate.

Jaimie stood watching her, his eyes watery and glazed.

'Very enjoyable, Julia. If I was you I would not take what Cassandra said too lightly, Hernandez is really aching to get his hands on you, I feel.'

Night time drew in again and Julia huddled up into the corner. She felt freezing, but she knew she was on fire. There was nothing she could do, she couldn't get out. If she told them what they wanted to know, they would just kill her. And she didn't know anything, she didn't have anything to tell them that they didn't already know. She felt hysteria bubbling up inside her and she began to laugh. She was finished. Was Christophe working with them? Isn't that what Cassandra said. But he couldn't be, he'd been so kind and… she must be hallucinating. That coffee maybe that coffee hadn't been there at all. She could hear herself laughing hysterically like a witch cackling away in the background.

'Shhhh,' came a whisper over by the gate and Julia looked around for the source of the voice.

It was Goutal. My God, it was Goutal. *He'd* left her the coffee.

'Goutal, is it you?' she said, rushing over to him. 'Is it really you?' She never would have believed she would be so glad to see the little man.

He smiled at her, put his tiny hand through the bars of the gate and stroked her hair, caressing it so gently it almost made her cry.

'Goutal, you've got to let me out,' Julia whispered. 'Do you understand? You've got to get the key and let me out.'

She could see he was not listening to her. His hand touched the cut on her face and then Julia saw a tiny tear run down his cheek. She was almost sobbing herself.

'Goutal, it's okay, really it will be alright. You've got to get the keys.' Oh, how the hell could she make him understand? Christophe had always been nice to him. Maybe...'Goutal we have to go and see Monsieur Christophe, understand?'

At the sound of Christophe's name, Goutal stopped touching her face and looked at her.

Julia hesitated. She was confused. It was the fever. Was Cassandra telling the truth? Was Christophe involved? It didn't matter, she had to get out 'We have to see Monsieur Christophe, now. We have to go *now*.'

Goutal smiled and putting his hand in his pocket, he blithely pulled out a bunch of keys.

Julia wanted to shout for joy. The little angel had got the key.

He selected one of them and, fumbling with the lock, opened the gate very slowly so that it didn't creak. He took her hand and putting his finger to his mouth made the shush sound, rather like a young child would. She gave him a big hug and whispered. 'We have to go; you have to take me to Monsieur Christophe.'

Goutal pointed down at Julia's feet and made the shush sound again. When Julia's shoe made a distinct sound on the stone step Goutal pointed at her feet again and made her remove her shoes.

They started up the stairs and there was a sudden commotion from outside as Hernandez's deep tones mingled with Jaimie's high-pitched excitability.

Julia glanced at Goutal – he looked as terrified as she felt.

The voices grew louder – they were coming towards them and Julia and Goutal were trapped. There was no way out but up the stairs and that was the direction Hernandez and Jaimie were coming from. Goutal suddenly grabbed Julia's hand and, pulling it furiously, he dragged her to a small arch on a landing to the left of the stairs. It was a small, disused fireplace, which must have been for the jailer's comfort in medieval times. Goutal's small frame disappeared inside the chimney as he climbed up like a little monkey, using all four limbs. He leant down and pulled Julia's hand to follow him, dragging her roughly with incredible strength after him into the chimney. His hand guided hers to the stones jutting out inside. It was a very tight squeeze but with Julia's fear driving her and Goutal's determination and strength they got her hidden inside. She could feel Goutal above her and when she looked up she could just make out his shape squatting with his feet resting on the stones either side of the chimney.

She did likewise and they waited.

Her heartbeat seemed to be ringing out as loud as Big Ben and she felt sure Hernandez and Jaimie must hear it. Their footsteps and voices got louder as they came down the stairs.

'We'll go ahead exactly like Cassandra said,' Jaimie's voice sounded more slurred and trance-like now. 'But I want first go and then you can have her and finish it off.'

Julia stuffed her hand into her mouth and bit it as hard as she could to quieten the terrified sobs that threatened to erupt, giving them both away.

All hell broke loose as they discovered her gone. Jaimie was shouting angrily at Hernandez who was stamping up and down. They both came charging back up the stairs. 'Where's Goutal?' demanded Jaimie. 'He's behind this – I'll kill the little runt. I'll cut him into a million pieces.'

Julia heard Goutal whimpering above her; he understood the threat alright. She carefully let go of the side of the chimney for a moment and squeezed his foot reassuringly. He calmed down and they waited a bit longer. Eventually all was quiet and Goutal nudged Julia to climb down.

They were both filled with terror as they crept up the steps to the courtyard. For a moment they stood silently not daring to go out, but too terrified to stay inside. Eventually Goutal decided that it was quiet enough and in the dark of the moonless night they crept across the courtyard. Goutal was very quiet, being accustomed to moving unobtrusively and Julia followed, feeling rather like a herd of elephants by comparison. She prayed that Goutal knew where they were and could find his way out. He seemed to go more on his child-like intuition than on adult understanding.

Goutal continued pulling her hand frantically as he guided Julia. There did not seem to be any paths away from the stone outbuildings and they walked out onto a large solid plain of scrub strewn with drifts of gravel and boulders. Goutal continued on his way seemingly with a purpose definitely in mind.

Suddenly Goutal stopped and held his head in the air like a horse smelling the wind. He seemed to be listening too. He glanced around him in panic and began to whimper loudly, pulling furiously at Julia's hand to make her run.

'Vite! Vite!' he said, sobbing, setting Julia into a panic as well. As they ran on, Julia too heard what Goutal had been listening for; the sound of Jaimie's voice ringing out across the plain and the sound of dogs.

The boulders cut into her feet but she ran on, adrenalin numbing the pain. Eventually they reached a large outcrop of boulders standing alone and Goutal pushed Julia into a hole between the rocks. It was so tight she could barely squeeze into it but he kept pushing and after much wriggling she emerged into a dusty, cave-like room that was formed between three of the larger boulders. Goutal scrambled in after her and together they crouched down, their hands clutched together and their eyes transfixed on the entrance of their hideaway.

There was complete silence, apart from Jaimie's voice ordering Hernandez to search more to the left. He sounded ominously near.

The sweat was pouring off Julia from all her running and from her fever. She was drained of all energy. If they found them now, she would just give up.

Although Jaimie's voice sounded nearby, Julia sensed that Hernandez was even nearer. She could almost smell the heavy acidic odour of his flesh. She clutched Goutal's hand even tighter and they sat deadly quiet, but suddenly a hand exploded through the gap in the rocks, grasping at Julia's hair and both Goutal and Julia cried out in terror. The pressure increased as Hernandez's grip tightened, dragging Julia inexorably towards the entrance of their shelter.

Hernandez called out to Jaimie but there was no reply. He called again for help. The sound of the dogs seemed to be disappearing and then suddenly a shot rang out. Julia screamed and struggled against her captor to move further back into the hole. She closed her eyes, knowing the next shot was the last.

Nothing happened, then the grip on her hair suddenly slackened.

There was a commotion outside – voices shouting and then there was a face at the hole. It was Christophe. Tears of relief poured down Julia's face as he pulled her out of the hole, straight into his arms.

'I thought I was going to die and I'd never see you again,' she said, sobbing.

CHAPTER 27

Julia sat on the bed of her cell-like room and flung the magazine to the floor. She picked up a pen and paper and drafted yet another letter to Alan in a vain attempt to explain things. But she couldn't explain anything because she didn't know herself what was going on. It had been over a week since they had rescued her from the Crau. The doctor had checked her over and then she'd been left in bed in her two room cell ever since. There was no telephone so she could not call anyone and, with the exception of a guard who, in a white uniform, could have been a nurse or a prison warder, she did not see anyone. Jacques had sent a message saying that it was for her own protection, but an Egyptian mummy in the heart of a sealed pyramid couldn't have had more protection. It was terrible, it was worse than being in a proper prison.

She looked down at the blank paper in front of her. Maybe if she just got the address and 'Dear Alan' down, it wouldn't seem so daunting a prospect.

'Dear Alan. I'm sure you must be wondering what the

hell is going on – and quite frankly that makes two of us.'

No that was no good, it was far too glib. Julia screwed up the paper and threw it into the wastepaper bin. She wanted to be totally honest with him for once and tell him the true reasons why she couldn't marry him.

She tried again.

'Dear Alan. This is a very difficult letter for me to write. If I could speak to you in person I would, but at the moment I am unable to speak to anyone. I think we both know that our engagement was very spontaneous. We had both had a lot to drink and I think the cosy atmosphere went to our heads a bit. I don't think either of us thought things through properly. I love you dearly, you are the nicest man I know but I'm sorry, I don't think our marriage would work and I cannot marry you. I know that deep down I would be marrying you for all the wrong reasons and you deserve better than I can give you. You deserve someone who is devoted to you and shares your ideals. I wish you all the luck in the world, Alan. Please forgive me.

Well at least there was one person in the world she'd made happy – Lady Bloomsbury would be over the moon.

Julia lay back down on the bed and let her thoughts tick away. They drove her mad. She could not even cry anymore. She'd watched more television than she had believed could have existed and she was completely fed up. She punched her pillow – they should have told her it would be like this.

She sighed and turned over on the bed. Locked up and no sign of Christophe. Why hadn't he been to see her? Half the time she worried that something dreadful must have happened to him and the rest of the time she worried that he was indeed in league with Cassandra and Jaimie. Jacques would not give her any information. If he'd come to see her, life in her cell might have been bearable but she hadn't seen him since they'd rescued her and Goutal. He couldn't care less about her. Was Cassandra telling the truth that he was in on it all with them?

There was a knock on the door and Julia shouted, 'Come in,' her voice listless. It was probably only the silent warder with her lunch.

'You might as well just leave it on the table. I'm not really hungry thanks.' she said, her voice slightly muffled by the pillow.

'They tell me that you are not eating and that if I am not careful you will fade away before I can get you into court to present your evidence.' Jacques Morell sat down on the settee opposite the bed.

Julia sat up abruptly. 'Jacques, where is Christophe? Why haven't either of you been to see me? Why haven't you told me what's going on and when can I get out of here?'

Jacques raised his hand in defence at Julia's barrage of questions. He was unshaven and there were great dark shadows beneath his weary eyes. 'Julia, Julia, so many questions all at once.'

The tears brimmed up into Julia's eyes. 'Well, answer them. Tell me everything. I can't stand it here any longer. I can't believe it. It's as if I'm the one that's guilty who's been locked up.'

Jacques stroked his chin, thoughtful for a moment.

'Jacques, for God's sake,' said Julia. 'I did what you asked, I risked my life. You owe it to me to tell me what's going on. Please I'm begging you'

He smiled as if resigned to his fate and leaned back in the chair.

'I'm sorry you have had to wait for so long, but although you were discovered, you set up one of the best operations we've had in years and all this week we have been collecting more evidence and tying up the loose ends. The numbers you obtained were not of much use but actually we had a small recording chip in your sunglasses that they didn't find. You left your sunglasses at Lacoste in the laboratory and we were able to pick up vital evidence on the contents of the concentrate that they were bringing in from South America, from one of the drug cartels.'

'Great so now I can leave.'

'Not exactly, I'm afraid. We haven't made our move yet because we don't have enough to set extradition proceedings into operation.'

'And Christophe?'

Jacques Morrell shook his head. 'I'm afraid Christophe has disappeared Julia, along with Cassandra and Jaimie.'

'What??' Julia couldn't stop the sick feeling in her heart. 'So it's true? He is in it with them? That's what Cassandra said. I just don't believe it. After what his sister went through, the fact that he tried to kill Jaimie... it just doesn't make sense.'

Jacques Morell smiled a sad smile. 'For what it's worth, I agree with you. I've known him since we were children but all the evidence indicates that he has gone off with Jaimie and Cassandra.'

'Maybe they kidnapped him. Maybe something has happened to him.'

Jacques shook his head. 'I don't think so Julia. I can't tell you any more than I have but we are trying to track him.' He stood up. 'Anyway Hernandez is safely under lock and key and it is only a matter of time until he cracks and tells us everything.'

'That's brilliant. So can I go home now?' Julia just wanted to be back in her flat. She wanted to see Liane, explain everything to Alan then maybe go away for a while to think things through. She wanted to wake up in her own bed, walk through Kensington on her way to work like she used to as if nothing had happened. She might even suck up to Boucher and try and get her job back. And Jean-Claude, she needed to see her old mentor, see the warmth of his smile and be pulled into one of his fatherly bear hugs.'

'Err, I'm afraid not, Julia.' He looked at her sadly then suddenly stood up very business-like. 'I know this is hard for you to understand and believe me, my decision to involve you in the operation was not taken lightly. You will be in danger from this gang for the rest of your life. You are a key witness in the trial and eliminating you is crucial if the Juan Mareno cartel is to survive in Europe. But even after the court case, it is a matter of family honour with these people, you are an enemy who is the key to having Mareno imprisoned and the family will not rest until they have their revenge.'

Julia couldn't quite believe what she was hearing.

'The gang will do anything they can to get hold of you and use you as a bargaining chip. Realising that we would not exchange you, they would try to pay you off – pay you to not give evidence against them. If you agreed they would try to control you with drugs and if they can't they would kill you because while you are alive you will always be a witness.' Jacques paused before going on.

'I am arranging for you to be taken to a safe house which is heavily manned and which will allow you to use a pool and other facilities, but it will take another couple of days to arrange, so you will have to stay here until then.'

Julia looked at him horrified. 'But for the rest of my life. You said they would be after me for the rest of my life. What will I do?'

'You will be alright for money, we will see to that. There are other things that can be done too, changing your name, changing your appearance, plastic surgery is very sophisticated these days.'

Julia sat with her mouth agape staring at him. Plastic surgery? Plastic bloody surgery? OK so she'd wanted a nose job but a full face change. Surely she couldn't have heard him right.

Jacques continued efficiently, as he had when briefing her on the operation. 'I have some papers here for you to sign. It is best if you arrange to sell your flat in London and deposit the cash in a high interest account which you can use when you start your life with a new identity. In the meantime it is better that nobody contacts you. Friends and family are the easiest leads that the gang may use to find you. Where are your parents living?'

'Nowhere. I … I mean my mother died and I haven't seen my father since I was young. I have no idea where he is.'

'Good. What about your friends? Is there anyone in particular you would like to contact? I don't know if it is possible but I will try.'

'Well there is my fiancé. I've drafted a letter to him. Things aren't really going to work out between us, I feel.'

Jacques nodded.

Julia couldn't help it she had to ask again. She could not believe Christophe was involved.

'Jacques please tell me honestly. You don't think Christophe is involved do you. I can see it in your eyes.'

Jacques looked her in the eye. 'Where Christophe is concerned, Julia, I cannot lie to you. Who knows what goes on in Christophe de Flaubert's mind? When he makes a decision to do something, it is rare for any of us to find out the reasoning behind it. But I can tell you, no, I don't but I have no other explanation for his disappearance either and there is a paper trail that we are following that all points in one direction.'

Jacques looked at Julia's stricken face.

'I'm sorry Julia.'

Jacques turned towards the door to go. 'If you wish to send that letter and others I can get them posted from another area of France. I am sorry, Julia, that it has to be this way.'

Julia sobbed what was left of her heart out into the pillow. What life had she got now, anyway? She had no family, no friends she could contact – and no Christophe. There were many times when she'd lived in the *Rue Pigalle* when she would have given everything to be able to start again, to be a new person with a new identity. Now, ironically, she had got just that and she didn't want it. She wanted to be Julia Connors working at Jacquard – even Madame Boucher would be a welcome friend. She wanted to be with Christophe back at Rochelle and Bernard's, she wanted to be with Jean-Claude arguing over dinner. Surely they couldn't make her stay there, they couldn't hold her against her will? She'd got to find a way to leave, to disappear on her own. Christophe didn't care about her and nothing mattered anymore.

The following day, appearing outwardly calm, but still churning inside, Julia lay down and tried to absorb herself in a book. There was a knock on the door and the uniformed warder informed her that she had an unexpected visitor. For a second, a flicker of hope rose up from Julia's stomach.

The door opened and in came Marie, dressed up in her best black and clutching a batch of freshly baked *pan chocolat*. Julia's tear ducts threatened to overflow yet again as she gave Marie a big hug.

Marie wiped Julia's tears away, tutting to herself, then started to fuss around the room, checking that the sheets were clean and fresh and shooing the warder back outside the door.

'Tch,' she said; a sorry state Julia was in and she was far too thin. Jacques Morell should be shot and Christophe was a very bad boy. She sat down in the chair and grinned her toothless grin at Julia. Julia couldn't help but smile back and Marie nodded her approval at the improvement. They chatted about Le Castellet, Julia's brain doing the best it could to decipher Marie's strong accent. Pierre's roses were just budding and he had picked out the best to save for Julia. Thor was in a bad way and needed a good gallop but he was left in the paddock. He would need re-breaking when Monsieur Christophe finally paid him some attention.

Julia took Marie's hand in hers. 'Marie, where is Monsieur Christophe? Why does he not come to see me?'

Marie shrugged her shoulders and pouted. She did not know.

Julia sighed. She'd got to get out of there. Then she

had an idea. If she could only get some money she could leave there. They could not stop her. They could not *make* her stay.

She smiled her most winning smile at Marie. 'Marie, I need some money. I cannot stay here. I have to go home, don't you see? I have to leave here. I am so unhappy and I'll go mad if I stay here. You understand, don't you?'

Marie looked at her uncomprehendingly.

Julia's tears brimmed over again and she could not hold them back. She didn't want this new identity. She knew who she was and she'd rather go it alone than live in a new face for the rest of her life.

'Please, Marie.' Julia knelt on the floor in front of her, virtually begging. 'Marie, I cannot stay here without Christophe. Don't you see I have to leave?'

Marie stood up and nodded. Alright, she would come again and bring the money.

The following day Marie was as good as her word and she arrived with a bunch of beautiful white roses from Pierre, a small shopping bag containing Julia's clothes, and a large wad of euros. She did not stay long, but gave Julia a big hug and said Pierre had told her to be very careful.

Julia spent the next afternoon attempting to put together an escape plan. Most of it relied on the fact that she believed everyone would be looking the wrong way because they were expecting someone to break in and murder her, rather than for her to break out. And if she did escape they wouldn't want the gang to know that she was running about loose so they would probably carry on pretending she was in a safe house.

About seven o'clock her police guard changed shifts and the familiar figure of Anton, her guard, was back on.

So far things were going in her favour – she could tell Anton was as bored with watching her door as she was with watching television. It should be easy enough to get him to come in for a chat and a drink.

Julia asked for a bottle of champagne and a bottle of brandy and put the champagne on ice. She had a shower and changed into a short, simple black dress that Marie had brought in that afternoon. She put on a deep red lipstick and a little light blusher to highlight her cheekbones. Her pale, drawn face stared out at her from the mirror: you could have run an Olympic ski jump off her cheekbones and gone potholing in the hollows. Julia hung large diamanté earring from her ears and swept her hair on top of her head. Happy Birthday to you, she said to herself and then turned and called Anton through the door.

Anton looked surprised but appreciative when he entered the room. Julia had been banking on the fact that Anton was getting tired towards the end of his shift and it would be easier to charm him.

She smiled, half sadly. 'Anton, it's my birthday, and I have no one to celebrate with, so would you share a drink with me?'

He hesitated for a moment, taking in her pale face and sad turquoise eyes.

Julia smiled again. 'Just one won't hurt you've nearly finished your shift and, after all, it is my birthday.'

He nodded and sat down beside her. Julia mixed brandy and champagne cocktails, and crushed one of her sleeping tablets into Anton's. Aided by a couple of trips to the loo during which she tipped half of her drink away and diluted the rest with tap water, and given Anton's natural

JULIA

thirst, he was soon well on the way to achieving a very relaxed attitude to his guard duties.

By midnight Anton was snoring soundly in the chair and Julia quickly changed into her trousers, sneakers and sweatshirt. She grabbed her bag, in which she had packed a few things, including her driver's licence, and the money from Marie. She crept quietly out of the door.

At the end of the corridor there was a door with a frosted glass window that led into the main reception desk. She could see from the dark shadows that moved the other side, that there appeared to be two people on duty and she could hear muffled conversation but could not make out the words. She had no idea how she was going to get past them unseen. She'd got to think quickly, Anton might wake up soon and his duty was over in an hour.

Help arrived in the form of a couple of drunks that a young officer was having trouble dragging up to the reception desk and into a cell. She could hear their drunken singing and the irritated conversation of the policeman. One of the duty officers went to lend a hand and the other went to get the cell open. Julia opened the door as slowly as she could and crept past them unseen, out into the warm night air of Marseille.

CHAPTER 28

The first train out of Marseille was bound for Limoges. Julia did not hesitate. She bought her ticket and climbed aboard. She didn't care where she went just so long as she didn't have to stay holed up in the police station and have a face change. The train was virtually empty and Julia found she had a whole carriage to herself. She leant back in her seat and watched the sunrise over the mountains as the train whisked her away to freedom.

Limoges was already quite busy when she arrived and Julia's choice of onward trains was substantial. She supposed she could stay in Limoges, or maybe she should go to Paris – but then again maybe that was an obvious place that they would look for her.

She looked up at the departures board. There was a train for Brittany due in ten minutes that sounded okay. There would be English people on holiday and she could merge into the tourist population, or she could disappear into a little cottage somewhere. She might even be able to get a job, and she would need to work, for the money that

Marie had given her would not last forever.

Julia tried desperately to sleep on the journey from Limoges to Rennes but her mind took over. As the hours ticked by she found herself believing less and less of what Jacques had said. She understood the logic of it but she really could not believe that they would try and kill her. She thought about Christophe. He was the only person that she would have asked for advice, believing he'd tell the truth, how ironic.

She wiped the tears away from her eyes. Any thought of him and she just cried. She felt pathetic but she'd never been in love before and she'd never known it could hurt so much. It was as if her whole body had been crushed, she ached all over. They say you use fifty-two muscles in your face to smile – well you must use every muscle in your body to cry, Julia figured, if pain was anything to go by. She spent the final leg of the journey talking to herself and trying to pull herself together. Christophe wasn't worth it; he was a lying cheating drug trafficker and he'd used her, he didn't care about her, so why was she wasting so much brain and muscle power on him?

It was a while before Julia even noticed that they'd arrived at Rennes, she was so busy thinking about Christophe. She dragged her bag over her shoulder and stepped listlessly off the train. She hated him. As she began to walk towards the exit, some kind of instinct made her look up. Two men were talking to the ticket collector and they appeared to be showing him a photograph. Julia stopped in the middle of the platform. She was being ridiculous; how would they know she had come this way? Because they were policemen, that's why, and they always seemed to know everything, she responded silently. Well, she hoped they were policemen and not Jaimie's mob, but she decided not to risk bumping into either of them and walked across the platform to where another rather rickety train was just getting ready to pull out. Julia jumped into the front carriage and settled herself next to a middle-aged man who was reading a paper.

As the train pulled off she turned to ask him where it was going. He looked at her as if she was mad for a moment and then said St Malo. He then seemed to realise he'd been rather abrupt with her and relented slightly. Putting down his paper he smiled apologetically at her and said that he was taking the hydrofoil to Weymouth for the weekend, as he had friends there. Julia smiled back, and her mind began to chew over the information. If she could get to Weymouth she could get the bus to London.

'How much is the hydrofoil?' she asked. She didn't have much money left and she would still have to get to London.

'About forty eight euros I think, and the next one is at twelve o'clock.' Julia nodded her thanks for the information. London. She'd go back to London. The trouble was she had no passport, but they did let people over on day trips and she did have her driver's licence for identification. She'd go back to London and find a job, even if it was just working in a wine bar or something, and then she'd figure out what to do with herself. Maybe if she dyed her hair it would be better – they would have less chance of finding her. She looked at herself in the dirty mirror hanging on the carriage wall. She seemed to have aged a hundred years; her face was so lean and grey, she probably looked like Boucher.

By the next day Julia was trudging along Oxford Street in the humid heat of the afternoon. It seemed she managed to hit two people out of every three coming in the opposite direction and she ended up either side-stepping, apologising or just bursting into tears. She had been stupid to come back. Being in love with Christophe had just turned her brain to water. How can you be in love with him, you stupid, stupid woman, she muttered to herself. She felt disgusting because she hadn't had a bath since she'd left Marseille. She'd managed to wash her hair once, using soap as shampoo, in the public lavatory sink when she'd got to Weymouth but the attendant had come back and told her to get out. She'd had to plead with the old harridan to at least let her wash the soap out even if she didn't let her dry it with the hand dryer. And she had no money left for a room as she'd changed her last euros into pounds and had used it to pay the bus fare to London.

Dry-eyed for a while, Julia looked in Selfridge's window at a large display of floral dresses on frosty faced, emaciated models with Rapunzel hair. I should have applied, thought Julia, I could do that job – I'm as anaemic and about as animated as they are. She was so miserable. She had no money to eat anything and she didn't have any friends. Well she did, but she couldn't get in touch with them in case some Hernandez type hatchet man was waiting to give her a one way trip to the Pearly Gates. And what could she say if she did get in touch. She had no explanation she could give without putting them at risk.

After much thought about what she was going to do, Julia finally decided that the only safe option was to become a bag lady, so she headed off for Soho to stake out a perch. It was a very practical solution. After all if this 'greenhouse effect' was true and England did become as hot as Spain, being a bag lady would not be such a bad life; in fact everybody would probably be wanting to be one …

Julia turned down Bond Street for one last look at the boutiques. A few people glared at her, largely because she walked into them – her big blue sweater and baggy trousers did not attract nearly such a polite response as the slick, sophisticated Julia who used to emerge from the Jacquard offices. Halfway down Bond Street she found herself looking across the road at the Jacquard window. Liane was in the process of taking a dress off of one of the dummies. When she suddenly turned around Julia had to duck down behind a car so that she didn't see her, but Liane seemed to be staring unseeing right at her through the window. Julia waited until she went back into the interior of the boutique, and then carried on down towards Piccadilly, crying as she went.

The streets bustled with platinum blonde women hiding beneath dark glasses as they dived out of polished chrome shop entrances into polished chrome cars. Most of them seemed to be followed by various short men hidden beneath a hundredweight of designer packaging who were permanently gasping for cups of tea that never materialised.

Julia trudged on, deep in thought and finally found herself smack in the middle of Soho. She hovered around for a while outside a peep show trying vaguely to find a particularly cosy doorway. She sat relatively undisturbed for a couple of hours, watching the world go by, before two young Scottish guys came over and stood near her.

'Are you waiting for the hostel?' the taller one asked.

Julia looked up for a minute, stunned that anyone

should speak to her. 'No; what hostel?'

'There's a hostel for the homeless, just over there. It opens in about an hour. We've been trying to get in for a week but there's no room.'

'Oh. No I wasn't waiting and I don't have any money to pay for anywhere to stay so ...'

'If you can get in, it's free. There's just too many people looking that's all.' The taller one sat down beside her on the step, the other stood leaning against the wall, listening but not saying much.

'Well where do you normally sleep?' Julia asked.

'We sleep rough. Been sleeping rough now for a year. Came down to look for work but you can't get work if you haven't got an address and you can't get an address if you've no money to pay in advance. You can't get money if you've no job. Can't sign on if you've no address either.'

'That's terrible.'

'Just the way it is. There's loads of people like us, that's why you can't get in here.' He nodded towards the door that was opening up across the road.

A tall man came out, and seemingly from nowhere a couple of dozen people bolted out from doorways and shopfronts to surround him. The shorter Scots guy had already crossed the road and was at the front of the queue.

'Sorry,' said the tall guy trying to get back into the hostel and shut the door behind him. 'Sorry, folks, nobody's moving out tonight; we're full up again, sorry.'

'Oh, hell,' said the young man sitting next to Julia. He stood up and brushed the dust from his jeans. 'We're going down to the Southbank. There's a good soup kitchen there; do you want to come with us?'

What had she got to lose? Julia stood up and smiled

hesitantly, she'd be glad of the company.

'Yes, yes I will thanks. What's your name by the way? Mine's Julia.'

'Stevie, and this here's Ricky.'

Julia smiled at Ricky as he crossed back over the road carrying a blanket.

'Well, come on, Julia,' said Stevie taking her arm. 'Ricky here's got a little something he's been saving for a special occasion.'

Ricky grimaced. 'Yeah, finding a job, that was gonna be special.'

Stevie grinned at Julia. 'But seeing as he 'ain't getting a job, we've decided to celebrate surviving a whole year on the streets.'

Ricky pulled a bottle out of the inside of his coat, unscrewed the top and gave Julia a swig. The liquid burnt as it flowed down her throat and then left her with a warm feeling all over.

'It's from the Isle of Skye that. My Grandad gave it to me.'

They set off towards the embankment, as warm inside as the summer evening outside.

'If you've got family back in Scotland, why don't you go back there?' asked Julia.

'Because there's nothing there fer us and we've no fare back,' said Stevie.

'We're alright though see, because we can look after ourselves; we've lived in Glasgow. It's the really young ones, that are in trouble and the poor buggers who don't speak much English. There's pimps, drug pushers and all sorts hanging around near the hostel waiting to pick 'em up. Us, we've just got no bed, we're not young and gullible.' He stopped in his tracks.

'Anyways. What about you? What are you doing sleeping rough? You're a bit old for it, aren't you? And you haven't been doing it long either – homeless people don't have nicely streaked blonde hair and posh wool sweaters.'

Julia smiled sadly, 'I don't know what I'm doing and that's the truth.'

They walked over Waterloo Bridge and a sharp, cool breeze blew across from the river. The lights of London sparkled below, the distinctive dome of St Paul's fought to stand up for itself against the large, impersonal buildings of the City.

'Looks grand, eh? Streets paved with gold and all that' said Ricky giving her another swig of whisky.

As they stepped down beneath the concrete jungle of the South Bank, Julia was astonished to find easily a dozen or so people already bedded down under the walkways. And they weren't all youngsters either.

Ricky pulled his coat off and put it and the blanket on the ground while Stevie went off in search of some cardboard.

'It'll be okay tonight,' said Ricky. 'It's warm and it doesn't look like rain. Well, it'll be nice if we don't get moved on.'

Stevie came back with a large cardboard box. 'This'll do. It stops the cold and damp coming up through the concrete. We'll get three of us on it won't we, Ricky?'

They all sat down and continued to swig Ricky's whisky. A few people wandered by and more people turned up to sleep rough. Some of them said hello to Ricky and Stevie, others just bedded straight down.

At about quarter to eleven the theatres and concert halls began to empty. Many people rushed past them hurriedly, not wanting to see them or linger any longer than they had to. One or two people wandered over and put money in the cups that Ricky and Stevie put out but most just carried on past, embarrassed.

'Thank you kindly, good night to you,' said Ricky as a middle-aged man smiled and threw a couple of pounds in the hat.

The street was now quite crowded and a city type was forced to walk quite close to them. He frowned at them and rushed past.

'That one's scared we're gonna steal his toupée,' said Ricky, wryly.

'I came here once,' said Stevie. 'My gran won a trip to see that Tennant actor doing Hamlet. Knocked out she was. I thought he was a bit hyper myself, but she didn't care.'

Julia was beginning to feel quite mellow. All that whisky on an empty stomach had gone straight to her head.

'So how come you're homeless, then?' asked Stevie.

And next thing she knew it was all pouring out. Living in the *rue Pigalle*, Alan, Christophe, the drugs, running away from the police and being under threat from the drugs gang.

'Christ,' said Stevie. 'That Christophe guy, what a bastard. The drug dealing shit set you up. The bastard.'

Ricky shook his head in disagreement. 'Julia said he asked her not to do it, didn't he? It was Julia's choice.'

'Well I still think he was in on it.'

'I dunno. If he was really in on it he would have just

let her do it and reported back everything to them others, wouldn't he?' Ricky took a final swig of the whisky and wrapped the bottle in his coat. 'Won't need to fill it tonight, eh?' he said to Stevie.

'Some nights we can get into the lavs and fill it with hot water,' said Stevie. 'Keeps us warm for hours.'

'I think Julia should ask the guy herself,' said Ricky.

'What? That whisky has gone to yer head mate. What if that Cassandra woman is right and he's in on it. He'll do her in, won't he!'

'He should be made to tell her what happened. He shouldn't have led her on. He should be made to tell her the truth: he can't just run away from her like that without explaining.'

'Well I still think it's too dangerous.'

'How can it be dangerous? If he's in on it, he's done a runner off to his drug cartel mates, and he won't even be there will he?'

'Maybe he's hiding there, thinking Julia will turn up and then he can shut her up for good. I'm telling you she's in danger.'

'Not.'

'Is.'

'Isn't.'

'Is then.'

'Well I think Julia should decide.' They both turned around to ask her.

But she'd gone.

CHAPTER 29

Julia's pace got quicker and quicker as she wound her way along the inky black pavements towards Eaton Square. Don't let yourself think about all the horrible possibilities she told herself, otherwise you'll turn around and go back. But she couldn't stop herself worrying – what if Christophe wasn't there? What if he was there but really was part of the gang. The truth was she didn't care anymore. He was the only man she'd ever been able to love and he was worth dying for. She'd die if he wasn't there, and maybe she'd die if he was. God that whisky really had her confused.

It was three o'clock in the morning by the time she reached Eaton Square. As she walked along the pavement a black cat suddenly shot out in front of her, wailing loudly and setting Julia wailing back, she was so startled. A black cat walking across your path was supposed to be lucky though, wasn't it? She looked up at the stars scattered like glitter across a clear sky. The full moon glared down at her warningly. Maybe that wasn't so lucky.

By the time Julia reached the front door of Christophe's flat, she was in complete turmoil. Her head and heart were all at odds, her stomach was churning and tears were already leaking out from beneath her eyelashes. She took a deep breath as if she was expecting to drown at any second and launched herself upon the front door, sobbing.

Christophe had the door open in ten seconds flat. He stood in front of her in his dark blue bathrobe, with an enormous brandy in his hand. His face was drawn and grey, his eyes glazed and for a second it was as if he didn't see her.

Suddenly his face lit up in recognition and his arms shot out and he pulled her towards him.

'Julia ... Julia!' For once he was lost for words, but he didn't need them because his mouth came down on hers, kissing her hungrily, kissing away all the salty tears that were running in rivulets down her face. As he hugged her to him, Julia thought she would faint, but she didn't know whether it was due to the breath that was being squeezed out of her or due to the sheer joy of being in his arms.

'Oh, Christophe, I can't stand it anymore. I love you and it's all been awful. I don't care if I have to have a face change so long as I can be with you. I don't think I even care if you are part of the gang.'

Christophe started mumbling in between kissing her as hungrily as a starving man falls on a feast. 'I thought I'd lost you forever. I've had everyone out looking for you, and I've been going mad. Don't ever run away from me again.'

Eventually Christophe pulled her inside and shut the door before starting to kiss her all over again. 'I don't know if I'm drunk on you or the brandy,' he said grinning at her and Julia was amazed at the depth of love apparent in his eyes. He really *did* love her.

Without further ado he whisked Julia up into his arms and carried her up the stairs, kissing her all the way to the top.

'Julia darling, I don't mean to be rude, but where have you been? You reek of whisky.'

'I went to become a bag lady but I failed the interview.' Julia babbled.

'Thank God for that. I think I'd have died if you hadn't come back. But now that you are back, the first thing you are going to do is take a long hot bath, while I make myself some strong black coffee...' Christophe deposited her in the bathroom and headed for the kitchen.

Julia ran a bath full of bubbles and began to wash her hair. God it was bliss. She was home with Christophe. She couldn't quite believe it yet. She sank into the foaming water, feeling utterly content as Christophe came into the bathroom with two large mugs of coffee. He handed her one.

'So how does it feel knowing that by leaving me you nearly turned me into an alcoholic?' he asked, settling on a large wicker chair beside the bath.

'I'm sorry about that, but I didn't know where you'd gone did I? I didn't know what was going on.' She sank further into the hot water. 'My God this is so good. I haven't had a shower or real wash in I don't know how many days.'

'Well I think you deserve a good back scrub then, Miss Connors.'

Suddenly reality hit Julia like a cold shower – she was

sitting totally naked in the bath in front of Christophe and she became horribly embarrassed. She ran some more hot in and frantically started making more bubbles. Christophe turned around and grabbed a back scrubber.

Julia's skin tingled as his hands firmly soaped her back and neck. She thought she'd melt into the bath tub and never be seen again.

'Jacques has been going spare ever since you disappeared. I think he felt very guilty about using you, because he pulled in some favours with the chaps at Interpol and it didn't do his reputation any good at all that you managed to give your protectors the slip. How did you do that by the way?'

Christophe wrapped a huge towel around her as she stepped out of the bath and he began to towel dry her hair.

'No don't tell me … beauty, charm …a seductive glance of turquoise eyes…'

'I had help actually, from Marie.'

'Really? I can't imagine Marie bless her could have helped with any of that.'

'No but she did bring me money and the sleeping tablets so that I could drug the police protector and get away.'

'So I have my housekeeper to thank for losing me the love of my life.'

'Actually I think Jacques should blame you for my disappearance because it wouldn't have been necessary if you'd come to see me.'

'Julia, believe me I couldn't come to see you. You are going to have to trust me on this. I had to go and do something really important, something that would save all of us. This is much bigger than you and I and Simone. ' He drew her towards him and kissed her deeply.

Eventually Christophe stopped kissing her for a second, and Julia called time out by sitting up abruptly.

'Christophe, I know you think I'm experienced at this but I'm not ... well not with doing it with someone I love.'

'That's OK, more than OK. Brilliant in fact.'

'Really? Why?'

'Simple, because I don't want you to have ever loved anyone but me,' he said absently, nuzzling her neck.

'Look what I'm trying to say is that I've been frigid ever since the time when the landlord raped me.' Julia was amazed – she'd said it, she'd *said* it without going mad. She could actually speak about it rationally.

'It's alright, Julia,' said Christophe, stroking her hair. 'We'll take it nice and slowly. If you want, we'll just get used to touching each other. We won't go any further until you want to, okay?'

Julia nodded and then was horrified as Christophe fluffed up his pillows and grabbed a book from the other side of the bed. He leant back with the air of a man to whom time has no importance, and proceeded to read.

Julia lay beside him astonished and unmoving.

Christophe turned the page and read on.

Oh no, he doesn't find me attractive anymore, intervened Julia's subconscious. He can't possibly, otherwise he wouldn't have stopped so easily. I was only trying to explain things. I didn't mean I didn't want to. Now *he* doesn't want to.

She lay rigid, with the covers pulled up under her armpits and then glanced swiftly over at him. She was sure that he'd been watching her and then had quickly looked away.

Maybe …

Julia ran her hands under the covers to stroke the smooth tanned muscles of his chest. She was trembling all over but she wasn't sure if it was from nerves or anticipation.

Christophe turned the next page of his book.

Her hand slid down his body and she trailed her finger lightly along the inside of his thigh.

Suddenly, Christophe threw the book aside, rolled her over and pinned her beneath him. His brown eyes were dark with emotion. 'I'd have died if you'd just gone to sleep,' he muttered huskily.

As his lips met hers, Julia's mind finally shut down for the evening and let her heart take over the night shift.

The next morning Julia's mind woke long before her body which was hibernating in the duvet cover. She lay immobile, thinking about the previous night. Oh my god, that's what it was all about. That's why people came in late to work, that's really why they had siestas and probably why they eloped and had duels and ripped their clothes off. That's what I've been missing! She then rolled over to find a note left on the pillow.

'Gone out to get some things, back in an hour, so don't you dare go anywhere, love, C.'

An hour was just exactly the right amount of time required for Julia's insecurities to come racing back. What if he was just being nice to her because it would keep her near him to control her before he could get the gang to take her. He had never fully explained why he hadn't been to see her in Marseille and nobody else could tell her why – neither Jacques nor Marie. *Oh God, Julia, you're such a fool.*

He had said he loved her though – but that was easy to say and he hadn't come to see her in Marseille and she'd still have to have plastic surgery and become a crow-face like Boucher.

The telephone rang. Julia glared at it as it sat beside the bed ringing and ringing. Julia glared at it some more. What about Cassandra too. Maybe that was her. Julia glared at the phone, but it kept on ringing. In the end she braved it and picked it up.

A female voice with a French accent asked in a panic, 'Christophe? Christophe? Are you there?' Julia hesitated. It didn't sound at all like Cassandra.

'No, he's not here, he's gone out.'

'Oh no. Where? Is he alright? We've been so worried about him.'

And then Julia recognised the voice. 'Rochelle, is that you? It's Julia.'

Rochelle shrieked so loudly down the phone that Julia had to move the earpiece away for a second.

'Julia, where have you been? It's been terrible ever since Christophe came back from South America and found you gone. Bernard's been so worried. He was terrified Christophe was going to do something really stupid'

'Oh God, Rochelle really, has he really been missing me?'

'Missing you? I've never seen a man so desperate. He falls in love with you, having sworn he'll never love anyone, and then you go and disappear. He was terrified the gang might have taken you or that they would find you.'

'Rochelle I thought … thought when he didn't come

and see me at the Marseille Gendarmerie, I thought he didn't love me. And Cassandra said that he was working with them. And he just hasn't said anything about why he didn't come and see me. You say he went to South America?'

'Look, Julia, I was sworn to secrecy by Bernard, but you, of all people, should know. Christophe went to South America to talk to Juan Moreno and get him and his family to leave you alone. He used all of his contacts, he even talked to the president. Bernard said that even drug barons need banks. Anyway with all the pressure on them, Moreno's family agreed to leave you alone if you didn't give evidence. Jacques Morrell went berserk when he heard. Christophe disappeared, you see, without telling anyone but Bernard, and Jacques wouldn't have let him go if he'd known.'

Julia wiped away a tear and her voice trembled. 'Oh, Rochelle.'

'Don't cry, Julia,' said Rochelle, 'you'll set me off. Anyway Bernard said that Jacques was not as mad as he was because Christophe drugged Jaimie and brought him back with him. He was in custody and was supposed to spill the beans.'

'Was? *Was* Rochelle..?'

'Yes but apparently he's escaped. Or maybe Moreno's men got him out, we don't know. Bernard's gone to find out what's going on but we're worried about Christophe, in case he goes off again or gets involved. Jaimie or one of his cronies might even come after him.'

At that moment Julia heard shouting and the front door opened. There was the sound of a struggle and things breaking in the hallway outside.

'Where is she?!!! Where is she?!! Tell us where she is?'

Another voice joined in. 'Tell us, or you'll get a face full again.'

There was the sound of punching

Julia began to panic.

'Oh my God! Rochelle I think they've got Christophe!'

Julia didn't know what to do. The sound of pounding feet was getting nearer.

'Rochelle what shall I do?'

She heard a thud then Christophe's voice, 'Aargh'.

Julia dropped the phone and frantically looked for something to use as weapon. She grabbed a porcelain sculpture that was on a hall table and hid herself behind the door.

The door was flung open and Julia swung the sculpture, just as Christophe's head appeared around the door.

'Stop! No!' shouted Christophe, seeing the sculpture just in time. 'It's me!'

Julia dropped the sculpture and stared in shock. Christophe was being manhandled through the door by Stevie and Ricky

'Stevie! Ricky! Let go of him!'

They immediately let go and dropped the big heavy books they held in their hands. Christophe had a black eye and there was blood coming from his nose. Ricky and Stevie didn't look much better.

'Oh. Julia you're OK,' said Stevie embarrassed.

'I take it these are friends of yours,' said Christophe

Christophe sat in a chair groaning as Julia put ice and arnica on his head.

'Oh Christophe I'm so sorry'.

Christophe mumbled something undecipherable through his split lip.

'Do you think we should go to A and E?' asked Julia. 'Maybe you need stitches.

'Noh, just kiss … kiss it better.'

Julia gently placed her lips on his.

'Mm better,' he said.

'Oh Christophe. What were Stevie and Ricky thinking? What a mess! It was so good of you to put them up in a hotel too, I'm sure you didn't need to…'

'Yes… needed to. They have nowhere… were only trying to protect you.'

'Well it was still good of you. How does your head feel now?'

'Better, the painkillers are working.'

'Good. And I am so going to look after you, Christophe de Flaubert.'

'No, I look after you. My job.' he said pulling her onto his knee. He tried to smile his most seductively charming smile but winced. 'That's what you do to people, you make them want to look after you.'

'Do I?'

'Yes. Jean-Claude, Alan, Liane … even Marie and Pierre and now that pair of Scots bodyguards.'

Julia suddenly felt overwhelmed. It had all been so awful and now it was over. She felt the tears start to fill up in her eyes and one started to roll down her cheek.

Christophe put his hand to her cheek and gently wiped it away.

'What is this, Julia Connors, so short a time together and is it so awful?'

Julia sniffed. 'Nnno ... it's wonderful. Rochelle called and I don't have to have my face changed.'

'Oh yes. I was going to talk to you about that. I rather like it the way it is, so I think we should keep it.'

Julia buried her face into his sweater. 'Oh, Christophe, I'm so awful. I started to believe what Cassandra said and I couldn't believe that you loved me'

Christophe held her away from him for a second and looked stern. 'Julia Connors, I love you more than I've ever loved anyone in my life. I love you because you're you, because you're full of life and you're funny and brave. I think I started loving you the minute I saw you standing there on Alan's doorstep, looking so beautiful and dressed so completely outrageously.' He pulled her back into his arms and stroked her hair. 'You're completely mad. How could you possibly think that I didn't love you? I couldn't keep my hands off you in this very apartment, remember? I couldn't keep my hands off you at the ball, I nearly blew my cover and all the time you were still engaged to Alan. I couldn't just waltz in and ask you to marry me, could I – although it did cross my mind.'

Julia looked up at him through her tears. 'I wish you had it would have solved an awful lot of problems.'

'How silly we've been. I should have just run off with you that very first day.'

Julia looked up to find him smiling down at her lovingly and she blushed. God must finally be on her side she figured.

'And if you don't believe I love you,' said Christophe, 'you can go and have a look in the wardrobe. There's a few things there that should help to convince you.'

Julia pulled Christophe's bathrobe around her and

went over to the wardrobe. Inside the cupboard was piled high with parcels wrapped in Welcome Home paper. She gave a squeal of excitement and dragged the smaller ones onto the bed and began to open them.

The first was a bottle of Chateauneuf du Pape.

'And don't you ever use it in your cooking again,' said Christophe sternly, swatting at her bottom which was pointing in mid-air as she leant over to open the parcels.

Julia looked sheepish. 'Sorry.'

The next parcel contained her mother's china doll, fully discharged from the doll's hospital with honours. You could barely see the join.

'Oh, Christophe,' said Julia hugging him.

'And this one,' said Christophe passing her a large cardboard box, 'is from Jean-Claude.'

'How is he? Does he hate it with Boucher?'

Christophe grinned. 'He loathes it. But we've managed to persuade him to go it alone. I have already sorted out the initial financing of the new business, but I think he'll need you with him if he's going to make a go of it.'

'Oh, Christophe, that would be great. You won't mind me working then?'

'Not at all. You're brilliant at what you do.'

'And once the business is really going,' said Julia excitedly, 'we can get Liane in on it.'

'Err … Julia, I'm not sure Liane will be interested in changing jobs – in fact I don't think it will be long before she leaves anyway.'

'Really? Why?'

Christophe pulled Julia around to look at him. 'She's getting married – to Alan.' There was a pause. 'Do you mind?' asked Christophe quietly.

Julia jumped up and kissed him passionately. 'God, no. If their chemistry is anything as good as ours, I wish them loads of luck.'

Christophe proceeded to prove what an excellent chemist he was, so it was almost midday before Julia managed to get around to opening Jean-Claude's box.

Even then Christophe found it very hard to let her out of his arms, even for a second.

'Do you know,' he said, pulling her back down so that she collapsed against his bare chest and couldn't get anywhere near to opening the box, 'Jean-Claude has been on the phone constantly ever since you disappeared. He said our self-destruct tendencies were supposed to provide us with something in common, not lead to the annihilation of both of us.'

Julia laughed. 'He'll just be so pleased with himself that his matchmaking project worked. He'll be impossible.' She sat up in bed. 'But he'll be even more impossible if I don't open his present.' She tore off the lid of the box. Inside was the wedding dress from Jean-Claude's last collection.

'Oh Lord. Is this for me?' asked Julia.

Christophe laughed. 'Well, no matter how eccentric Jean-Claude is, I don't think he expects me to wear it.'

Julia looked warily at him for a moment, suddenly serious.

'Christophe do you mind if ... if we don't get married yet?'

Christophe looked equally serious. 'It depends why you don't want to get married.'

'Well I just feel that I wanted to marry Alan for all the

wrong reasons. But with you; I want to be with you, live with you and I love you for all the right reasons, but I still want to be me. There's plenty of time for marriage – and Jean-Claude's dress will wait.

'OK. But you will just have to accept the fact that for the rest of your life I will just keep on asking you a thousand times a day.'

The End

CHRISTOPHE
BOOK 2 THE JULIA SERIES

'I still can't believe you've got through a whole ten days, without any major disaster at all. In fact I've been thinking about all this jogging in the park. I think it's too dangerous you being out early in the mornings on your own. I think we should get a dog. We could make it a guide dog for the blind then you might not run into any more traffic light posts.' He wandered off into the kitchen, his voice fading slightly. 'There's an added advantage too,' he said, shouting back down the hall from around the kitchen door. 'Then when I come back from my trips, if the dog wags its tail friendly to any men, I'll know it knows them and you've been unfaithful to me.'

'Very funny,' said Julia. 'I've never heard of a dog being called as an expert witness in a court of law, not even in America.'

'Are you kidding?! In America dogs have their own attorneys.'

Christophe watched Julia opening the front door, appreciating the pleasant way the line between her tan and the curve of her bottom just peeped out from the bottom of the bathrobe.

'You have a suspicious mind,' she called back to him.

Two men in brown overalls stood at the door. The younger one blushed seeing Julia in just a bathrobe, and the older man smiled apologetically, pushing the card into Julia's hand. Two security guards with guns stood behind them, looking up and down the street.

Before they even spoke, Julia had a sinking sense of déjà   vu...

ABOUT THE AUTHOR

Chrissy Perry spent her post graduate years in London living the high life and working in the fashion industry and advertising. After publishing her first novel she jumped ship in the Panama Canal and sailed away across the Pacific with a French yachtsman. She has lived in French Polynesia, Brittany and Corsica. She now lives on the island of Mallorca with a constantly changing menagerie of children, dogs, cats and rabbits

25729458R00208

Printed in Great Britain
by Amazon